The SEEKER

S.G. MacLean has a PhD in history from Aberdeen University, specialising in sixteenth- and seventeenth-century Scottish history. She lives in Conon Bridge, Scotland, with her husband and four children. She is the author of a highly acclaimed series of historical thrillers, starring Alexander Seaton. *The Seeker* is the first of a new series.

Also by S.G. MacLean

The Alexander Seaton Series

The Redemption of Alexander Seaton
A Game of Sorrows
Crucible
The Devil's Recruit

The SEEKER

S. G. MacLean

Quercus

First published in Great Britain in 2015 by

Quercus Publishing Ltd
Carmelite House
50 Victoria Embankment
London
EC4Y 0DZ

An Hachette UK company

A CIP catalogue record for this book is available
from the British Library

ISBN 978 1 78206 165 6 (HB)
ISBN 978 1 78429 223 2 (TPB)
ISBN 978 1 78206 166 3 (EBOOK)

10 9 8 7 6 5 4 3 2 1

Typeset by Jouve (UK), Milton Keynes
Printed and bound in Great Britain by Clays Ltd, St Ives plc

To Lara

HISTORICAL NOTE

England in 1654

In 1654, England was nominally a republic. The Civil Wars of the 1640s had resulted in Parliament's execution, on 30 January 1649, of Charles I and the establishment of the English Commonwealth. The decisive factor in Parliament's triumph over the King had been its military superiority in the shape of the New Model Army created principally by Sir Thomas Fairfax and Oliver Cromwell. Cromwell, an East Anglian yeoman and Member of Parliament, descended from the sister of Henry VIII's notorious chief minister, was the supreme general of the Civil Wars. A military genius, he was also prone to bouts of almost manic energy and depression, and read success and failure alike as manifestations of the will of God.

As the Civil Wars had progressed, and the control of the Stuart administration over religious practice, the army, and censorship of a new and influential press was loosened, the new liberties led to extremes of fanaticism. Parliament and, increasingly, the generals who had led its armies, sought to reassert control with an ever-greater restriction on the freedoms of the people. The Commonwealth would reach its nadir in December 1653, when Cromwell's supporters forcibly dissolved Parliament. A newly drafted constitution, the *Instrument of Government*, soon afterwards appointed him Lord Protector, affording him power virtually without limits. Resident in the former royal palaces of Whitehall and Hampton Court, Oliver Cromwell was King in all but name.

As their defeated supporters awaited the opportunity to restore Charles II to his father's throne, the remnants of the Stuart royal family maintained their refugee courts in continental Europe. Their agents were at work throughout the Commonwealth period, as were those of the Commonwealth itself. Under Cromwell's Protectorate, a virtual secret service was operated under the direction of John Thurloe, Secretary to the Council of State. Not only Royalists at home and in exile, but radicals and dissidents who found their voice and a means to express their views in the multiple news-books and the new milieu of the London coffee house, came under the close attention of Thurloe's agents. England in 1654 was a place in which trust could be a dangerous idea.

Dramatis Personae

Whitehall

Damian Seeker	Intelligence Officer in the Government of Oliver Cromwell
John Thurloe	Secretary to the Council of State
John Winter	Lieutenant in the New Model Army
Lady Anne Winter	John Winter's Wife

City of London

Samuel Kent	Old Parliamentary Soldier; Keeper of Kent's Coffee House
Grace Kent	Samuel's Niece
Gabriel	Coffee House Boy
George Tavener	Merchant in the City of London
Mirjam Tavener	George Tavener's Wife
Elias Ellingworth	Radical Lawyer and Journalist
Maria Ellingworth	Elias's Sister
Will Fiddler	Peddler

Visitors to London

Jakob Hendricks	Dutch Scholar
Archibald Campbell	Scottish Minister
Zander Seaton	Scottish Soldier

PROLOGUE

England, early in 1645, a village near Exmoor

In the village, gathered round their cold hearths, the people could hear their own breathing. Babies were swaddled tight, held fast against their mothers, that no sound might escape. Older children knew not to open their mouths, knew to make no movement. What men were left – too old, too young, too ill – stood in the doorways of their huts and cottages, whatever weapon they had managed to salvage or fashion for themselves gripped in trembling palms, for tonight it would be their turn, they knew it: the night-men were coming.

Through the darkness, across the Moor, they could hear them. Not a fire, not a light in the village for twelve nights now, and twelve grey dawns that told them they had been spared, one more time. The people of the village cared for neither Parliament nor King. It hardly mattered – still the beasts must be tended, the soil turned, the rents paid. But their lord had chosen his side, and tonight, for these people, it was the wrong one. They could hear the hooves coming closer, louder. Soon there would be the steam from the stamping beasts' nostrils, the glint of moonlight off a cavalryman's sword. But devastation might yet be averted, and only in one soul that night was there true panic. The men had had their meeting, twelve days since; they knew what would be demanded and they knew what would be done.

And it was done. And better forgotten.

ONE

London, 1654

Sixth year of the English Commonwealth and
first of the reign of Oliver Cromwell,
Lord Protector
1 November

Damian Seeker read the words on the paper: three words, and a date. The cypher was intended to hide their meaning, but Seeker spent many hours in daylight and more in darkness uncovering things hidden. John Thurloe, Cromwell's Secretary of State and master of a network of intelligencers that reached to every corner of Europe, had said nothing as he'd handed him the paper. He hadn't needed to, for there was only one matter of business between Thurloe and Seeker, only one thing of interest to either of them: the safety of the Protector.

It was late, and Thurloe, who had much business yet to attend to, did not linger; he had done what was required in this matter, and he could forget about it. A plot, one in ten, a hundred, a thousand, to unseat, remove, put an end to the

Protector, but this one would die in its birth pangs, for in a world where men believed in everything and nothing and where madness walked the streets declaring itself sanity, Thurloe knew Damian Seeker believed in the only thing that mattered: Seeker believed in Cromwell.

After the Secretary had left, Seeker considered a long while. He pictured the wherry that was always waiting for him, at the foot of Whitehall Stairs, but he preferred the solid, tangible feel of stone and hard-packed mud underfoot to the dark and shifting infinity of the river. The smells of the night air told him things, the noise of closing doors, creaking shutters, the hasty snuffing out of a candle took their place in his head, waited their turn to make their revelation. He walked in his mind the streets and alleyways that would take him to the place named on the paper. Through each he heard the sound of his own boots reverberate in what passed for the silence of the city at night, he saw faces appear at windows, caught the end of whispers passing through courtyards, up stairs: take care, the Seeker is about. And tongues that might otherwise be loose would pay heed and silence themselves a while, lest they be heard by the Seeker. No, he would bide his time yet. He would send another.

He picked up the paper and passed his eyes one time more over its contents. A new cypher: every time a new cypher, for fear of mishap, discovery, betrayal. And there would always be one or the other, for men were fools. Three words this time, and a date, tomorrow's date. 'Again,' he said to himself as he held the paper to the flame of the one candle that burned in his chamber. The flame consumed it carefully, thoroughly. Letter by letter, symbol by symbol, and it was gone, ashes. But Seeker did not trust even to ashes; he swept them from the table and poured water over them, grinding the grey mess into the grain of the wood under his heel.

Far away, in the heart of the town, in the garret of a house in Dove Court, between Poultry Street and the Old Jewry, the scratch of Elias Ellingworth's pen across paper was never-ending, like the rats scrabbling amongst the rafters, night after night. Word after word, multiplying, going out into the city, running by its lanes and alleyways into homes, into mouths, into minds. Not just of the merchants and traders, the hawkers, apprentices and masters of the city, not just in the alehouses and taverns and coffee houses and across the Exchange floor, but westwards, past St Paul's, down, swirling in and through the Inns of Court, caught in the mists rising from the river, whispering their way along and through the fine households of the Strand, of Pall Mall, and at last to the great palaces of Whitehall, and Westminster. So travelled Elias Ellingworth's words, and there they fell like specks of dust to be swept aside into unseen corners, or caught up in the providential fury of the Lord Protector's wrath.

It was cold, it was always cold, the warmth of their supper long since forgotten. Elias coughed and the pen juddered in his hand, leaving a streak upon the page; the rats paused in their scrabbling a moment, and through the brief silence of the city, he could hear the soft breathing of his sleeping sister.

Elias wondered what dreams Maria might have, that she slept so sound, what dreams could be left, for she, it seemed to him, had never been naïve, as he had been. He allowed himself a smile as he recalled his nineteen-year-old self, going through the portals of Clifford's Inn for the first time, fired with all the enthusiasm of youth rather than the disillusionment of a man of near thirty. Clifford's had not been in the best of repair even then. Weeds grew through the cracks in the outer walls, and here and there a bush seemed, incredibly, to have taken root in high corners and gutterings between the sloping tiles. Rooks lodged ominously on the roof, looking down on the young men in the courtyard below, like elderly doctors of law waiting to pronounce their judgments. And still, there was learning in these very stones, and the right principles of the law. Elias loved the place, for all its faults, for all the dankness, the stench from the Fleet, the cavalcade of poverty and sin that passed on the street outside. He would have been living there now, eking a living from teaching students, strolling with his fellows in the small garden in the evening, debating the issues of the day, had it not been for Maria. But when their father had followed their mother to the grave, Elias's choice had been to take his sister under his care, or leave her to live on her wits. It had been no choice – for all her wits, he could not have abandoned her to the great maw of the city alone.

And so, he had moved out of his homely chamber at Clifford's, and away from its comforting fellowship, and taken his young sister to live in this garret, promising that one day he would be a great man, and that the cream of the city's bachelors would be queuing up for her dowry.

But Elias was not a great man, and though they might pause and turn their heads in the street to look a second time upon the striking girl with the jet-black hair and eyes that might have belonged to a Castilian princess, the cream of the city's bachelors had not found their way to the crumbling stairway of Dove Court and the proud young woman who would never have a dowry.

The rats began to scrabble in the rafters again; Maria pulled the thin blankets tighter round her as she turned in her sleep, and Elias took up his pen once more.

In Whitehall, it was never silent; Lady Anne Winter knew that: there were always feet marching, echoing somewhere in its never-ending corridors. Soldiers — cornets, captains, lieutenants-general — marching by twos, helmets under their arms like Roman legionaries on their way to pay homage to the Caesar of whom they had long since begun to tire. Or softer feet, quieter feet, of men shuffling in corners, doorways, looking about them for those who might listen to their words, their careful whispers, these men accustomed once to declaim in Westminster. But Westminster, with its chambers for Lords and Commons, was a place only of echoes and muted voices now, for those men had shown themselves to be ignorant of the mind of God. Indeed, only one man in this great English Commonwealth, it had appeared at last, knew the mind of God.

Anne Winter could see him now, Cromwell, far, far along those corridors from her apartments, along many passageways, around many corners, up countless steps. Across courtyards, beneath archways, through doorway after doorway until at last there he was, in all his coarse, be-warted glory: his sparse, wiry hair and ill-fitting clothes, his monstrous nose perhaps the only noble thing about him – this country squire, this rough-shod soldier, this scion of a brewer's line who sat now where once Tudor, Stuart, had sat; this man, this Cromwell, who had taken upon him the trappings of a king.

Lady Anne looked from her mind's eye back to the mottled glass in front of her, and began to pull the brush through her hair. She did not know the woman looking back at her, and had not the interest in her life to enquire any further. The brush had been a gift from her mother, years ago now, ivory, with her own initials worked in silver scroll beneath the family crest. She laid it down before the glass and snuffed out the one light there was to see by. Her husband would be somewhere in this vast morass of buildings, attending night councils, taking orders, giving orders, rising, ever rising, in the service of the Protector. The night was freezing, a hard frost threatening to stop the relentless river beneath her window, and her bed would be cold again tonight, but it did not matter; she preferred it that way. She would pretend to be asleep, whenever he came in at last, making as little noise as possible as he removed his boots, his sword, all the trappings of his rank. He would touch her hair, her face, gently, and she would remain rigid, as stone. And then she would listen a while as he lay awake in the darkness, and know that in the morning some of the hurt would still be in his eyes.

In Samuel Kent's coffee house on Birchin Lane, the fire beneath the roasting pan and cauldron had long gone out, and the pots been cooled and cleaned and set back upon their hooks by Grace as they were every night, but the embers still glowed in the hearth by the serving table. The walls too, infused with the smoke from coffee pan and pipe tobacco, breathed some of their warmth back into the room, carrying with it aromas of far-off places, of chocolate from the Americas, coffee from the Levant, spices from the Indies and the Molucca seas, where cold and frost were not known, and men felt the warmth of the sun on their faces. As he had lain in a Cornish ditch ten years ago, half-dead with cold and hunger and the wound in his leg, Samuel Kent had vowed that should he live, he would never be cold again.

He moved quietly, so as not to disturb the boy, Gabriel, who slept soundly on his cot by the hearth, and whose dreams no doubt swirled with the voices, the prattle of the day: endless talking, rumour, news – prices, trades, gains, losses, the catastrophes of foreign armies, the absurdities of fashion, the duplicity of courts and kings, the petty adulteries of the great and the lowly – what could they mean to a boy of twelve who had never been further than the market at Leadenhall, the dock at Billingsgate? And yet they were his world, as he scuttled from counter to table with his pot, filling, refilling, cups, bowls, pipes, passing papers and news-books from one table to another, earning his cot by that fire and the roof over his head.

In her small bedchamber above the coffee room, Grace listened to her uncle go about his nightly routine of calling time on another day. She was happy. For all the world that passed by on their lane, for the murders, the robberies, the violent assaults and hangings that scandalised and entertained their patrons, day to day, as they drank their coffee and smoked their pipe, none touched her here. It was a continuing story, telling its tale again and again in the city, a background sound to the world of the coffee house.

And indeed, the world did come to the coffee house. A merchant had taken the time to tell her once how the beans she roasted and ground had travelled from Arabia by way of Constantinople and over many seas. How at that very moment, the Mussulmans of Cairo, the Paschas of Baghdad, the traders of Damascus and Aleppo were sitting, cross-legged in booths in the street or on cushions in opulent coffee houses in the bazaars and the midday shade of their mosques, drinking this very same brew. He had told her how the pots and bowls, the special, delicate finians, from which her patrons drank had been shaped and fired and painted by artisans across the China seas who did not know there was such a place as London, dark, damp and miserable, where a lovely young woman turned their wares in her fingers in awe. She did not need to travel the oceans: she held them in her hands.

And every day in the coffee house, there were new people. Some stayed and became regular customers, friends, drawn in by London, to belong, as she and her uncle had been, with no thought of returning again to where they had come from. Others lingered perhaps a few days, before they moved on. Others came once and were never seen again.

There was nothing in the news of the world that Grace did not know. She had even, over the last few years behind her counter, picked up a few words of Dutch, of Flemish, of French. She did not show it, but she practised them alone at night in her bedchamber, liking the rhythm of the alien words on her tongue.

'What would I do without you, girl?' Her uncle said it to her every day.

'You'll never need to know,' she would answer him.

They had never been parted since the day, nine years ago, he had marched into Bristol with General Fairfax's army, having flushed Prince Rupert's occupying forces from the city, and found her, scrubbing pots and waiting tables at an inn by the cathedral precincts. Samuel delighted to tell the story to any who asked.

'There she was, my brother's girl, orphaned. Hadn't seen her since she were nine years old, but I knew her straight away and she me, and that was that. The battle for the city had done for my leg, no mending this time. A barber-surgeon tried to break the bone and reset it – near lost me the damn thing – and that girl there held on to my hand the whole time, and has never left me since.'

The battle had finished the old parliamentary soldier for fighting, but the General had seen to it that he got his back pay, and he and Grace had gravitated towards London. They'd taken a tavern first, down by Blackfriars, but Grace hadn't liked to be so close to Bridewell and all that misery, and then they had heard of the clean living there was to be made of selling the new, mesmerising brew from the Levant. To Samuel, the coffee pot, for the life it had given them, was an object of veneration. 'We got ourselves in here, and here we do just nicely, do we not, my dear?' he was fond of asking.

'We do, Uncle,' she would reply.

She had come close, once, to telling Elias the rest. But what good would it do to pass on to another the burden of her secret? Soon, she was sure, the words on foreign tongues, the gifts of far-flung worlds, brought on the winds to her uncle's door, the smells and sounds of the coffee house would be all that was real to her, and all else become but a fable.

Downstairs, Samuel carefully put up the bolt on the coffee house door and snuffed out the candle above the sleeping boy, before ascending the wooden stair to his own chamber, his left leg dragging a little, as it had done last night and would tomorrow, for tomorrow would be little different from today, or so Samuel Kent thought.

But Samuel did not know of the ashes lying at the base of a candlestick somewhere else in the breathing, creaking darkness of London, ashes, cold now and ground to wet muck, that only an hour ago had been a note bearing three words, in cypher, that spelled out to its careful reader: 'Kent's coffee house'.

TWO

At Kent's Coffee House

2 November

Seeker was awake long before the first fingers of grey dawn light had begun to make their way through the cracks in his window shutters. It was not some tension, some anxious anticipation of the day to come and what it might hold that had woken him, but the desire to rein in his mind from its night-roaming. Awake, he could reassert his will over those things that, if they could not be forgotten, could at least be pushed for a few hours to where his thoughts had not the leisure to consider them.

In the daytime hours, and those of darkness when Thurloe's business, Cromwell's business, occupied him, he was surrounded by people: in the city, in his rooms at Whitehall, on horseback at the head of his troop, and yet none, not even Daniel Proctor, his trusted sergeant, could breach the defences he had set round himself. Few tried, none more than once. But here, in his own room, in his sleep, faces, voices from the time before he had known to set that barrier around himself, came to him. He woke, sometimes, to the sound of his own voice trying to call out, but he was determined that he would master that too, eventually.

On the Shoreditch road, two Scotsmen left their inn early. As ever, there were many travellers on that road, and few took the time to notice that the tall young man clad in a worn but well-cut suit of Flemish cloth and his older companion, who was dressed entirely in black, were wrong, somehow. The older man, thin and sallow-skinned, might have been a man of learning. The younger carried what luggage they had in two packs upon his back, like a soldier, and indeed, he had something of the air of a soldier, for he was certainly not a servant. Zander Seaton did not walk as a servant would, did not address the other as a servant might his master.

Something of the city had begun to seep into them long before they saw it. By the time they approached the Bishop's Gate, they could feel the heat and the noise, the stench, of the great metropolis rise from its walls, past fields where women dried their linens and windmills turned, carrying the odours of every shade of humanity towards them on the breeze. Seaton glanced at his older companion. From their first sight of the sea of spires piercing the sky, and the naked steeple of the great church of St Paul's rising on its hill above the rest, Archibald Campbell had not spoken, had not taken his eyes from the panorama unfolding before them. Only once, as they passed the crumbling, morose walls of a place called Bethlem, beyond whose gates they could not see, did the minister's step falter, and a momentary shiver as of intense cold seem to possess him.

'What is that place, do you think?' he said at last.

Seaton knew. He had seen other such places in France, in Germany, Holland, Spain. God help them. 'It is a hospital for the lunatic, the distracted, the sick of mind.'

The black-clad Campbell regarded it a moment before turning his eyes back to the road ahead of them. 'I do not think so.'

And indeed, half an hour later it seemed that the madness was within the gates of the city and not without. In all his travels, Seaton had never known a place of such constant movement and noise. Smiths, carpenters, butchers, groaning and shrieking beasts, the calls of hawkers of every conceivable ware, and everywhere, the ringing of bells. The babble grew louder the further in they got, delivering themselves to a swarm of streets and alleys and strange cacophonic voices. Seaton listened to the great beast of the city that awaited him and thought how in its very bowels he might find his revenge.

The aromas from Samuel Kent's roasting pan were already snaking their way down Birchin Lane to meet and mingle with those coming from Pasqua Rosee's coffee house in nearby St Michael's churchyard. Others ground their beans and heated their brew in The Rainbow on Fleet Street and The Postern by Moorgate. Samuel knew it did not matter:

there was trade for them all, as merchants and traders from the Royal Exchange, lawyers from the Inns of Court, printers, booksellers, pamphlet-writers around St Paul's, physicians, apothecaries, poets — all felt themselves compelled each day to their favoured coffee house, to take their dish and pipe and hear all the news and rumours of the world, arrange their trades, increase their business, practise their wit, have themselves seen, know what was to be known in London that day. There were those who thought the new beverage to be an abomination, the Devil's drink, that the dark and smoky serving rooms were but precursors of the Hades to which their patrons would inevitably be consigned; they complained about the noxious smells and clouds of smoke from fire and roasting pan and pipe that enveloped the streets and lanes around a coffee house, warned of the sedition harboured within. Kent paid them no heed: most men were drawn there, eventually.

Samuel poured out a dish of coffee for the pale and shabbily dressed lawyer, Elias Ellingworth, who was laughing good-naturedly with a wealthy-looking merchant twenty years his senior.

'We'd given up seeing you here again, George, when we heard you'd gone to Hull. How did you find it?'

George Tavener, another regular at Kent's, grunted as he accepted a pipe from the coffee boy. 'Miserable as one of Mistress Cromwell's dinners and damned if I could sell the place.'

Ellingworth and Will Fiddler, a packman, laughed, but

Grace, behind the serving counter, looked up warily. 'You know we are to call her the Lady Protectress,' she said quietly.

George Tavener looked about him. There were some new faces in the coffee house this morning, and you could never tell who might be a spy for the Council of State, sniffing out signs of sedition. 'Aye, you're right, Grace: this tongue of mine will land me in Newgate one of these days.'

'More like the Tower for your treason,' said Ellingworth.

'Then we'll hunker down together, Elias, for I don't think Old Nol much likes the tenor of your pamphlets.'

'Then he should remember what was fought for, and stop aping the king so many died to be freed of.'

'Elias . . .'

'Well, where is our liberty of conscience, our free parliament, equal access to the law?'

'Elias,' Grace cautioned again.

'What? Did your uncle lame himself in the war that we might bow and scrape to a Huntingdon housewife?'

'Ach,' said Samuel good-naturedly as he lifted the grill pan from the fire and poured the beans into a pestle for the boy to crush, 'I lamed myself because I was too stupid to do anything else.'

Tavener shook his head. 'You have never been stupid, Samuel, although,' and he took his pipe from his mouth and pointed with it to something on the wall a little behind Samuel's head, 'the standard of decoration in here gets no better.'

Samuel looked again at the landscape of ancient church and churchyard that he had hoped might lend the right degree of *gravitas* to his establishment. It had pleased him on sight: the huge skies and desolate moor beyond had reminded him of his native West Country, as had the poor fellow who'd sold it to him.

'You don't like it?'

Tavener snorted. 'If you had wanted something for the walls you should have come to me. I have boats in and out to Amsterdam every other week, and I know every dealer in the place. I tell you, Holland is brimming full with poor fellows who would sell you a masterpiece for the price of those daubings, is that not so, *Mijnheer*?' His appeal was to the soberly dressed Dutchman who had come in but half an hour earlier, and with whom, in the way of the coffee house, he and the packman had already made it their business to become acquainted.

Jakob Hendricks attempted diplomacy. 'Perhaps a Dutchman would not have painted an English scene so well.'

'What?' scoffed Tavener. 'When Dutchmen have so thoroughly painted our kings!'

Hendricks looked uncomfortable and bowed his head to the merchant. 'I am a mere scholar. I know little of art.' He turned his attention away from the painting, and engaged the packman in a conversation about where certain books he sought might be found at the best prices, while Tavener regaled the rest with his thoughts on the relative merits of van Rijn and van Dyke, of de Hooch and Vermeer.

Samuel Kent smiled as he bent once more to fill the roasting tin. All was well: George Tavener could always be trusted to turn the talk of the coffee house away from the path of sedition. The regime had eyes and ears everywhere, in the very court of the exiled King even, it was rumoured, so that a man might barely speak free with his neighbour. This hard-won liberty was a fearful thing.

And there were other strangers in the coffee house today. When the door opened in from Birchin Lane, Samuel knew the two newcomers for Scotsmen at a glance. He had seen their like in the War, though not, it struck him, on the same side. No matter: his war had been over nine years now, and it did no good to dwell on the past. The Scotsmen seated, their penny paid, Grace saw to the preparation of their coffee and the boy Gabriel began to fill their pipes.

Samuel noticed Tavener regarding the older of the two curiously. 'You have travelled far I think, Mr . . .?'

'Campbell,' answered the other. 'Far enough.'

'Scotland is it?' joined Will Fiddler, the packman.

A nod.

'And what has brought you to London?'

'My own two feet,' said Campbell sourly, reaching for an edition of *Mercurius Politicus*, fresh off the presses that day, and steadfastly ignoring the packman.

George Tavener glanced around the table and then addressed himself to Campbell. 'You must forgive us, Sir. You will not be familiar with the ways of the London coffee house. It is a place of discourse amongst strangers as well as friends. We will talk on anything from the price of a Holland bulb to the lace on the Queen of Spain's cap. News flies in through the door, around the tables, and out again. There is no precedence, no respecting of persons.'

Campbell grunted in acknowledgement, and Tavener, encouraged, continued. 'Here you have Will Fiddler, a humble peddler,' and at this Fiddler doffed his cap to the newcomers, 'and should the Lord Protector himself put in an appearance, no one would expect Will there to shift for him. Here by my side is Elias Ellingworth, a young lawyer of great gifts but few means, and to your left, *Mijnheer* Jakob Hendricks, docked only yesterday from Amsterdam. All are welcome and all are equal.'

Campbell had shown little interest in Tavener's encomium, although he now displayed some in Tavener himself.

'You have not the look of a man who is either humble, or of poor means.'

The merchant smiled. 'I was, once. I was born to the stench of the Thames and all its detritus, but I soon began to understand what the river is, and then it was not filth and tar that I smelled, but the scents of the Levant, the Indies. Oil, wine, spices. I smelled money. Now I trade English woollens for Flemish lace; I carry bibles from Amsterdam to the Americas, tobacco from Virginia to Bilbão, Spanish wine back to London.' He clapped his hand on the smooth oak surface of the coffee house table. 'As the world spins on its axis, its wealth spins round on bargains I strike in this very room.'

Campbell sniffed and took a first, tentative sip of the coffee that had been set down before him. He winced at the scorching, bitter taste, but took another sip before addressing Tavener again.

'And is that all you trade?'

Fiddler laughed. 'Lord, Sir, is there anything left?'

Campbell turned his full gaze on the packman. 'Oh, I think so. Indeed I think so.'

As Campbell lifted the cup a third time to his lips, there came a terrible screeching from outside on Cornhill, followed by the sounds of a crash.

'You stay here, girl,' said Samuel to his niece as he hobbled out on to Birchin Lane after a good number of the coffee-drinkers.

All was chaos. A hackney carriage had collided with a bookseller's shop front, overturning and throwing its driver to the ground in the process. The flimsy wooden façade of the shop front had crashed down, trapping an unfortunate passer-by under the weight of smashed shelves and tumbled books and pamphlets. The horses were rearing and squealing in terror, to the imminent danger of any who drew near, and there were loud cries for the Watch, and for something to be done. A surgeon was called for, to attend to the unfortunate soul beneath, who was making a tremendous amount of noise. From the broken cab there came no sound at all.

A little more than ten minutes later, by which time the accident on Cornhill had threatened to turn to riot as carts and carriages found their way blocked and tried to make their ways instead down too-narrow lanes and alleyways, putting pedestrians, animals and shopkeepers' booths alike in peril, Grace Kent was attending to the one person who amidst all the noise and confusion had simply waited. The lady, who gave her name as Anne Winter, had finally emerged from the righted cab almost unscathed. Her hair and clothing were only a little dishevelled, and she appeared to have escaped any injury at all. At least, this is what she herself insisted, utterly refusing Grace's entreaties that she should allow herself to be examined by the physician whom her uncle had sent Gabriel to fetch.

'I assure you, there is nothing.' The voice was soft, distant.

Grace thought that if there was nothing, then it was a miracle. The slim, pale arms and hands glimpsed from the sleeves of the lady's plum-coloured velvet jacket were fine as porcelain and yet did indeed appear to be unmarked by bruise or graze. Grace could not tell whether the pallor of the woman's face beneath the deep brown hair was habitual or the result of the shock she had just had, but there was a brightness to her pale grey eyes that surprised her.

'Will you take a dish of chocolate, my Lady, to warm you, while we send word to your husband?'

It was a moment before the woman showed that she had heard her. 'I do not wish you to send word to my husband. But I would like to try your chocolate and then I will find my own way home.'

'I really don't think your husband would like you to wander out alone, your Ladyship.'

The woman regarded Grace with a strange smile. 'Do you know my husband, then?'

'No, I, don't think so. Unless he has ever been in here—'

'Ah, you would remember him, if that were the case. Some say he is the best-set man they have ever laid eyes on. But he is a very busy man, too, and there is no call to inconvenience him over so minor a thing as this.'

Grace gave off trying to persuade her, and, leaving Anne Winter in the private booth near the rear of the coffee room, she went to begin the preparation of the chocolate. As she passed, Elias touched her lightly on the arm. 'Best for Samuel to send her on her way, before her husband hears of it,' he muttered, but not so low that Archibald Campbell did not also hear him.

'Why? Who is she?'

'Lady Anne Winter. Her husband, John Winter, is a lieutenant in the army and has Cromwell's favour. He will not like his wife to be seen in a public coffee house.'

Campbell was still watching the woman. 'He must be wealthy man too, by the look of his wife's clothes.'

Will Fiddler shook his head. 'Not him. An ostler's son, lower born than the Protector himself. But her, now that is a different matter.'

Elias Ellingworth tilted his head in Fiddler's direction. 'There's no one in London whose story Will cannot tell. And sometimes they're even true!'

Fiddler ignored the remark and leaned closer to the two Scotsmen. 'Lady Anne's father, Lord Baxton, came out for the late King. After the father's death at Naseby the son tried to hold Baxton Hall, near Oxford, against the parliamentary forces. The boy was only seventeen, refused to surrender, died defending the place. The house was sacked, and the soldiers would have had the sister too, had John Winter not intervened. He was just a sergeant in those days, but still he held firm and the girl was unmolested. She'd no one left then, though; God alone knows what would have become of her if he hadn't married her.'

The woman quietly sipping her chocolate in the private booth still had the look of someone alone in the world. Grace watched her from her counter.

'She won't let me send word for her husband,' she said to her uncle.

'Don't worry, it's already done,' he assured her.

'She will not like it,' said Grace.

'Hmmph,' Samuel grunted. 'It's not her head the trouble would fall on if I allowed her out to wander these streets alone.'

★

Yet, sitting there in the booth of Kent's coffee house, Anne Winter did not feel alone. She could hear the rising voices of the men in conversation, and it brought her back to her home in Oxfordshire, and her father's table, where men, and women too, had talked without fear, and where there had been laughter, and rows and shouting and all things natural to a home. Baxton Hall had not been a place of silences, of carefully measured words. Much had been said there that was not politic, not wise. She had not understood it then, but that was freedom, and she had not known it since John Winter had brought her to London, but she saw it here, now, in this city coffee house.

The conversation at the table had turned to John Milton, the Dutchman having fallen into earnest debate with the young lawyer over the role of Milton in the state censorship of the press, and of his merits as a writer. Anne Winter knew John Milton and she did not like him. Hendricks spoke warmly of Milton's gifts as a poet, but Ellingworth was having none of it.

'He's a hypocrite and a traitor to his own beliefs. Once, you know, he was a champion of free speech, now he sits in the censor's office, declaring which of their thoughts other men might, and might not, be permitted to set in print. Ten years ago he did not scruple to put his name to things that might have landed him in the Tower; now, he courts Cromwell and polishes his pension.'

Anne Winter remembered, ten years ago, her father and brother arguing in the library, the pamphlet *Areopagitica* in her brother's hands. 'Anarchy,' her father had declared at last. 'Anarchy is what there would be, if your Mr Milton should have his way, and men be free to publish whatever nonsense came into their heads.' But he had not crumpled the pamphlet her brother had brought home, nor set it on the fire as she had thought he might. Instead, before leaving the library, a glass of wine in one hand, his other arm around his son's shoulders, he had set it on a shelf, with others of the like, and there it had remained, gathering dust, until Cromwell's soldiers came to smash every shelf and cabinet in the place, and trample Milton's fine words underfoot.

Ellingworth's rising voice brought her back to the present. 'He is twice culpable, to prostitute his gift as the chief propagandist of a regime that would stifle the freedoms of other men . . .' For some time, the lawyer went on in this unguarded manner. Once or twice Anne Winter glanced at Grace Kent, and saw the growing anxiety on her face.

'She loves him,' she thought. And the realisation that such a thing might still be possible warmed her more even than did the chocolate in the bowl.

The Dutchman had sat quietly throughout Elias's diatribe. 'I see you are a Leveller, my friend. I thought your Cromwell had crushed the Levellers along with everyone else who did not agree with him.'

'So does he,' muttered Ellingworth quietly, before gathering up the papers in front of him. 'But there is my sister at the door to remind me I have business to see to at the Temple. I have enjoyed our conversation, Mr Hendricks. I hope to meet you here again.' And he left, hastily ushered out into the lane by the young woman who had been waiting for him in the doorway.

It was only a little later that Hendricks also left, to be followed soon afterwards by Lady Anne, dismissing a last entreaty from Grace that she would not go out into the streets alone.

'Who would ever lay a hand on John Winter's wife? His name opens doors quicker than a key, it clears the street in front of me. If any importune me, I have but to say, "I am John Winter's wife," and they are gone.' She laid a shilling, far more than was required for the cost of the chocolate, on the table and left before any could think of a reasonable way to stop her.

The Scotsmen had not lingered long after their second dish, and once Will Fiddler had collected some packets of coffee from Samuel for distribution to a few private houses across the Bridge in Southwark, he too was gone. Samuel and Grace had not much time to reflect upon the events of the morning as the benches at the table filled up time and again with new drinkers, new stories. And yet Grace did wonder about the piece of paper, a cutting from a news-book, by the look of it, that had fluttered to the floor of the private booth from Lady Anne Winter's sable muffler, and wished she might have had time to look at it before the younger of the two Scotsmen had found it, and put it away in the folds of his cloak.

THREE

Blood

Seeker ran a hand across his forehead after reading the report a second time. The chapel bell had just tolled three, but there was nothing for it, the thing could not be left until dawn. He cursed the false intelligence that had dragged him out to Romney and kept him there all day while his informant's report from Kent's had lain and festered on his desk.

His men were at their barracks, in their beds at last, the ante-chamber to his room near the Cockpit was empty, but that was all right: what he had to discuss with John Winter was not something he wanted a junior officer to hear, anyway.

Winter's apartments were away over on the other side of the morass of buildings that was Whitehall Palace, and Seeker had time to go over in his mind the main points of the report from Kent's as he made his way there. His source was a good one – dependable, thorough, and to the point. Seeker's business was the communication, the processing, of facts; he had limited interest in the opinions of others, and this informant knew well enough by now not to offer any. Half at least of what Thurloe brought to him proved to be grounded in false trails, rumours begun to divert attention from some other plot, planted by enemies of the Protectorate less subtle than they imagined themselves to be. There was too much, however, in the report he had just read that could not simply be ascribed to coincidence. It was to be regretted, for Samuel Kent had been a good soldier and an honest man, but he should have chosen for himself some other trade than keeper of a coffee house, for dissidents were drawn to those places as bees to a hive.

Merchants, lawyers, newspaper men: Seeker would be more suspicious of a coffee house that did not boast such a clientele. It amused the Council that the lawyer Ellingworth appeared to believe his alias of 'the Sparrow' shielded his true identity. 'Give him enough rope and he will hang himself,' one of the generals had said, and the others had laughed. Milton, taking down a record of proceedings, had not laughed. Seeker had not laughed, either, when he heard of it.

Travellers – so many travellers passed through London that it was a wonder they did not carry the place off with them. The Dutchman: a scholar journeying to Oxford, visiting some friends in the city before he did so. Seeker would have the names of these friends soon enough, from his contacts in the Dutch quarter of St Katharine's, and their church at Austin Friars. Cromwell might be at peace with the Dutch just now, but peace was made to be broken. And then there were the Scotsmen. What a creeping plague on this nation – no interest in the good of England, the welfare of the Commonwealth, no interest in anything but their own petty schemes, their Covenant or their King, and never knowing from one day to the next which they wanted. Cromwell had scarcely more stomach for them than he did the Irish. But why had these two come to London? The minister, Campbell, had been called to the pulpit of the Presbyterian chapel at Goldsmith's Court. Good luck to him – the days of his sort were done, thank God. But what of the other – a Royalist, 'even smelled like a Royalist,' his informer had noted. 'Has been abroad' – well, most of them had by now. 'Clothes are Flemish, good, but worn. Didn't speak to the Dutchman, but understood him all right when Hendricks slipped into his own tongue.'

All these individuals would require Seeker's attention, and yet, none of them was particularly out of the ordinary, for imagined plots against the Protector usually featured a foreigner, a returning Royalist, or a Scotsman, somewhere. What worried him were the things he could not have predicted: a clandestine search of the packman's bag had revealed things that shouldn't have been there. Seeker had long suspected Will Fiddler of circulating pamphlets for Ellingworth and his like, and that such had been in the bag was no surprise. There had been another item though in amongst the chapbooks, broadsheets and almanacs: a folio of sheets of music and songs by Henry Lawes and William Davenant. Lawes had composed for the court of Charles Stuart, and had had the sense to live quiet until such time as

Oliver had declared a liking for him; Davenant was a Royalist plague, who should have gone to the scaffold long ago. This late collaboration of theirs was permitted by the indulgence of the Protector alone, and not a thing for public consumption, far less to be touted round the country by the likes of Will Fiddler.

Most troubling of all was that John Winter's wife should have been alone there, in a coffee house in the middle of the city, and intent on going afterwards to Whitefriars, of all places. Over by Temple Bar was outside the Lord Mayor's jurisdiction, and many living there were beyond the law, desperate types. It was not a place for any decent woman to go alone, but for the Royalist wife of one of Cromwell's most favoured officers, there could be no good reason to go there at all.

It was a frustration to him: there could be no good ordering of society if people would not keep to their proper places, if they would persist in masquerading as that which they were not. But Seeker would find them out: he always did.

He knew that the Army Council meeting had gone on until almost two; if John Winter was at last abed he could not have been there long, but no matter: his wife lived too close to the centre of power, and if she should be mixed up in some plot against the Protector, it was not a thing that could be left until the morning.

Seeker mounted the last flight of stairs leading to the corridor where the Winters had their apartments, alongside those of Cromwell's other favoured officers and their families. He never felt comfortable in this part of the Palace, and came to it as seldom as possible. Turning down the corridor he wished he had brought a light with him, for half at least of the candles along the walls had burned down or been snuffed out. The Winters' lodgings were at the far end, at the top of another flight of stairs, and that end of the corridor was almost totally in darkness. Something of Seeker's old huntsman instinct came back to him. There was a prickling of the hairs on his arm, at the back of his neck, as when wounded prey was close somewhere, in the darkness. He slowed his pace a little, looked more deeply into the gloom, listened. He sensed them then: something living and something dead. A man with his back to him was standing up slowly, never shifting his attention from the object crumpled on the floor. As Seeker drew closer, Elias Ellingworth at last turned to face him, his open mouth emitting only a strangled moan as the knife in his hand fell to the floor where John Winter lay collapsed, bloodied, dead.

FOUR

A Woman's Room

3 November

'I swear it, Seeker, I swear it . . .' Ellingworth's protestations of innocence became fainter and fainter as he was dragged through the corridors away from John Winter's body and towards the closed and heavily guarded wagon that would take him to the Tower. The lawyer had been scarcely coherent in the short time between Seeker having come upon him and the arrival of the guards Seeker had shouted for. The commotion had brought three other officers, neighbours to the Winters, bleary-eyed but ready-armed, through the doors of their own private apartments, and they quickly took charge of the prisoner while Seeker hammered on the Winters' door.

A terrified girl opened the door a few inches, and her terror only increased when she saw the bloodied mess on the floor a few yards from where she stood. She began to scream.

Seeker put a hand on her mouth, firmly, but without violence, until she calmed and he could see that her eyes were fixed on his, and that she was listening. His voice was low.

'Where is your mistress?'

'I, I don't know . . . I think . . .'

She looked towards a door set into the wood panelling to the right of the fireplace.

'In there?' he said, nodding to the door.

The girl seemed unsure. 'I think, maybe.'

Seeker tried the handle. 'Open it,' he ordered, on finding it locked.

The girl scurried to the ornately carved mantelpiece and ran her hand along the high shelf with increasing confusion. She turned at last to Seeker, tears brimming on her lashes and starting to travel down her cheeks. 'I cannot find the key, Sir.'

An uncharacteristic oath escaped Seeker, and he ordered the girl to move aside. A moment later, after a massive thud and a splintering, the thick oak door swung open on to another scene of blood. It was on the sleeves of Anne Winter's white linen nightgown, and all down the loosened front. There was some even in the hair that lay across her cheek and brushed her exposed breast. She was sprawled across the damask coverlet of her marriage bed, the heavy velvet curtains of the canopy not closed, one wet silk slipper on her right foot, the other fallen on to the floor.

At the sight of her mistress, the girl had slumped to the ground, jabbering, incapable. 'Get her out of here,' Seeker said to one of his men. He removed the black leather glove from his left hand and put two fingers to the side of Anne Winter's neck. 'Pass me that jug of water.' Another of his men handed him the silver ewer from the sideboard. Seeker checked it briefly and then threw it over the face of the woman lying across the bed in front of him.

She flinched and turned her head, moaning slightly.

'Get up,' he said.

Another moan.

Seeker stood up and turned his back on her. 'Lift her up against the pillows.' He lifted a green brocade dressing gown from a chair by the wall and threw it over to the bed. 'Make her decent.'

In a few moments, the men had Anne Winter upright, and had called her maid, who had recovered herself a little, back into the room to help dress her. 'Don't wash her, yet,' he said.

As she came to, Anne Winter rubbed her hands over her face, wiped them on the Italian damask coverlet, examined the sodden strands of her hair as if she had never seen them before. Slowly, she looked up at Seeker, taking a little time to focus on him. Her forehead furrowed in incomprehension. 'Captain Seeker, why are you here?'

'Why is there blood on your gown?'

She looked at her garments, again a picture of genuine curiosity. 'I don't know.' And then, 'Oh, I think it must be my husband's.'

The calmness of her tone astonished him.

'You know he is dead?'

She nodded, making an effort at being exact. 'Oh, yes. He was not at first, when I found him, not quite. He was in the corridor, outside our door, slumped over and the blood was everywhere: there was a great deal of blood. I held him a few minutes until he died. Poor John, he had so long longed for some sign of tenderness from me, and he had it at last, but I do not think he would have wanted it that way. Never mind.' She looked again at her hands, the blood on her white lace cuffs. 'Poor Dinah will have some work to get these stains out of my clothes.'

Seeker wondered if the woman was mad. He had heard it said she was ill, a melancholic, vacant even, but now he wondered whether she might actually be mad. She made to get out of the bed, but he put out a hand to stay her.

Anne Winter looked at the hand on her shoulder and glanced at the two men guarding the doorway and again at Seeker. Something of the seriousness of her situation at last appeared to register.

'No, I suppose not.' She sank back against the pillows.

'You cannot have come upon him alive. I just found him myself, dead in the corridor there, his killer kneeling over him.'

Seeker was certain he saw a brief flash of fear in Anne Winter's eyes.

'No,' she said.

'No?'

She shook her head, adamant. 'He was still alive when I found him.'

'And the man – the lawyer, Ellingworth, was not there?'

Again she shook her head, again adamant. 'No.'

The effort appeared to be as much as she could make, and Seeker feared she might drift out of consciousness once more. He took hold of her chin with thumb and forefinger, and forced her to look at him.

'At what hour did you come upon him like that?'

She bit her lip. 'Late, very late.'

His patience was threatening to fail him. 'How late?'

She shook her head, raised her hands, helpless. But then, 'I think I heard the chapel bell. I think it was perhaps two.'

'He was calling for help?'

'What?' She didn't seem to understand him.

'Did you hear him calling for help? Is that what awakened you, or were there sounds of a struggle?'

She looked at him a moment then comprehension dawned. 'Oh! No, I wasn't sleeping. I was coming back along the corridor when I found him like that.'

'You were out in the corridor?'

'I was coming home.'

'From where?'

Again she gave the question her consideration. 'I wish I could tell you, but I really do not know. My head is an agony – where is Dinah?'

'She can come back in when I've finished. Was anybody with you? Were you alone when you found your husband?'

'Yes.'

'There was not a man there with him?'

'No.'

He could see she was flagging, drifting in and out of sense, but he was not finished yet.

'And you are certain he was still alive when you found him?'

She smiled. 'Oh, yes. He tried to say my name. Poor John.'

Seeker cast his mind back to the scene he had so recently come upon. One of Cromwell's finest officers lying dead, his cheek against the wooden panelling of the corridor, his body twisted, slumped on black and white marble tiles turned brown with dried blood. At Winter's neck had been one deep gash from where his life had flowed. His eyes, that had been fine eyes, were wide not in horror but in sadness. She had not even bothered to close them.

'You did not think to call for help?'

Anne Winter twisted the ruby ring on her finger, like fresh drops of blood gleaming in the candlelight. She appeared fascinated by it, and didn't raise her eyes to look at him as she spoke.

'It was so late, and everyone sleeping. And it wouldn't have made any difference, anyway.'

'You cannot have known that.'

Now she left off playing with her ring and regarded him directly. 'Believe me or not, as seems best to you, but that is the truth.'

Seeker couldn't look at her. All round her were the trappings of a luxury she didn't even appreciate, silk stockings, women's underthings lying carelessly dropped on the floor, jewels – rings set with emeralds, a brooch and earrings of ruby and pearl, a silver clasp in the form of a rabbit with amber eyes. There was little in here of the man he had once supped with. His mind went back to that time: they had met one night, late, on the Old Staircase leading from the Tilt Yard up to King Henry's Gallery. Seeker had just returned to Whitehall from business across the river, and Winter had just left from a meeting of the Council of Officers in the Cockpit. Seeker was not in the habit of issuing invitations, and rarely sought out the company of other men, but there was something in the other man, perhaps a reflection of his own weariness and hunger at the end of a long day, that had prompted him to ask John Winter if he would have a bite to eat with him. And so they had done, no more than some bread and beer and cold mutton, and they had talked of the country, and the army, and just a little of themselves. Seeker had liked John Winter, and at another time, in another England, they might well have fallen more into one another's company. But this was not another time, nor any other England.

And now, tonight, looking on the man's widow, Seeker would rather have been many places than John Winter's bedchamber, but although he had no great confidence he would get any sense out of her, there was something else he needed to know from this woman.

'Why did you go to Kent's coffee house yesterday?'

'The coffee house?' She was surprised. 'I had not meant to go there, there was an accident. But who told you I was there? Oh, Sir Gwyllm, I suppose.'

It was Seeker's turn to be thrown off guard. 'Sir Gwyllm who?'

'Crowther. I thought I saw him there.'

Seeker cast his mind back to the list of names on the report from his informant. There was no Sir Gwyllm Crowther on it, and Gwyllm Crowther was a name unknown to him. He filed it away for later consideration.

'And after Kent's?'

After Kent's. Anne Winter searched through the clouds of her mind until they began to clear a little. She remembered where she had gone. Not to the fashionable shops and booths of the Royal Exchange as she would have had people think, but down towards Whitefriars, and further into parts of London than a woman whose husband walked the corridors of Whitehall and had the ear of Cromwell should ever be found in. The further from the city proper she had gone, the closer to the stinking Fleet ditch and the river, the more she had felt an indefinable sense of anxiety in the air that only served to heighten her own agitation. With every step, she had become more conscious of herself as a thing out of its element. The press of people on the street might have been scarcely less, closer to the river, than it had been on Cornhill, but she'd become more and more aware that the quality of her clothes, the way she walked, marked her more clearly here as she delved deeper into passages and alleyways where neither she nor her fine clothing belonged. What she had not been aware of, then, was that she was being followed.

She remembered the slight panic when she had gone to check again, for the tenth time at least, the cutting from the news-book, and not been able to find it. But it hadn't mattered: she had read it over so often, she had it by heart. 'The Countess of Kent's powder, efficacious against fever, plague, small-pox, the pains of labour and colic in the newborn.' Only to be purchased at a certain apothecary's shop, at the sign of the Pineapple, in Magpie Alley, Whitefriars. In this world of codes and deceptions, she knew what this one offered. After a few false turns, she had at last found herself in the narrow alley, and seen the sign of a pineapple hanging some way down it, away from the street.

How furtively she had made her way there, yesterday; how pointless it all seemed now, today, that John was dead. Here, in her bedchamber, surrounded by the baubles of her life, she looked at Seeker. Out in the streets, her maid had once told her, the man was a myth, a story to frighten children to their beds. So much for the streets. He stood before her now, no myth, no children's tale, but a living man of flesh, blood, bone and muscle on a frame six feet four in length, clad almost entirely in black. His cropped dark hair shot through with steel-grey, Damian Seeker was aged somewhere between forty and fifty years old, and in his eyes was reflected a world he did not care for. Looking at him, calculating, Anne Winter decided to tell him the truth, or some of it.

'You went to Whitefriars, for an apothecary?' Seeker found it difficult to keep the trace of contempt from his voice. 'There must be two dozen apothecaries at least between here and Magpie Alley. What did you want from this apothecary that you could not get within a half-mile of here?'

Despite everything he had thought about this woman – and he had rarely thought about her, other than when the Protector had once remarked that she was not good enough for Winter – he was not prepared for her answer.

'Opium.'

So that was it – the deadness of her eyes, her clouded recollection, the rumoured wanderings: the woman was an opium addict.

Seeker thought again about John Winter. 'Your husband knew of it?'

She was looking down at her feet, over to the grey ashes of the fire. 'He, I didn't think . . .' Finally, she looked directly at Seeker. 'Yes. In the end, yes.'

Seeker could have done without this. He had not the time for this. The usual motives of man – greed, lust, power-hunger, jealousy, revenge – were the paths he would track his prey by. He would cut through the tangle of obfuscation and deception set out before him and eventually find the culprit at its heart, but a woman whose mind was not under even her own control changed the rules of the hunt to the extent that they were unknowable.

'Tell me then,' he said.

Anne Winter clasped her hands in front of her and focused again on the dead hearth. She was making an effort to be clear, to get things right, he thought.

'It is not a secret, in these corridors, or further afield, I imagine, I was not happy in my marriage. I do not say John was a bad husband – he wasn't. But I would never have chosen to marry an officer of the army that murdered my father and my brother, and destroyed my home.'

Seeker had resolved to keep silent as she spoke, so he did not correct her; her father had died in battle on the field; her brother had been offered the chance to surrender and had refused. That was not murder, it was war. Other things were war too, and John Winter had saved her from those.

'I knew of herbs and plants to deal with many ailments of the mind and body, but none that would make me forget my soul. When John brought me to London, I began to seek out apothecaries who could provide what I needed. Little by little, they began to understand what I wanted, but most, when they realised how deep was my desperation, or who my husband was – I could never really be certain which it was – drew back, and would not help me. So I had to go further, into the dark places, places where others go to find what cannot be had honestly.' She smiled at him. 'There are other women, you know, who do the same. You are not the only one who deals in codes, Mr Seeker. I found the man on Magpie Alley through an advertisement placed in a news-book, in plain sight.' The thought evidently amused her. 'Mr Milton's office is clearly too busy censoring the news-books for other things.'

'Keep to the matter in hand,' said Seeker.

'Yes,' she nodded, thinking. 'Magpie Alley. I had been warned this man was not like others – the payments he demanded were very high, and not easily mitigated. I had with me some money, but when I got there, he wouldn't take it.'

'He wanted more?'

'He wanted something else. I had taken a jewel with me in that bag' – she looked to her bedside cabinet, on which a black velvet bag embroidered in plum and gold threads had been laid – 'a brooch, but in my panic, I couldn't find it, so I offered him one of these earrings instead.' Her fingers went to her neck, pushed back the still damp mahogany curls that fell on it, and began to unclasp an ornament from her ear. She held towards Seeker a pearl and ruby drop, a match for the brooch on her dresser and the ring on her finger which had so occupied her attention earlier. He glanced at it briefly and she slowly returned it to her ear.

'He wouldn't take it?'

She shook her head.

'What was it that he demanded of you?'

She bit her lip and said nothing.

'Lady Anne, have you been—' He was not a man comfortable in these circumstances, or easy in conversation with women. The words came out more harshly than he had meant. 'Did he abuse you?'

Again she shook her head. Her voice was almost inaudible. 'I don't think so. Perhaps when I can wash properly – but I don't think so. Not then, I know that, but as for later, I don't know. I can't remember.'

He took a breath, summoned his patience. 'What can you remember?'

She was on firmer ground. 'I agreed to some sort of bargain, some payment I would make, and he let me have what I wanted. I was in a hurry then to be out of that dingy place, to get back here and take what was in the phial, but I was hardly out of the shop, not even out of the alley, when a man took my arm. Stopped me.'

'The apothecary?'

'No.' She was emphatic. 'Not him. It was a Scotsman I had seen in the coffee house. He must have followed me from there, been outside all along.'

'A Scotsman? The minister or the soldier?'

Her eyes widened in surprise. It never ceased to amaze Seeker that people thought their movements, the company they kept, would stay long a secret from him. 'It was the younger one, the soldier. He spoke to me by name, took the phial from my hand before I even had it in my bag, told me I should not be in that place, and that he was taking me back to my husband.'

This Seeker had not expected. 'He knew who you were? Had your husband sent him?'

'Oh, no, that is what I thought at first. I'd never seen him before in my life until the accident at the coffee house, but he knew who I was, and he was determined to take me directly to John. I asked him questions, tried to persuade him to give me my opium back, as we made our way back here by river, but he would say nothing at all. At the Privy Stairs, and all the guard posts between there and this apartment, he told them he was escorting me home to my husband, and he said it with such an air of authority none questioned him further and I was hardly in a position to argue with him.'

'And what happened when you got back here?'

'John was home, as luck would have it – he was sitting by the window, going over some documents. He stood up when I came in, but then when he saw the man behind me, the colour drained from his face and I knew he hadn't sent him to follow me. When he spoke to the man, it was as one would speak to a dangerous dog.'

'What did he say?'

Seeker could see she was making an effort at being exact. 'He said, "You, what are you doing here?", and the Scotsman answered, "I have brought you your wife." John told me to move away from the doorway then said to him, "What have you to do with my wife?", and the Scotsman answered, "Nothing, but you should have a better care of her and see that she does not wander the streets." Then he threw the bottle I had got across the table, and John got to it before I did. He didn't even taste it, I think he had half suspected it anyway. He said, "Opium," and before I knew it he had opened the casket window and poured the contents into the river below.' She was rubbing at her hands, becoming agitated. 'I begged him to give it to me, but he wouldn't listen . . .'

Seeker had no further interest in her opium craving. 'The Scotsman's name is Seaton. How did your husband know him?'

'What? Oh, I don't know, he wouldn't tell me, and by the time he had managed to pull me away from the window the man was gone. John gave me over to Dinah. Told her to watch that I didn't leave our bedchamber, then went to call the guards, but it was too late, they didn't find him. '

Seeker felt a coldness begin to crawl on his skin. 'And have you seen him again since then, Lady Anne?'

She took more time to reply than he had expected her to. 'No. No, I haven't.'

He'd heard as much from her as he wanted for the moment, and was keen to be out of the disordered bedchamber. Without further comment he turned and went through to the parlour, where the maid was still sniffling. 'See to your mistress,' he said.

Seeker pulled the broken door to John Winter's bedchamber shut in as far as it could be done, and began to examine the parlour. It was richly furnished – not from the days when King Charles's officers of state had occupied these apartments, for what had not been put to the war effort had been taken into security and redistributed as had seemed wise. The paintings, silverware, carpets and good furniture in the room were, he suspected, the remnant of what Winter's wife had been allowed to keep from her father's house at Baxton Hall. So rich, so heavy – how had John Winter, who had been scarcely higher born than Seeker, sat in this room? What comfort could there ever have been for him in all these reminders from her forfeit home of why his wife hated him? There was a bureau by the window, French in design, a delicate thing, but Seeker could appreciate the craftsmanship. Anne Winter's, again, no doubt. But who would Anne Winter have written to, and Thurloe not found her letters? The Council of State had gained control of the postal service over four years since, and for the last year and a half Isaac Dorislaus, under cover of Solicitor to the Admiralty Court, from his rooms next to the principal sorting office, had examined all intercepted mail. Adept in several languages, Dorislaus had learned to recognise handwriting and seals, to spot a cypher and to send it for decryption to John Wallis in Oxford. Anne Winter would not have got past Dorislaus.

Seeker crossed the room, his boots soft on the carpet underfoot where he preferred stone, and opened the lid of the bureau. There was paper, ink, a set of quills, paperweights and sand for blotting. Seeker examined the top sheet of paper – nothing, no markings, indentations, impression of anything written on top of it. He held the sheet to the light. Still nothing. A small drawer inside the bureau was locked. Seeker took a knife from its sheath at his belt and broke the lock. Inside the drawer was a small book, a journal. Seeker brushed off the splinters and opened it. Not Anne Winter's writing, but her husband's, for he had seen it on enough orders, counter-signatures, lists of stores. John Winter's writing and John Winter's name, and two words further, *My Atonement*. He turned the pages. Nothing, until he came to the last and there was a list of names and numbers, books of the Bible and selected verses. Seeker knew them, knew them all – how would he not have done? He slipped the book into his pocket. In a second, deeper drawer, beneath the lid of the desk, again locked and opened by Seeker in like manner, a bundle of pamphlets, news-sheets – different printers, different types, some with copperplate illustrations, most with none. The titles ran for a few weeks it seemed, before they went into abeyance and another appeared, under a new title, with a new author, but Seeker knew them: they were all by the Sparrow, Elias Ellingworth, every one.

On top of the desk, lying as if left to be picked up soon again, was another small book, little more than a pamphlet. Seeker took it in his hand, opened it. He turned the pages, slowly at first, and then more quickly, until he did not see what he read. He sat down in John Winter's chair – a man's chair, how could he have thought this was her chair? – and opened the pamphlet again. It must have been a few minutes before he became aware of Anne Winter, still sickly pale and weak, standing in the doorway, watching him.

'I would not have thought you a reader, Mr Seeker.'

She was dressed in black, now, with a white gauze collar and a row of pearls in her hair. She had exchanged her rubies for mourning rings.

He stood up, held the pamphlet towards her. 'Is this yours?'

She glanced at it, did not take it. '*Colasterion*. No. It was John's. Someone gave it to him.'

'Why would anyone have given him this book?'

'To tempt him, perhaps, to encourage him? Perhaps it was Mr Milton himself.'

Perhaps, thought Seeker. Perhaps Milton, blind Milton, Latin Secretary to the council at which John Winter was often in attendance, had heard in the man's voice that truth which he, Milton, had so long wrestled with. That truth which he had proclaimed, in books and pamphlets, to the scandal of a society that bought up those books and pamphlets in their thousands: a marriage without love was no marriage, and Christ had not intended that a man and woman so united should spend their lives in despair. *Colasterion* was a manifesto for divorce.

'Perhaps it was,' said Seeker, crumpling Milton's divorce pamphlet in his hand and throwing it on to the fire. 'Did you kill your husband, Lady Anne?'

The woman's eyes widened. 'Kill him? No. Why would I have killed him? As I said, he was not a bad husband, if I was to have one at all, and in this Commonwealth I might have fared a deal worse.'

'But you did not love him?'

'Love him? What would that matter? What do you know of love, Mr Seeker?'

Seeker watched the flames consume the pamphlet, considered the power of words, the inefficacy of flames to destroy words once read or spoken. And Anne Winter's words burned in his mind. More than you have ever known, he might have answered, but when the pamphlet was at last ashes, he rose and left the apartment without making any response.

FIVE

The Girl at Dove Court

First light had not yet broken over London, but it was still later than he would have wished that Seeker's troop made its way with a clatter of hooves over the cobbles of Horse Guard Yard out on to Whitehall and the road to Charing Cross. Mounted soldiers were a common enough sight at any hour of the day in London, and yet something of this party took the special attention of any passers-by who chanced to turn or lift their eyes towards it. The New Model Army was famous for its discipline, its order, the quality of its arms and horse, and still this troop was something apart. Eight soldiers who sat their mounts with a confidence born, not learned, and at their head their captain, on a black German stallion seventeen hands high. It was in the stables of Horse Guard Yard, perhaps more than anywhere else in London, that Damian Seeker let slip the mask to show tenderness, and that tenderness was towards this magnificent beast. But today, his long black cloak flowing behind him as he spurred his horse towards the city, there could be no doubt that there was business of great import somewhere, and those few who saw Seeker pass gave silent thanks that whatever it was was no concern of theirs.

In the garret of Dove Court, Maria Ellingworth was stirring. The birds outside her window had not started their song, and even the Angel Tavern up the lane had yet to waken to a new day's business, but the coldness of the air was insidious and pulled her to consciousness from an already unsettled night. Elias must have been very late last night; she had not heard him come in. She wished he would not wander abroad so long after curfew, but he had told her that there were matters which he and his fellow thinkers could no longer discuss freely in daylight hours. He was radical and careless enough in his speech at the coffee houses, more so in print. What he discussed with his companions in the hours of darkness, she did not even want to know.

She had known from the look on Grace's face when she had gone by Kent's yesterday to collect her brother that Elias had been unguarded in front of strangers again. There had been a number of coffee-drinkers in Kent's whom Maria had never seen in there before, and any one of them might have been a government informer. Once out in the street, she had noticed that Elias was carrying the papers he'd been working on the previous night. It had taken her some time to prise the bundle from him.

'I will take them to the printer's. You shouldn't walk around with them on your person like this, Elias.'

'And what would you have me do,' he had protested,

'trust them to carrier pigeon? One of Cromwell's hawks would have it in its claws before it took flight, and it would be on a silver platter before the Lord Protector by dinnertime.'

'I would have you give them to me.'

He would have argued with her further, but the bells of St Paul's had begun to chime twelve, setting off other bells all through the city.

'And now, see, you will be late!' she had said, wrenching the papers from him as she gave him a peck on the cheek and sent him to dodge through the crowds on his way down to Clifford's and then the Temple, as she continued on to the printer's.

Elias out of sight, Maria had taken the piece firstly to Calvert's on Ludgate Hill. It was as ever busy, busy with the desperate who could get their work printed nowhere else in all the printers' and stationers' that surrounded St Paul's. But even Calvert would not take the pamphlet this time. 'I'm sorry, my dear, but the Council of State have had their officers all over this place like a swarm of ants the last couple of days, they're mighty jumpy about something. I've heard that Damian Seeker is on the prowl, too. You keep the Sparrow in his nest a while, that's my advice.'

The Sparrow. That's what they all called her brother – the Putney Sparrow, who kept on chirping long after the others had fallen silent. She remembered the day, seven years ago, with what hopes Elias had set off down the river for St Mary's church in Putney, where the great debate was to be held: the King was defeated, and the army that had fought for the liberties of the nation would be rewarded. The generals – Cromwell, Ireton, Fairfax – whom they had raised to power would defend and extend those liberties, so that all men might have a say in the governance of the country in which they had been born. She remembered the look on Elias's face when he told her the rule of the great God, 'Property', was over, and that the labouring man would have the same rights as the man for whom he laboured, that every honest citizen would have equal access to the law, and that every man and woman would have their liberty of worship. It was the propertied men in Parliament who had held these things back, even now, but it would be different after Putney, because the generals would listen.

And then, a few days later, in disbelief and with a sinking heart, she had heard what had happened at Putney: the generals had listened, and they had been appalled by what they heard, for this was not what they had fought for at all, not this levelling of men – how could men be equal when plainly they were not? How else could a nation be governed if not by right of property? And in the course of the war, the generals had acquired a great deal of property. There would be freedom of worship, of course, for some, but there must be none of the wild blasphemies of the Ranters and the Diggers and all the rest of that crew who threatened the stability of the nation. But the soldiers would be paid their arrears, of course they would have their arrears, how could they think that their Cromwell, their Old Nol, didn't love them?

One by one the dissenters had been mollified, bought off, sidelined, dispensed with, court-martialled, persecuted, broken. The madness unleashed by the lack of censorship, by freedom of speech, of worship, the endless shifting of armies, the overturning of property, was brought to an end, for the good of a people that did not understand what was in its own interest. They were to thank God, she was given to understand, for Cromwell, who did.

And so her brother had gone back to his legal studies, and to his garret, and taken up his pen, and the writings of the Putney Sparrow had been a thorn in the flesh of the Protector and his decreasing inner circle ever since. Other writers of pamphlets and news-books would change their views to accommodate themselves to those in power, but Elias never would, and she loved him for that.

Having been turned down by a first, a second and then a third printer on Paternoster Row, Maria had trudged down Sermon Lane towards St Benet's and the one printer left in the whole city whom they might trust. She had not even read this latest pamphlet; she was not sure that she wanted to, for Elias was becoming increasingly desperate, and she wondered how far away he truly was from advocating something that might bring him to the gallows. She needed to get him away from London, away from England. He had spoken of Virginia, and Massachusetts, but he had no time for the Puritans. There must be other places in the Americas where they might go, where he would be safe. She would talk to George Tavener about it.

So lost had she been in these thoughts as she'd turned into Knight Ryder Street that she hadn't notice the journeyman carpenter step out of a doorway a little ahead of her, and by the time she was aware of him she had collided with him. Though tall and, from the force of her collision with his chest, very strong, the man seemed more startled by the encounter than she was. He bent to pick Elias's papers from the gutter they had fallen into, and returned them to her, his eyes lowered, mumbling an apology. Something in the moment transfixed her, but before she could speak he had briefly touched the rim of his beaten leather hat to her and was gone, had merged into the crowd on the street and disappeared, a large hound trotting at his heels.

But now, thoughts of the carpenter were far from her mind. Elias was almost as restless in his sleep as he was in his waking hours, and there was an unaccustomed stillness in the room that frightened her. She spoke his name, but there was no reply. Even as she repeated it, pushing back her own blankets and swinging her feet to the floor, she knew it: her brother had not come home last night.

Seeker had sent guards early, to stand at the entrance to Dove Court, before he'd even left for the city. As he dismounted, his men were, as ever, impassive. They did not try to anticipate his wishes. They would do what they had been told to do, and nothing else, until commanded otherwise.

'Has anyone tried to come in?'

'No one, once they saw us.'

Seeker glanced towards the garret. 'Or leave?'

The older of the guards indicated his fellow at the top of the steps. 'Thomas dealt with it.'

Seeker nodded, and strode up the crumbling stairway that led to the attic chambers of the house in Dove Court. He dismissed the man at the door, and paused for a moment. He lifted his hand and knocked firmly, three times.

From inside, silence.

Another three raps. Still silence. He was on the point of putting his shoulder to the door, when a woman's voice finally said, 'Come in, if you will.'

Seeker pushed open the unlocked door into a room where the light was very dim, but he registered a young woman sitting at the table. She said nothing and he went over to the fire where he took a spill from a pile by the hearth and lit it from the dying embers, before putting it to the candles on the mantelpiece. The garret was cold and spare: two beds, against opposing walls, a small, scrubbed table, stained by ink, with two chairs set at it, a hearth where the fire was almost dead, a few pots around it. A plain dresser stood against the wall, some earthenware bowls, a pitcher of flour and a basket of onions and carrots on the top. Above it were three shelves, the bottom one ranged with pots and tubs that might contain butter, cheese, and other provisions, and tankards and jugs of differing sizes. The two upper shelves were crammed with books and papers. Some herbs struggled for light at the room's one small window.

It was difficult, in the shadows cast by the other buildings of the court, to see if there was any colour at all to the place. It reminded him of where he himself slept, when he sought anonymity from Whitehall.

He lifted another candle from the dresser, lit it, and carried it over to the table where the young woman was seated. She lifted her eyes to meet his, and he saw the same confusion flit across them that he himself briefly felt. She moved her head slightly, as if to dislodge whatever thought or memory had started to present itself there, and waited.

'Maria Ellingworth?'

She nodded.

'I am . . .'

'I know who you are,' she said.

Yes. Everyone knew. His notoriety served its purpose. There had been a time when he had been content with anonymity, but that had been in the days when he had thought the world a better place – his anonymity would do little good to any but himself now.

'You know why there are guards at your door?'

'Where is my brother?' she said.

'He's a prisoner. He's been taken to the Tower, and charged with the murder last night of Lieutenant John Winter.'

Her face blanched and he saw her swallow slightly. She shook her head. 'No, it must just be for some paper he has

written, surely.' She looked up at him in a sort of desperation as his words began to sink in properly. 'How could
you think it? How could anyone think it? Elias never murdered anyone.'

'I myself found him, bent over John Winter's body, the
knife in his hand. I doubt if they have washed all the blood
off him yet.' He didn't tell her about Anne Winter, about
that part he couldn't understand: her assertion that her husband had in fact died in her arms.

She shook her head. 'No.'

'It is not in my interest to lie to you, nor, you should
understand, in yours to lie to me. What was your brother
doing in Whitehall last night, Mistress Ellingworth?'

She was looking away from him, calculating something,
trying to work something out. Seeker felt a frustration rising in him. No man would have been given the time she was
taking to answer his question. He didn't enjoy interrogating
women, had no time for their subtleties and subterfuges on
the rare occasions when they intruded on his world, and
Anne Winter had already tried his patience enough. But
Maria Ellingworth did not strike him as such a woman, and
the questioning of her could not be avoided.

He repeated his question.

'Mistress Ellingworth?'

Still no response.

'Maria?'

At last she looked at him. 'What does it matter, if you
already have him in the Tower?'

'I don't believe that he killed John Winter.' He saw a glimmer of hope in her eye and moved to stifle it. 'But what I believe is of little importance: only evidence of the truth will save him from swinging as a traitor on Tower Hill. Now what was he doing there?'

She took a breath and he saw her make the decision to trust him. 'It was the coffee house,' she said at last. 'Something he had learned in the coffee house, yesterday. He was going to warn John Winter.'

'Something about Winter's wife?'

'Winter's wife?' Maria was puzzled, almost to the point of irritation. 'No, he said nothing about John Winter's wife. Elias has no interest in gossip. It was something else.'

'That endangered Winter?'

'That endangered "the cause".' For the first time Seeker saw the beginnings of a tear on Maria Ellingworth's lashes. She looked away from him towards the window. 'Dear God, only Elias could believe that anyone but him cares about "the cause" any more.'

Seeker put his hands on the table and leaned towards her – not to menace, but the better to see into her face; his massive frame almost blocked out what meagre light there was from the window. 'What cause?'

She frowned, and then smiled, in a mockery of disbelief. '"What cause?" Why, the one you are supposed to serve, protect. The cause of the Republic, of the Commonwealth, of our liberties and freedoms. You know, what was fought for ten years since, and then forgotten, as your pure holy goblin set about making himself a king.'

Seeker flinched. He had seen the slur in seditious news-sheets, but no one had ever so denigrated the Protector to his face before.

'There can be no liberty without order and there can be no order without government. And if there is to be government there must be governor and governed. To have liberty, men must be governed. That is what your brother never seems to have understood.'

Maria smiled. 'My brother has read Hobbes too, Mr Seeker. He is less persuaded by him than you are, that is all. And neither does he find Mr Milton's celebration of our "well-regulated liberty" altogether convincing.' But then the smile faded. 'Elias has seen, as we all have, how those brought to power by the desire for freedom have been corrupted by the power they usurped.'

Seeker was seldom disposed to the discussion of philosophy. To read, to consider, to comprehend with one's own mind was well enough, but open debate was something else. The enactment of the law, the maintenance of order, those were all his concern. He sometimes wondered if the last twelve years had taught his fellow countrymen and women nothing at all. What good purpose could there be in the poor of London discussing in their leaking garrets these matters that didn't concern them? What did the notions of power or corruption have to do with this girl, who had hardly the sense to keep a proper fire in her miserable home? What business had she to look at him with such defiance?

Unaware of his scrutiny, Maria continued. 'But despite all, Mr Seeker, Elias did not think John Winter had been corrupted, or forgotten what it was that he had fought for.'

No, John Winter had not forgotten, Seeker knew that. That had been his great weakness, that and his wife. 'How was it that your brother thought he knew John Winter's mind so well?'

'It was seven years ago, at the great debate at Putney, when there were still hopes the generals would support the soldiers and their rights, and the liberties of the people. Elias thought John Winter, of all the officers, had always come closest to turning, to supporting the rank and file against the generals, and that if he had, others would have gone with him. Pity he had not, then the world might have spared itself more dictators.'

Seeker let the barb go and turned his mind instead to what he had found in John Winter's bureau only a few hours earlier. The pamphlets locked away in there were not just of the Sparrow's writings before Putney, but since as well, some very recent. It would have been easy enough for an officer such as Winter to have obtained them from the censor's office, but it only now occurred to Seeker that none of those pamphlets had borne the censor's stamp.

'Did your brother and Winter have any contact after Putney?'

She shook her head.

'They hadn't met together since then?'

'Not to my knowledge. Elias never mentioned any such meeting.'

'And yet he went to Winter last night?'

Maria let wax from the candle in front of her trickle on to her finger, and watched as it cooled, before turning her eyes once more on Seeker. 'Elias took what he discovered to John Winter in the night, because he thought no one else on the Council would give him the chance to speak, never mind actually listen to him.'

Seeker knew this was probably true. If anyone had seen the Sparrow within half a mile of Whitehall, his mouth would have been stopped before he ever got to open it.

'And what had your brother discovered?'

For the first time, Maria's shoulders slumped a little, her voice was quiet. 'I don't know.'

'He didn't tell you?'

She shook her head. 'He said it was safer for me not to know: that we could not know who was to be trusted and who not. He said that should I ever come before the Committee of Examinations, it would be better that I could answer honestly that I did not know.'

Seeker was glad to know the Sparrow, who in all probability was at that moment being interrogated by that self-same committee, was not altogether a fool.

But then she remembered. 'It was something to do with a painting in the coffee house, and some things that shouldn't have been there.'

'In Kent's coffee house?'

'In the painting.'

Kent's again. He could delay going there no longer. There was nothing more to be had from Maria – indeed, he had learned more from her than he expected – and yet he found himself searching for something else to say to her.

She hadn't stirred from her seat since he'd come in. She didn't even have a shawl about her shoulders; the sleeves of her brown woollen dress came to just below the elbow, and each showed the thin white linen cuff of her shift, below which the skin on her arms was mottled with cold, and the long thin fingers of her hands almost colourless.

'You should build up the fire,' he said, suddenly awkward. 'It would do your brother no good for you to become ill.'

Then he was at the door, ready to leave.

'Mr Seeker?'

He turned.

'Why do you care about my brother?'

He could have lied to her, but he was not in the habit of lying. 'I don't. I care about the truth. I believe John Winter was dead before your brother ever found him. If he didn't kill John Winter, then the man who did is still about White-hall, or walking the streets of this city, or somewhere in the Commonwealth. That is not justice, and so it is my job to find him.'

And then he was gone, and Maria Ellingworth realised that she was indeed cold, and very alone.

SIX

Water

Jakob Hendricks would be glad of the dawn. He would be glad to be away from London. 'But you were not to leave until tomorrow,' his friend Wim de Boer had protested. 'Nette has invited friends to meet you tonight.'

'I'm sorry,' Jakob had said, thrusting his good silk suit into his pack, careless of the crumpling and creases. 'I must leave, now. I need to be away from this city.'

Wim didn't ask why. He had known Jakob too long to ask why; why a scholar should arrive, unannounced, to stay a few nights and then leave again, as suddenly as he had come. It was not just London – Wim knew that from other Dutch friends, traders in France, Germany, all over the Netherlands, Spain. You did not question Jakob; it suited everyone best that way.

Nevertheless, there were things his friend needed to be told. 'You cannot go out on to the High Road at this time. The place will be alive with thieves and cut-throats and no protection of law.'

'I'll go by the river.'

'You'll reach Oxford quicker by road, if only you will wait until it's light.'

But already Jakob was tying the strings on his pack, easing on his long boots, taking his thick woollen cloak from its peg on the back of the door.

'The river, Wim.'

And so, with a lantern to guide them and much head-shaking, Wim had led Jakob down through the quiet streets of St Katharine's to the wharf. Jakob did not look behind him. He had never understood why his countrymen had chosen to live in the shadow of the Tower, with its message of power and death. He would be glad to be away from it.

Wim was known to all the rivermen, and it hadn't taken long to find a barge carrying Portuguese wine and Flemish cloth upriver to Oxford. He paid the bargeman and thrust Nette's hastily prepared parcel of bread, cheese and ham into Jakob's hands, waving away the coins Hendricks held out to him to cover his passage. 'May God prosper you, Jakob, and protect you.'

With little fuss, Hendricks had found a comfortable and quiet part of the boat to settle himself. The bargemen had no interest in him – a stranger's business was none of theirs, if his money was good, and they had enough to attend to. It would have been better to have rested, slept, but his mind raced over the events of the previous day and night and would not let him. It had started at the coffee house, where it had been supposed to start, but he had found more at the coffee house than he had expected to and he did not quite understand it. And then there had been the night.

The clouds that had masked the moon through much of that night were shifting, and the jagged silhouette of the city stretching westwards revealed itself to him. It seemed a dangerous thing, a threatening thing, and he wondered for a minute that he had ever got out of it. He kept his eyes straight ahead as the barge went silently past Tower Wharf, as if the bargemen no more than he wanted to draw attention to themselves. At Billingsgate already there was life, and the stench of fish carried to him on the early-morning air almost made his stomach turn, his clenched stomach. The barge went carefully underneath the Bridge, Hendricks wondering about the weight of souls slumbering in the houses above them, whether they worried for the morrow in Cromwell's England or met each new day with a confidence that they would return, safe at night, to their sleep once more.

But why would they not sleep safe in their beds, when there was that mighty church of St Paul's rising so solid, so uncompromising, so *English* above the beast of the town that pressed upon it from all sides? It was difficult to comprehend that human beings, near half a million souls, could live, could breathe, in a place so crammed with those vertiginous buildings, storeys teetering one upon the other until it seemed they must topple over at any minute. And what unknown stories, intrigues, passions and failures played out their time in those streets and alleyways, up stairways, behind shutters and closed doors? What troubled fates stalked the unwary through those narrow, leaking passageways? As a grey light gradually revealed more of the town, it seemed that everything was turned to face the river as the only means of escape. It would not have surprised Hendricks to see men and women emerge from their darkened doorways, descend the steps from their riverside buildings into the waters of the Thames, and sink themselves beneath it.

But then, little surprised Hendricks. The places he had been and things he had seen over the past few years had led him to believe that nothing could shock him any more. That had all been changed by the events of last night.

It had begun innocuously enough: a promise of a pleasant musical evening in the presence of his countrymen, something to while away a few idle hours while he waited until the time was right to continue with his journey. A famous organist was in London, by permission of the Protector himself, and would give a performance of the music of Jan Pieterszoon Sweelinck in the Dutch church at Austin Friars, prior to a private recital at Hampton Court, it was rumoured, before Cromwell's own family.

As he and Wim had made their way to the church the previous evening, Jakob Hendricks had not been able to help but wonder at the blood of the Cromwells, the brazenness, the audacity that must run through the generations. He knew, of course, of old King Henry's seizing of the monasteries, the great scheme for taking the revenues and crushing the power of the church, all masterminded by that other Cromwell over a hundred years ago. 'The Augustinians had a friary here,' Wim de Boer said, as they hurried along Broad Street towards Austin Friars. 'Thomas Cromwell had it off them, for the King, he said. But up to the left there, the Drapers' Hall on Throgmorton Street, that was the fine house Cromwell built himself on the spoil of the church and other honest men's land. No one dared utter a word against him.'

'Until he went to the executioner's block,' murmured Hendricks.

'He was born too low and reached too high,' said Wim.

'And another of his line may well do the same.'

Wim shot his friend a look. 'Be careful what you say, Jakob. Nowhere in London is free of Oliver Cromwell's spies. Nowhere.'

Jakob nodded and composed his face accordingly as they turned into the old friary courtyard to join the throng of their fellow countrymen and women making their way into the church. Wim bought two programmes from Will Fiddler, the packman Jakob had met earlier in the day at Kent's. The packman made the pair an exaggerated bow, which Wim ignored. 'Sweelinck. I heard him play in the Oude Kerk when I was a boy, you know. You would be too young to remember I suppose, Jakob?' A nod. 'Magnificent. Magnificent. Let us see what nonsense Fiddler is peddling tonight, if any of it be true.'

As Wim entertained himself by reading through the programme and the supposed 'Life' of the great composer that
Will Fiddler had cobbled together, now nodding sagely, at
other times expostulating, 'Nonsense! Sheer nonsense!'
Hendricks looked around the rapidly filling church. So
many faces from home, known, familiar, vaguely familiar,
having made their new life and remade their own community here, in this teeming city. He had to own to himself a
certain pride in his countrymen – no one could do sober
prosperity like the Dutch. Jakob looked down at his own
clothing. He was never more comfortable than when garbed
in his familiar, slightly worn old Dutch scholar's robes, but
Wim had made it plain that the company they were to keep
tonight would require an effort of a higher order. Jakob
Hendriks did not like to go out in the city as he now was,
attired in his best silk suit, and even Wim had been somewhat taken aback at its fineness. Black, of course, as befitting
a good Protestant scholar, but of markedly better quality
than he was wont to wear around the halls of Leiden. The
doublet was fashionably short, with slashed sleeves, allowing more display of his long white shirt than he was
altogether comfortable with, and the billowing sleeves of
that shirt would have been filthy by dinnertime in the course
of a normal day. The wide breeches, trimmed with black
linen lace to match the doublet, were at least comfortable,
but the beribboned shoes he found the most awkwardly
ostentatious of all. The effect, overall, was something almost
courtly that did not sit entirely easily with the sturdy

mercantile quality of his countrymen. The trouble was, there was no middle ground for Hendricks between the roles in life he had been called upon to play.

Soon, a small man, who it was said had learned at the feet of Sweelinck himself, seated himself at the organ; it seemed almost impossible that his short arms and legs could perform the task ahead of him, but even as he tuned the instrument, Hendricks became aware that he was about to listen to one of sublime gifts. The singers were taking their seats in the choir, and the two carpenters who had been making some last-minute adjustments to the pulpit steps had tidied away their gear and secreted themselves into a dark corner, behind where Hendricks and de Boer sat, that they too might hear what was to come. Soon all were settled, the Predikant having prayed God's blessing on this evening to his glory, and formally introduced the organist, renowned throughout Germany and the Netherlands, who was to play before the Lord Protector himself during his visit to England.

A sense of anticipation washed through the congregation. They waited, and then he began, and truly, the sound was sublime, a gift from God offered back to God. As the magnificent strains of the Toccata in D rose from the pipes of the organ to fill the Dutch Church in Austin Friars, Jakob Hendricks closed his eyes and imagined himself back again in the Oude Kerk in Amsterdam, a young man almost swept away on the swell of sound from its organs. He'd known, even as a schoolboy in the scholars' loft, that the music's purpose was to focus his mind on the glory of God, but his mind, week by week, in those days almost twenty years ago now, had been taken up instead by a young girl who sat with her parents in the same pew each Sunday morning, across the nave and in full view of the scholars. Sometimes he would see her on Vijzelstraat or in Dam Square with her mother or a maid, buying chickens, or fish, or flowers. He had even smiled at her once, and she had inclined her head, very modestly, just for a moment. He had been possessed by her, left her flowers, notes, with never any reply. He had gone to his studies in Leiden thinking of her, come home in the vacations thinking of her, and then one summer vacation, three years after he had first noticed her, she was gone – another family filled the familiar pew in the Oude Kerk. After the sermon, he had asked his father about the family who used to sit there.

'Oh,' his father had said. 'Jan Snelders. Went down with his goods on a voyage back from Java. Everything lost. The wife drowned herself in the Herengracht.'

'There was a daughter, was there not?'

'She was sent to the Weesehouse, I believe. He should have made better provision, Jan Snelders.'

The Weesehouse, where orphans and the children of those fallen in the world were sent to be educated, taught useful skills, where girls were trained to become good wives. He had never seen her again. After he had graduated in the Laws and entered upon his profession, he had called at the Weesehouse, once, in the hope that he might find her. But no, 'I am sorry, *Mijnheer*. Mirjam Snelders left here almost two years ago. I cannot tell you where she went. No, I am sorry.'

He had never looked for her, never been able to persuade himself to marry another, but in this warm, packed church in London, as the toccata reached its triumphant end and he opened his eyes, Jakob Hendricks saw Mirjam Snelders for the first time in seventeen years. Her name was not Mirjam Snelders any more though, and the older, well-dressed merchant beside her, looking upon her with such proprietorial pride, was not her father, but her husband. More, it was the very same merchant, George Tavener, who had been so welcoming towards him in the coffee house that morning. Hendricks didn't hear the fantasia that came next, nor the canon, nor the capriccio that followed it. The famous organist played one flawless piece after another. Halfway through his programme, to give his hands and feet some respite, the singers took up their parts, not religious, but secular – chansons, rimes, madrigals – to the delight of their audience, but to Jakob Hendricks' ears, in his head, there was only unbearable noise.

When the final piece of music at last came to its end, approbation, at first respectful, became tumultuous. The little organist, exhausted, hung his head a moment over the keys, before turning and rising, crimson-cheeked and mopping his brow with a large linen handkerchief, to acknowledge the applause. Wim de Boer beamed happily. 'Very fine, very fine,' and all around them people were doing the same, until the organist finally made his exit from the loft. 'Now you must excuse me a moment, Jakob,' said Wim, 'for I see Geert Stiegmans over there – I have a proposal for him, and he's the very Devil of a fellow to get hold of. I'll meet you out in the courtyard.'

Hendricks nodded, and somehow made his way through the great body of people that moved slowly and awkwardly, like a bear lumbering relentlessly out into the night. The cold air took him full in the face as he stepped out into the old courtyard of the Augustinian Friars. After the blaze of light and the stifling warmth of the church, the crispness of the night, the possibility of concealment, had rarely been so welcome. And yet, it was not quite dark enough. The walls of the courtyard were lit with torches, which cast light into corners that would otherwise have been dark, and lent the glowing faces of the crowd emerging from the church a quality that might have something demonic in it. He leaned against the outer wall of the portico and looked for her, and eventually she was there, only three yards from where he stood.

'You will see your Mistress home,' George Tavener was saying in English to two young men, who had already been waiting outside the church when Hendricks had found his way out. 'I have some late business to attend to. See that she is not importuned, and that the doors in the house are all locked before you retire for the night.' He turned next to Mirjam, and said to her in his strongly accented Dutch, 'You go home now with Will and Peter, my dear. I will try not to waken you when I come in.' And then he had kissed her and was gone. She was taking a moment to put on her gloves against the cold of the night, and the two young men waited patiently at either side of her. Some desperation seized Jakob Hendricks then, and he stepped out in front of her, about to remove his hat. She looked up. 'Oh, I am sorry *Mijnheer*.' She was apologising for being in his way, stepping aside to let him pass while she finished putting on her gloves. No recognition, not the merest flicker. The same modest, detached politeness that had almost shattered his young self one afternoon almost twenty years ago, outside a bookseller's on the Kalverstraat, when he had ventured to speak to her. Jakob Hendricks was older now though, and knew the cost of an opportunity lost. He made to step towards her again, but the larger of the two clerks accompanying her moved towards him. 'You will excuse us, Sir.' There was little room for doubt that Jakob Hendricks should come no closer to George Tavener's wife. And then, flanked by her chaperones, happily chatting to them about the wonderful evening she had just enjoyed, Mirjam Tavener had left the precincts of the Austin Friars without once looking back.

And now, in the early-morning light, Hendricks was resolved that he, too, would not look back. The barge had left the city behind, and was passing in front of the red-brick sprawl of Whitehall Palace, where Kings had held their courts, played at tennis and bowls, ridden in the lists, married, loved, danced, slept, died. Where Oliver

Cromwell slept. Jakob pictured the Banqueting Hall of which he had so often heard, standing, brazen almost, beyond those walls, in the yard of which the English had separated their monarch's head from his neck. He tried to imagine Cromwell, who had had the stomach to pen the executioner's order that day, but not to witness the deed – how he had been then, in some council room, making a show of prayer as in that freezing yard the axe fell on his nation's anointed king. He pictured Cromwell as he must be today, what he might be in a week's time. But too fast; he was running ahead of himself, and there were many miles to travel yet to Oxford. They were approaching the Privy Stairs, and Jakob Hendricks hunkered down lower against the bolts of linen.

As the journey progressed, Jakob considered how he had always preferred water to land – he felt happier, safer. As a boy, looking down from his window high up in their house on the Keizersgracht, the water below had promised freedom, movement in a world restricted by convention, expectation, necessity. It had whispered the possibility of other places, other lives. Over the past few years he had come to understand that it could also be other things: a channel of communication, a swift means of escape. And now, on this barge making its way up the Thames, Jakob Hendricks knew he could trail his hand in the water and soon that water would be passing by London, almost unnoticed as London got on with the business of itself, out into the North Sea to mingle with the waters of the Elbe, the Maas, to crash against the dykes and fill the canals of Holland. All was connected: from tributaries, rivers, sea, to rivers, tributaries, canals. Jakob Hendricks, drifting past Hampton Court, where once cardinals and kings had played and now the Lady Protectress, that Huntingdon housewife, fretted for her husband, could dip his finger into the calm surface of these English waters and the ripples be felt in The Hague, Paris, Cologne, until Charles II might know he was free at last to take his father's throne.

SEVEN

Revelations

Samuel was calling. Grace could hear him. Always, a few minutes before the first of the bells, she would hear her uncle call the coffee boy. 'Up, lad, up! Why, when I was a soldier . . .' and so it would go. 'You would have been run through, the enemy would have been upon you, you would have been burned in your bed. Up!' Did the old man ever sleep, she wondered? Did he ever truly sleep, or did the pain in his leg, that twisted, useless leg, keep him marching the floorboards through the night, waiting for the respite of the dawn? But the war was over now, and the time for marching done.

Grace ached with tiredness. She would have liked to lie in her bed, she often thought it, just lie in bed and listen to the city awaken. On this morning too, she would have given much to lie in her bed, wait for the bells, sleep on and on, but the city was wakening, and would soon be at their door.

As ever, on waking, as on drifting to sleep, her thoughts turned to Elias. Just last night, Will Fiddler had been teasing her uncle, as he was wont to do, about terrorising every suitor who came her way. Samuel had defended himself by listing Grace's many virtues in the face of the innumerable failings of the generality of his customers. 'And only a good man will take her from me. None but a good man.' He had gazed fondly then at Elias, and Grace had not been able to keep herself from glancing in the same direction, and feeling a surge of warmth at the lawyer's bashful smile.

Elias had returned in the evening, as was his habit, full of the talk and doings of the day from Clifford's Inn and the Temple, anxious to talk about them again with whoever might be in the coffee house, seek new views, before going home at last to Maria to talk them out once more, and scribble down his thoughts as his supper grew cold.

Last night, he had been on a new topic: the rumours of Cromwell's desire for an empire.

'Do you truly think it will happen? A war on the Spaniards, for the Americas?' Samuel had asked.

'I hope not. Maria speaks more and more lately of the new beginnings that are to be made there. She would have us go and make a life in New England, in a freedom that is no longer to be had here.'

Grace had found herself gripping the counter as her stomach tightened. Only her uncle had noticed her reaction. He'd turned again to the young lawyer. 'You would be missed, Elias, if you left us.'

Elias had shaken his head, animated. 'But you would come too, you and Grace. Think, you could have a coffee house there, and I could have my own news-book, without censorship or fear of retribution . . .'

'And the Man in the Moon might deliver to you fresh green cheese every day,' a young clerk had laughed, before taking up his hat to go home for the night. But Grace hadn't cared about the young clerk's mockery because Elias hadn't been listening to him; he'd been looking at her, and smiling.

Shortly afterwards, the bell of St Michael's had sounded for six o'clock, and Will Fiddler had flown out the door to the printer's, to collect some programmes he planned to sell at a recital at the Dutch Church that night. Grace had gone over to plump the cushions in the private booth, thinking of the woman who had been sitting there earlier in the day. Anne Winter had spoken to her with envy of Grace's freedom, and of her own captivity in the gilded cage of Whitehall. And Grace had not, as others might have done, looked at the woman's fine clothing and compared it with her own plain and serviceable dress, not coveted the smooth pale hands of Anne Winter that were not roughened by labour as her own were. Grace had understood; she had thought she could feel the woman's presence still there, hours after she had gone. She'd almost finished her tidying when the door of the coffee house had opened, but she hadn't looked up – it opened a hundred times a day at least. But then all the clamour of the coffee room had fallen to a silence that was broken only by her uncle's voice. 'John . . . Lieutenant . . .'

'John will do, Samuel,' the man had said.

By turning her head slightly, Grace had been able to see through the turned wooden bars at the back of the booth. She'd caught her breath. Standing in the middle of the coffee room floor had been a soldier of Cromwell's New Model Army. He was certainly not the first soldier to cross her uncle's threshold – many of Samuel Kent's old comrades had found their way to Birchin Lane to take their pipe with him and talk over old campaigns before moving on. But this was no old soldier, nor ordinary infantryman either, but an officer of high rank, accustomed to command. Words spoken to her in this very booth only a few hours earlier had come back to her then: 'some say he is the best-set man they have ever laid eyes on.' Samuel had looked towards the counter, then the storeroom beyond; he'd called Grace's name, but she had stayed exactly as she was, immobilised by the sight of Anne Winter's husband.

Samuel had had no idea where Grace had got to. 'Where on earth is the girl?' Then he'd flicked a finger at the coffee boy. 'Be quick! Bring a dish and pipe for the lieutenant.'

John Winter had interrupted him. 'I have not come here for drink.' He'd looked distractedly towards the table where the patrons were seated, his eyes resting for a moment on Elias, who nodded briefly to him. 'I have come . . .' His voice had become hoarse and he was having difficulty speaking. 'I have come, Samuel, to talk of my wife.'

Samuel Kent's mind had gone back nine years, and he'd

seen before him not an officer, high in Cromwell's favour, but a young parliamentary infantryman distraught over the loss of comrades in the field, and tonight there was the same pleading despair in that young man's eyes.

Samuel's hand had gone out to touch the lieutenant on the arm. 'She was here, John, as I said in my note. She said she hadn't been hurt in the carriage accident, wouldn't allow that we called for you. She left, hours since. If you wish for help with a search . . .' Samuel was already looking for his hat and coat.

Winter had shaken his head. 'No, no, she is home, it is just – should she ever come here again, or should you ever hear tell of her alone somewhere in the city, will you send straight for me, keep her if you can? She – she is not well.'

'You have my word on it, John.'

Winter had taken a breath and closed his eyes. 'Thank you, Samuel.' Then the young infantryman was gone, and the high-ranking officer, sure of his place and the respect due him, had returned. He'd looked once more at the table of patrons, his eye pausing a moment at the Scotsman, Campbell. Elias he'd studiously ignored this time, looking directly at Samuel to say, 'And see you rein in the Sparrow too – he's as good as asking the Lord Protector to wring his neck for him.' Then he'd stridden from the coffee house, leaving not a few of the patrons staring at the coffee man.

'I fought with him. A long time ago. A decent man.' Those days were past and Samuel hadn't been disposed to say any more. He'd limped back towards the counter. 'Now where the Devil did Grace get to?'

The Scottish minister, Archibald Campbell, had also returned to the coffee house last night, this time without his younger companion. He'd looked with interest at Elias. 'I think he knew you too.'

'That was also a long time ago, in a church, in Putney.' Grace had heard about it from Maria. They'd faced each other, Elias and John Winter, in the great debate of the Agreement of the People. At Putney, Elias believed he'd come within a hair's breadth of winning Winter over. After Winter had left the coffee house, Grace had seen him look towards the door that only a minute earlier had closed behind the lieutenant. 'He may stand high with the Protector, but that is not a man who is happy with the regime he serves.'

Elias had stayed a while longer, only half listening as Campbell droned on about sin, the Elect, and the Damned. Another time, Grace knew, he would have baited the man, played the Ranter, claimed, as he had heard the Ranters do, that to overcome sin, a man must know it in all its detail, experience, savour, wallow in it. That was one thing Cromwell's crew had done, give them that; they had, with a few, well-published trials and torments, silenced the mania that their own dismantling of the established church had unleashed. But she'd seen that Elias had not had the stomach for it: it was as if seeing Winter again had reminded him of all the other chances lost. He'd extricated himself from the minister's company at last, and come over to the booth, where she'd still been sitting, to bid her goodnight. As he'd come closer, his eye had been caught by the picture on the wall above her head, but Grace herself had been too intent on something she had found amongst the cushions to ask him what it was.

'What?' he'd said, dragging his eyes from the picture to look at the object she'd been holding up to the candlelight. 'Like blood in the snow,' she'd repeated. 'She must have lost it when she was in here earlier today, John Winter's wife.' It was a brooch, a ruby heart surrounded by pearls. It was worth more than anything Grace Kent had ever touched. She'd been transfixed. 'Just like blood.'

'Samuel will see it gets back to her,' Elias had said, distracted, his eyes back on the painting. 'I must go now.'

Grace had a vague memory of replying to him, 'Yes, Maria will be waiting, you should go.'

Often, they would prolong these last exchanges before Elias finally left for home, but neither of them had been disposed to last night. And now, it was another day, and there was much to make ready for the first customers of the morning. Grace wearily swung her legs out of bed and began to prepare herself to go down and help her uncle.

By the time George Tavener arrived at Kent's, the first pot was ready, the second under preparation, and the coffee room was filling up. Gabriel had been round the table already, refilling bowls, fetching more pipes. Samuel watched as Tavener heaved himself wearily into the first available seat and nodded gratefully as the boy placed his dish in front of him.

'A bad night?' guessed Samuel.

'Three hours of dismal organ groaning and wailings in French and Italian and God knows, all endured from the comfort of a hard wooden pew with no cushion. These Dutch have a great fear of enjoying themselves, Samuel, I'll tell you.'

'Ah, but your Mirjam is as light and joyful as a bird, George, I have never seen her one day miserable.'

Tavener's face softened. 'You're right, Samuel. And it is because you are so often right that I come to your coffee house above all others, that and the best coffee in the city,' and he took an appreciative sip that seemed to restore him further. 'And what news do you have for me today, my old friend, to send me on my business full-informed?'

'Very little.' Samuel shrugged apologetically. 'We were tardy in opening up, and missed poor Will Fiddler, who will have spread news of our sloth all over town by now, I am sure.'

Tavener grunted and looked round at his fellow drinkers. 'And Elias? It is not like him to be a slug-a-bed.'

Samuel glanced at Grace, who did not turn around from the dresser, where she was setting out new crockery. He saw her hand pause on a small finian of fine Chinese porcelain, come there from Java on a Dutch ship docked only yesterday. She traced the rim of the cup with her finger. 'Elias has not been in yet this morning.' Samuel worried for his niece, should anything befall him, and wished the lawyer would make his feelings for her clear.

A moment or two later, the street door opened, and several curious pairs of eyes turned towards it, only to be disappointed by the sight of Archibald Campbell. He was more unkempt than he had been the day before, his hair not so well-brushed, his shoes dusty, his eyes red from lack of sleep.

Staring wildly round the room, Campbell dismissed the conventional pleasantries. 'Is he here? Has he been here?'

'Who?' asked George Tavener.

'Zander Seaton. Has he been here?'

Samuel shook his head. 'I have not seen him since he left here yesterday afternoon.'

Campbell sat down, breathless suddenly, and a little deflated. 'No more have I.' By the time Grace set a dish of the steaming black liquid in front of him, he had become a little less agitated. He took a gulp that Samuel thought must surely have burnt his throat, and then a second. He scanned the table. 'No news today, then?' he said, pushing aside a copy of *Mercurius Politicus* already thoroughly read.

Someone at the bottom of the table started to tell a well-worn tale about a prophetess who had set up in Holborn, and pronounced the doom of the Protector, but he was interrupted by the sudden arrival of Will Fiddler, hurrying through the door as quickly as his pack would allow him.

Usually, he was buzzing with every rumour the streets and alleys around the Exchange had to offer, and a few of his own fancy to boot, but today there was a different look on his face. Before anyone could ask him, 'What news?' his hat was off, and leaning on the bannister for breath he said, 'Have you heard? Surely you have heard?'

Samuel hobbled over to him. 'Calm, yourself, Will, we have heard nothing. What has happened? What is amiss?'

Will Fiddler took another breath. 'John Winter is dead, murdered. Last night, in Whitehall. His throat cut a yard from his own door.'

Samuel took a step back, colour draining from his face. 'No.'

Will nodded vigorously. 'But aye, Samuel, I tell you, it is so. Cromwell roars like a thing demented and vows vengeance on every sinner.'

'And his wife?' asked Tavener, half risen from the table.

'Winter's? Out of her senses. Covered in blood.' Fiddler was carried away with his tale. 'It was she, they say, that found him. Wouldn't let go, even after he was long dead, I heard. Had to be pulled away. Wouldn't have the blood washed off her . . .' The coffee boy was helping Fiddler off with his pack, showing him to a chair, and still the packman talked. 'The soldiers will be everywhere now, you see if I'm wrong.'

By the end of half an hour, Samuel knew there would be few in London, in England in fact, who had not been named, in his and in every other coffee house in the city, as being behind the death of John Winter. Royalists — they were always first, and safe to cry down. And then the Republicans, old Levellers, angry that the army had gone out of their control; dislodged parliamentarians, with a grievance; radicals, sectaries, Presbyterians — he cast an eye towards Campbell; old generals, angry at being replaced; new generals, anxious to come closer to power.

The babble of the coffee house, which had risen to a considerable height, was soon brought to a sharp end when the door flew open, and a boy, one of George Tavener's runners, burst in. 'Sir, you must come out.'

Tavener stood up. 'What is the matter? Is there a ship down? Not the *Black Hind*?'

The boy shook his head, still struggling for breath. 'Worse, much worse.'

The merchant's face greyed, and his voice was little more than a whisper. 'What could be worse, boy? Not the Mistress . . . tell me.'

'Damian Seeker. They say Damian Seeker is on his way here.'

Samuel stopped in his stoking of the fire. 'Here? To my coffee house?'

The boy gulped and nodded.

'Dear God,' said Fiddler, almost to himself. 'We are done for.'

EIGHT

Visitation

The human noise of the coffee house died to nothing, and all within were motionless, their eyes turned to the door, as the sound of heavy boots marching in unison down the lane towards them came closer. Behind her counter, Grace felt her breathing grow shallower. She had heard of the Seeker, everyone had heard of the Seeker, but she had never thought, for all the tales that were told of him, that he would find his way here, to the sanctuary of her uncle's coffee house. She swallowed as the footsteps outside came to a halt and the door handle turned. The door swung open, and the frame of the man who stood there almost blocked out the light. Even as he reached up and removed the steel helmet from his head, Grace felt she was looking upon some biblical avenger.

Her uncle was the first to recover himself.

'Captain, how may we help you?'

Seeker was surveying the room. His expression gave nothing away, other than that little he saw pleased him. He turned his attention to Samuel.

'You are Samuel Kent?'

'Aye, Captain.'

Seeker nodded slowly, as if Samuel, at least, did not offend him. 'I must ask some questions of you and your customers.'

Samuel nodded and motioned the boy to help him in readying the private booth.

Seeker shook his head. 'No, here, in plain sight.' Samuel started to move a table but Seeker, noticing his leg, stopped him. He told two of his men instead to set up a table and two stools two feet from the end of the serving table.

While this activity was going on, Will Fiddler tried to slip out unseen. 'Sit down,' Seeker commanded, without appearing to have moved his head. The packman slunk quietly back into his seat. Seeker stood in front of the counter, his back to Grace. He looked to the coffee boy. 'The door is closed?'

The boy nodded vigorously.

'Lock it.'

As the boy ran to do his bidding, one of the armed men went with him, and took up position by the top of the steps.

Seeker surveyed the coffee room. Its murmur had been utterly silenced, and all that could be heard was the sound of the pot on the fire and the life of the world shut away outside on the street. He addressed the drinkers at the table. 'No one is to leave this room without my say-so, is that understood?'

A general nodding of heads affirmed that it was.

'Good.' He murmured something to his sergeant, who flicked his head towards two of the soldiers. To the evident puzzlement of the coffee-drinkers, they started to remove the paintings from the coffee house walls. Seeker noted that Samuel Kent had the sense to say nothing. An old soldier understood when to speak and when not to.

Once the paintings had been removed, Seeker turned once more to the coffee boy. 'There is no need to be frightened,' he said, 'if you tell the truth.'

The boy made plain that he understood.

Seeker indicated the serving table. 'Which of these people were in the coffee house yesterday when Lady Anne Winter came in?'

The boy took a moment to consider. 'Will Fiddler, George Tavener and the Reverend Campbell there.'

'Your master and mistress also?'

A nod.

'And tell me, do you remember who else was in here yesterday when she came in, that are not here today?'

'Yes, Captain,' said the boy. 'There were only three: a Scotsman, Zander Seaton – a soldier, I think, Sir. And there was a Dutch gentleman, a scholar on his way to Oxford – Jakob Hendricks was his name.' As he spoke, it occurred to Seeker that a coffee house boy was a useful thing, for they evidently missed nothing. But Gabriel was not finished. 'And there was Elias, of course.'

In his head, Seeker checked the names against those given by his informant. The lists tallied exactly. No mention in either of any Sir Gwyllm Crowther, the man Lady Anne Winter had alluded to earlier. He asked the boy, but no, he was sure.

First taking their names, Seeker dismissed all those who had not been present the previous day: in their grateful scramble for the door, none complained of their unfinished beverages or cooling pipes. The door once again locked, those who remained looked at each other. Six of them: Samuel, Grace, Gabriel, Tavener, Fiddler and Campbell.

Seeker began with Samuel, started with questions about his customers, those he knew well, and which were strangers. Who had come to the coffee house for the first time that day? What did he know of Lady Anne? He had fought alongside Winter, had he not?

'Aye, a good long time ago now, Captain, in forty-five, under General Fairfax, clearing the dregs of Grenville and Goring's crew out of the West.' He spat. ''Course, I was younger then and John Winter younger still, hardly more than a boy.'

'And what kind of soldier was he?'

Samuel considered and Seeker watched him. Most men would have answered too quick, or asked him what he meant, but not Samuel Kent. He understood, and Seeker felt something in him warm to the coffee man.

'One who did not like war,' Samuel said in the end. 'One who looked for the end of it. Soldiering was not a way of life for him as it was for me. He could fight, mind, oh aye, he could fight. Taken by a fury almost sometimes.'

'A fury at what? The Royalists?'

'Perhaps,' said Samuel. 'He'd come out with the Club-
men at first, never minding Roundhead nor Cavalier, just
trying to protect their own communities. But then they
met in with Fairfax, and joined the general on Parliament's
side. Loyal, he was, from that day on. Did his duty, never
shirked a fight. Saw too much, too young, like so many of
'em, Captain. Not many a Royalist came across John Winter
and lived to tell the tale. But there wasn't hatred in it – he
understood: it was war and that's what war is. Sometimes I
did wonder if his fury wasn't against himself.'

'For what?'

Samuel sighed. 'That I never knew.'

It was stifling hot in the coffee room, and Seeker rarely
kept a fire. His cloak he had removed before he'd ever sat
down. Now he loosened the ties on his black leather doublet. He wore no sleeves with it, just a plain white shirt
underneath, and no collar. He unbuttoned the plain cuffs of
his shirt and folded them back an inch or two, revealing
dark hair on wrists from which the tanning of last summer's
sun had not quite faded.

'Were you with Winter at the taking of Baxton Hall?'

Samuel tapped his twisted leg, shook his head. 'Bristol
finished me for soldiering, but I always listened out for
news – the New Model Army, under Old Nol – what would
I have given to fight with them! Never mind. But I started
to hear tell of John Winter, eventually, rising through
the ranks – Dunbar, Worcester, and then that he was at

Whitehall.' He looked directly at Seeker, as few men ever did. 'I was glad of it; he was a good man, and Old Nol needs good men around him, Captain.'

Seeker chose not to consider what Samuel Kent might mean by this, and continued with his questioning.

'And what of religion? Did John Winter talk much of matters of faith?'

Samuel considered. 'Kept it to himself, and that was all right. There were sectaries enough in the army then, even before the New Model – though not so bad as in the North, begging your pardon – and they were tiresome. John Winter just read his Bible and didn't bother anyone.'

Seeker nodded. But he had one more question before he let the old man go. 'And what of atonement? Did he ever talk of atonement?'

Samuel sat up straighter, appraised his interrogator carefully. 'Not then, no.'

Something in his voice alerted Seeker. 'When then?'

It was a moment before the coffee man finally answered. 'Last night.'

Seeker put down his quill pen. 'He was here last night?'

Samuel nodded. 'Not long before we put up the locks. He came to ask that we should tell him if ever his wife came here again, not let her out in the city on her own.'

'Who was in here?'

'Just myself, Grace, the boy there, the Reverend Campbell,' he said, nodding at the Scotsman, 'and Elias.'

'And what had he then to say of atonement?'

It was a moment before the coffee man answered. 'He said, just to me mind, "I thought if I married her, I might make atonement." I supposed he meant for what had happened to her family in the war.'

'But you do not think it now?'

Samuel smiled. 'I'm not accustomed to being asked what I think, Captain, and what I think about it hardly matters now, does it?'

Seeker nodded. He was done with the coffee man for now. He asked Grace to bring him a cold draught of ale, and called for the packman. 'Bring his pack too,' he said, writing down Fiddler's name.

'Sit down' he said, without looking at the man as he noted down Fiddler's occupation. And then he began his questioning.

Where had he been travelling to two days ago?

Nowhere. He had just returned from two weeks to the West Country.

What business had he had there?

The usual, Fiddler replied, with an ill-advised attempt at a grin.

In a second Seeker had pushed back his stool and was on his feet. Will Fiddler looked nearly out of his skin.

'If I ask you a question, you will answer it. Do you understand me?'

The ruddy cheeks of the packman were now blanched white, and his hands were shaking. 'I, I . . . I had taken some pamphlets to Bristol, and brought back some quina bark and some jars of aloe vera juice, for the supply of several apothecaries between there and the city here, off a ship in from the Canaries.'

Seeker looked up from his writing. 'Do you have any dealings with the apothecary at the sign of the Pineapple, on Magpie Lane?'

Fiddler shook his head.

'You did not visit him yesterday?'

The packman was emphatic. 'No, nor any other time. He has not a good name.'

Seeker grunted, then hefted Fiddler's heavy sack up on to the table with ease. 'Empty it,' he commanded. Slowly at first, with fumbling fingers, but then more quickly under Seeker's impatient promptings, Fiddler began to lay the contents of his pack along the table. One section contained several packets of spices; bought, he said, at Leadenhall that morning for the housewives and cooks of Hackney. Then there were ribbons – blue, green, scarlet, yellow – got from a trader on Petticoat Lane. Seeker restrained himself from growling with impatience. At the last came what he had been waiting for: the pamphlets. He glanced over the title page of each one, then called to one of his men, 'Have these packaged up and taken to Secretary Milton's office, for the censor. List the names of the printers.' When the pile had been removed, and Grace got to fetch brown paper and string, Seeker turned his attention back directly to the packman. 'And?'

The man affected innocence. 'And?'

There was a palpable silence in the room.

'The bottom packet.'

'There is no bottom packet,' said the peddler, ostentatiously turning the pack upside down.

What might have been a grin slowly began to disappear as he saw the look on Seeker's face. The grin was gone altogether by the time Seeker had stretched a long arm deep into the pack, found the concealed folds, pulled open the laces on the pocket underneath, and brought out a small package, a little larger than the size of the pamphlets Fiddler had been planning to sell. When Seeker pulled the first of the quarto sheets from the package and unfolded it, Fiddler started to say something, but Seeker silenced him by merely lifting one finger of his left hand as he read.

Seeker pulled out another sheet, and another and the peddler's agitation subsided, either through relief or an acceptance of the hopelessness of his situation. At last, he was emboldened to speak once more. 'As you can see, Captain, it is only some music – a few harmless songs.'

Seeker made no response, but continued to examine the sheets, one by one.

Some of the colour had returned to the packman's face, and he expanded his audience to include his fellow coffee-drinkers, sitting, thoroughly bemused now, around the serving table.

'Davenant's an old rogue, of course, but Lawes has kept him right – nothing there to offend the ladies. Why, the Lord Protector himself . . .' but his voice trailed off, as he saw that Seeker had finished looking through the song sheets and was observing him carefully.

'You have a fondness for music, have you not, Fiddler?'

'Why, yes, Sir, who would not . . .?'

'You were at the Dutch Church last night . . .'

Fiddler's new-found confidence deserted him. 'I was selling programmes. To hear the playing was a bonus.'

'And yet I think your interest was more in the players than what they played.'

Fiddler swallowed. 'I hadn't realised that you were there.'

Seeker let silence hang in the air a moment. 'I didn't say that I was.'

He folded the last song sheet, but kept his hand on it. He was done with the packman, for now. He handed him his now half-empty pack, and told him he was free to go. As Fiddler reached the door that would take him back out on to the lane, Seeker said his name and he turned back round.

'And do not think of leaving London until I tell you otherwise, no, not for a minute.' Fiddler was half out on to the street when he heard his name again. 'And do not think I will not know your every footstep.'

As the packman stepped once more into the flow of people that passed up and out of Birchin Lane, nobody spoke, the scratch of Seeker's pen across paper dominating all other sounds. Then, from the table, came Archibald Campbell's voice.

'Another dish of coffee, surely, if I am to be held here half the day.'

The coffee boy looked to Grace and then to Seeker. The scratching of pen across paper slowed and stopped. Seeker looked up at Campbell, took a draught from the tankard of ale that Grace had brought him, and pointed to the stool in front of him. He told the boy to bring the man more coffee.

The first thing was the name. Highland? Yes. Argyll? Yes.

'What is your allegiance?'

Campbell didn't flinch. 'To the Covenant.'

'No longer relevant. And to Charles Stuart, calling himself King, son of the traitor Charles Stuart?'

Campbell spoke slowly, and with a degree of bitterness. 'I have no interest in the doings of those men.'

'Did you fight in the wars?'

'I am a minister of God.'

This was no answer to his question. Seeker repeated it. 'Did you fight in the wars?'

Campbell's reply was scarcely audible. 'I fought at Dunbar.'

'For Charles Stuart?'

Campbell's mouth was twisted. 'For the Covenant.'

Dunbar, an impossible victory, impossible for all but God, and Cromwell. Seeker wondered whether he himself might have faced Archibald Campbell, four years ago, at Dunbar. But no, because if that had been the case, Archibald Campbell would not be sitting across from him now. Archibald Campbell would be dead.

'Why are you in London?'

'I was called to the pulpit of the Presbyterian chapel in Goldsmith's Court. I am a minister of the word of God.'

Seeker knew of the place, hidden away in Goldsmith's Court, reached by a long, narrow passageway at the end of Fetter Lane. It was an odd place, he had often thought, for the worship of God, tucked away behind a ramshackle thoroughfare of inns for the transient, booksellers, quack doctors, dubious lodging houses from which painted women emanated at night. On the margins of the city proper, there was a breath of danger, an atmosphere of well-judged fear that hung around those who passed by or plied their trade there. And yet perhaps it was as apt a place as any for a house of God or for a Christ who had come to call sinners.

He studied the man before him a few moments. He had seen his like before, often enough. The Scots had crossed and recrossed the border countless times, seeing themselves on a mission from God to secure a covenanted King or Commonwealth, ready to throw in their lot with whomever might promise them what they wanted to hear. He had seen their soldiers hungry, exhausted, cold, be sermonised for two, three hours at a time by the likes of Campbell, only to be led to oblivion. But in Campbell, in his eyes, there was something more, and it was that something more that Seeker determined to know.

'Where is Zander Seaton?'

Campbell was taken off guard. 'I don't know.'

Seeker asked the question again. Again the protestation of ignorance. 'How should I know where he is?'

'Because you travelled together all the way from Edinburgh to this place.'

Still Campbell said nothing.

'He is a known Royalist,' said Seeker, without looking up from the paper on which he was writing.

'I, no, I . . .'

'He is a known Royalist who rode with the rebel Montrose in the cause of the traitor Charles Stuart and of his son, the pretended King, now in exile. It is not six months since he escaped from the rebels' defeat at General Morgan's hands at Dalnaspidal. He evaded the notice of the authorities until he appeared here only yesterday, in this coffee house, at your side. Don't waste my time by denying that you knew this.'

Campbell took a gulp of his coffee and looked right at Seeker, his mouth a little twisted. 'I guessed some of it, but what of it? His cause is lost. Montrose is dead, Charles Stuart wandering like a beggar round Europe, and the flags of my nation hang in Westminster Hall. There is nothing left for Zander Seaton to swear allegiance to.'

'So what was he doing with you, here in London?'

'I met him on the road. We came to an agreement – I paid to have his protection on the journey. It is not safe to travel alone on the open roads of this Kingd—. . . Commonwealth, especially for one such as I.'

Seeker accepted the truth of this. 'And so I ask you again, where is your companion, your hired sword now, Mr Campbell?'

Everyone in the coffee room waited. Campbell looked to the side and muttered, 'I don't know.'

'I did not hear you,' said Seeker.

'I don't know,' said Campbell, almost defiant this time. 'Our bargain is fulfilled and I have not seen him since he left this place yesterday afternoon, just after that woman, that harlot—'

'Lady Anne Winter?'

'Her. Just after she left.'

'And before her husband came in?'

'Aye, a long time before.'

'Did he return to the Black Swan?'

Campbell looked only mildly surprised for a moment that Seeker should know where he and Seaton were lodged. 'He didn't sleep there last night, but he had been back at some point. Some of his belongings are gone.'

'Some?'

'His sword. A pistol. He always carried his knife in his stocking anyway.'

Seeker held the quill pen, unmoving, over the ink bottle. 'Why did Zander Seaton come to London?'

Campbell was looking at his hands. Seeker followed his gaze, noting the scarred fingers, the broken, disfigured nails. Eventually, the minister raised his eyes to meet his. 'I never cared enough to ask.'

Just as Seeker dismissed the minister, the bell of St Michael's joined in the peal all around the city that rang out for ten o'clock. George Tavener shifted in his seat.

Seeker looked up at him. 'You have business to attend to?'

Tavener nodded. 'I am expected at the Exchange.'

'Very well. We will talk this afternoon, after your meeting at Westminster. Wait in the committee room until I come to find you.'

The look that fell across George Tavener's face told any who cared to notice that he had not expected Seeker to know his movements and business so well. It never ceased to surprise Seeker how little people understood about the world in which they lived. Tavener was one of the wealthiest merchants in the city; his knowledge of trade, and particularly of the Caribbean and the Americas, had drawn him to Cromwell's attention and into Cromwell's counsels on the matter of the Protector's plans for expanding his power westwards, across the ocean. Could Tavener really not know that his day-to-day movements were a matter of interest to those who concerned themselves with the security of the Protector?

Seeker watched the merchant leave. It occurred to him that the man was trying too hard to conceal his relief at being allowed to go.

And then they were alone, save the guards: Seeker, Samuel Kent and his niece, and the boy, Gabriel.

'Is that you finished now, Captain?' asked Samuel, only a trace of apprehension in his voice.

'Almost.' Seeker looked at the coffee boy. 'Go you out into the yard now, and wait until you are sent for.'

Gabriel hesitated only a moment, glancing at Samuel, who frowned at him thunderously in response. The boy scuttled through the hatch towards the storeroom and the yard beyond.

'Where did you find him?' asked Seeker.

'On the street, an urchin. He earns his keep here, and we are fond of him.'

'He'll do well.' Seeker took a draught of his ale and brought out a clean sheet of paper. 'I'll speak to your niece now, but you stay also,' he said to Samuel.

Grace had known her turn would come. She'd been watching Seeker. Everyone had been watching Seeker, but whereas they had all been wondering what he would do, whom he would call next, what he would say, and after that and after that, she had been wondering about Seeker himself. Where did he come from? The North. She had heard it before, somewhere, she thought, and she had heard it here, today, in his speech, in the way the words fell with a sort of understood contempt for the hearer. He was not a gentleman. Plenty of gentlemen found their way to Kent's, but he was not one of them. When had he come, from the North, into the mind, the fears, of Londoners? That she didn't know. Had he been there when first she and Samuel had arrived, more than eight years ago now? No, she didn't think it. When had there come the time when people might disappear in the night, and it be said the Seeker had come for them? It would not always be known what they had done, but it would be agreed they must have done something, for Seeker was for Cromwell, and Cromwell was the law. She sat down across from him and placed her hands together on the table.

'You are ready?' he asked.

'Yes.'

A nod. 'Good. Now think carefully over my questions, take your time and answer me honestly.'

She took a breath to compose herself. 'I will.'

He began by asking her the same sorts of questions he had asked her uncle about the events of the previous day, about the customers, regular and new-arrived, who had spoken to whom. The answers she gave differed little from those he had had from her uncle, but as he listened, Seeker had the feeling there was more behind them. The girl who spent her days at the counter of the coffee room did not simply serve her customers: she studied them. Will Fiddler, Tavener, Ellingworth – all of them she knew well and of long standing, and her thoughts on them would have been coloured by feelings over time; information on their words and actions on the previous day was what he required, and that he had been able to extract, though it did not differ greatly from what he had learned from her uncle or the coffee house boy. What interested him most was what she had observed about the strangers.

'Tell me about the Dutchman.'

She considered a moment. 'He was reserved,' she said at last. 'He listened more than he spoke.'

'Who was he listening to?'

'He spoke a little in Dutch with George Tavener – but soon they reverted to English.' Here she gave a small smile. 'George's Dutch is not as good as he would have us think.'

Seeker felt something in him warm to the girl: very few people considered inviting him in on their private humour, however gentle that might be. Grace returned to the matter in hand. 'He talked a while with Will Fiddler, about book-sellers, and the best inns to call at on his way to Oxford – he was journeying to Oxford to meet with some of the learned doctors there, that he's been writing letters to. But it was Elias he was most interested in – he listened a good while to Elias.'

'And what did Elias have to say?'

The girl coloured. 'I—I don't pay much attention to talk of politics Mr Seeker. It doesn't interest me, and I don't understand it.'

So, a lie, that much was evident. He had seen by the look on her face, the tone of her voice when she spoke Ellingworth's name that Grace Kent had feelings for the lawyer. Clearly Ellingworth, the Sparrow, had been at his unguarded worst in his conversation with the Dutchman, or the girl would not have pretended otherwise. If she would lie to protect him over that, he would need to tread carefully in what he let her know of the lawyer's fate, or there would be nothing more useful to be had from her.

He moved on. 'And the Scotsmen?'

She relaxed visibly. 'The minister was as you have seen. His manner didn't fit well with the . . . tone of the table; he made the other customers uncomfortable, and didn't seem to care about it. My uncle is hoping he'll find somewhere else to go soon.'

'Hmm,' said Seeker. 'And his companion?'

'The soldier?' Her brow furrowed slightly. 'I don't know what he was doing here. He seemed a man ill at ease.'

'With the company?'

'Yes, but with himself, too. He was not interested in being drawn into conversations, and I had the impression he did not like his companion either.'

Seeker recalled something his informant had reported of Zander Seaton: 'Didn't speak to the Dutchman, but understood him all right'.

'Did Zander Seaton speak with Jakob Hendricks at all?'

Grace thought carefully. 'No, I don't think so. At least not that I could see. But I had the impression that he – I'm not sure . . .'

'That he what?' prompted Seeker.

She thought harder for the right words. 'That he took an especial notice of him.'

'And the Dutchman? Did he return the Scotsman's interest?'

Grace was more certain here. 'No. I don't think he even looked at him.' But then something seemed to bother her. 'But you should know, Captain, I don't see or hear everything. I keep to my counter most of the time. I never join the men at the table.'

'No. But yesterday was different. You joined Lady Anne in that booth, did you not?'

Grace looked over to where she had sat with that other woman just the day before.

'Yes.'

'And none of the other customers spoke with her?'

'No, she would have liked to but—it would not have been proper. This is a respectable house, Mr Seeker, but the coffee house is not a place for ladies to frequent.'

'And did any of the other customers try to speak to her?'

Grace shook her head. 'They all knew or were soon told whose wife she was. They knew better.'

'So she spoke only with you?'

'Yes. She would not let the physician see her, or allow that her husband be sent for, but I persuaded her to rest a while and take some chocolate. I thought she must be in some shock, after the accident. We spoke a little while and then she left.'

'What did you speak about?'

Grace furrowed her brow. 'Childhood. She said the coffee house reminded her of her father's house, which must have been nonsense, because I know her father was a wealthy man, a gentleman, and that his manor was worth the taking.'

Seeker looked up from his writing. 'Her father's manor

was forfeit because it was being held by rebels against Parliament. Go on.'

Grace continued, a little nervously. 'Well, she said it was because of the noise and the talking, and that people did not talk at Whitehall. She asked if I liked the coffee house, and I told her yes, for that reason. And then she asked me about my own childhood, and if people had talked, and I told her they had worked.'

Seeker looked at Grace Kent a moment. He knew the silence that came with work, the focus on survival, the silence that could become a habit, so that many things thought were never said, until it was too late to say them.

'Did she speak of her husband?'

'A little. Of his childhood, what she knew of it, and that he too seemed to live in a world of silences.'

'And then?'

'And then she left. She had been making purchases at the Exchange, and said she had something still to get at White-friars, from an apothecary's shop, at the sign of the Pineapple. I tried to make her wait, let me send the boy, but she would not have it and I could not keep her here and she was gone.'

And then he asked her about when John Winter had come in, and who had been there, and she gave him the same answers as her uncle had.

'And that was when Elias Ellingworth became agitated and left?'

Back to Elias – Seeker noticed her composure slip a little. 'Sometime later – not very long.' Then she looked around her, pointlessly. 'I don't know where Elias is today, why he hasn't been here.'

Seeker sensed he didn't have long until he lost her, and there were things he still had to know from her. He proceeded cautiously.

'John Winter was known to Elias was he not?'

Again Grace swallowed, looked around her.

'Grace?'

'Yes,' she said. 'Yes, they had exchanged words at Putney, many years ago.'

'Did Winter acknowledge him last night?'

Her fingers grasped each other on the table. 'Yes. I think so.'

'And Winter's wife? Had Elias ever spoken of her before? Did he know her?'

'What?' Her panic was rising. 'No, no, he'd never met her before.'

'Is Elias Ellingworth the Sparrow?'

'Yes, what of it?'

'Did Elias Ellingworth ever make threats against John Winter, against anyone?'

'No, of course not! Why don't you ask Maria? Why don't you ask Elias?' And then, at last, he could see that she understood. She was gazing in terror at Seeker, her mouth stumbling over her words.

'Where is he? What have you done to him? Where is Elias?'

Her hands were gripping on to the table, she was beginning to stand up, all pretence at composure gone. 'What have you done to him?'

There was no more to be had from her. She would have to know the truth. 'Elias Ellingworth was taken past here under guard five hours since, from Whitehall, and will now be under examination in the Tower. I myself found him, in the early hours of the morning, stooped over John Winter's dead body, a bloodied knife in his hand. He will be . . .'

But Damian Seeker could say no more of Elias Ellingworth as Grace Kent stumbled backwards from her stool and cried out 'No!' He lunged across the table as she fell, and caught her just in time to stop her head hitting the hard stone floor.

NINE

The Sights of London

Lady Anne Winter looked down at the water of the Thames flowing far beneath her window. She took a breath before taking the stopper from the phial in her hand, and pouring the liquid away. As she watched the drops disperse, come to nothing before they ever met the surface of the river, the events of the previous night played themselves through in her mind, but what she had been involved in before coming upon her husband in the corridor outside their apartments she did not like to think of. It hardly mattered any more: he was dead, and she would visit the apothecary no more.

Her mind was becoming clear now – clearer than it had been in a long while, and she made her decisions quickly. Seeker had not long left her, could scarcely have had time to call for his horse, before she'd been seated at the desk – John's desk, John's quill pen in her hand and writing the first letter she had written since the day nine years ago when a parliamentary soldier had run a sword through her brother before her very eyes. Her letter now was to Cromwell; she could force down the bile that rose in her stomach to think of him; she could use the terms his monstrous pride demanded. This once, she could prostrate herself before him, and today, as he raged in his grief and fear, she would have from him what she wanted. For he had loved John, she knew that, and been kindly to him, and he would not deny his widow this one thing: what she asked of the Lord Protector was his leave that she might pay one visit to her husband's murderer.

His reply was in her hand within the hour. In frustration, she tossed aside the near-interminable profession of grief and exhortation to prayer. 'Seek the will of God in this terrible Providence of His displeasure,' the Lord Protector said, 'that we might be reformed of our iniquities and stay His hand a second time.' And so it went on, as she had known it would, but that didn't matter, because at the end was the permission, under his seal, that she sought. She traced her finger over the bumps and mounds on the seal, Oliver on horseback, a panorama of London behind him, and mouthed the words, 'Thank you.'

She called for her black woollen cloak, with its trimming of mink. Some mourning would be expected of her, and so be it, she would comply, but there were other matters she must attend to, and with Oliver's pass in her hand and the escort he had insisted on at the door, she would lose no time.

They went by river. Cromwell had decreed it would be safer, and he was probably right: the city was its own power, truly loyal only to itself, and when stability at Westminster came under threat, London could not always be trusted. Long before their barge had travelled as far eastwards as Blackfriars even, she could sense the heightened tensions on the streets, and wondered what whisperings, what fears, were being voiced behind the garden walls, the high windows, of the houses on the Strand, as those who might suffer or benefit from her husband's death weighed their chances. None of it was of any concern to her: her business was at the Tower.

It was cold on the river, and all the long progression from the Privy Stairs at Whitehall to the Tower Wharf, neither guards nor boatmen spoke. But all that long progression, Anne Winter heard the voices of wronged women, the pawns of men or objects of their desire: at Bridewell, the inconvenient Katharine of Aragon defiantly asserting her innocence and her right; it was a prison now, a House of Correction for strumpets and vagabonds and insubordinate wives; a little further on, at Baynard's Castle, over the sound of the bargemen's oars she could just hear the fading voice of Lady Jane Grey, asking: why me? She couldn't hear the women's voices so well as they went by the city – too busy, to talk to her – but as they passed at last beneath London Bridge and the Tower came clearly into view, the chattering started again, the desperate chattering of desperate women who had overplayed their hand, who had forgotten, or not understood in the first place, that they really had no power at all. They had been silenced, at last, by the simple expedient of severing their heads from their necks.

Anne Winter shivered. Sometimes, in the night, she had wakened her husband by crying out, terrorised by her dreams of London's palaces and prisons, and now she was preparing to walk of her own will through the gates of the most terrible of them all.

The guard at the top of the wharf stairs examined the seal on the pass Cromwell's soldier had handed him. He looked at Lady Anne.

'Is she sure? Why would any woman want—?'

But the soldier cut him short. 'Not your concern. She has the Lord Protector's pass.' And so they had let her through, under one gate and then another, along walkways, through sentry posts, until they reached the Sale Tower. When they came to the final door, she told her escort to wait outside. They protested. 'But the Lord Protector—'

'Has entrusted me with this particular task. You know who I am?'

The soldier glanced at his companion and nodded.

She turned to the Tower guard, who was about to unlock the door. 'Is the man in there shackled?'

He spat. 'Hands and feet. He'll not give you any trouble. He's not saying much; mind you, they haven't started at him with the instruments yet: the Seeker wants to see him first.'

She hesitated. 'Is Damian Seeker here?'

He shook his head. 'No, but he will be. Luckier for this fellow. The Seeker doesn't talk to them once they've been tortured, doesn't see the use in it, he says. Mind you, I'd rather have the screws on than have that one bearing down on me for an hour. Two minutes, and I'd break.'

As Anne Winter stepped through the doorway, one of her escort said, 'We'll wait at the door, but don't close it. And do not draw near to him.'

But Anne Winter did draw near to Elias. She knelt down in front of the wooden chair to which he was bound, and drew a small flask of brandy from a pocket in her skirts, which she held up to his swollen and bloodied lips. It hardly seemed possible that this was the young lawyer who had spoken with such animation and carelessness in the coffee house only the day before.

'Do you remember who I am?' she asked quietly.

He could not lift his head properly. He moved it slightly, and made some effort to speak. She saw that one eye was red and swollen, closed up entirely, the brow above it cut. He was stockingless and barefoot, his hose and shirt soaked through with the same ice water that had evidently been poured over him, plastering his hair to his head. What, she wondered, did they consider torture in this place? He winced as the brandy dribbled on his lips. 'You are Winter's wife.'

'Yes, and I know you have been imprisoned here for his murder.'

'I didn't . . .'

She reached out a hand to the side of his face. 'Ssh, do not trouble yourself. I know you did not kill him. But you must listen to me. Can you listen to me? I have come here as your friend, but you must trust me. Will you trust me?'

He managed to make some reply that said he would.

'Good,' she said, keeping her voice as low as possible, that the guards on the other side of the door might not hear. 'What I am going to tell you is the truth. I cannot make you believe me, but I swear before God it is the truth.' Clearly, and with no unnecessary embellishment, she explained to him how it was she knew that he had not killed her husband.

At the end, he searched her face, but she could see in his eyes that he had already heard enough to believe her. 'I will do all I can, but you must trust me, and you must give me time. I do not think it can be much longer before Damian Seeker is here to question you. You must tell him the truth, such as you knew and understood it, up until the point that I walked through this cell door, and then you must tell him no more. If he asks why I came here, tell him I said it was so that I might look upon my husband's murderer, and that I said nothing else.' She looked carefully into his face. 'Do you understand?'

His head still lolling to one side, he let her know that he did, and she got up to leave. Before she reached the door, he managed to call her name.

'Lady Anne?'

She turned.

'If you cannot make it right, it doesn't matter.'

She looked at him a moment, at his beaten body and the red bloom on his shirt where the blood from his lip had seeped into the sodden linen, and knew that he meant what he'd said. She nodded once, and left the cell.

Seeker was back in Whitehall, pacing, agitated. He looked out through his windows to the park, closed up and empty, on Thurloe's orders. The Protector would not be able to ride out today. Seeker knew Cromwell was growing unsettled, hemmed in by the town, anxious to be out in the countryside, riding in the open, hawking, but things at the centre fell apart every time Oliver turned his eye away from it and the government of England would become the plaything of lesser, squabbling men. And so the Protector had to make do with the Parks, and Hampton Court, and put his memories of his glories on the march behind him.

Seeker also knew what it was to be sick of the city, and sometimes, in spite of himself, he found himself looking to the North, imagining, remembering. There had been a time when 'London' had been little more than a word to him, a reference to a place he had no thought of ever seeing. There had been a time when he had hunted, trapped for animals, for sustenance, for their hides, a time when he had not known that one day he would hunt for men, for what was in their minds. But remembering did no one any good. He turned his back on the window and strode to the door.

'Where the Devil are those paintings?' he bellowed at the guard outside.

The whereabouts of the paintings were demanded through a series of doorways and stairwells until they reached those charged with fetching them. 'Forgets that his horse is twice as fast as everybody else's, that people get out of his way double quick. Doesn't live in our world, the Seeker,' muttered one soldier to another as they carried the pictures from Kent's up the last few steps of the stairs leading to Seeker's apartments near the Cockpit.

Seeker hid his smile as he cleared the pewter water jug and salt cellar off the table and dismissed the soldiers after they had laid down the paintings. He inspected them one by one. Surely they were the poorest daubings ever to find their way within the walls of this palace. Fuel for the Lord Protector's fire, at best. He surveyed them a few minutes, and began to wonder if Maria Ellingworth had misunderstood what her brother had been saying, or if she had been foolish enough to lie to him. But she was not foolish: she was careful and, he thought, clever. He looked again.

The German woodcuts were not so bad, no doubt from the coffee man's time fighting on the continent, a happy reminder of more brutal days, but more interesting to Seeker was a large framed map, almost twenty years old, purporting to encompass 'Nova Totius Germaniae Descriptio' and covering an area from Schleswig, Friesland and Flanders in the north-west to Hungary and Bosnia in the south-east. On it were marked, by hand, rough crosses, the sites of famous battles, another reminder to Seeker that Samuel Kent had not always been old and lame, and that he had been a seasoned soldier long before Parliament had ever taken up arms against a treacherous king. Seeker looked a long time at the map, traced with his finger what he knew of the wanderings of Charles Stuart, the pretended King in exile, but could find little correspondence between them and old Samuel's markings. At length, he set the map to one side and looked at the remaining pictures.

There were some scenes, little edifying but not grotesque, of Londoners at their pleasure. The locations were not well chosen: the Bear Garden, the Globe, the Swan, the Spring Gardens – all demolished now or closed up. Ill-advised reminders of the days of disorder, before the Commonwealth and Protectorate had been instituted, they would not be returned to Kent's. Then there was an imagined scene of a Turkish bazaar, pipes and coffee pots, turbans and flowing silks, heat and colour. In the cascading fall of the garments, the curl of smoke from pipe and coffee pot, the curve and sheen of those vessels themselves, was a softness, a luxuriance, alien to Seeker's experience of the world. He spent more time looking at it than he had intended to, before setting it aside with the others. And now he came to the last. It might have been the most poorly done of all, and of little interest to anyone. An English church and churchyard, like a thousand to be found the country over. In the background, a cottar guided his oxen across a shallow stretch of river. Seeker recognised neither river nor church. Rivers were obstacles to be forded, and churches, as places of worship, were something alien to him, and ever had been.

Churches were places he had slept in, taken shelter in, hunted down others to in time of war. Some, he knew, were considered by others to be things of great beauty; for others, that man-made beauty was a distraction from the truth, but to him they were buildings. Even in his young days, when the search for God had been enjoined upon him, churches had never been anything more than buildings where others, more certain, congregated.

His eye had begun to wander back to the German map, but the unbidden thoughts of childhood brought images to his mind of woodlands, endless travelling, one community and then another, the Cumbrian hills, the moorlands of the North. This church was set by a moor, but it wasn't in Cumbria, nor Yorkshire, nor any other of those places he knew so well. There was a different quality to the light, to the landscape, and it spoke to him of the south-west. Samuel Kent was from the West Country, more nostalgia. Seeker would have dismissed it with the German woodcuts had curiosity not drawn his eye closer to the gravestones in the churchyard. Three, the middle one of them rendered in the form of an angel, stood out; they were not the largest, nor the furthest to the foreground, but whereas the engraving on the rest had been rendered as no more than a smudge, on these the lettering was defined. He took his glass and looked more closely. Three names, on three stones, the same date on each stone – 5 November 1654. Seeker put down his glass and sat back in his chair, his chin resting on his left hand. He was looking at the gravestones of three men not yet dead. Three known Royalists in the West Country who had been remarkably quiet this last year, and a date two days from now. He could feel his heartbeat quicken and leaned back in towards the picture. It was a letter, a message in a crude but clever code, and one that Elias Ellingworth had seen through and gone to warn John Winter about. But what else? The word from the Tower was that Ellingworth was saying nothing, nothing at all. And perhaps he was right to have trusted no one but Winter. There was nothing for it but Seeker must go, as soon as his business here was over, to the Tower, to put an end to Elias Ellingworth's silence.

He had to wait here a while yet, though, until George Tavener had finished with the business at Westminster. This regime, like every other, needed the City of London, the wealth and the power of merchants, but no regime ever fully trusted the city, still less did the city ever fully trust the nation's government. That was why Cromwell needed men like Tavener; more, Cromwell liked George Tavener, and it was rumoured that John Thurloe even trusted him, but Seeker was not ready to, not yet. He looked again at the painting, examined every detail, searched for something he might have missed. And then he found it, so simple, so obvious, once you knew. Very faint, on a wooden board by the door of the church, could be deciphered the words 'St Peter's'. Seeker traced his hand in a line from the church door to the cottar taking his beasts across the water in the background. The oxen fording the river. He sat back and allowed himself the trace of a smile, before calling to his guard in the corridor.

'Go down to Horse Guard Yard. Tell Proctor I will need Acheron ready at first light tomorrow, and a troop of eight men, fully armed.'

'Do they need to know where they are headed to?' asked the man, his heel already turning.

'Oxford,' said Seeker. 'We are going to Oxford.'

Archibald Campbell had taken care that the image he presented to the world as he entered the Rainbow coffee house by the gateway to the Inner Temple was quite different to that of the dishevelled fanatic seen in Kent's a few hours earlier. He had brushed his hair with a silver comb found amongst the remnants of Zander Seaton's belongings, and cleaned his shoes. He had dusted down his sober coat and hose to a respectable black. His buckles and buttons shone, and after the conventional pleasantries of the coffee house, which he now understood, Archibald Campbell wanted it to be known that he had money to invest.

He was a Scottish minister, not long come to London, and knew little of trade, he said. He had a fancy, he said, for the East Indies trade. The house of the East India Company on Leadenhall Street had appeared to him very fine. Perhaps that would prove to offer worthwhile stock?

'Don't touch it,' a merchant at the far end of the table advised him. 'That house on Leadenhall Street, and a rock in the middle of the Banda Sea, is about all they have left, and Cromwell's taking God's own time deciding what should be done with the whole company, lock, stock and barrel. If you'll take my advice, you'll plump for the West Indies.'

'Barbados?' asked Campbell.

'For now,' said another, removing his pipe and putting down the list of stock prices he had been surveying. 'But the Lord Protector has a mind for an empire – the Spanish one, I've heard.'

Campbell affected surprise. 'Hispaniola? Cuba?'

The man nodded, lowering his voice to a whisper. 'There's a fleet being gathered now, to sail under Desborough. They'll make for Barbados and then Hispaniola, but only for a start. It's to be Jamaica, next, I hear. And them that can get a foot in that trade will be made for life.'

Campbell leaned in towards the man. 'And how is that foot to be got?'

'If you have money, put it into sugar, tobacco, slaves . . .'

Campbell flinched. 'As a man of God – and I am a man of God – it would not sit well with my conscience to profit in the trafficking of my fellow Christians.'

'But if they are not Christians . . .'

And so started a debate around the table, where Aristotle was called into play, Augustine quoted. Campbell attended closely to the speakers, keeping his counsel, a fact that his animated companions appeared not to notice. He listened more carefully than was usual in the Rainbow to what others had to say. Dishes were emptied and refilled, pipes taken and replenished, voices raised. Soon, the rights and wrongs were forgotten in tales of profit, fabulous profit. Campbell almost held his breath, careful to say nothing that would interrupt the flow.

'But the risks are very great,' said one merchant. 'The perils of a voyage to the Gold Coast, of dealing with the traders there.'

'Ah, but not for those who truly keep their wits about them – what need to go to Africa? Let Cromwell go in again to Ireland, let the Scots make war in the name of their King again, and there's money to be made for the man that has his eye on events.'

'Prisoners taken in battle?'

'Thousands of them – how else do you think Old Nol got rid of them?'

'But to sell your fellow Christians into slavery,' protested a young printer.

An older fellow laughed. 'The Irish are hardly Christians – barbarous savages that must be tamed, and as for the Scots, well, they rebelled against the Commonwealth, didn't they? Went back on their bargain when they took up with Charles Stuart, marched into England. They knew what they were doing when they took themselves beyond the Lord General's protection. And should they do it again, well . . .'

'I for one wouldn't stoop so low,' said the young printer roundly.

'No,' said the other, all humour gone from his face now,

'and that is why you'll get no further than your hovel on Pudding Lane, dodging the slops of dung at your feet, while George Tavener advises Old Nol on Barbados, and is carried home from Westminster to his fine house on Cheapside by sedan chair.'

And so, in the way of things, conversation moved on to the state of the streets, the inadequacies of the night soil men, whose carts dripped effluent from one ward to the next, and the great inconveniences of traffic.

Archibald Campbell had heard enough. He finished his dish of coffee, pushed his empty bowl aside, and walked out into those dirty streets, his unasked questions answered.

TEN

Merchant

It was nearly four by the time George Tavener came out of the meeting of the Advisory Committee for the Western Design. Cromwell had been in a predictably foul mood to begin with. There had been long prayers, invocations to God that His will in the terrible death of John Winter might be revealed to them. The Lord Protector was not a man of subtlety, but some of those around him were, and knew how to play to his doubts and fears. Tavener had observed with increasing apprehension as Thomas Cage, a great pro- moter of this 'Work in the World' that was the Protector's desire for a foreign empire, for spreading the Revolution across oceans, for garnering the world's wealth for this one, true, godly nation, condoled deeply with Cromwell on this irredeemable loss to the nation and to the Lord Protector himself, but then, word by word, look by look, Cage had hesitated. Tavener could have predicted what was coming next: John Winter had been against the Western Design, had he not? He had not been in favour of taking the

Revolution to other lands, and had often counselled against it. Was it not a sign of God's will, perhaps, His dread Providence, that Winter's dissenting voice in this matter had been so decisively silenced? And so Cromwell had found some comfort and encouragement in this, and Tavener had realised that the balance of power on the Committee had tipped even further away from men of reason towards those whose counsel of greed could lead only to disaster.

Keeping his voice low, Tavener told all this to Seeker as they walked from Westminster Hall across New Palace Yard. The place was always heavy with the presence of soldiers, but usually at this hour they would be at their dinner in one of the taverns or eating houses that fringed the yard, laughing, arguing, watching carefully who among their officers was in favour, who not, content that their presence was felt by the politicians or whoever else might have business at Westminster. Today, though, it was different: today, on Seeker's orders, they were at every corner, every passageway in twos or fours, fully armed and waiting for something. Tavener noticed that they all seemed to stand a little straighter when the Seeker passed.

'What was John Winter's objection to the Western Design?' asked Seeker once Tavener had finished.

'He believed that if the Protector embroils himself in dreams of foreign empires, lands where he has never and will never set foot, and where the people have no interest in loyalty to the Commonwealth, the centre can only be weakened.'

Seeker nodded, and Tavener thought he could see a degree of agreement in the soldier's eyes.

'And Winter's views were not debated after Cage spoke?'

'No,' said Tavener, 'it was made clear they were no longer a point for discussion. And that is no good thing, for the hotheads, and those who know nothing of the true condition of the Indies, now hold sway, and they will persuade the Lord Protector to disaster.'

'How so?' asked Seeker.

'They dangle before him prizes he cannot win, without much bloodshed and loss of life, if at all. And if he wins them, he will hardly keep them. Our colony at Barbados has no desire to move to Jamaica or Hispaniola or anywhere else. And how is it proposed we should people our new acquisitions, should we ever win them? How should we secure this great Christian enterprise – for I told him straight solid Englishmen and women would not go.'

Tavener was becoming animated, some of his frustration with those who would not see things as he did coming to the surface. 'Irish orphans, the children of rebels, to be rounded up and shipped off two and a half thousand miles, to build Cromwell's empire. Highlanders – savages of savage tongue and savage dress with loyalty only to a dead king and his dissolute son.'

'But you yourself have sold into slavery prisoners of war, rebels against the Commonwealth, have you not?'

Tavener looked like a shadow had just fallen across his path and took a moment to respond.

'Aye, I have. To work until they drop on tobacco plantations, or amongst the sugar canes, not to be the builders of
empires. I tell you, Seeker, it is disaster that waits for the
Lord Protector on this Western Adventure, and with
John Winter gone, there is none left with the stomach to
tell him so.'

They continued along back towards the King Street Gate
and into Whitehall. Parties of soldiers, civil servants, on
foot or on horseback, household servants, clerks, secretaries
to army committees, all made way for the Seeker. Tavener
wondered how aware the man was of his own reputation,
whether he sought to cultivate it, or took it for granted. As
they passed within the Palace precincts, no sounds came
from the Privy Garden – those of the Protector's family
who were not safe already at Hampton Court were under
close guard in their private apartments – for although Thurloe was confident they had their murderer in Elias
Ellingworth, Seeker had put some doubts in his head, and
strongly advised him to caution. Only as they began to
climb the stair to the Cockpit did Tavener realise that Seeker
had not yet said a single word to him about the events of the
previous day and Kent's coffee house.

They arrived at his room, where Seeker dismissed the
guard outside before turning the key in the lock. Tavener
looked about him: no fire in the grate, no pictures, books,
no furnishing other than was strictly necessary – of good
solid construction but little interest in aesthetic or design,
or indeed comfort. Nothing of the man to see, or perhaps

everything. Perhaps, thought Tavener, this is everything there is to see of Damian Seeker. And yet, even as he thought it, he doubted it.

He was offered nothing to drink, no pipe, nor chair even. When Seeker himself sat down on the high-backed oak chair at one side of the table and began to write, Tavener waited and then sat down on the bench across from him; this provoking no reaction, he supposed he had done the right thing. Tavener removed his hat and was in the process of laying it down on the table in front of him when Seeker looked up and indicated with his quill pen a long nail on the back of the door.

After a moment or two of writing, Seeker pushed a sheet of paper towards Tavener – it was a list of all who had been in the coffee house the previous day, both when Lady Anne Winter had been in, and later, when her husband had come.

'Do you agree with the names written there?'

Tavener scanned them quickly. 'For the earlier time, yes. I was not there when John Winter came in.'

Seeker nodded, then reached behind his chair and brought out a picture, which he laid on the table. It was the English churchyard scene. Tavener sat back, thoroughly confused.

'It's from Kent's, is it not? That piece of rubbish Samuel bought from some charlatan two days ago?'

'Tell me what you know of it.'

Tavener shrugged. 'Very little. Samuel can be a soft touch at times. Some down-on-his-luck traveller from the West Country sold that to him two days ago, for the price of a dish of coffee and a shilling in his pocket. Waste of money, and it'll do the fellow no good to let him think he might live without working.'

'Where is this man now?'

'I don't know – I never saw him, and Samuel said he was looking for the money to get himself home.'

'Where?'

Again Tavener shrugged. 'West. That is all he said.'

'When did it appear on the wall at Kent's?' asked Seeker.

'Yesterday.'

'Did anyone pay particular attention to it?'

'Not that I noticed. It was on the far wall from the table, above the private booth; we spoke for a moment about what a poor piece of work it was, poked a little fun at Samuel for his soft heart, and the conversation moved on; we spoke of Dutch artists then, I think.'

'Did anyone look at the picture close up?'

Tavener considered a moment. 'I was not aware that they did, but anyone would have passed close by it on the way to the privy.'

'Jakob Hendricks? Elias Ellingworth?'

Tavener shook his head. 'That I couldn't tell you. I don't go to the coffee house to observe my companions on their journey to the close-stool.'

A brief change in Seeker's expression, a rearrangement of the papers in front of him, alerted Tavener to the fact that they were now coming to another matter, and he felt unaccountably on his guard.

Seeker spent a moment looking over the sheet now on top of the pile of notes in front of him. 'And when you yourself were leaving Kent's, you told others there it was to see to a piece of business at the Royal Exchange?'

'Yes,' answered Tavener cautiously.

'You didn't go to the Royal Exchange.' A statement of fact, not a question.

Tavener hesitated, but clearly there was little point in denying it. He would tell him no lie, although there was no need to tell him the whole truth.

'After I left, I remembered something that I had to attend to in my offices at home, and then I took my dinner with my wife.'

It was no lie, other than that on leaving Kent's the previous day, George Tavener had never had any intention of going to the Royal Exchange, less than two minutes' walk from the top of Birchin Lane. He had, instead, turned westwards, down Cornhill and along Poultry Street to his own fine town house on Cheapside. Towering five storeys above the street, every storey was a mark of George Tavener's life, and declared his success to all the world that passed, and it was said that all the world that mattered would pass this way, eventually, between the Tower and St Paul's and Whitehall, one way or, God help them, the other.

It was Tavener's habit to go first to the basement when he returned home, to cast his expert eye over the storing of his goods – no drip from the street above, or damaged barrel or furtive rat escaped his notice: George Tavener lost fewer goods to spoiling than almost any other merchant in the city. He would then, as a courtesy, and from genuine affection as well as a careful reminder of his oversight, call in to the kitchens, where his wife would be directing the work of cook and maid and kitchen boy. She was a very pretty woman, a good deal younger than he, and a good wife, and George Tavener often said it. But yesterday, he had not gone to check on his stores nor call in on his wife. He'd passed instead to the first floor of the house, as message boys from the docks and the Exchange had scampered out of his way, and gone straight to the counting room, where his two clerks had been working upon the ledgers and inspecting bills of lading for a ship just in.

Tavener had addressed the nearer of them. 'Peter, you go down to the mistress. Tell her I will take my dinner at home with her today, in the small parlour. For now, I have some work to do here with William. We are not to be disturbed, until I send word.'

The boy had been gone in seconds.

William, the senior of the two clerks, and the one Tavener trusted more, had put down his pen and blotted the account book he had been working on, and waited.

'The books for 1650. The Americas.'

The young man had gone directly to a large oak cupboard, set into a recess in the wall, the key ready in his hand. 'Going out or coming in?'

'Going out,' Tavener had said.

'The *Henry* or the *Eagle*?'

Tavener had scrambled in his mind a moment, then shaken his head impatiently. 'Give me both,' he'd said.

The boy had handed him the two identical-looking, red hide-bound ledgers, quite alike but for the yellow silk ribbon attached as a marker to the spine of the second.

'The *Eagle*,' Tavener had murmured before recollecting himself and handing the other back to William. 'Put this away again with the others. Is the *Eagle* marked in the catalogue?'

The boy hadn't needed to check. 'All the ship's ledgers are catalogued, Sir.' George had guessed this would be the answer: it would have been more than William's position and the roof over his head were worth for it to be otherwise.

'Excise it then,' Tavener had said before turning, ledger under his arm, from his astonished clerk and leaving the counting room without closing the door behind him.

Once upstairs in his private study, which could be accessed only through the bedroom he shared with his wife, George Tavener had turned the key in the door. He'd lit a candle on the small walnut desk by the window, then closed the shutters. He'd laid the ledger on the desk and looked at the cover a long time before opening it at December 1650. He'd checked the cargo list, although he knew it already. He could remember watching it loaded, every item. Not London, but Bristol it had gone out from, and it had made his fortune. He'd traced his finger down the list and found what he was looking for. Some men might have destroyed that list, But George Tavener's caution was more far-sighted: he might need that information yet.

He'd taken a small key from its chain around his neck and gone over to the cabinet in the corner, to the left of the window. He had placed it there purposely, that it might not be damaged by sunlight. His wife was not an ostentatious woman, but she loved that cabinet, and could not understand why he would keep a thing of such beauty from public view, or at least from that of their friends. He had come upon her in this room on more than one occasion, sitting on a little stool, just gazing at it, the ebony veneer on pine and oak, with a myriad of *pietra dura* panels that were mounted with gilt and bronze and painted plaques, each one a drawer or cupboard. Fruit, flowers, exotic birds from countries his Mirjam could only dream of – he had known as soon as he set eyes on it that he must have it for her, although the shipping of it from Florence had cost him a small fortune at the time. But Mirjam was never given a key: the cabinet was hers only to look upon, and she did not know what treasures, what insurances against future disasters, he kept in there, in the drawers and behind the little locked doors. She had often, in the night, fingered the tiny key on its chain about his neck, but she had never once asked if she might have it. She was a good wife.

Checking once more that the study door was indeed locked, George Tavener had slid the key into the centre of a magnificent peony with a black bee at its heart that only the very observant would have noticed was a keyhole, and gently eased open the long, shallow drawer at the very base of the cabinet that, again, the untrained eye would hardly have guessed was a drawer. Into this space he had placed the ledger. He'd shut the drawer, locked it again and returned the key to his neck, before snuffing out the candle, opening the shutters once more, and going down the stairs to take his dinner with his wife.

None of this, however, did he tell Damian Seeker.

'So,' repeated Seeker, recalling him to the present, 'you remembered some business you had to attend to at home, and remained there to take dinner with your wife?'

Tavener nodded.

'Hmm,' said Seeker, then he put down his pen and leaned back in his chair, surveying Tavener in such a way as to leave the merchant in no doubt that his inquisitor was no respecter of persons. After a moment of this silent appraisal, Seeker said, 'And where did you go last night, after the recital at the Dutch Church?'

'I . . .' Tavener again considered lying, but then remembered something he had once heard Cromwell say of Seeker: 'He watches the enemy so continuously that they eat, drink, sleep not, but he can give us an account of their darkest proceedings.' No, a lie would make matters worse. 'I went to the White Nutmeg coffee house, in Bleeding Heart Yard.'

The White Nutmeg coffee house in Bleeding Heart Yard was a very different order of establishment from Kent's on Birchin Lane. By day it was the respectable haunt of many young lawyers and gentlemen's sons from the Inns of Court, but at night, after the bellman had been through the streets to ring the curfew, the lawyers returned to their chambers and it became a quite other place entirely. The shutters were closed, the front door locked, but the fire was kept going in the hearth and the coffee pot kept on the boil. It had been well after eleven o'clock that Tavener had arrived in the yard, to join those who murmured amongst themselves and shuffled quietly towards the back door of the coffee house. On his entering the room behind the serving counter, voices had drifted towards him not from the stillness of the coffee room next door, but from beneath the floorboards. He had given the agreed word, and been allowed down the narrow stairway that led to the cellar storeroom below.

'The White Nutmeg?' queried Seeker. 'At that hour of the night?'

'There was an auction by inch of candle. It is a common enough way of doing business.'

'What had you gone there to buy?'

Tavener hesitated. 'There were some goods I had heard were for sale . . .'

'What else would there be? Answer the question!' snapped Seeker.

Tavener saw it again his mind: sacks of coffee beans and chocolate, crates of green tea and other dry goods pushed to the side wall of the cellar. One or two benches had been brought down from the room above and candles lit in the sconces on the wall. On a barrel by the foot of the stair stood a single, tall church candle, marked by the inch. It had not yet been lit. At about ten minutes to midnight, the goods for auction had been brought in. Some of the buyers crowded into the cellar had leaned forward a little, the better to view the items, but been respectfully requested to keep back, that all might see.

On a bench set against a far wall, with two ostentatiously armed men at either side of it, were laid out a range of items that could not have been sold in open light. An apothecary out of Whitefriars, a charlatan if ever George Tavener had seen one, had on display a vast number of preparations that might alter the mind or blind, debilitate, or paralyse the body, bring rapture or agony to those who partook of them. He said it openly, and apologised that he could not demonstrate the properties of his finest compounds, but he had brought with him a poor soul, an idiot who babbled about wild wolves and monkeys, whom he assured the intrigued patrons had formerly been a Fellow in a renowned Cambridge college. 'But he made a rival of the wrong man, a client of mine, and here you see the result.' What the truth of it was, Tavener had not cared to judge, but there could be no dissembling in the man's idiocy.

Tavener's interest had been in the next lot offered for sale that night. Three men, their hands tied behind them, their feet shackled, were brought forward: Irishmen, soon to be slaves. He'd listened, only half hearing, as the agent selling them went through a litany of outrages and barbarities, half-truths and outright lies, purporting to be the crimes of these three men and their like against the godly English occupation of Ireland. Tavener thought the agent might have saved himself the trouble: none of those there to buy had any interest in the morals of the case, and here, at this time and in this place, surrounded by their own kind, had no need to pretend. They were sizing up the men for the strength of their bodies, the health of their skin, teeth.

Seeker's sigh of impatience brought Tavener back to the present. 'I went to bid on Irishmen, rebels from Wicklow taken on their way to the continent to join in the cause of Charles Stuart. Three of them. Fair game. I have a buyer in Barbados . . .'

'So you do not scruple to profit from the very thing you warned the Lord Protector against?'

'These men will cut tobacco till they drop in the sun. I am under no delusion that they will build me a Christian empire.'

Seeker grunted. 'And did you make your purchases?'

'They're in the hold of a ship leaving St Katharine's Wharf on the next tide.'

Seeker asked for the name of the ship and wrote it down.

'Who else was there that will vouch for the truth of what you say?'

'The light in the cellar was very poor . . .'

Seeker leaned closer and spoke very deliberately. 'I have a great deal of business to see to, Tavener, and men more important than you will ever be to answer to. Do not waste my time.'

Tavener swallowed. 'All right. All right,' then, looking Seeker straight in the eye, he said, 'Lady Anne Winter.'

It was clear that the Seeker had not had even the merest idea that he had been going to say this. He got up from his seat and walked over to the window, turning his back on Tavener while he appeared to look out over the empty park. In the silence of the room, the merchant became more and more aware of his own breathing. He watched the fingers on Seeker's right hand drum slowly, again and again, on the casement, and wondered if the man realised that he was doing it.

'And what,' asked Seeker at length, still apparently surveying St James's Park, 'was Lady Anne there to buy?'

There was no option now but for Tavener to tell the truth, and pray God that he might be believed, and so he did.

He had been considering how much he should bid for the Irishmen when production of the third item for sale that night had brought the noise in the room to silence and stopped him in his tracks. The shadowy apothecary from Whitefriars had appeared again, no longer touting the preparations — laudanum, tobacco of coca leaves, snakeroot — by which he brought desperate men and women under his control, but instead leading Anne Winter by the hand. She had stood before them, her eyes strangely bright and a bewildered smile on her face, as in a slow and clear voice the auctioneer had laid out the precise details of the bargain.

The candle had then been lit, and the auctioneer had pointed to the first notch on it, an inch below the wick. 'One hour, gentlemen,' he had said. 'You may start your bids.'

Tavener looked to Seeker. 'She was not there to buy anything. Lady Anne Winter was amongst the goods for sale.'

Seeker did not question the truth of what Tavener said. In fact, he did not seem altogether surprised by it, simply asking after a pause, 'And so John Winter's wife prostituted herself to feed her craving. Well, let us have it: who bought the whore?'

There was silence in the room. Even the incessant sound of footsteps on the stairs outside and the corridors below seemed to have been suspended. Seeker turned around, his fingers no longer drumming. The late-afternoon sunlight coming through the window formed a haze around his head and shoulders and obscured his features. Tavener steadied himself on the chair, thought about Mirjam, his lovely Mirjam. At last he spoke and his voice was low but clear. 'I did.'

*

Some way from his lodging on Knight Ryder Street, between Fetter Lane and Shoe Lane, and hidden from the street, there was a garden where the carpenter liked to sit. No one could tell any more whether it was left over from the countryside and had been built around and forgotten, or if Londoners past had planted and tended it, then died and left no mark behind them but this sanctuary of trees and flowers. Herbs grew here, run wild over the centuries;

two apple trees, a cherry, ferns in dark corners, and stocks that scented the night air in the summer so that even the stench of the diseased city was held at bay for a while.

He had made a bench of pine, carved it night by night, and set it here in the night. Sometimes old women sat here, drunks slept here, children climbed. The carpenter would come occasionally, the rumble of carts and carriages, beasts and men continuous in the background, but kept from intruding on the sounds of insects and birds. Where did the bees go to, he wondered, when they had drunk their fill, a hundred years after the destruction of their hives at Black-friars? Where does a man go, when he has no place any more? The city; the city, where he can change and begin again. Men, women, names, dynasties came and went and disappeared in the city, and no one asked why or where they had gone, where they had come from in the first place.

Ten minutes of solitude here were enough to restore him. The dog knew, only the dog could see. The stray, the mon-grel of indeterminate ancestry he had come on here once as a puppy, that had followed him ever since. A young couple came into the garden, laughing. The dog looked up at him, knowing it was time to go, and the carpenter lowered his hat and raised himself from the bench, murmuring an unheard 'good evening' to the lovers as he passed.

ELEVEN

Of Women

'Is she still sleeping?' Even in the stifling heat of Grace's small bedchamber, Samuel Kent's face was ashen.

'Aye, but not restful,' said the old nurse, dabbing Grace's forehead with a cool, damp cloth. 'Is the boy back yet from the apothecary?'

'Just this minute.' Samuel peeked for a moment at his niece and then looked away; he had never held illness in high regard – it would kill you or it wouldn't. He had seen men die in so many different ways that the prospect of Death at work held little fear for him. And yet in Grace – no, that he could not countenance. He who had seen so much suffering could not watch her suffer a moment.

He didn't hold the Seeker to blame – someone would have had to tell her about Elias, and yet he would not have had it so, he would have made up any lie to protect her from the knowledge of where Elias was now, and what his fate must surely be. He himself had been useless when she had fainted, and her condition now would have been much worse had Seeker not moved so quickly to catch her before she dashed her head on the floor. It had been a good few minutes until they had brought her to with the aid of a little powdered briony root in some wine, but it had soon made her sick and she had fainted again. No sense at all could be got from her after that, and he had had to have the clock-maker's wife from across the lane put her to bed. He had busied himself with all manner of things he thought might aid her, anything but have to look on her as the fever took hold and began to addle her mind. And so the fire she did not light from one year's end to the next was built up and roared in her room, for fear the fever would turn to chill, the boy sent for best beef broth from the cook shop on Pope's Head Alley, and the physician called for. But the physician would not come to Kent's coffee house, not for any money, once he heard the Seeker had been in there an hour that morning, the door bolted and under guard, to question them on Elias Ellingworth's murder of John Winter.

Samuel, furious, was intent that that physician would soon find out what he was made of. Gabriel was helping Samuel on with his buff coat when a knock came at the street door.

'We're closed!' he growled between oaths as the boy struggled with the bandolier.

But the knocking continued, and eventually, cursing in frustration, Samuel told Gabriel to open up. His cursing stopped in his mouth when the stuttering boy made him understand who was standing there.

'You . . .'

'Mr Kent . . .'

He shook his head. 'Oh no. Now, I mean no disrespect to you, my Lady, but you have brought a world of trouble on our heads. Your husband was a good man, a good soldier, but the likes of us have no business being looked to for his death, and it's your ever setting foot in here that brought it all on us.'

Anne Winter took a step further into the light. 'I know it, and I am heartily sorry for it, but I have come here to make some reparation . . .'

Samuel stopped in his struggle with his bandolier. 'What? What reparation can you make for Elias being shut up in the Tower, waiting to hang like as not – for they don't give our kind a nice swift death with a sharp axe, you know! Or my niece, lying in a fever up there, hardly knowing where she is, and no physician will come to her for fear of the Seeker? Go back to your Palace rooms, Madam, and leave us be.'

Anne Winter flinched a little under his tirade, but she swallowed and tried again. 'I have been to see him.'

'The Seeker?'

She shook her head. 'Elias. The lawyer.'

The boy could not stop himself. 'The Tower? You have been to the Tower? Is it like they say? Are there . . .'

Samuel silenced him, and at last sat down on the stool the boy had put out for him ten minutes earlier. He looked at Lady Anne. Could he believe her? She was standing there, waiting, holding her breath almost, like a woman who knew her hand of cards would beat all others at the table.

'I have come to tell his friends, his sister, not to worry – he cannot be convicted of my husband's murder because John was dead before Elias Ellingworth ever came upon him, and I have told that to the Seeker too.' She looked away from them. 'I cannot tell you your friend has been well-treated, but he will not die while the Seeker doubts his guilt; the man is ruthless enough, but it is the truth he is determined upon uncovering – not some convenient lie that would leave the real assassin still a threat to Cromwell.'

Samuel felt calmed a little. He looked around him and gestured apologetically towards the counter. 'I'm sorry, I am sorry. You have been very kind and had no need to do this, but my niece, you see . . .'

Anne Winter came closer to him, spoke slowly. 'Your niece is ill, you say?'

'Aye. And no physician will come.'

'Might I see her? I often assisted my mother at Baxton Hall; she was skilled in healing and nursing. There may be something I can do.'

Samuel stared at her a moment, then nodded. 'It cannot harm.'

Gabriel led Anne Winter up the narrow wooden stair from the coffee room to Grace's small bedchamber. Her black mink-trimmed mourning clothes rustled as they brushed the edges of those stairs. At the door near the landing, the boy knocked quietly, and in a moment the clockmaker's wife appeared. The boy glanced past her to where Grace lay, fevered and restless, on the bed.

'There is a lady here, wishes to see Mistress Grace,' he said.

The old woman surveyed Anne Winter with an air of suspicion.

'Oh, yes? Well, she's sleeping now, but not sound. You'll get no sense out of her – and there's been none these last hours since the Seeker was here.'

'I would just like to sit with her a few minutes, if I may.'

'Well . . . if it's all right with Samuel . . .'

'Oh, it is, Mistress Haddon, it is,' affirmed the boy.

'I'll just be across the lane, when I'm needed then.' She looked back towards the bed. 'Poor lass, I doubt she'll ever be a bride now.'

Anne Winter looked enquiringly at the coffee boy. When the clockmaker's wife was safely out of earshot he said, 'They say that Grace and Elias will marry one day, if he ever gets round to asking.'

'Has she no other suitors?'

'Plenty, but she won't give them the time of day, says me and Samuel's enough for her to be looking after. She likes Elias, though.' He looked at his feet. 'We all like Elias, your Ladyship. He wouldn't have killed your husband. Elias wouldn't kill anyone.'

Anne Winter put her hand on the boy's chin and lifted it up. 'I know that, child. All will be well.'

Once Gabriel was gone, she took off her cloak and sat on the stool the old woman had left. She gazed on Grace's face and when the girl became anxious in her sleep, passed her hand over her forehead, used soothing words. She looked around the tiny room, so different from her own at White-hall. A simple looking glass of poor manufacture, no drapes at the window or above the wooden cot that served Grace Kent for a bed, but plain wooden shutters and thick wool-len blankets. No wardrobe, but three hooks on the wall where hung two plain, clean linen smocks, and one black gown, of a little better quality than the brown woollen gar-ment the coffee man's niece had been wearing when first Anne Winter had met her. A small chest, unlocked, revealed clean linens, wool stockings and mittens. There was a plain linen tucker, with matching cuffs, such as Anne Winter thought Grace might wear with the dress hanging on the wall, and another set, much finer work, bordered with scal-loped bobbin lace, that looked as if it had never been worn. Perhaps Grace had meant it for her wedding day.

Anne Winter looked closely at the black dress hanging on the wall then, glancing only briefly at the two smocks beside it, looked carefully around the rest of the room. Nothing. She sat down by the bedside and regarded the girl a moment longer. 'So where have you put it, Grace?' she asked softly. Then a thought struck her, and she carefully slipped her hand under the thin straw mattress on which Grace Kent slept. Her hand paused, and she glanced at the door, but there was no one looking into the room, for she had taken the trouble to put down the latch. She tugged a little, moved Grace very gently towards the other side of the bed, and tugged gently again, this time bringing out a smock of quite another order of quality and workmanship than those that hung on the wall, with its wristband and collar embroidered in chevrons of pink silk and edged in bobbin lace. Quickly, Anne Winter rolled the smock up as tightly as she could and placed it into the black brocade bag she had carried with her, drawing the cords tight shut.

Then, she leaned over to the chest by Grace's bed and picked up the small pewter mug that had been set on it and sniffed – an aromatick of sugared wine and spiced fruits. Swiftly, she unscrewed the top of a small bottle she had drawn from her bag, and poured three drops of liquid into the drink. After stopping up the bottle again, she spoke the girl's name.

'Grace.'

A murmur.

Again, more sharply: 'Grace.'

A slight flicker, a soft moan.

Anne bent forward and lifted Grace up a little by the shoulders. Supporting her against the pillows with her left arm, she lifted the cup to Grace's lips with the right, very careful that a few sips of the fragrant liquid should find their way into Grace's mouth.

'Swallow,' she said. Again: 'Swallow.'

Then, satisfied in the two purposes of her visit, she gently let Grace down again. She thrust the small bottle back into her bag with the smock, tied on her cloak once more, and with only the briefest of glances back towards the bed, left.

George Tavener would have given any money not to have had the conversation he had just had with Damian Seeker. He had been worried he might have been seen, escorting Anne Winter back to Whitehall, that the hackney-driver he had paid to take them or the guard to whom he had handed her over at the Palace Gate might have misunderstood why he was abroad with John Winter's wife at such an ungodly hour. 'Lady Anne has been taken ill – she is Lieutenant Winter's wife: see to it that she gets safely back to her apartments,' was all he had said to the men on watch before having the cab-driver return to the city. How the woman had come to the pass he had found her in he had not wished to consider – it could hardly be for want of money. But then, he had known others, also in thrall to their addictions, who would have done whatever was required of them by those with the power to supply them. However she might have called this fate down on herself, he could hardly have left her there at the White Nutmeg, to be pawed by the highest bidder.

He had feared, for a moment, that Seeker had seen him, and come to those very same wrong conclusions that anyone else would have done. But no, it seemed Seeker had been elsewhere, and witness to a different scene entirely, and one that might lose George Tavener a great deal more than his good name. How could Seeker know what he did? How could he take a half-dozen words and shatter a man's life?

Tavener had been planning to tell Mirjam about the house in Covent Garden today. She would have everything in readiness for their dinner; selecting a necklace as the maid laid out her best gown. It would be the oyster silk, that he had had made up to her exact measurements by Mme Leclos in the Galerie du Palais Royal in Paris, and she would wear with it her new Mechelen lace. He had bought many dresses for Mirjam, but that one was her favourite, he knew. At her neck would be the table-cut diamond he had had a Bread Street goldsmith set for her in an ornate mount with a drop pearl. Mirjam asked for nothing, wanted almost for nothing, yet every small gift he gave her brought an effusion of happiness to her face. All that lacked was a child, and he knew that she prayed each night that God would grant her that one thing that he could not buy for her.

And that was why he had bought the lease, only two days ago, of the house in Covent Garden, away from the foul air and dirty streets of the city. Mirjam would walk the pleasant square and wide streets and gardens around the piazza. She would be surrounded by people of quality, and not look out any more on the poverty and squalor, taste the bad water, of the city, for it was that, he had been assured by more than one physician, that prevented her from conceiving the child they both longed for.

But what Seeker had just said to him made that dream seem as transient and fragile as a fallen snowflake. When he had finished questioning him on his involvement with Lady Anne Winter on the night of her husband's death, Seeker had suddenly said:

'Tell me about your wife and Jakob Hendricks.'

Tavener had been taken aback. 'My wife doesn't know Jakob Hendricks. I only met the man myself for the first time at Kent's yesterday morning, and my wife never has.'

Seeker had looked at him directly for a few moments and then said, 'That isn't true. Your wife is thirty-two years of age and was born on the Herengracht in Amsterdam, is that not correct?'

Tavener nodded. 'She was taken into the Weesehouse when she was orphaned, at fifteen.'

Seeker appeared uninterested in this detail. 'Jakob Hendricks is four years older than your wife, and lived around the corner from her family home on the Keizersgracht for seventeen years. He spent almost the whole of the organ recital at Austin Friars last night watching her.'

Tavener shifted in his seat. 'It's hardly an unusual thing for a man on his own to look at a pretty woman, and when I mentioned Hendricks to my wife, after I first met him at the coffee house, she had clearly never heard of the man before.'

'Do you trust her?'

'Trust . . .?' Tavener could feel his colour rising, his anger too. No man had ever dared ask him such a question. 'Trust my wife? What would you know of—'

'Answer the question.'

Tavener was having difficulty masking his anger.

Seeker was not to be put off. 'Did she tell you that Hendricks twice attempted to speak to her, when she was leaving the church?'

Tavener opened his mouth, but could not find the words he had been searching for. Seeker didn't appear to have much interest in hearing them anyway. 'You should know that Jakob Hendricks is suspected of plotting against the Lord Protector's person, and acting in the interests of Charles Stuart, son of the late traitor of that same name. If your wife is found to be assisting him in any way, it will not go well for her.' Tavener knew what this meant and felt himself go cold to the bone. Should Mirjam be found guilty of treachery, she would either hang or burn. Seeker blotted the page he had been writing on, and pushed the book to one side. 'Look to your wife,' he said, and dismissed him.

Seeker strode back through the corridors of Whitehall with a look of thunder on his face that perfectly reflected the anger he was feeling inside. When he got to the door of the Winters' apartments, he hammered on it, and went past the astonished maid with little ceremony when she opened it.

'Your mistress is at home?'

'Yes, but—'

'Tell her I want to see her, now!'

'But she is—'

'Now!'

The maid scurried through the door to the bedchamber, and very soon was back again, followed by her mistress. Anne Winter's hair was uncoiled, and the front of her gown partially unhooked.

'Mr Seeker, I am not—' she began.

'Spare me your attempt at modesty. Sit down,' he said, pulling out one of the hard oak dining chairs rather than indicating the more comfortable embroidered seats by the fire. 'You, girl,' he said to the maid, 'wait outside until I am ready for you.'

He loosened his cloak, handed it to one of the soldiers he had left by the door, and laid his broad-brimmed black leather hat on the table. The curious hard, dull sound of it making contact with the wood irritated him further. It was only at Thurloe's insistence, due to several attempts on his life, that Seeker had finally agreed to the insertion of the 'secrete', the small, round steel helmet that had been worked under the crown of his hat.

'You are in transit somewhere, I see, Mr Seeker,' said Anne Winter, indicating the hat.

'I am on my way to the Tower, to talk to Elias Elling-worth.'

Her face was unnaturally pale and she was shivering, even though the room was warm. 'He didn't kill my husband, you know.'

'Yes, you've already said that. Why didn't you tell me George Tavener brought you back here last night, after he had "bought" you to save you from further abasing yourself at the White Nutmeg coffee house in Bleeding Heart Yard?'

She stared at him, caught. 'I, I didn't remember at first, and that is the truth. And then when I did, I was . . .'

His impatience was growing. 'You were what?'

'Ashamed. As I told you before, I was . . . beholden to the apothecary, for the laudanum he has been supplying to me of a particular strength that I could not get anywhere else of late.' She turned her eyes towards the window. 'I never thought in my life to have sunk so low.' And then she said, almost to herself, 'But I am determined that will be an end to it.'

'Whether you continue to indulge your weaknesses or not is of no interest to me.' Then he hesitated before continuing. 'That you might not be mistaken, though, you should be informed that a woman of suspect report will not be permitted to remain in the proximity of the Protector's court, whoever her husband might have been.'

'I understand.'

He nodded. 'Good. But as to the matter at hand: did George Tavener leave you at the Palace Gate or did he bring you further inside?'

'He left me at the gate, with a guard. The guard accom-

panied me to the outer stair of this wing, then allowed me
to come up myself.'

Seeker nodded. It would be easy enough to check.

She rose slowly and began to turn to her bedchamber. 'If
that is all, Mr Seeker . . .'

'Wait!' he commanded. 'One thing more. Do you recall
you told me you thought you had seen Sir Gwyllm
Crowther at Kent's coffee house?'

'Did I?' she said. 'That is very extraordinary. The tears of
the poppy, Mr Seeker – they make a person say foolish
things. I have not seen Sir Gwyllm for many years. Goodnight.' She continued to her chamber and passed through
the doorway out of sight. This time Seeker did not attempt
to stop her.

It was several hours later, and three miles or so across to the
east, that Damian Seeker finally dismissed his guards for the
day. They had shadowed him more than eighteen hours,
since word had come of the murder of John Winter, and
they would be ready at first light to ride with him to Oxford.
It was when Seeker emerged from the Sale Tower, that part
of the Tower in which Ellingworth was held, facing away
from the city that gave his writings their life blood, that he
told his men to stand down for the night.

'I have some business yet to see to in the city. You take
the barge back to Whitehall. I will meet you in Horse Guard
Yard at dawn.'

He watched them go; like faithful dogs, they did not like

to leave their master. He knew he was feared throughout the city, in Whitehall, by parts of the army, but these men, he thought, did not serve him through fear. They served him through pride, and he had chosen them, every one, because he judged them incorruptible. It mattered little to Seeker that laughter ceased and his men sat straighter when he entered their guardroom; he did not seek their companionship but their loyalty, and that, he knew, he had. More, there was devotion. He knew of a time when a soldier of another regiment had slighted him, Seeker, in the hearing of two of his own men. The defence had been brutal, short and unequivocal. He doubted that there was anything he might ask them to do that they would not do. And tonight, although these men, who had followed Cromwell from the Fens and with him mastered England, trusted London no more than did Oliver or Seeker himself, they would know of long experience that there was no point in arguing with him. They would know they could tell him that they should accompany him, that they would be ready to ride tomorrow, sleep or no, but it would make no difference, they would be dismissed all the same. As he'd known they would, they simply nodded their assent and turned down towards the Water Gate, to the waiting barge and the black ink of the river that would carry them westwards past the sleeping city.

Seeker considered what Ellingworth had been able to tell him in their long interview, interrupted, of necessity by many pauses while the prisoner summoned the strength to go on. He would have liked to have been able to question the lawyer before the Committee of Examinations had had their first run at him, but the delay could not be helped, and in the end, he had learned little from Ellingworth that he did not already know. Elias confirmed what Maria had already told him – that he had gone to Whitehall to warn Winter of the coded painting that had appeared at Kent's. He had told no one else in the coffee house what he saw in it.

'Not even Grace?' Seeker had asked. 'It was when you went to bid her goodnight that you noticed the painting, was it not?'

The lawyer had been instantly on his guard. 'Yes, but she was more interested in a brooch she had just found amongst the cushions of the booth. I told her Samuel would send word to Whitehall the next day for someone to come for it. I said nothing to her of the painting.' He had then repeatedly asserted that he had discussed the painting with no one else. He would not be shifted either in his denial of the murder of John Winter, or the fact that the man had already been dead outside his own apartment when he, Ellingworth, had come upon him. He had seen no one exit or enter the corridor when he himself had turned into it. And he had not seen Winter's wife, either.

Seeker could see there was nothing to be gained from pursuing the point further – he had seen many men lie, and he had the impression that Elias Ellingworth was telling him the truth, if not all of it. Another day or two in the Tower should make him reconsider that.

Something else was troubling him though. 'How is it you got so far into the Palace?'

Ellingworth had ventured a broken smile, and looked down upon his torn, dirty and bloodied clothes. 'They are not at their best just now, I'll grant it, but last night they were the grandest I could muster for a man of the law on business for the Committee. I gave a good performance, but not, of course, my own name.'

Seeker cursed inwardly. There would be hell to pay in the guardrooms of Whitehall when he had the time to deal with them. That would not be tonight, though, as there were things he still had to do before leaving for Oxford in the early morning. He left the lawyer, reminding him that only the whole truth could free him, and that time was rapidly running out.

Out in the night, Seeker knew where to walk and where not, which streets were lit and which not, where the foulest gutters ran, where bridges over brooks and ditches were sturdily made or rotted. He knew where the thieves lurked, the beggars slept, the whores plied their trade: the city at night held no fears for him. He purposely left by the Iron Gate and, in the shadow still of the Tower, he passed by the fine tall house in St Katharine's where Jakob Hendricks had lodged two nights with his countryman Wim de Boer. Oh, that house was well-lit tonight; there would be little sleep, few Dutch dreams under that roof. De Boer had known, or suspected at least, what Jakob Hendricks was up to, and had talked himself dry telling Seeker's men everything he knew about his friend, which turned out, as de Boer himself had come to realise fairly quickly, to be much less than he had thought he knew. Every lamp in the house was lit, as de Boer's wife flew from room to room, floor to floor, supervising the packing of everything they could carry. Seeker knew that by the time he was halfway to Oxford, Wim de Boer and his family and his account books would be aboard a merchantman bound for the safety of Amsterdam, the keys to the house in St Katharine's and his goods at the Wharf left in the hands of a steward to do with what he would. Well, that was de Boer's concern: he should have chosen his friends better.

Seeker came back around and down into the city by Tower Hill. One or two lights still burned in the Navy offices on Seething Lane, but around them most was dark and quiet. Deeper into town, the coffee houses were closing and the taverns emptying their detritus out on to the street. Seeker saw one or two men he recognised lurch from inns they should not have been in, in the company of women they should not have been with. He took note of it, for future use. He was alone, but he might have walked with a phalanx of men around him. Those who inadvertently staggered into his path hastily got out of it again when they saw what they had done. Beggars pulled back their hands and whores withdrew their promises. Laughing groups quieted themselves until he was a long way past. Even the constables of the Watch, with their lanterns and poles, found other things to take their attention when they caught sight of him. It suited him that way.

All was at rest for once at the Exchange: a pause in the selling of fripperies, the making of money, as if the heart-beat of the city itself had been briefly stilled. Parliament, Protector, King, it didn't matter to the merchants, if only they might make their money. There had been a time when Seeker had been for sweeping them all away, making them work as other men worked, but Cromwell had shown up the folly of the Diggers, the Levellers, and besides, he needed their coin.

And then, almost before he knew it, he was at Dove Court. He nodded to the guards who were there for the night-duty, the daytime sentries having long since gone back to their barracks. Again he climbed the crumbling stair. This time, when he knocked on the door of the top-floor dwelling, he did not have to wait so long for a reply.

She was dressed in a thick cambric nightgown, her hair loose under the cap on her head, a woollen shawl around her shoulders. No lace trimmings, silk stockings or brocade slippers for Maria Ellingworth. Her brother's politics, his known disfavour with the authorities, had left him with few clients and even fewer students and this was the result: poverty. And yet, he had chosen his side and stuck with it, and Seeker could understand that.

He hesitated in the doorway. 'I did not mean to waken you.'

'You didn't,' she said, going back into the room and leaving the door open behind her, for him to follow or not as he wished.

She crouched by the hearth and threw some coals on the fire to bring it back to life, as if somehow that would warm this chill place.

'I have just been to see your brother.'

She didn't turn around, but asked carefully, 'How is he?'

'Well enough.'

'He is not dead yet, you mean,' she said with some bitterness.

'That will be for a judge to decide. Your brother's fate is in his own hands.'

Now she faced him, her anger palpable in the few feet of space between them. 'In his own hands? When you yourself know he is innocent and yet continue to hold him there?'

He was not used to being questioned by anyone other than Thurloe or the Lord Protector himself. This woman did not appear to live by the same rules as anyone else he came into contact with. 'You should understand,' he said, 'that any assassination brings with it much restiveness, not only in the army and in the city but in the country at large, until the perpetrator is caught. The longer such restiveness is allowed to go on, the greater the likelihood that the centre will be seen as weak, that grievances will rear their heads, disorder be encouraged. It is better for the common good that the executive arm is seen to act quickly.'

'How safe we will all sleep in our beds if only we might see an innocent man hang,' she said.

How was he to make her comprehend? 'I don't believe your brother murdered John Winter, but I don't know it for certain yet, and that is something different. More, though, Mistress Ellingworth, I do not believe him to be entirely innocent of complicity, somehow, in the act.'

Some of the fight started to go out of her. 'But how . . .?'

'I am certain your brother is lying to me.'

'About what?'

'About how much he knows about Winter's death. Are you aware of who has visited him, who has undertaken to pay for his food and light while he is in the Tower?'

'Your guards would not let me as far out as the street, and they have let no one but you come near me today – no, not even his students. How could I be aware of anything?'

'It's for your own protection. If your every movement is noted, you cannot be accused of anything you haven't done. If you are not in commune with your brother, whatever happens from now on cannot be laid at your door. The same applies to his students, which they will see for themselves, if they have any sense.'

'Sense? To ally themselves to Elias? In our brave Commonwealth, where is the sense in that?'

He registered the irony in her remarks, but chose to ignore it. 'None.'

She furrowed her brow. 'It must be George who has paid for him, I cannot think that any others amongst our friends would have the money to spare, however well they might wish us.'

'It was not George Tavener. It was Lady Anne Winter.'

The full measure of her surprise registered on her face. 'But how could it be?' she said after a moment. 'She doesn't even know him.'

'Perhaps,' said Seeker steadily, 'you don't know your brother as well as you think you do. Whether he knows her or not, you will understand that it does not appear well for him to be visited and sustained in gaol by the woman whose husband he is accused of murdering.'

She was shaking her head, some question unformed on her lips. Seeker forestalled it. 'She is also his alibi.'

'How so?'

'She claims her husband was dead before your brother ever came near him.'

'But then surely . . .'

Again Seeker forestalled her. 'It is not enough. Anne Winter's credit in Whitehall withers by the hour. He needs something else.'

Maria sat down at last, on a stool in front of the fire she had just kindled, her face a picture of despair. Seeker had had such interviews before, looked on such faces before, and left them to their misery once he had finished with them. Maria Ellingworth had nothing left to tell him.

He needed to get away, to wash, eat, sleep. He couldn't

remember when he had last stopped for a moment and taken something to eat, and yet something was preventing him from walking out of the door, descending the stairs, leaving the night-guards to their duties.

'You should not stay alone here,' he said at last.

'Alone? Are you calling off your watchdogs, then?'

'My men and I leave London in the morning and will not return for a few days. Have you no friends you can go to? Kent's? Somewhere you would not be alone?'

'I am happy enough with my own company, Mr Seeker,' she said.

'Do you not understand? Some officer or soldier might take it into his head to exact revenge on Winter's killer, to make himself a name, curry favour in higher places or amongst the ranks. You would be his revenge.' He looked around the sparse room. 'Your brother has nothing else.'

'And I nothing but him. I thank you for your protection, but I do not want it.'

There was evidently to be no reasoning with her. He said no more, but nodded briefly and walked out of the door.

Left alone by the cheerless fire, Maria listened to him descend the endless flights of stairs to the courtyard and then out on to the street. She kept listening until, eventually, the sound of his boots on the cobbles faded and were lost in the other noises of the night. She wondered whether she should have offered him some of the stew Elias had never come home last night to eat, for Damian Seeker had looked hungry.

★

The carpenter seldom dreamed, but tonight his sleep was tormented by visions of his wife, of the cradle he had made. Somewhere a little way away, possibly in the small physic garden of the house two doors away on Knight Ryder Street, the bough of a tree creaked in the wind. The carpenter always slept with the shutters opened to the night, and the noise of the bough became the rocking of the cradle in his dreams. On the floor by his bed, the dog whimpered, and lifted its head to be nuzzled by the gentle hand.

TWELVE

Old Acquaintance

4 November

After disembarking at Folly Bridge and entering Oxford by the South Gate to make his way up Fish Street, Jakob Hendricks did not pause, or play the tourist, or newcomer or anything else that might attract attention to his being but lately arrived in the town. To blend in was the trick, and his talent. And so he did. He travelled from the Castle in the west towards Magdalen College in the east, mapping in his mind every crooked lane and dank alleyway until his feet were sore. By the time he finally came upon the church of St Peter-in-the-East, on Queen's Lane, the streets and byeways of Oxford were imprinted on his brain.

The Angel coffee house was not hard by the churchyard, as he had expected it to be, and it took him a further few minutes to locate it, across from the bottom of the lane, on the High Street. A little more public than he might have hoped, but it was not to be helped. An inviting glow emanated from its windows, but Hendricks did not go in.

Rather, he walked casually around it, noting is position, its front and side exits, before crossing instead to Tillyard's, at the sign of the apothecary, next to All Souls.

Tillyard's coffee house was a place of quite a different order from Kent's. No merchants here, talking of profit and loss, risk and adventure, over their coffee and pipe, nor newsmen even, but everywhere scholars and Fellows, disputing, declaiming, persuading, laughing and some even listening. At one end of the table, a great discussion was underway on the problems of measuring time at sea, at the other, a dispute over whether the violin was an apt instrument for polite musical gatherings, or fit only for unlearned fiddlers. At a smaller table near to the street window, a young man was earnestly explaining to his companion his ideas for the remodelling of some old student hall fallen out of use since the beginning of the troubles. His companion was laughing,

'A new theatre, Christopher? In Oxford? Only once Dean Owen and the Lord Protector are in their graves!'

The young man looked abashed. 'All men must go to their graves, someday,' he said, in a voice not intended for others to hear. But Hendricks was used to listening carefully to what was not meant for his ears. He turned his head slightly, the better to see the speaker, and resolved to remember his face. He liked Tillyard's; something in the tone of the talk, the dress of the coffee-drinkers, the ease of their movements even, told him he was in a place well-affected to the interest of the King.

★

Leading his troop on to the High Street by way of Magdalen Bridge and the East Gate, Damian Seeker glanced upwards to meet the unseeing eyes of saints and kings, of men and monsters, awaiting those who would come to Oxford in those days. Unseeing eyes, unhearing ears, impassive faces set in stone. There was much, he had often thought, they might tell those who came through their city gates, about how the best-laid schemes of even the cleverest of men generally played out. There was little they had not been witness to over the centuries, could not have warned of, had not their mouths also been made of stone. As he rode on, Seeker marvelled at the great gifts of humble men who had chiselled and carved such beings out of the most elemental of materials, of sandstone and of granite.

'A vipers' nest!' An hour after entering the town, Vice-Chancellor Owen's words were still ringing in Seeker's ears as he impatiently descended the great vaulted stone stairway from the King's old headquarters in Christ Church college to the quadrangle below, where his soldiers awaited their orders. Owen had not minced his words. 'Oxford is a vipers' nest: trials, visitations, ejections, purges, and still half the colleges crawl with Royalists. As for the rest, there is far too much inter-mingling, far too much – in taverns and coffee houses, on the tennis court and the bowling green. There are music clubs, and scientific societies. Those ejected at the trials and visitations live openly in the town with sympathetic friends, they take private pupils and live off God alone knows what. There are others, believe it or not as you will, but I tell it you for the truth, that are still in their college rooms, still take their meals at the college table and not a word said about it. And to what purpose? Nothing good!'

Seeker had heard the same question asked of the whole enterprise that was Oxford, by men who made Elias Ellingworth seem moderate. There were those who would have dashed these colleges, these fermenters of exclusion and privileges, these citadels, to the ground. As a young man, Seeker might have thought the same thing, but now he understood that such views led only to chaos and disorder. The universities were necessary for control. Oliver understood this: he had had himself made Chancellor of this place three years ago, but never set foot in it since. If all that Owen told him was true, and Seeker had no reason to believe it was not, stringent measures would yet need to be taken before it would be safe for the Protector ever to do so.

Owen knew nothing of a Dutch scholar by the name of Hendricks, or that such a one was expected in the town, but he undertook to enquire of the heads of all the colleges whether any knew anything of him. On the matter of Sir Gwyllm Crowther though, he was more certain.

'Crowther? I am surprised they could not tell you of him in London.'

'I had little time between hearing of his name and setting out for here. Have you ever heard him spoken of in Oxford?'

'Of course,' said Owen. 'He was a Welshman, a hothead, like most of them. He was for a time a scholar at Jesus

College – it has always been overrun with Welshmen. He abandoned his place as soon as word came to the town of Charles Stuart landing in Scotland from the Netherlands three years ago. Crowther and many others of his sort threw off their gowns and took up arms in support of the rebel. But he was killed fleeing from Worcester in fifty-one, was he not?'

'That was the story given out, but Gwyllm Crowther was seen in a London coffee house, by John Winter's wife, on the very day John Winter was murdered.'

Now Owen was surprised. 'Winter's wife? One of the Baxtons, was she not?'

Seeker nodded.

'Baxton Hall is not ten miles to the west of here. Sir John was a Royalist through and through. His son after him. I can't speak for the girl. The army did well to wrest the place from them – it would have been a breeding ground of sedition.'

'Who holds it now?'

Owen furrowed his brow. 'The Protector granted it to Winter, only this year, as a sign of his special favour. And now, I would imagine, it will revert to his wife, unless . . .' He did not finish his sentence.

'Unless Anne Winter burns at Smithfield for his murder.'

The Dean watched him carefully. 'And will she, Captain?'

'If she is found to have murdered her husband, she'll be chained to a stake with her feet in a barrel of tar and burn as any other woman would.' He took up his helmet. 'But my business here is not the murder of John Winter. I have a Welshman and a Dutchman to find.'

Jakob Hendricks finished his bowl of chocolate and reluctantly prepared to leave Tillyard's coffee house. He would have liked to have lingered a little longer, listening to the conversations of his fellow drinkers, to have persuaded himself a while that he was, after all, the quiet and earnest scholar he claimed to be. But that was not what his life was, and it was not safe for him to linger anywhere he did not need to be.

An Oxford college could be a fortress, and Hendricks calculated that an Oxford college understood to be loyal to Cromwell's government would be much safer than one suspected of loyalty to the King. Besides, he knew Warden Wilkins of Wadham College of old, by correspondence, at least. That Wilkins had long thought himself to be communicating with a Cologne physician on the interesting flora of the Rhineland had been a necessary deception. As he left the inn, Hendricks made himself start thinking in German.

Instead of going by Catte Street, he found himself walking a second time that day up Queen's Lane. The light was fading, and scholars were hurrying up the lane from the town and through the small door set into the great arched doorway of their college. Lamps were being lit in the windows of the chambers and studies above him as he walked past, and they made it a little easier to see where he put his feet. There was smoke coming from the chimneys of St

Edmund Hall opposite, and it mingled with that from the nearby coffee houses, promising light and warmth in stark relief to the cold churchyard of St Peter's beside it. He thought for a moment that he might have done better to have lodged the night in that Hall: closer, should anything go wrong, and little more than a hop and a jump from the East Gate of the city and the London road, but it was too late to change his arrangements now: Wadham it must be.

By the time he came to New College, he found he had quickened his pace. The old feeling, the one that had seldom failed him, was upon him: he was being watched. He stopped a moment. No footsteps. He continued then turned quickly, but could hear nothing, see nothing. His ears were strained to every possible sound, movement, as he turned into the grimness that was New College Lane. There was nothing to do now but wait. He stopped, and the figure emerged slowly from a darkened doorway to his left.

'You,' said Hendricks, his voice deliberately even.

'You do remember me then?'

The Dutchman nodded. 'I recognised you the moment you walked into that London coffee house: Zander Seaton.'

The Scotsman nodded. 'I think it is time we talked, Jakob, don't you?'

Hendricks had half suspected this interview might be forced upon him at some point.

'I am expected at Wadham within the half-hour . . .'

'I know.'

'How could you know that?'

There was a ghost of a smile, just a ghost. 'Do you think I could have survived this long without friends? I will come to you there about midnight. Warden Wilkins should have extracted everything you can tell him of the beauties of Cologne by then, I imagine.'

'I would imagine so,' said Hendricks. 'Midnight, then.' And then Jakob Hendricks was alone again on New College Lane, and not looking forward to his night under the roof of Wadham College as much as he might have wished to.

Seeker would have cursed, had he been a man to curse. The search of Jesus College had revealed little of any use, achieved nothing other than to render his men more tired and hungry than they already had been, and he was glad to order them out of it in the end. For all that the Principal, Jonathon Roberts, was a firm Puritan, the place still reeked of Royalists. Seeker knew Welshmen well enough to read the mockery behind their protestations of loyalty to the Protector, and their shock at the news that Gwyllm Crowther might not, after all, be dead. Had any there known him? 'Oh yes.' And what had he looked like? 'A tall man, fair hair, had he not?' 'Nonsense, Crowther had been of stocky build, a redhead.' 'No, indeed, a slender fellow, dark, quiet.' The smirks had been less in evidence by the time Seeker had finished outlining for them the penalties for anyone knowingly harbouring a traitor. That he would take a personal interest in seeing that those penalties were applied was also made abundantly clear.

As his troop made its way back to Oxford Castle, Seeker dismounted near the Bocardo prison at the North Gate. He removed his helmet and gave Acheron into the care of one of the younger men who he knew had a way with the beast and could manage him as most couldn't. Once the sound of his men's horses had faded down the cobbles of the Cornmarket, Seeker unrolled the brown bundle he had taken from his pack, a woollen cloak and worn leather hat, such as a labourer might wear. His boots were mud-spattered enough as not to draw undue attention.

The inn just within the gate of the town seemed as good a place to start as any, its wood-framed gables a homely rejoinder to the chiselled grandeur of the colleges. Seeker adjusted his bearing, lowered his head slightly, hunched his shoulders, slowed his pace. He walked with less assurance, moved aside to let others pass. His own men would hardly have known him. He attracted little notice as he stooped beneath the doorway and found his way to the counter. He asked for a jug of ale and some bread and cheese, and found a place to sit near to the door and began to eat as townsmen and travellers talked around him. After a while, as usually happened, one of a group near to him thought to draw him into their conversation.

'New arrived in Oxford, friend?'

'Passing through, west.'

An old fellow who hadn't said much looked him up and down. 'What's your trade? Steel?'

'Wood,' said Seeker.

'Ah, your voice spoke to me of steel.'

'You've travelled the country then?' said Seeker.

'Who hasn't, these twelve years?' Another old soldier. 'Had my best sword off a Sheffield steelman. And what takes a carpenter from Sheffield all the way to the West Country?'

Seeker took a long, deliberate draught of his ale. 'The North has nothing for me now. I heard there might be some work this way, manor houses to be built up again, wood-work restored.'

'Oh, yes, there's plenty of that, where the Parliament hasn't burned everything to the ground,' said a young ostler bitterly.

'Hush, Gerald,' chided the older man. 'How many times do you need to be told?'

'Told what?' asked Seeker.

'To keep his trap shut when he doesn't know who he's talking to.'

Seeker grunted. 'Parliament's nothing to me. All I know is I was told there might be work a few miles to the west of here. Baston House or some such has a new master and is in need of repair.'

'Baston?' said the old fellow. 'Baxton Hall you mean?'

Seeker nodded. 'Aye, that.'

'Well, you're too late, my friend,' said a smith who had

just joined them. 'I heard word from London today, traveller on his way through. John Winter's dead. Stabbed in his
bed in Whitehall, they say.'

'No.'

'Good riddance.'

The older man was thunderous. 'Gerald, if I have to tell
you again, your head'll be down that water butt in the yard,
and it won't be coming out again.'

But the young ostler was not to be silenced this time. 'I'll
have my say, Seth Jenner. What were John Winter to you?
He were no Baxton. Sir John were a proper gentleman.
Winter were nothing but an ostler's son from Exmoor, same
as me. Cromwell give him that house because he knew his
way round a horse.'

'And because he'd taken it for the Parliament,' said the
old man. 'Got Baxton's daughter, too. You picked the
wrong side, Gerald.'

The young man was scarlet in the face. Seeker thought he
might have the table over in a minute. 'Not me,' he said.
'Not me, and I don't care who hears it.' He cast Seeker a
furious glance.

'Well, you should,' said the old man, 'because the King's
lot were just as bad. Goring and Grenville. Their men did
some terrible things down the west, terrible, and you
know it.'

Gerald was now staring down at the table, his fists
clenched, refusing to look Seth Jenner in the eye.

'Aye, but you'll hear me out, all the same,' said Seth, 'and then you'll shut your trap and no more of it. Pillage and plunder. Arbitrary hangings. Nothing to do with war, just straight debauchery. When Goring was trying to take Taunton for the King, they'd go out in raiding parties in the night, and it wasn't cattle or horses they were looking for. All over Exmoor – Luccombe, Selworthy, over by Dunster way. Aye, look away, but you weren't so young you didn't know it. You and plenty others. Young women, girls just, with no one to speak for them, handed over, traded for the sake of the rest of the village.' He spat on the floor. 'War's over and let that be an end to it.'

Seeker pushed away his plate, his meal only half eaten. 'Nothing here for me then.' He got up and left the inn, no one at the table trying to stop him, or ask him where he went; he had disturbed the comfortable rhythm of their evening and he knew they would not be sorry to see him go.

A tour of the rest of the inns of Oxford revealed nothing of the whereabouts of Jakob Hendricks, but Seeker reflected that it didn't matter that he didn't know where Hendricks was tonight: all that mattered was that he knew where he would be tomorrow.

At St Edmund Hall, his pack had already been left in his chamber: he was well enough positioned here for the approaches to both St Peter's church and the Angel coffee house. He unrolled his cloak and lay down on the bed. The heavy, dank air of Oxford seeped through the stones of the Hall, under the window frames; all day it had threatened to sap his energy, his will almost – he had seen it in his men too – until at last it had settled like a stone at the pit of his stomach. Now, as he breathed it in in its nocturnal guise he could feel it begin to clog his mind with images of other places, of crumbling stone and mouldering vegetation, of being forever on the move and yet too weary to move anywhere any more. That had been the life of his people. He closed his eyes but the images persisted, as they always did.

Up at Wadham College, Warden Wilkins clapped his guest warmly on the shoulder. 'No, indeed, it is I who should thank you. Good conversation, fresh news of the doings in the world are more than enough recompense for a few morsels from our kitchens and a catch or two of music. But tomorrow, after convocation, I will show you our gardens, and my beehives – I'll warrant you have never seen the like in all your travels.'

Only once in the evening had Hendricks feared discovery. As the small consort the warden had arranged to entertain them had been tuning their instruments, rehearsing their pieces, a scholar of Christ Church had been admitted to the hall with an urgent missive from the Dean requiring the Warden's attention. Wilkins had accepted the letter with a hint of irritation. 'A man might almost think Dean Owen knew I was at this minute in the midst of a fine meal, about to give myself over to the pleasures of music.'

He sighed. 'And yet he is the Vice-Chancellor, and especially in these days is not to be ignored, I suppose.'

He had frowned a little. 'No,' he said, sighing as he marked his response on the letter and returned it to the boy, 'we have no Dutchmen here.' Hendricks felt his fingers tense around the goblet in his hand, and thought for a moment that the others gathered in the hall turned to look at him, but they hadn't, of course, they were all watching the Warden, waiting for some hint as to the contents of Owen's note. Wilkins merely shook his head as the boy was being shown back out. 'Our good Vice-Chancellor is an earnest and learned man, but he is wont to see enemies of the state around every corner.'

And so the evening had gone on with much music and engaging conversation under the high, hammer-beamed roof of the hall, warmed by a good fire and what seemed to be a hundred candles set along the tables. There was not a subject of interest, it seemed, on which Wilkins and his guests could not easily discourse, although the matter of politics was avoided. Wisely, thought Hendricks, for in this room of good and learned friends were men of almost every political and religious hue. A man sitting here might never have known there had been a War, nor any Revolution: the name of Protector or King was never uttered. For a few hours, in a gilded place, Hendricks saw a dream of something else. But those hours came to their end with the ringing of Oxford's bells, and Hendricks knew he must meet his next appointment.

As he made his bow to the musicians assembled in their gallery, Hendricks silently regretted that he would never see the Warden's famed glass beehives, or ever again be able to spend an evening in the company of this genial and fascinating man. It was sometime past eleven now, and he reluctantly bade his host and the assembled Fellows a last 'goodnight' before passing through the carved wooden screen from the hall and commencing his eerie journey to his rooms along dimly lit corridors and up and down the cold stairways of the sleeping college.

His chamber was silent as he entered it, but he knew Seaton was there already — he could feel the other man's presence. He looked towards the study; the door leading to it was very slightly ajar. He took a step towards it and held his candle up a little higher.

'I'm here,' he said.

Zander Seaton moved into the light.

'Yes, Jakob, you are here,' said the Scotsman. 'But what I would have you tell me is why.'

Hendricks said nothing.

Seaton spoke again. 'I think the same question is on your lips as on mine, Jakob. Since you are not disposed to speak, I will ask it. Have you turned? Are you still for the King?'

'Are you?'

'Always,' returned the Scotsman.

'And I,' said Hendricks at last.

Seaton's eyes crinkled and he let out a laugh. 'But, oh me, Jakob, how are we ever to believe each other?'

'There are passwords,' said Hendricks.

Again Seaton smiled, shook his head. 'I do not know them.'

'That's a start, then.'

'How so?'

'Well, if you were a spy, you would surely know them.'

'Then we have no option but to trust each other?'

'We have many options,' Hendricks told him, 'but let us start with trust. No one at the King's court has seen anything of you since you vanished from The Hague, three and a half years ago. And then you turn up in London. I doubt if even after that passage of time Cromwell and his crew have forgotten Dorislaus.'

Seaton laughed. 'I should hope not; that would, after all, negate the point. Can you believe even they could have been so stupid as to reward the lawyer who had drawn up the charges for the King's trial by sending him to The Hague as their emissary? To send one with *that* blood on his hands to the very place the exiled son of the murdered King kept his court? Even you were outraged – I remember it.'

Hendricks remembered: the fury amongst the courtiers of the young prince, now King himself, had been immeasurable, and in none had it been so ungovernable as in Zander Seaton's master, the Marquis of Montrose. The men selected by the Marquis to carry out his vengeance on Dorislaus had not disappointed him. The Dutch authorities had been appalled, and Charles had had to shift his fledgling court to France. Montrose had then wandered Northern Europe, trying to garner support for his young King, and Zander Seaton had been his shadow, sharing in his master's triumphs and his sufferings. Hendricks had never ceased to wonder at Montrose's foolhardy determination, his devotion to the Stuarts, his passion. A hero, for those who believed in heroes, unworthily abandoned at the last. But not by Zander Seaton, who had been forced to watch the last hope of the Stuart cause go to the scaffold alone. Hendricks had not heard or seen anything of Zander Seaton since. Not, at least, until three days ago, when he had walked into Kent's coffee house.

Hendricks surveyed the man properly for the first time in over three years. Where once there had been fire in the amber eyes, now there were haunting shadows. 'After Montrose – you disappeared. There was talk you might be dead.'

'What?' said Seaton, who was staring at the floor. 'Of shame?'

'There was nothing you could have done: his time was come and that was it. He knew it. They say he faced it like a prince.'

Seaton's head whipped up. 'Better than any prince.'

'Perhaps,' said Hendricks evenly. 'And did you blame the Prince?'

'Charles? For that he abandoned him? Aye, perhaps, for a time.'

'But no longer?'

Seaton shook his head. 'He was badly counselled, and he knows that well enough now.'

Hendricks didn't even try to argue that point.

'So what have you being doing these last years? There have been rumours . . .'

'There will always be rumours.'

'I think some of them are true. You have been operating on your own, have you not? Continuing the Marquis's revenge.'

The Scotsman did not even begin to deny it. 'What else should I do?'

'But of your own design – you know there are networks, chains of command, of communication . . .'

Seaton laughed. 'Aye, I know it and so does half of White-hall. What sweet nothings do you think Thurloe whispers in Cromwell's ear? The man's spies are in the very entourage of the King. Letters fly to Thurloe in his lair as fast as they can be written, from Cologne, Rotterdam, Paris, Madrid. It is a wonder there is one amongst you left standing. Do you *know* who is in Oxford tonight, looking for you? Have you never thought why every attempt at a rising in the name of the King dies in its very birth pangs? Your networks are rid-dled with the seed of their own destruction, Jakob. That is why I work alone. No man knows my plans, my work; none, save myself.'

'We have means of circumventing Thurloe. We have begun to plant false intelligence. This new liking of coffee houses is wondrously useful in that respect. And half the news-sheets that fly about the country carry in them some message, some code. We are learning, all the time.'

Seaton shook his head. 'Not fast enough. You know that Dorislaus' son sits in an office in London and opens all the foreign mail? Thurloe is always one step ahead of you.'

Hendricks held up two fingers and brought them towards one another. 'We inch closer, ever closer. We have other methods than the mail now. Besides, you can hardly hope to foment a rising on your own.'

'No,' said Seaton, offering him nothing.

'But then, perhaps that is not your aim. There have been reports, from Switzerland, Italy, France, Holland – the Americas even – more than rumours, of an assassin who works alone.'

Seaton inclined his head slightly.

'And now you have come home.'

'You misunderstand me greatly if you think England my home, Jakob. But it is the heart, the centre of all that is rotten in these islands. Whatever else their faults, my countrymen never compassed the death of their King.'

'And that is why you went to London?'

Still Seaton offered him nothing.

A thought that had lodged itself in Hendricks' mind the previous day now became a certainty. 'Winter. That was you. But why him? He was never numbered with the regicides, never listed by Montrose or anyone else.'

Seaton went over to the window. 'I know that. I didn't

come for Winter.' He turned and looked at Hendricks. 'I came for Cromwell.'

Hendricks could not hide the sudden jolt he experienced. So many times, so many attempts, plans, and this one foolhardy Scotsman thought he could do it alone. 'So what went wrong?'

Seaton laughed, and there was little humour in it. 'That coffee house. I stepped into that blasted coffee house. The very day I arrived in London.'

'And you saw me.'

'Oh, I saw you, Jakob, but you, my dear friend, were not the problem, although it did give me pause for thought to see one of the King's best agents sitting sucking at his pipe while an old parliamentary soldier fussed around him making coffee. No, it was not you, Jakob, it was that woman.'

'Winter's wife?'

Seaton nodded. 'Did you know Winter was in Edinburgh, to witness the Marquis's execution for Cromwell? I remember looking into his eyes that day and he mine. I had expected to be two weeks, a month, in London, putting together my plans, and here now was a means to the heart of the Usurper's court served up before me within an hour of me entering the town.' He snorted. 'I could scarce believe my good fortune.'

'And yet?' prompted Hendricks.

'And yet, Winter's wife was not quite the gift I had thought. Things went too quickly, far too quickly, beyond my control, and I was entangled before I knew it. I could almost smell Cromwell, and my wonted caution left me. A few hours after I followed her from that coffee house, I found myself admitted, with never a word of suspicion, into the corridors of Whitehall itself. I knew where Cromwell lay—'

'Of course,' said Hendricks, 'the plans.'

'Yes, the plans.'

Hendricks had never ceased to wonder at the carelessness of Cromwell, allowing it to be known that he slept in the King's own chamber in a palace whose every nook and cranny, every door and passageway, was so well-known to his mortal enemies. The first thing any of them learned in the exiled King's service was the plan of Whitehall Palace.

'I concealed myself until darkness fell, then began to make my way towards the apartments of the Protector.'

'Unchallenged?'

'Of course not. How long do you think it took me to disarm a guard and garb myself in his clothing?'

Hendricks should have remembered. He had rarely seen anyone play a role with more assurance than Zander Seaton.

'So what went wrong?'

'Nothing, I stood in the man's very chamber – I might have murdered him in his bed, had I wished.'

'But?'

'Cromwell was gone.'

Hendricks was trying to work it out. 'And so you murdered John Winter instead? What was to be achieved by that, other than to put the whole army on alert?'

Seaton was grave. 'I am not so indiscriminate as you would have me, nor yet so foolish. I should have wondered why the Lord Protector's bedchamber was so poorly guarded. By the time I reached it, he'd been called from his sleep with the news that John Winter was already dead.'

Hendricks had not expected this. 'I was certain it was you who'd killed him.'

Seaton shook his head.

'Then who?'

'That I don't know, but in doing so, they saved the life of Oliver Cromwell.'

THIRTEEN

The Angel and the Crypt

5 November

Seeker had not slept well and had woken long before dawn. He had breakfasted early in the Hall kitchen as the cook and his boys got ready for the day. No one paid him much heed – the sight of a soldier in Oxford was hardly anything new, and neither was an officer billeting himself somewhere in town rather than roughing it with his men at the castle.

His breakfast finished, Seeker went out on to Queen's Lane and smelled the air. Oxford was waking. Bells all over the city had begun to ring, calling scholars and teachers to their devotions and their study, craftsmen to their work-rooms and yards, tradesmen to their shops. Already he could hear cattle and sheep, restless in their pens, ready to begin the next stage of their long trek to London, where the butchers of Smithfield awaited them. Smoke had begun to curl from holes in roofs or stone chimneys, and to mingle with the damp autumn mist clinging to the Cherwell and the Thames. The air was heavy with anxiety; it was not like London: London was always awake and ready, always moving, doing what it must do without pause for doubt or thought. Here, he thought, the possibility of failure enveloped everything. It whispered on his skin in the morning damp and Seeker did not like it. He preferred certainty, but in Oxford, when he looked into men's eyes, listened to their voices, however they might try to hide it, he saw apprehension, heard doubt.

Somewhere in this town, Jakob Hendricks would also be waking, at the terminus of his journey, not realising, Seeker thought, how close to its end-point his mission now truly was. Somewhere here, too, Gwyllm Crowther might be. If so, he would be well-warned by now, his countrymen of Jesus College having seen to that.

Seeker's men would have left their barracks up at the castle a good while ago, and have made their separate ways, quietly, down the mound and past the houses, shops and inns of Carfax right into the learned stone heart of the city until they were already in their places, unnoticed, all within fifty yards from where he himself now stood.

A light westerly breeze was stirring the leaves, exclusive once to Fellows and scholars behind the walls of college gardens, but drifted now on the wind to lie in the streets and threaten to clog the town gutters. The breeze told him things: it told him that the coffee man in Tillyard's was already at his work. It was almost time. Soon, the boy at the Angel would also be stoking up the fire, the coffee man there roasting and grinding his beans, and the great business of the day begin to unfold.

The waiting, the lack of action, was a frustration for his men, he knew that. One was even now in the Angel, having slept the night in a chamber at the head of the stair. No message of anything unexpected had come to Seeker from that quarter. Another two, in the guise of gravediggers, laboured in the churchyard of St Peter's. The church warden had been dealt with, the usual men set on another task, and no one questioned the need for a new grave: death was an old familiar in the town. Two masons worked at some crumbling stonework at the corner of the east range of Queen's College, where it met the back walls of the houses facing on to the High Street: their aprons held implements a good deal more deadly than a chisel or hammer, although those they could also wield to the required effect. It had been a good thing, a wise thing, for so many reasons, Seeker had often thought, that Oliver had taken men of craft and talent, rather than birth, for his New Model Army. Their old trades had served them well, had served Seeker well in his hand-picked band, many times before now. Two more, not much more than boys, but proven worthy already, were in the garb of young scholars. They knew their Latin both, he had checked that before he had ever selected them. The last, the eighth man, Daniel Proctor, played his own part: a soldier. A soldier walking the streets of Oxford, about his business, bothering no one who did not bother him. Seeker smiled when he thought of it: Proctor could never have been anything other than a soldier, and he was the best soldier Seeker knew. So: they were ready.

From his vantage point in the shallow porch of a house to the south of St Edmund Hall, where the lane met the High Street, he could see with no great difficulty all that came and went, both by side and front exits, to and from the Angel coffee house. An hour passed, and several scholars and Fellows arrived to take their morning dish and pipe. John Wallis, Professor of Geometry and chief cryptographer to the Protectorate, came down the lane, discoursing enthusiastically to a companion on an evening spent at Wadham the night before. Seeker stepped back into his shadows: Wallis might have a brilliant mind, but he knew Seeker well and was no master of subterfuge. Time passed, and yet of Hendricks there was no sign. The dropping of a hammer by one of the masons at work on Queen's caused him to glance up the lane, and he saw, approaching from the direction of New College, the first of the dead men: the Royalists whose names had been engraved on the gravestones of the painting in Kent's coffee house, with today's date. The fellow had made no attempt to parade himself as anything other than he was. Silk ribbons fluttered from his boot-hose and another, a gaudy yellow, circled his waist. Chestnut locks hung luxuriantly on the shoulders of a moss-green velvet cloak. Seeker knew him by sight: Daffyd Morgan. Morgan was one of those who had, or so it had appeared, accommodated himself to the regime of the Commonwealth and the Protectorate that followed it. He had displayed that most reliable trait of human nature, and one that had served the new regime well in its dealings with its former foe: the desire to be left in peace in exchange for offering no trouble. 'Clever, Daffyd, never to hide what you were,' thought Seeker, 'that we might not notice you at all, when you finally stepped forward to play your part.'

Events followed quickly one upon the other after that. A dropped chisel, and there was Ethan Caduggan, whose father had held the watch of half the Cornish coast for the Stuarts, sauntering across the High Street, after a comfortable night as the guest of a cousin at All Souls. He too, it appeared, had been taken by an early-morning desire for a dish of coffee and the news of the day. Last of all came Richard d'Oilly, a black sheep to his family, for all of them but he had upheld Parliament's cause. The d'Oillys had held much of the land round about Oxford for centuries, some of it as far down as Exmoor. D'Oilly was a Fellow of Oriel College, a place the Dean had declared to be 'teeming with Royalists' and with a Royalist for its head. 'How many will you bring down with you, Richard?' wondered Seeker, as the man passed quickly through the portals of the Angel.

The bells of the city began to strike nine, the hour marked, so faintly, on the church clock in the painting from Kent's. Still there was no sign of Hendricks. Seeker waited five minutes, ten. The gravediggers in St Peter's became a little slower in their work, the masons at Queen's more pensive, and inside the Angel, two young scholars were losing interest in their rehearsed discussion of matters scientific. The soldier on his circuit of Merton Street, Magpie Lane and the High passed the Angel a third time, and paused for a word with a traveller who had just left the coffee house. But ten minutes was as long as Damian Seeker was ever prepared to wait, and as he emerged from his porch, the masons put down their tools and the gravediggers their shovels. In a handful of strides, Seeker was at the door of the Angel, two of his men behind him, another pair guarding the side exit of the coffee house.

He entered the place alone. The scholars glanced at him, then nodded slightly towards a group of four men gathered round a bench near the serving hatch. Seeker followed their eyes, and in that first look began to understand that something was wrong. The three Royalists were there all right, but even from the back, Seeker could see that the man they were talking to was not Jakob Hendricks. He went over to his two men and spoke in a low voice, never taking his eyes from the group by the serving hatch. 'Who is that man?'

The younger of the two spoke. 'He was here by the time we came down this morning. There has been no sign of the Dutchman.'

Something went through Seeker, like a stone dropping. Before even his own men knew what was happening, he was across the coffee room, his sword drawn. On his approach, Caduggan, Morgan and d'Oilly, who had all been sitting with their backs to the wall, jumped up, reached for their weapons. As the disguised soldiers rushed in towards the table, the man with his back to Seeker never moved, but at the first touch of Seeker's gloved hand on his shoulder he turned slowly around, and Damian Seeker found himself looking into the face of a man whom he had never seen in his life before.

Zander Seaton's hand was already on his own knife. '*Mijnheer* Hendricks asks that his regrets be passed to Mr Thurloe, but he is at present unable to make the pleasure of his acquaintance.'

'Where is he?' growled Seeker.

The man shrugged. 'That I cannot tell you, Captain, but he is most certainly not here.' The voice was Scots, slow and feigning amusement.

As Seeker lunged, the Scotsman whirled round and threw over the bench he had been sitting on. Seeker kicked it aside as if it had been a child's toy, but in the time it took him to do so, the Scotsman had mounted the table and launched himself through the window of the Angel. Seeker was after him in an instant, wood and glass splintering beneath his heel and catching on his clothes as he forced himself through the narrow opening. His opponent had speed, but for a man of his frame, Seeker was astonishingly agile, and in no time was across the High Street and up a long narrow alley opening into the churchyard after him. The gravediggers, posted close to the east wall of St Edmund Hall, took a moment to realise what was happening, and even then were hindered by a student who wandered into their path just at the wrong minute. They got past him just in time to see Seeker disappearing into the south porch of St Peter-in-the-East.

The sudden diminution of light brought Seeker to a temporary halt; very few candles were lit in the nave, and the dismal November light hardly seemed to permeate the windows at all. It took his eyes a moment to become accustomed to the gloom of five hundred years' accumulation. What was not thoroughly dark was in shadow. Above his head, over the doorway to the nave, the curling beak and godless eyes of some hideous creature, the work of a centuries-dead stonemason, announced this as a place of evil. Seeker allowed it the briefest glance as he began to advance carefully into the body of the ancient church. He could see nothing of the Scotsman. More, he could hear nothing of him. He remembered them from past campaigns, Highlanders, so light and fleet on their feet you would hardly know they were past you until you heard their retreating laughter or the sound of a comrade's throat being cut. This one, however, was not barefoot: he was fully booted in good Spanish leather. Seeker listened harder. He listened for the breathing, and in a time that seemed much longer than it must have taken, he heard it. Down at the east end of the chancel, by the altar, there was the suspicion of a sound, of a disturbance of the air. Seeker began to move. The moment he began his run down the nave, the other man sprang forward, seemed to fly past the east window, ran a few paces, and then disappeared. Seeker checked and changed direction, coming quickly upon a small door leading to a descending stone stairway. He could hear two of his own men entering the church; others would be posted outside, waiting for re-enforcements from the castle. He took the stairs three at a time, and very soon found himself in the bowels of the church, an ancient vaulted crypt that smelled more pagan than Christian, and spoke of death.

The relic chamber was long empty, no mouldering bones nor saint's head here now, no Scotsman either, but Seeker could feel the presence of the other man somewhere close by. He stepped further into the crypt proper, and struck flint to light a torch in the wall sconce nearest him. Instantly, what might have been any cold stone cellar was transformed into a vaulted chamber redolent of the prayers of the long-dead. Four pairs of columns, the length of the aisle, supported the groined roof. Some had been carved with fig-ures, fantastic beasts, but most left blank, as if the mason had feared at last to spend any longer in this place, and left off his work unfinished. He could almost hear the fading swish of priestly robes on the paving of the floor.

He flicked a hand to the side, as if to brush the priests away.

'There is no escape from here,' he said, 'nowhere to go.' A slight sound drew his attention to the farthest column from him, and he waited, as the man stepped from behind it, no fear, but a kind of smile on his face.

'They tell me your name is Damian Seeker.'

'And yours?'

'Zander Seaton, in the service of the King. Do you surrender?'

Seeker almost laughed. 'There is no King,' he said levelly.

'Oh, but there is, and before one of us walks from this church, he will have killed the other because of him.'

Seeker lit another torch on the wall. 'No, you can walk from here, at the point of my sword, and tell what you know. The Lord Protector is not vengeful.'

'No? I saw his mercy at Drogheda and should I ever come within three yards of your Lord Protector I will show him what I learned there. Better that you let me pass now, or I will be walking from here with your blood on my sword.'

'I think you know that will not happen,' said Seeker.

'Then we must fight it out.'

All the while, the sounds of Seeker's men approaching through the church above them had been growing louder. His adversary's eyes flicked to the relic chamber and the flights of stairs behind Seeker.

'Captain?' It was Daniel Proctor, at the head of one of the stairways. Another of Seeker's men was at the top of the other.

Seeker spoke again. 'You're trapped. Surrender now, or you will not leave this place alive.'

The Scotsman made a show of appraising the exits from the crypt. 'Better meet my maker here than on a stinking London gibbet,' he said, and drew his sword.

Proctor and the other soldier launched themselves down the stairs but Seeker held up his left hand to stay them. 'I will do this myself.'

It was a short work, though not so short as the run of these things for Seeker. He had killed in the field of open battle, in the forest, he had killed desperate men hiding in ditches, clinging between the branches of trees, in barns and outhouses, by their own hearths or attempting to jump from the windows of locked rooms in miserable inns. Battle was one thing – there could be no negotiation, no offer of one last chance; but the other times, the killing had been a last resort – the men had chosen to have one last throw of those heavily loaded dice. No man had escaped once Seeker had decided that his only remaining option was to kill him. He saw it now in his opponent's face: Seaton had come to the end of his road.

The Scotsman was quick, agile, expert. Twice, it seemed, he almost had Seeker, twice Seeker had to shout at his own men to hold off, to stay back. There was an exhilaration in fighting for the first time in so long one who was so nearly his equal. Flashing in the other man's eyes as they whirled around the columns of the vault, forced each other up steps and down again, feinted, turned, side-stepped, surprised from above, behind, Seeker saw memories, passions, vengeances. For one moment, when the tip of the Scotsman's sword grazed his throat, Seeker glimpsed his own desire for death; he looked on its enticement almost a moment too long, before pulling away and sending his opponent flailing backwards on to the cold stone paving of the crypt. The Scotsman's sword clattered on the floor and as he reached for it Seeker brought a heavy boot down hard on his wrist. He tried to wrest his arm away, to twist his body, but was rendered immobile by the placing of Seeker's sword at the base of his throat.

'One last chance, for your valour. Will you surrender now?'

The Scotsman smiled. 'Did my King surrender? On the scaffold in the yard of his own palace? Did he give up his friends, those who had been loyal, risked everything, given everything, lost everything for him, save their honour? Did my general surrender, as they hoisted the gibbet thirty feet high at the market cross of Edinburgh? Did he abandon his honour and his King? What would you do, Seeker, would you surrender?'

Seeker looked into the eyes of the man who spoke to him, and they both knew the answer. There had only ever been one answer.

'Tell me, did you murder John Winter?'

A smile and 'No.' An honest 'no'.

Seeker nodded. 'And is there anyone to whom a message should be sent?'

A hesitation, then another 'No.'

Again Seeker nodded and a moment later, a mercifully short moment, his sword did its work.

As two of their men carried the Scotsman's body from the church and laid it on a cart for carrying up to the castle, Proctor turned to his Captain.

'He wouldn't have spoken then?'

Seeker shook his head. 'We'd have got nothing from him. He made his choice: he'd done all his living. He was ready to die.' But Seeker hadn't wanted the man dead.

The body had been carefully searched, but nothing found.

'It's the man who was seen in Kent's, and at Winter's apartments at the Palace?'

Seeker nodded.

'You think he was passing on papers?' said Proctor, as they followed the cart out of Queen's Lane and on to the High Street in the direction of the castle.

'More like the other way around. We'll see when our birds up there sing. What I want to know is why it was him rather than Hendricks, and where Hendricks has gone.'

'Will they sing, do you think?' asked Proctor, nodding towards the castle, where Morgan, d'Oilly and Caduggan would already be secured and awaiting their interrogation.

'They'll sing,' said Seeker. 'Oxford gaol isn't a place for heroes.'

The early mist had lifted at last, and the sky was a brilliant blue. Seeker could see a sort of beauty in this town now, but it was a beauty closed off to him and he turned his thoughts away from it to the corpse on the cart. He wondered about the man who had inhabited that form, about the family he must once have had, and what had happened in his life that there was no one left to be told of his death in Oxford.

'Did he kill John Winter?'

Seeker shook his head. 'He said not, and he had nothing

to gain by lying.' He felt a sudden shiver cross him. 'In any case, there's enough to occupy us today. John Winter's ghost will have to wait.'

Up in the castle, the birds, not liking their cages, were singing soon enough. Caduggan was the first to break and that had not, in truth, taken long: he was followed soon afterwards by Morgan. Seeker wondered at the desperateness of Charles Stuart's cause, when it was reduced to looking to such men. Their stories did not differ much. They had known nothing of Seaton until he had made himself known to them in the Angel. Even then they had not indeed been sure that he was not Hendricks, masquerading under another name. But then d'Oilly had arrived, and d'Oilly had known the truth, for Seaton had visited him in his rooms at Oriel very late the night before.

As Proctor and two of his men were questioning Morgan and Caduggan about what d'Oilly had told them, Seeker in another cell was questioning d'Oilly, who held out a good deal longer than he had expected him to.

'You're wasting your time: Seaton didn't get away and the others have given you up already. What did you tell your fellow conspirators in the Angel coffee house this morning?'

D'Oilly prevaricated a little longer, but at last saw that it was hopeless and capitulated. 'Seaton came to my rooms very late last night. He brought with him a message, a verbal message, from Jakob Hendricks, the Dutchman who had been coming here to meet us. He told us that our plans were compromised and Hendricks being followed.'

'By?'

A flash of youthful bemusement crossed d'Oilly's face. 'By you, of course.'

'How did you know he was telling the truth?'

'He had the password.'

Seeker did not even bother asking what it was, for it was redundant now, and would not be used again.

'And yet you still made your rendezvous?'

'It was too late to warn Morgan or Caduggan, and I would have been of little good on my own – our plan was like a locked box with three keys, and I held only one of them. Besides,' he said with some bitterness, 'we did not know that you knew any more than to follow Hendricks. We had to take the chance.'

Seeker looked around the cell, the filthy rushes on the floor, the tiny barred window that let in no fresh air but only the fetid odours from the stalls and yards of Butcher Row below. He did not bother to ask d'Oilly whether he now thought that chance had been worth the taking.

'So Seaton took Hendricks' place?'

'Yes.'

'Why?'

D'Oilly examined his fingernails. 'He said that Jakob was of much greater use to the King than he, and that should all go wrong, his own loss would be so much the less than Jakob's.'

Seeker had suspected as much. 'Because Jakob Hendricks

is a principal agent in Charles Stuart's network of treachery and Zander Seaton was a mere foot soldier.'

'Was?' asked d'Oilly.

Seeker merely raised an eyebrow. 'You think this is a game? This is no game, d'Oilly. It never was.' He walked around the small cell, observing the man who had just lost everything for absolutely nothing. 'What was your purpose in meeting with Hendricks?'

D'Oilly looked up, and there was something almost self-satisfied in the look. 'It never took place, so you'll never know, will you?'

Seeker put a hand to his throat, pushed him up against the wall and held him there, just held him.

'You will answer my questions. Do you understand me?'

The man continued to stare at him defiantly.

'As you will.' Seeker let go of his throat, and left the cell, hearing, rather than seeing, d'Oilly slip down the wall to the floor. He nodded to his man on guard and said, 'Two minutes.' Two minutes were usually enough, but not too much. His men were trained well enough to know the difference.

When he went back into the cell d'Oilly was lying, rather than sitting, on the floor. He was slumped over now, on his side, and appeared to be holding his ribs. There was no blood – there was rarely the need for blood, but the ribs would most certainly be broken.

'Are you ready to answer me now?' asked Seeker.

Some noise signalling agreement rose from d'Oilly's throat. Seeker made a small motion with his hand and his man scooped a ladle of water from a bucket in the corner and brought it to d'Oilly's lips. The answers began to come more smoothly then.

'The money is secured?' Seeker was mounted and ready to ride out of Oxford Castle. Beneath him, he could feel Acheron, as anxious as his master to be out once more on the London Road.

Proctor nodded. 'Bander and Coyle brought it from Hendricks' rooms in Wadham an hour since. It is secured now in the sheriff's strongbox, and will stay there until the transportation to London can be arranged. I don't think he likes the commission.'

Seeker never took his eyes from the gate ahead of him, waiting for it to be cranked up and allow him to pass out of the town. 'He does not need to like it, just to do it.' Already, the sheriff's men, and the four Seeker had left to oversee the task, were searching every college for signs of Jakob Hendricks. The search of Wadham Seeker had overseen himself. Warden Wilkins had been appalled when he had learned of the true identity of his guest of the previous night, and offered every assistance to the soldiers. Even so, Seeker had suspected theirs was a hopeless task: given Seaton's warning, Hendricks had probably left the college and indeed the town the night before.

The list of names of each of the conspirator's 'assured men' was in Seeker's saddlebag – the names of those promised by d'Oilly had taken a little longer to extract than those offered up by the other two. Each man had secured a number of men who either held strategically placed land or were fighters of proven ability and courage, prepared to play their part in assisting a planned invasion from the West Country by Charles Stuart in the spring. Their names, and their place in the plan, were what was to have been transmitted to Jakob Hendricks in the Angel coffee house in Oxford, and in return, money somehow scraped together by Charles from supporters and relatives abroad was to have been handed over to d'Oilly, Morgan and Caduggan that they might begin in earnest their preparations – the buying of good horses, the securing of arms. The gold had been left in Hendricks' rooms at Wadham, apparently. D'Oilly was to collect it and distribute it to the other two after they had passed on the information.

The plan was that Charles should land on the Cornish coast, on a stretch of land where Caduggan's family still held influence. The invading army would then march through the West Country, gathering up forces and meeting up with those brought from Wales by Morgan. Strongholds would be taken on the way – Seeker noted that Baxton Hall, family seat of John Winter's widow, was on the rebels' list of targets. Oxford, stuffed full of Royalists as it already was, would be primed: those who had remained quiet and escaped notice for so long would rise up and deliver the city to Charles. And then they would make for London, where else but London?

It was all very simple, each piece of the plan meshing beautifully with the next. It was persuasive, almost a lovely thing to look upon, lovely as the spider's web and just as apt to be brushed away. It all fell apart like a spider's web the moment Seeker touched it. It was all worthless: the money raised abroad by Charles would within two days be in the Protector's coffers, and the list of names and locations in Thurloe's hand by nightfall. Whatever list Hendricks had escaped Oxford with would be incomplete and useless, now. The names on it, and those of the men promised by Morgan and Caduggan, would be adorning death warrants or the cargo lists of transportation ships before the Dutchman ever found his way back to Charles's German court.

'That's our mission completed, then,' said Proctor, as they rode at last over Magdalen Bridge and away from Oxford.

'Not quite,' said Seeker.

'How so?'

'We have not got Hendricks.'

'Granted, but he is known to us now, and it will take him months, years even, to bring another plot against the Protector to the place this one was. He'll get no merry welcome when he turns up back in Cologne with no money and a list of dead men's names.'

'If he does return to Charles's court,' said Seeker.

'You don't think he would stay here, in England? That would be madness on his part.'

Seeker thought of the look on Hendricks' face as he had

watched Mirjam Tavener with her husband. 'For myself, I don't know that the Dutchman isn't a little mad. And then there is Crowther.' On none of the three lists that had eventually been extracted from the men soon to be executed at Oxford Castle did the name Gwyllm Crowther appear, but they had recognised it, every one of them, of that Seeker was certain.

'I'll be glad to get back to London,' said Proctor.

Seeker gave an 'aye' in agreement and spurred Acheron on. There were things calling him back to London, and with every mile that passed beneath the horse's hooves, they drew at him more urgently.

FOURTEEN

The Presence Chamber

6 November

She supposed she would not walk these corridors much longer, and she was not sorry for it. Anne Winter was thoroughly sick of having doors opened before her by armed and liveried men. She wanted to open her own doors, to walk into a room and find discussions not of matters of state, but of life. Chamber after chamber she had passed through, and she faced the last door now. At this one, she knew, she must wait a little longer.

Grown men, it was said, trembled to stand where she did now, but that could only be, she thought, because they wished to please him, or because they had something to lose. Anne Winter felt only a mild curiosity as she awaited her summons from the Guard Chamber to the presence of the most powerful man in England. If she trembled, it was that her body had not yet comprehended that there would be no more opium. Those around Whitehall who observed her sickly pallor, her haunted look, read in them signs of grief.

It was perhaps ten minutes from the sending of a message that she had arrived before the doors were opened again, and this time it was that another might leave, rather than she enter. It was hardly unusual – he was at business almost all day, every day. What she could not have predicted, though, was that the figure leaving a private interview with Oliver Cromwell would be George Tavener.

Tavener himself looked startled to see her there, and paused a moment to nod to her, as if yet uncertain of who she was, before putting on his hat and continuing on his way down the passageways of Whitehall. Anne Winter watched him go, and wondered.

The Foot Guard in front of her nodded. 'You may go into His Highness now.'

She straightened herself as the guards put up their weapons and stood aside, leaving her to step alone into the presence of Oliver Cromwell.

He had his back to her, and was poring over two large charts rolled out and weighted on a table of green marble with fantastically wrought gilt legs. She took a moment to look around her; the sight caught her breath. She had heard, of course, but John had not liked to speak of it so she had given up questioning him upon it, but now she saw that it was true: Cromwell, this Usurper, this champion of the cause of the people, surrounded himself with the majesty of Kingship. Here was a Mantegna tapestry, there, alongside Walker's portrait of Cromwell himself, was a Titian, on a desk by the window the Lord Protector's private seal. The hangings, carpets and furnishings were as exquisite as ever they had been, and as fit for a king, as in any royal court in Europe. Anne Winter thought of the desecration of churches – their statues and glass and ornament, the ripping out of their organs, the destruction of fine libraries, houses, all in the name of godliness, at this man's command. How ironic then that he should surround himself with a beauty and fineness that he so vehemently denied his people.

She had said it once to John, who, unlike her, had been in this room many times. 'He makes himself ridiculous.'

'No,' John had said, his face suddenly stone.

'What? A fenland farmer that preens himself as King? He is the laughing stock of the courts of Europe.'

He had appraised her a moment before saying, 'You have no idea how wrong you are.'

'How so?'

'Cromwell is the stuff of their nightmares. How seriously do you think they would take him, take this people, this government, were the ambassadors of Spain, France, the Netherlands, to be received in some hunting lodge, inn, barracks? They need to know that *Cromwell* is the man with whom they are to deal, that this Protectorate is the government of England. I tell you, Anne, they see what this fenland farmer, as you would have him, has wrought, and they tremble.'

And yet, as she looked on him now, the strong back, the sturdy legs that sat a horse as well as any she had seen, the power that had cowed parliaments and led armies to feats beyond all human expectation, she thought there was indeed something ridiculous in the sight. Hanging silks and heavy velvets, Venetian crystal chandeliers, gilt-framed portraits, chairs of gold: they were fripperies and they belittled him. Cromwell should have met any who dared to approach him in a draughty castle hall, a plain, Puritan church, a stable yard; he should have faced all-comers honest, dared them to brave him for what he was.

'Do I disturb you, your Highness?' she asked at last.

He turned around, straightened. 'My Lady. I am sorry, you find me deep in thought. Please, sit.' He motioned towards a sedan embroidered with a hunting scene, and then the mighty orator who could make armies tremble at his voice, and cow entire parliaments seemed unsure as to how he should proceed.

'My wife,' he began at last, 'the Lady Protectress, asks that I should pass on to you her condolences and prayers.'

'That is very good of Her Highness,' said Anne Winter. She had met the woman once, and found that she had nothing to say to her.

'It is not goodness; she was fond of John.'

'Fond?'

'Aye, fond. There was much in him to love.'

Anne Winter found she could not hold his eyes and looked aside, at a Bohemian gilt clock whose time, she thought, was wrong.

Cromwell let his words hang a moment then continued. 'The Lord chastens us by taking from us that which we have grown too much to love on this earth, that we might consider it, and the greater love we owe him.'

'Then he has chastened me greatly,' said Anne Winter.

'The loss of your husband . . .'

She lifted her hand a little. 'Your Highness misunderstands me; I was talking of my father and my brother, whom the Lord saw fit to take from me, for their love for the King. Though that done with your Highness's assistance.'

She saw the kindness — and there had been kindness — pass from his eyes, and a slight twitch appear at the side of his mouth.

'My armies have oft-times been chosen by the Lord for His mighty work, and for that I have often rejoiced and given thanks.'

He walked back over to his desk and pulled open a drawer from which he lifted a parchment. 'I will not bandy words with you, Lady Anne. I have not the time for it, as your husband always understood and perhaps you do not. It is known all over Westminster that you showed John Winter little affection — it was spoken of openly. I myself, with Secretary Milton, counselled him to look to the laws on divorce.'

Now he had her full attention, and Anne Winter was no longer directing the game.

Cromwell continued on his course. 'Did you think yourself so wronged and he so friendless? No matter. He would not have it, would not hear it. He loved you was the simple truth, although all that knew him knew he deserved a better wife. And so it is for the love he bore you that I grant you this that was his.'

He held out the document he had lifted from his drawer. Anne Winter, who had come to listen to professions of grief and perhaps, inwardly, to mock, had not expected this. She remained motionless.

'I give you Baxton Hall, that was your husband's for his service to the people. He wanted it for you, and so you shall have it.'

Anne Winter stared at the document, afraid, almost, to touch it. Cromwell pressed on. 'I would advise you to shift to there as soon as you are able. There is more than one amongst the late lieutenant's men who suspects you of a hand in his killing.'

She tried to speak: 'I did not . . .'

'Oh, be assured, Lady Anne, it shall not long remain hidden if you did, and in such a case, my men will know where to find you. Damian Seeker has only now flushed the dregs of some Royalist plot from Oxfordshire. I would counsel you to live quietly and consider carefully of your friends when you return there.'

She stood up, took a step towards him. 'Do I remind you so much of those you have wronged? Does my—'

But he held up a hand. 'Your husband had many friends, Lady Anne, whatever your contempt for him might have been. Betake yourself to Baxton, or the consequences will be your blame alone.'

He turned his back on her, and returned to the

consultation of his charts. Anne Winter stood, in the middle of this room where so much had been petitioned, so much granted. She held in her hand the deeds to her childhood home; Oliver's seal was appended to them, granting all that was left of what had once been her father's to her.

She spoke quietly now, curbing her defiance, seeing possibilities she did not want to lose. 'And am I free to sell it?'

He didn't turn around. 'Do with it what you wish.'

Almost without realising she did it, she sank a curtsey to his back. A guard opened the door, and she left the presence chamber, her future in her hand.

George Tavener's head was pounding. The Americas. Was there anything on anyone's tongue today but the Americas? Not in those who had spoken to him, at any rate. Sugar cane, cotton, tobacco, furs. Was there still a glint of gold? Dear God, not that old myth.

Oliver was the worst: nothing would have it but he would export his revolution, fight the Lord's battles overseas, win himself an empire. Or take it from Spain. Tavener and others like him had laboured to make the Lord Protector see sense, but the man's mind was more set every time he saw him, and Tavener knew it could not be long until the decision was made that would send many men to their miserable deaths thousands of miles from home and disrupt all profitable trade into the bargain. He had tried to tell him: swamps, malaria, savages – not fitting for an Englishman. Others who had never seen the Caribbean, never walked the streets of Jamestown or travelled the waters of the Chesapeake with a musket in their hands and starving men at their backs, whispered other things: export the godly revolution; export the dregs of society – the shiftless, the criminal, Irish savages, prisoners of war, Royalists that would not take a telling. Glorify England, cleanse England, make her rich. Tavener had come to Kent's, to see what other news and trades were on the air today, and loose himself a while from this business of the Americas.

Sitting at the coffee table, with all the babble and news of the world going on around him, he felt the absence of Elias. He would be hard put to think of a single matter of importance on which he agreed with the man, but his daily debates with the lawyer sharpened his wits and enlivened his day. More than that, he liked him. If Elias were to hang – and Tavener did not see how that was to be avoided – there would be a void in the merchant's life which it would be difficult to fill. And then Maria had come down the stairs from seeing to Grace. Maria, like her brother, made Tavener smile; if he had ever had a daughter, he would have wished her to be like Maria. He called her over to him.

'How does Grace today?'

'Little better. The medicine Anne Winter brought has cooled her fever, but done nothing to rouse her from her sleep.' She lowered her voice, that neither Samuel nor the coffee house boy could hear. 'I can hardly get two mouthfuls of broth down her, or a sip of ale. She will die if she does not wake and take proper nourishment.'

'And what do the physicians say?'

'No physician would come to her, once they heard the Seeker had been here. Samuel tried, but to no avail.'

Tavener cursed and called to the boy for paper and ink. The note took him two minutes to write. 'You will take that, now, to the house of Dr William Jamesone at the sign of the Lancet on Hart Street. If he is not there, tell his wife to send it to him wherever he is at, forthwith, if she would not have her neighbours see the fine French writing desk that she is so fond of, and that her husband has not yet paid me for, carried by the bailiffs out of her front door.' The boy had his apron off and was out on to the street in seconds, the gravity of his mission making him almost forget his note.

'There will be a physician here within the hour,' said Tavener.

Maria put her hand over his. 'God bless you, George.'

Tavener looked at the hand, fine, thin, roughened by too much hard work. 'If anything should befall Elias, you know you would have a home with Mirjam and me.'

She shook her head. 'Elias will go free, I am certain of it. And when he does, I must ask for your help, George. England is no place for him any more. God knows what Cromwell's government will turn to next, but whatever it is, it will not bode well for men like Elias. I am determined we will go to Virginia, begin again.'

There it was even on the lips of a young woman who had known only three square miles her whole life. Let her dream. Let Elias believe the fables of liberty put about by the adventurers and stock-holders who had sent so many others to their squalid deaths. Elias would never see America. Nor Maria either, God willing. He tried again. 'But should anything befall him, we . . .'

He wondered if she was even listening properly. 'But Elias *will* be freed. He will not die for this murder of John Winter.'

There was something utterly certain in the way she spoke. 'You cannot know that, Maria.'

She didn't flinch. 'But I do. He will not hang for John Winter. Damian Seeker will not let it happen.'

Tavener was astonished. 'Seeker?'

'Yes. He knows Elias didn't kill John Winter. He will not see him hang while the guilty one goes free.'

Tavener sought the right words. 'Maria, he may have no choice. If they do not find another, Elias will be their scapegoat.'

But she was unshakeable. 'The Seeker will not let that happen,' she said as she lifted a tray of dirty cups from the table and turned away with it. 'I saw it in his eyes.'

'Others have been assigned to the matter of John Winter's killing; you need concern yourself with it no longer.'

'But . . .'

Thurloe put down his quill pen impatiently. 'The investigation into the death of John Winter was never your business, it was only the coincidence of his wife's presence in Kent's coffee house that brought the matter of his murder into your path. Your termination of the Oxford coffee house plot and the exposure and interrogation of those involved make clear that John Winter's death was by no means connected to it. The search for Winter's killer is no longer your concern.'

He lifted his pen again, but Seeker did not move.

'There are too many connections – Winter's wife, the Scotsman, her father's house so close to Oxford, Jakob Hendricks . . .'

Anger and astonishment were contending for supremacy in the face of John Thurloe. Seeker acknowledged to himself that never once, in all their many dealings, had he questioned his superior's judgement, still less baulked at a command. Thurloe stared at him.

The mud of the western road was still on Seeker's boots. His face was unshaven and he had hardly slept or eaten properly for days.

'Go home, Damian. Sleep. You did well in Oxford. The Scotsman was vermin, and well rid of. If Hendricks has the good fortune to escape these shores, he will never dare return, now that he is so well-known.' He indicated the list Seeker had given him, and which he was engaged in copying into a ledger. 'Even now, we have platoons flushing out those men whose names you extracted from the plotters. Those who do not hang will spend the rest of their days sitting at home watching their wives embroider, and gladly.

Caduggan, Morgan and d'Oilly will be looking out over Oxford from spikes on the castle wall before the week is up. The coffers of the Protectorate have been buoyed by Charles Stuart's gold. Besides,' he said, leaning back in his chair, satisfied, 'we have a man we can hang for Winter's murder, should the need arise. If some other later be found to have done the deed, no matter: the Sparrow will hardly be missed.'

Seeker stared at him, unable to believe Thurloe could so casually discard the life of one who might be innocent. 'But—'

Thurloe shook his head. 'No, there can be no "but". There's been trouble enough in the army of late, questioning of the Protector's authority – Alured and his Levellers, Overton in Scotland, Ludlow in Ireland. Any delay in dealing with Winter's murder will only fan the flames of agitation. There is a greater good. You have always known that.'

'Aye,' said Seeker, turning at last to leave. 'I have.'

Keeping close to the walls and out of the light, and making as little sound as possible, to avoid notice by the night Watch, Maria Ellingworth turned into Dove Court for the first time in three days. Samuel had pressed her to stay, not to go home alone, while Elias was not there, but Maria had assured him all would be well, and that she would be back to tend to Grace and help him in the coffee house in the morning. Leaving Grace in the care of the night nurse, for whom George Tavener had paid, she had slipped out into the darkness and made her way home, a huge mongrel dog that had shadowed her three days now loping at her side.

There was no guard now at the entrance to the passageway, none now on the stairs, and none at the door to the only place she could think of as home. She almost regretted it: for the last few hundred yards of her journey Maria had felt an uneasy sense that she was being watched. Quickly and quietly, careful not to attract any attention, Maria Ellingworth turned her key in the rusted lock of the old door.

FIFTEEN

Transactions

6 November

As he had walked from Thurloe's chamber back to his own, Seeker had considered that while the Secretary had warned him off pursuing the matter of John Winter's murder any further, given that a suitable culprit had presented himself so easily and was now held in the Tower, he had said nothing about looking more deeply into the matter of the coffee house plot centred on Kent's. Zander Seaton might have been dealt with, and the Oxford plotters be facing a swift justice, but questions remained, and those troubled Seeker. Why had Kent's been chosen for the placing of the coded painting, and who had communicated the location to Hendricks? Seeker was not so arrogant that he trusted completely his own instinct, nor so foolish that he trusted what other men told him when he had not the proof before him, and although he had sensed there was truth in the claim that Archibald Campbell and Zander Seaton had come upon each other on their way to London by chance, he could not be sure of it, and there was something the minister had not told him about his reasons for coming – of that he was certain.

On his return to his own chambers, Seeker had checked on the reports that had come in while he'd been in Oxford. Campbell was due to give a sermon to his congregation in Goldsmiths' Court that evening. Seeker's shoulders had sunk at the thought of it: Thurloe had been right about one thing at least – he was exhausted. He was not certain that he could even sit through one of the Scotsman's – or indeed any other preacher's – sermons; besides, during his interrogation of the minister in Kent's three days previously, he had been fully aware of the Scotsman's close scrutiny: Campbell would certainly recognise him and be on his guard. He had called for two of his younger soldiers who had not been on the Oxford expedition, and told them to garb themselves as apprentices and take note of proceedings that evening at the Presbyterian Chapel in Goldsmiths' Court.

Archibald Campbell surveyed his congregation. They wanted to hear about Hell, he could see it in their faces. He could tell them about Hell. They were waiting for denunciation, eager to tremble at the promise of eternal damnation. They hungered – they had told him so from the hour he had arrived – they hungered for proper chastisement in a city where the sects had run wild, even to government, and each man claimed to carry God within him. They thirsted for the terror of sin, the righteous roll call of the punishments of the Reprobate.

And it was, indeed, scarcely credible, even to one who had seen what he had seen, the torrent of blasphemies that had been unleashed by the march of Cromwell's New Model Army. Unlettered ploughboys, wandering labourers, packmen, the lost and hopeless decanted into the cities by the taking of their common lands; wood people, itinerant craftsmen from the North. No Heaven but on this earth, no Hell, no elect, no damned, no sin, no resurrection, God in everything, God in every man, each man his own God. No God. Cromwell himself had taken fright; *he* might commune with the Almighty, but the common man knew not whereof he spoke. Parliament had passed law after law, the punishments on those judged to have blasphemed had been terrible, but it was too late: the infection had been unleashed.

And so the pestilence of heresy, blasphemy and licence had been walked into the streets of London on the boots of soldiers and of the displaced. Its miasma had permeated the air, the wood, plaster, stones of houses and workshops, infected the water in conduit, pump and well, crawled on to the backs of dogs, mice, cats and into the homes where mothers nursed their babies at their breasts.

Campbell had not lost his power to preach, and within half an hour his congregation was aglow with his certainties. The text had been well chosen, the psalms too. By the end of the two hours they were well-satisfied, and justly terrified of the punishments of Hell he had delineated for them. They could return to their homes, their well-made, secure homes, thoroughly confirmed in their faith and their election, and as they settled by their welcoming hearths, they could denounce their neighbours in their hearts. They were well-pleased in their new minister.

Perhaps he should have been content with that, because that was what he had come for, was it not? That was even what he had believed himself, in the beginning. But London had revealed its workings to him, and in his heart he could no longer deny that he had come to this city for something else. As he went from place to place snuffing out the candles that lit the chapel in Goldsmiths' Court, he considered the deception he had wrought upon himself, and upon those people, and the deceptions still to be worked. Before he could snuff out the last of the candles, there came a voice behind him.

'A word, Sir, if you please.'

The voice had a tinge of familiarity, and so, as he stepped into the last pool of light in the chapel, did the man. Campbell had to make some shifts of place in his head, and finally he located him, the packman from the coffee house.

'There was much meat for a hungry soul in your sermon.'

'God strengthens me in the preaching of His word.'

'Of course,' said the packman, 'of course. And the congregation much edified.'

Campbell wondered what the man wanted, and wished him to be gone. Fiddler seemed to sense his irritation, and signalled by a shift in position and the slightest change of intonation that he was coming to his point. 'I know from my travels that many thirst for such a word; of places where a minister cannot be found agreeable to the government so that the people are abandoned to the unlettered rantings of shepherds and passing weavers.'

Campbell waited.

'But I know many printers in the city,' continued Fiddler, 'who would be glad to print sermons such as yours. I myself could then disseminate them throughout the country. It would be a godly work, and it would pay.'

Campbell was tired, and there was something in the packman he had not liked from the start, but what did it matter? And if there was money to be made, he might as well have it as another. One copy of each sermon he gave and half the profit to the minister, they agreed upon, and the packman went away, well-pleased, it seemed, with his bargain.

Campbell locked up the chapel and went back out on to Fetter Lane. The air was cold and the promise of frost was whispered already along the ground. A young boy, yoked with buckets of water that almost doubled him, hurried from the direction of the Fleet conduit up a darkened stairway at the side of a house. Two ragged children scurried to whatever might be their home. The honest business of the day, where there had been honest business, was retreating to its slumber and the night city was coming out of the shadows. At the bottom of the lane, two young apprentices who had been listening intently to his sermon, and who had left shortly before the packman had spoken to him, were turning on to Fleet Street. He wondered what lesson they might have taken from his words, from the lies and fallacies he had propounded for nigh on two hours to the approbation of the people, but the thought soon passed and the apprentices were forgotten. Campbell began to make his way up the lane towards the Black Swan, ignoring all that passed him on the street, their sounds muffled by the incantations in his head that would not be silenced: Hell was on Earth, the Devil was in man, God had been vanquished and there was no means to perfection but through sin.

'Do not tell me it is nothing; I can see it in your face.'

Mirjam Tavener turned away from her husband, walked to the window, her hand travelling absently to the lock on the shutters. From that window of their parlour, high on the third floor of their house, all the life of Cheapside could be seen passing below them. Often, when her work for the day was finished and George not yet returned from business at the docks or the Exchange, she would sit and watch that world, and make up its stories in her head. George, who liked to shut out the world when he left off his business for the night, would always have the shutters closed, but Mirjam preferred them open. Tonight, he noticed, they had been firmly shut and bolted by the time he had come up from the counting house below.

'Mirjam?'

She swallowed, still did not turn to face him. 'I think somebody is watching us. Watching me.'

He took her by the arm and turned her slowly around. 'What do you mean?'

'I sent Esther out on errands three times today – I kept forgetting things. After the second time she mentioned there was a man standing across the street who had been there before. It had struck her as odd, because she did not know him and he didn't seem to be doing anything, just standing there. The third time – for dripping from the Shambles for ours had gone bad – she came back convinced that he was watching the house. I went with her to the door and he caught my eye, then hurried off into the crowd.'

Tavener was very still, his voice low. What Seeker had told him of Jakob Hendricks still weighed heavily on his mind.

'This man across the street – did you know him?'

She shook her head. 'He wore a heavy dark coat and his hat was pulled low on his head. I could hardly see his face, and it was only for a second, but I felt those eyes.'

'He never came to the door? Spoke to any of the household?'

'No.'

'But there is more?'

She hesitated.

'Tell me, Mirjam.'

She summoned her courage. 'Later, I was out in the garden, gathering hazelnuts to stuff the pheasant his Highness sent for you the other day, and I had the same feeling, that there was someone there, watching me.'

Apprehension was written clear on George Tavener's face.

'In the garden?'

Tears were brimming in her eyes now. 'I think so. In the apple grove, by the east wall. A sound, a movement. I turned back to the house, to call for Jem, or Harry Grey, and then I heard footfalls, and by the time Jem came out there was no one there.'

Tavener's fists were clenched.

'Was the gate not locked?'

'It had been, earlier, I am certain of it, but Jem found it swinging open on to the lane, and no one there.'

For a moment George Tavener said nothing. The rage mounting in him had temporarily deprived him of the power of speech. His breathing came heavy and he was shaking with anger. His felt his face fill with crimson before he turned and marched from the room, and for the next ten minutes Mirjam heard him bellow at every servant he could find, and use language he must have learned as a boy carrying lobsters from Billingsgate wharf to Leadenhall market, until no one in the house can have been left in any doubt that he should have been told, he should have been *told*.

The bellowing ended, Esther arrived, ashen-faced, with instructions that she was to escort the mistress to her chamber and wait there with her. Harry Grey would stand guard at the bedroom door and others – clerks, maids, footmen, stable-boy – would be at every door in the house, none of which was to be opened until the master returned with the constable of the Watch.

Esther looked at her curiously. 'But who is this man I saw across the street, Mistress, that the master is so enraged?'

Mirjam Tavener sat down on the coverlet she had begun to embroider while still at the Weesehouse, for her marriage bed. 'I don't know, Esther. I really do not know.'

In Whitehall Palace, Anne Winter studied the deeds to Baxton Hall and what remained of its policies. She had wasted no time since her interview with Cromwell, and sought out a land agent who was known to haunt the corridors of Westminster, like a hound in a gentleman's hall, waiting for tasty morsels to drop from the table. The price he had suggested would do her well enough.

The other papers were plans John had brought back, some time ago, seeking to interest her in the idea of a house that would be their home, in London. She had hardly even glanced at them; she was sorry for that now. New developments around Lincoln's Inn Fields and the square, the piazza, at Covent Garden. He had pointed to a fine row of tall, elegant stone houses over vaulted arcades: 'You would have all the finest goods London has to offer on your doorstep. There would be new acquaintance for you – you might not be so lonely, so trapped behind the walls and guard posts of this place, surrounded always by soldiers . . .'

She had shown no interest in any of it, given him no

encouragement, and now, unblinkered, she looked at it again and saw what John Winter had seen, the possibilities that would never come to be. Too late now, too late. He was gone, and all the blame she had silently laid on him, the resentment, the studied cold indifference, was gone also. And it had been a studied indifference, it had been a work of effort. Cromwell, Milton, all who thought they understood her marriage had been wrong, because she had come to realise, quite early on, that in another time and another country, she could have loved John Winter. She rolled up the plans of Covent Garden and of Lincoln's Inn Fields. It was deeper, further east, into the heart of the city she would go. But that must wait, for first there was the business of the coffee house to see to. It had been John's final request to her, and that, at least, she would do for him.

SIXTEEN

Ink

7 November

The two young soldiers' report of Campbell's sermon had been on Seeker's desk before first light. Seeker read it with a degree of distaste – nothing that surprised him, but nothing that suggested any complicity with the Oxford plot. And then he came to the last lines of the report, and read them over twice.

After the end of the service, when the congregation had departed, a peddler hung back and made himself known to the preacher. Campbell looked displeased to be importuned by the man, and reluctant to accord him much time. They spoke only for a few minutes, and none of their conversation could be overheard. The peddler left the chapel several minutes before the minister, and went off in the direction of the river, while Campbell locked up his chapel before returning to his lodgings at the Black Swan.

Seeker then read the instructions that awaited him, as they did every morning, from Thurloe. In three days' time, the Protectorate family and court would travel to Greenwich for a celebration of the forthcoming birthday of the Lady Frances, the youngest of his Highness's daughters. Seeker should concern himself only with the assistance he was to give to the Protector's Life Guard at that event. The details would be in his hand tomorrow. The instructions ended with a reminder that, until that time, Seeker was not to exhaust himself further by meddling in matters that were the province of others, but should instead conduct himself as any private citizen might.

Seeker screwed the paper into a ball and threw it on to the grate to be burned, then, taking down his cloak and helmet, went down the Old Staircase and by the Tilt Yard to Horse Guard Yard, as he was in the habit of doing when leisure was forced upon him. At the sight of him, Acheron lifted his head from his nosebag, like a soldier caught off-guard, and stood straight, whinnying, ready. Seeker put out a hand to the horse's neck, and stroked it tenderly. 'Not today, I fear, boy. You are in greater need of rest than I am.' He surveyed the other horses in their stalls, but had not the heart to lead any of them out for a run in the park while his own beast looked on.

As often happened at such times, he felt himself drawn to the city, and that was where he now headed. As he went through the Ludgate and towards St Paul's he thought again of Thurloe's instruction. But how should a private citizen conduct himself? What should a man do if not fulfil his duty, his function, in a society? He watched other men;

none were at leisure. Lawyer, baker, hawker, cutpurse, beggar: all were about their business, legal or not. He was in the wrong part of London to observe men at their leisure: he should have been on the Strand, Pall Mall, or south of the Bridge perhaps, beyond Southwark, to observe the likes of John Evelyn at home at Sayes Court. Evelyn and all the others: gentlemen, Royalists, drones; Seeker did not know how men of so little purpose could fill their days. The State had forbidden most of their idle pastimes: theatres, pleasure gardens, baiting pits, bowling greens, tennis courts – spawning grounds of the rich and useless. Oliver had been right to close them.

It was in his mind to go to Dove Court and question Maria Ellingworth once more. It was not impossible that Ellingworth might have got some letter, some word, from the Tower to his sister, and if he had, Seeker was determined he would know what it was. The usual throng was about St Paul's, and it struck Seeker that should Christ have walked there that day, he would have torn it stone from stone, for the place was a very mockery of the House of God. Everywhere, there was buying and selling, business, endless business. Booksellers and printers – the censor's office worked night and day, almost all but the government's own news-sheets were banned. How could it be, then, that there was so much left to print?

A familiar figure in russet coat and woollen cap caught his eye: the peddler Will Fiddler, only a small pack on his back, disappearing through a side-gate on Paternoster Row. On

leaving his chambers, Seeker had ordered that two of his
men should follow Fiddler: he scanned the throng around
Paternoster Row and the nearby area of St Paul's churchyard, but saw nothing of his men: clearly they hadn't found
the peddler yet. Seeker knew the alley the fellow had gone
down to be a dead end and that Fiddler must emerge from
it again, and so waited, and indeed it was not much more
than ten minutes before Fiddler emerged back out into the
street, his pack no heavier than when he had gone in, and
disappeared once more into the crowd.

Seeker crossed the street and went through the gate. The
alley led to a printer's workshop. It was not one familiar to
him from the many raids he had led into places of the sort.
For all they were often disseminators of sedition, Seeker
liked the smell and noise of printers' shops – they were at
work in the world, they sounded and looked like work.

The workshop had been set up in what must once have
been a stable. Two pressmen were at work on the press, one
turning the bar that brought the platen of the press down
on the bed – or coffin, as Seeker had heard it called – the
other seeing to the placing of the paper on the frame above
the set type. An apprentice was engaged in lifting a sheet
just printed on to a line above his head to dry. Two compositors sat on stools placing pieces of type on wooden
composing sticks, which they set into a large metal frame.
At a lectern, nearest to the window, a corrector checked the
finished sheets. Between them all, looking for all the world
as if he knew of no existence outside that of the workshop,

ran the printer's devil, a boy covered in ink so ingrained it surely must never wash off. So engaged was he upon fulfilling the commands being shouted at him from all corners of the workshop that he did not at first notice Seeker, who stretched a hand out to his forehead to stop him mid-run. 'Where is your master, boy?'

Once he had recovered himself, the printer's devil, saying nothing, ran through to a back room from which a hint of hearth smoke emanated. A moment later, the printer himself emerged, some sheaves of paper in his hand. As the recognition of Seeker dawned, the mild irritation at being interrupted changed subtly to an alertness, a wariness that must have served him well in his trade.

'What business have you here, Captain? There's nothing comes off my presses that's not approved. You check with the Stationers' Hall: there's nothing with my mark on it to trouble the censors.'

'That will be for the censors to decide,' said Seeker. 'That man who just left here . . .'

The printer relaxed. 'Will Fiddler? I've told him his fortune often enough, not to come to me with the ramblings of the Sparrow and all that crew.'

'So what did he want here?'

The man snorted a laugh. 'I'll show you.' He called to his devil to fetch him the papers lying on the table in the back room. The boy was back with them in an instant. 'Wants me to print that,' he said, handing the sheaf of papers to Seeker. 'I had just made a start on it.'

Seeker examined the pages, ten in all, crammed with a tiny, neat italic script, and blighted by several blottings out and added notes. In the margins, in heavier ink, were biblical references. Seeker read over the first two paragraphs. 'Who is the author of this?' he asked.

'Jack, fetch that title page I wrote.'

This time the writing was in a large cursive hand, evidently the printer's. ' "God's Judgement Delivered: the Rewards of Iniquitie at the Day of Judgement", a sermon preached to the congregation of the Presbyterian Chapel, Goldsmith's Court, Fetter Lane, London, 6th November 1654, by the Reverend Archibald Campbell.'

'I warned him,' said the printer, 'I warned him it would be straight to Milton's office if I thought anything seditious in it. I haven't had the time to cast my eye over it fully, but he has assured me by all he holds dear that there's not a word in it that Cromwell himself could object to. But if you tell me it is . . .'

Seeker was scanning through the pages, thinking. 'Print it,' he said at last. 'Print it, and once you have done so, have your boy take a copy to this address.' He wrote down directions and a street name and handed it to the printer, who nodded and placed the paper in his apron.

'And Will Fiddler?'

Seeker shook his head. 'Delay twelve hours before you tell him it is ready.'

The man agreed, without question.

'Good.' But instead of leaving as the increasingly wary printer clearly had hoped he might, Seeker began a slow tour of the workshop, examining everything that took his interest. He watched as one of the pressmen finished levelling the type in its frame then carefully wielded a mallet and stick to drive into place the wedges holding it together. He was just about to leave when he became aware of a small movement, too quick, of one of the compositors at the other side of the room, in response to some agitation in the demeanour of the master. Seeker turned to bring the compositor fully into his view. The stick he had a moment ago been working on had been pushed under a sheet of paper, almost out of view. The fellow was not moving now and his face was crimson. Seeker walked over to where he was working and slid the composition stick from its hiding place. He saw the man's eyes glide to the shelf to his left where another, already completed, had been placed. Seeker set one above the other and peered a moment at the metal forms of print before calling to the printer's devil to bring him an inking ball and a sheet of paper, cut to octavo.

'Ink them,' said Seeker, indicating the sticks of type.

The boy did as he was bid.

'Now the paper,' said Seeker.

The boy nodded, and placed the sheet of paper over the inked type and pressed a weight on it for a moment. Then he carefully lifted the sheet and handed it to Seeker, who turned it over and read.

'William Davenant, *The Tempest, or the Enchanted Island.*'

The master printer's face was grave, his assurance of earlier altogether disappeared.

'It . . . it is a private copy, for Sir William himself. He hopes to work on it, he says, and produce a musical version as a gift to His Highness . . .'

The printer trailed off as Seeker stared him down. Evidently, he realised how unlikely that event seemed. An old Royalist playwright, up to his neck in plotting and running guns for Charles Stuart and his mother, Sir William Davenant, had not long been released from the Tower of London, due entirely to the good offices of powerful friends and his ability to charm even Oliver Cromwell. Many in Parliament would cheerfully have seen him hang, and Seeker was not alone in thinking the Protector's leniency towards the debauched old Cavalier a step too far in trying to win over surviving Royalists. Davenant's meddling with this old play of usurpers and lost kingdoms did not bode well.

'Where is the text?' asked Seeker.

'We don't have it,' said the printer, 'and that's God's own truth. Sir William said he still has much work to do on it, but he had a fancy to see how the title page might look. He nodded to his devil. 'Fetch the woodcut, Jack,' and in a moment the boy was handing Seeker a block of wood into which had been carved a device, a circle within which a ship was being rocked in a storm. 'That was to go beneath the title,' said the printer. 'Here, Harry,' he addressed one of the compositors, 'show the Captain how they would be fitted together on the frame.'

Seeker watched, and got the boy to print the title page again, this time with its image.

'Very good,' he said, nodding. 'Very good.'

And as the master printer and his workers were turning to each other, reassured and smiling with relief, Seeker took hold of the composition sticks and overturned them, the letters falling like spilled nails to the floor. Then, wrenching the woodcut from its frame, he was striding towards the printer's open office door, where a healthy fire burned. He threw the block with its carefully rendered emblem into the flames, and as the printer opened his mouth to protest Seeker shook his head. 'There will be no *Tempest* from this or any other printing house. You can let Davenant know that from me. If I find anything of the like in here again, it will be the presses.'

Having put the one printed title sheet of Davenant's work into his bag, Seeker made his way back on to the alley, with the printer still nodding gratefully. 'And remember that sermon,' he called over his shoulder. 'Tomorrow, at the latest.'

Back out on Ludgate Hill, the sounds and faces seemed clearer to Seeker, sharper than they had been earlier. Behind each pair of eyes were secrets, in each hand the possibility of threat, danger. The thoughts and words born in men's minds and given form and life by the printing houses could not be

properly controlled. Cromwell himself didn't fully understand the danger: he was not yet secure enough in the seat
of power that the likes of Davenant could be released from
the Tower to take up his pen again and scribble what they
pleased. He might never be secure enough.

The cold of the morning made no difference to the traffic
and footfall on the streets. The place teemed with purpose,
but no observer might have said what it was. A street vendor
selling hot chestnuts hurled threats at the clutch of barefoot
children drawn to his brazier for warmth, but to little effect,
they were like grains of sand: remove some and more came
pouring in to take their place. The city had no answer to its
stray children but to round them up and put them to Bridewell, sell them, ship them to the colonies, Virginia, the
Somers Islands, to labour till the day they died, which was
often soon. Seeker shook his head as if the thoughts of Elias
Ellingworth and his like might have begun to infiltrate his
mind along with the smell of the printer's ink.

Before he knew it he was almost at Dove Court. At a
cook shop on Old Jewry he bought a dish of potage.

'Where's your dish?' asked the old woman behind the
counter.

'You'll get your dish back,' he'd said, throwing down the
money for the food. Some hawker women eyed him suspiciously as he turned into the court and moved out of his
way. He put on his helmet and started to climb. A low
growling noise reached him from above, and became more
persistent the further he went. As he was almost at the top,

he saw a large shape bestir itself in the gloom. It was a huge hound, a shaggy beast more suited to bringing down deer or wolves in Irish woods than roaming the streets and passageways of London. It was between him and the door to Maria Ellingworth's dwelling. By the time its noise brought Maria to her door, it was standing, its growling unabated. Seeker observed the animal a moment then reached out his hand and said, 'Peace'. The dog whimpered, then lay down.

Maria looked at him, astonished. You might have lost your hand,' she said, 'glove or no.'

Seeker was dismissive. 'I know dogs.'

'You keep them?'

He continued looking at the animal. 'Once.'

Neither of them said anything more for a moment, as if the observance of the dog had been the sole purpose of the encounter. Eventually Maria said, 'Come in, if he will let you, but he has allowed no one else over this door these three days.'

Seeker moved past the animal, watching it all the time, as it did him.

'The beast isn't known to you?' he asked.

She shook her head. 'He appeared behind me as I left Kent's three days ago and has followed me everywhere ever since. He never comes in anywhere, always lies outside at the door. I wish I had something to give him.'

'He'll go looking for food when he's hungry, no doubt.' He looked around him. 'You have nothing here?'

'I've been eating at the coffee house,' she said.

'Kent's?'

'Yes. It is after all where you told me to go.'

'But you're not there now,' he said.

'Your powers of observation are indeed very great, Mr Seeker.'

He ignored the barb and set the lidded dish from the cook shop down on the table. 'There's some food there, if you want it.' He looked around the room. 'You don't keep this room warm enough.'

Her eyes were fixed on the steaming dish, incomprehension on her face.

'You brought that for me?' she said eventually.

He walked over to the window to look out into the courtyard below. 'I thought you would be hungry. With your brother in the Tower, I didn't know how you would be provided for.' He could feel her eyes, with their look of astonishment, now fixed on his back. 'You would do better to stay at Kent's.'

This was firmer ground for both of them. 'How did you know I wasn't there?'

He turned back, set his helmet on the table. 'Little passes in this city that I'm not aware of. People think it to be a place of secrets, but secrets exist to be found out.'

She fetched a spoon and lifted the lid from the dish. 'It was no secret that I came home – I will return to Kent's this morning. I just thought it strange that you should know even that.' She waited a moment. 'Do you wish some of this?'

He shook his head.

'Might I give a little to the dog?'

'Do what you will with it, but he doesn't look the sort that eats anything other than meat.'

She spooned some of the warm food on to a tin dish and set it aside to cool near the window, where the greatest draught came in, then sat down to eat herself. 'Thank you,' she said.

The words took Seeker by surprise, and he realised with a jolt that it was because he so seldom heard them, because he so seldom had cause to hear them. He was not sure he trusted himself to make any response.

She took a couple of spoonfuls and then said, 'You haven't come with news for me about my brother, have you?'

'Only that of two others who were thought suspect, a Scotsman and a Dutchman, one is missing, and one dead.'

She put down her spoon. 'The ones from the coffee house? Which dead?'

'The Scotsman.'

'By the same hand that killed Lieutenant Winter?'

He swallowed. 'No,' he said. 'But neither is a good thing for your brother. The field narrows.'

'You cannot help him, then,' she said blankly.

'If he will not help himself.'

Seeker lifted his bag from the wooden seat he had set it on, and took from it the title page he had confiscated at the printer's shop. 'Does this mean anything to you?'

She looked at the sheet, traced her finger over the image

as Seeker had done, smelled the freshness of the new-printed paper. 'It's from Clarkson's, off Paternoster Row. I know his mark. He is an honest man. Seeker, he will not be mixed in with this murder.'

'Has your brother ever done business with him?'

She shook her head. 'Jeremiah Clarkson won't touch anything from Elias.'

In that at least the printer had been honest then.

'And what of Davenant?'

'William Davenant? What about him?'

'Has your brother, to your knowledge, had any dealings with him?'

This time Maria laughed outright. 'Elias and Sir William Davenant? Dear Lord, Seeker, have you truly no idea of our lives, in what circles we move? Davenant that put on masques for the King's court? That was a lieutenant-general in the King's army? Of what interest might such a man have been to Elias?'

Seeker shrugged. 'Davenant was born humble enough. An innkeeper's son. There is no King nor court for him now.'

'Is there not?' said Maria tautly.

Again he did not rise to the bait. 'Elias never discussed his writings?'

'Not that I recall.'

'*The Tempest*, even?'

She frowned. 'That was written by his godfather, Seeker. Will Shakespeare. Did you never have plays in the North?'

Across Seeker's mind flitted an image, a vague memory of

a troupe of players in a clearing in the forest, many years ago, sunlight dappling through the leaves. The memory was quickly dismissed.

'We saw it once as children,' she went on when he didn't answer, 'before the theatres were shut. An apt piece for our times, some would say. What does it signify?'

'Davenant is at work on a musical version, he claims it is for the Protector.'

'What?' She laughed in disbelief. 'Oh, but surely, that is too good! He will sing to Oliver of a ruler restored to his rightful inheritance? I would pay good dear money to see that!'

Still he did not rise to it.

'Did your brother possess a copy of the play? Speak of it at all, of anyone who did speak of it?'

'Elias speak?' She pushed the dish away from her. 'Elias does little but speak, and write. You really do not understand my brother, do you, Mr Seeker? You do not understand our world. In this liberty your Cromwell would impose on us, that is no liberty, the only freedom we have is in our heads, and in our speech, when amongst friends. But that is where Elias differs from the rest of us, where he is better than we are, for Elias does not ask if a man be friend or foe before he speaks to him, and speaks freely.'

She had excluded him, Seeker, so easily, so thoroughly from that 'we', from her world.

'I asked you if you ever heard your brother speak of this play.'

She flinched slightly at his coldness, sat up more rigidly. 'I – yes, I did.' She remembered now. 'It was only a few days ago, last week. I was at the coffee house – Kent's – helping Grace with the preparation of some herbs she uses in bracket and aromatick and the like. A merchant was in from the Exchange, complaining about the Virginia trade, the need for greater order on the plantations in Bermuda. It was soon evident that by better order he meant greater harshness of masters on workers, and more street children to be sent. George Tavener argued against the sending of children, and of course Elias was soon talking about the enslavement of men. It was not long before the talk was of foreign empires, the claims of the natives and whether they were savages or had the rights of free men. Tempers were rising, but thank the lord for Will Fiddler, he began to act out Caliban, the savage in the play, and soon all was reminiscence of the days of the theatres, and laughter, and argument over whether the Cockpit was more rowdy than Blackfriars, and who the finer Falstaff.' She was smiling now, and turned thoughtful eyes on Seeker. 'And so, yes, Elias did speak of this play, and in his words I saw Virginia, and felt the heat of Bermuda, I heard the laughter and the cat-calling of the crowd, and saw the finest actors bestride stages that now lie empty and silent. I tasted cherries and nuts and oysters from the girls with their baskets at the theatre doors.' She passed her hand over the title page again and looked directly at him. 'And I wept for a monster who had not known he was one until his master rendered him so.'

He felt as if he had been hit in the stomach, because he knew those last words had been for him. There was a brief moment of silence, a hiatus, between them, and then he pushed a sheaf of paper towards her and put the quill from her brother's inkpot into her hand. 'The names of those involved in the discussion of this play.'

She did not move. 'You make a great assumption in handing me a pen.'

'I don't think I do, Mistress Ellingworth. Now write.'

Once she had done so, he blotted the list with a scrap of her brother's paper and placed the sheet, with the title page of Davenant's *Tempest*, in his bag and left, the hound growling as he put on his helmet and disappeared down the dark stairway.

It felt colder in her small room now, and Maria Ellingworth put on her shawl before lifting the dish of potage from beside the window and setting it down by the dog at the door. He sniffed at it a moment, before turning his head away. An hour later, as she was leaving for Kent's, she saw that he still hadn't touched it.

SEVENTEEN

The Players

Seeker had intended only a brief visit to Kent's that afternoon, to question Samuel on one or two matters, but what Samuel told him had made him tarry a little longer.

Samuel had been seated on a stool behind the serving counter, absently wringing a drying-cloth in his hands. The sudden hush in the din of the coffee room made him look up, just for a moment. 'It's you, then, Captain.'

He seemed to Seeker to have aged about ten years since last he had seen him. Samuel made to stand up but Seeker indicated by a twitch of his hand that it wasn't necessary.

The old man looked at him, utterly defeated. 'I have nothing left to tell you that I haven't already told your men. I never saw that West Country fellow before the day he came in and sold me that painting and I haven't seen him since. I didn't ask his name and he didn't tell it. And as for Sir Gwyllm Crowther, I never heard of him in my life, and he's never set foot in my coffee house whatever she might say.' His eyes travelled towards the ceiling.

Seeker glanced upwards. 'She? Your niece?'

Kent shook his head. 'No, that John Winter's wife, I mean.'

Seeker leaned on the counter. 'She is here?'

'Every day since Grace fell ill. Nursing her, bringing her medicines, warm blankets. Looks as if she wouldn't be the worse of some nursing herself, sometimes. Can't say I'm easy with it, but she turns up, stays an hour, then leaves when Maria arrives. Those two don't have much to say to each other. Too alike, maybe.' He leaned a little closer to Seeker. 'The boy there don't think she's right in the head – Anne Winter, I mean – and I can't say I think he's wrong. Shock of her husband, I suppose.'

Seeker grunted. 'Does she still try to talk to the coffee-drinkers?'

'No,' said Samuel. 'Knocked all that on the head on the second day. Still looks like she'd like to, though.'

The wooden stairway to Grace's chambers was hardly wide enough to accommodate Seeker's shoulders, the steps too narrow for his feet. He'd seen men – women too – with broken necks at the feet of stairs such as these. A trip in the half-dark, carrying a heavy bundle. The procurement of death could be very easy.

The door to Grace's room was not locked. Seeker knocked, but receiving no reply gradually pushed it open. The light was a little better than on the stairs, but still too poor to bring the room into any sort of definition. He noticed the place didn't have the sour, warm stench of the sickroom, but a cleaner aroma, from the many sprigs of herbs hung from the ceiling and the infusion of lemon and thyme burning in a lamp on the dresser by the room's one tiny window. The candle at Grace's bedside was good bees-wax, not the cheap stinking tallow that made almost every home reek with the odour of old mutton fat.

Anne Winter was leaning over Grace, talking to her. She didn't turn at the sound of Seeker coming in, but continued to whisper the comforting words into the sleeping girl's ear. She was wearing a simple black woollen dress with plain white collar, and yet to Seeker everything about her spoke of privilege.

'Why do you come here?' he said.

His voice startled her, but she mastered herself quickly enough, sitting up straighter, adopting that look on her face that was always ready to give battle. Seeker had wondered at Samuel Kent thinking Anne Winter and Maria to be in any way alike, but he saw it now: defiant women; women pre-pared to be alone.

'I might ask you the same question.'

'I hardly think so,' he replied. 'Again: why do you come here?'

She allowed a softening in the mask of her face. 'John said you were not a man to be worn down. I come here because she was kind to me, and I have met few enough women since I was brought to London that I would have cared to call friend. Her uncle, as you must see, is hardly fit to care for her as she is just now, and the girl Ellingworth helps in the coffee room, which I cannot. There seems to be little else I can do of good. Who else has need of me?'

There was no self-pity in the question: it carried in itself an assertion of fact. No one else needed Anne Winter, no one at all.

He moved closer to the bed and looked at the girl lying there. In sleep she did look like the girl she must have been a few years ago, before womanhood and the work of the city had begun, as he thought it had, to erase her bloom. 'Has she spoken yet?'

'She murmurs. I can make little sense of it. I think she talks of Elias.' She looked up at him. 'She's in love with him, you know. God knows what word of his death will do to her.'

'It may not come to that,' said Seeker.

Anne Winter had just dampened a linen cloth in a bowl of rosewater and had been about to dab it on Grace's forehead. She stopped, the cloth still in her hand, dripping scented drops on to the crewel-work coverlet. 'What do you mean?'

'You told me yourself your husband was dead before Ellingworth ever came upon him.'

'And have you found someone else?' Her voice was trailing away.

'I will. I am determined he will not hang for something he didn't do.'

Anne Winter let the cloth drop altogether. 'But how can

you stop it? Indeed word in Whitehall is that little more is being done to find another suspect, and that you have been told' – she seemed to lay an unintended emphasis on the word – 'to see to other things.'

Seeker's reply was forestalled by a voice from the open doorway.

'I do not think you properly understand the Captain. I think he is a man who will hold to what he believes is right, whether it suits others or no.' It was Maria Ellingworth, and although the light was very dim, when Seeker turned to look at her, he thought that she was smiling.

It was not a great deal later that Lady Anne left Kent's coffee house to make her way back out into the city. She left not by the main door from the coffee room on to Birchin Lane, but through the storeroom and the small back yard, out at the gate into St Michael's Alley. It had been at Maria's suggestion, who had told her blankly that it did no good to her name or that of the coffee house for her to be seen emerging from the front door of Kent's as if she had spent the morning taking her pipe and discoursing on the affairs of the world with all the men who went there.

She passed quickly up the alley, envying those who thronged the booths around the churchyard, doing business, gossiping, laughing with their neighbours. Time enough for that yet. Once out on to Cornhill, she scanned the crowd for Seeker's form, and could not see it, and so stepped out into the path of someone she had not been looking for.

The man in the russet woollen suit and cap stopped just in time to prevent a collision. His hat was whipped off in a second, accompanied by the best bow he could make, given the circumstances of the heavy pack on his back. He was grinning broadly.

'Your Ladyship.'

She looked at him in some astonishment. 'You . . . were at the coffee house . . .'

'Will Fiddler,' he reminded her, still grinning, 'peddler.'

'Yes,' she said slowly, recalculating, 'yes, of course.'

'Yes,' he smiled, encouraged. 'But I am heartily sorry to hear of the death of your husband. If there is anything I can do for your Ladyship, you have only to let me know.'

'You,' she said, still somewhat dazed.

'Yes,' he repeated. 'There is nothing to be got in London that Will Fiddler cannot get for you, no one to be found that he does not know where to find. You will not lack a friend, or a help in this city, if you but say it is needed.'

'Thank you,' she said, staring at him, feeling that somehow this offer merited some sort of like declaration from herself, but completely at a loss for what that should be.

'But,' he said, taking a step closer to her and lowering his voice, although already she had trouble hearing him over the clatter and endless rumble of the streets, 'the alleyways of the city are not a safe place for a lady to wander alone. Take a hackney back to Whitehall, Lady Anne.'

'Where my husband was murdered at our door? I think I am safer here.'

'Then to Baxton, as soon as you can, for the word is Cromwell has given you Baxton. Better back to Oxfordshire, where you have friends.' He had said it himself, and it was said of him, there was nothing passed in London without Will Fiddler knowing it.

'I would rather,' she said slowly, 'exchange Oxfordshire, where too many of my friends met their deaths, for London, where they might safely come. I am selling Baxton Hall, and will buy me a home in the city, and here do some good, perhaps.' She took a breath, committed herself. 'So if you should hear of a place, where one such as I might establish her household and do some good, I would be glad if you would let me know.'

The peddler, usually so garrulous, so eager to help always, said nothing, merely took a step back, bowed low to Anne Winter again, and receded back into the crowd.

Archibald Campbell left by the main door on to Birchin Lane. He walked quickly, away from the streets where the money glinted in the sun as it passed from the hands of one merchant to another, eastwards, and down towards the river that was the source of that wealth. The closer Campbell got to it, the more conscious he became of the heavy rhythm of the world, bearing its goods incessantly to London, taking away what London didn't want. Everywhere there was hurry, urgency: cranes, carts, baskets on men's and women's backs, even the rats were busy carrying off the booty of the world that the wind and the tide brought to these docks. At last he found himself in the taverns of Wapping, where every second voice spoke in a different tongue. No coffee houses here, no endless airy prattle of newsmen and lawyers: the dirt of men's work was not hidden here, but showed on their faces, their hands. About him were men and women of every known race. Campbell thought that if each could but draw a map of what they had seen, a map of the world complete would be had in the streets of Wapping.

Sailors always remembered the ships they had sailed in, where they had gone, what they had carried. In the third tavern, he struck lucky. That ship he was asking about, oh yes, it had sailed to Barbados then, twice a year it went. The merchants? He should ask the Spirits, they would know. And then they had laughed – he was a man of God, a preacher, a prophet maybe. Surely he was used to talking to the Spirits?

He let them have their laugh, bought them another tot of rum, and they told him what he needed to know.

'The office-keeper, that's who you need. Don't need to get your own hands dirty if you've got the money, eh? Let them deal with the Spirits – best not to get too close to the Spirits. William Thiene, up at Smithfield. Shoemaker to trade, so the sign over his shop says, at any rate.' The sailor had laughed, a deep gurgle that had some of the sea in it. 'Aye, shoes. Will Thiene'll see a man shod soon enough.'

The stench and noise of Smithfield took Campbell back thirty years, to the great market of Scotland at Perth, and he and his father at the end of their long drove, with their good black beasts ready for auction. He wasn't here to see about the selling of beasts though, rather of men.

The smell wasn't so different. Not just the dung, the butchered flesh, the hides waiting to be carted off for the tanners. No: in the streets and lanes around Smithfield, as beasts jostled with men for room on their relentless drive to death, Campbell smelled fear. And he knew that too, the fear of death, the unstoppable stampede towards it. He had heard dying men screech like hogs, known injured men stagger around like dazed bulls, ready to charge at whatever might come in their path, seen the same look in a man's eye as he did now in a heifer being driven onwards to the butcher's cleaver.

By the time he found his way to Thiene's shop at the sign of the cobbler's last in Hosier Lane, his own boots were filthy with the detritus of condemned animals. The boots ranged for display in the front shop window were workmen's boots, built to withstand the grind and grime of those who lived and laboured here. Campbell pushed open the door nonetheless. A young girl sat behind the counter, peering closely at the soft leather into which she was stitching a buckle. At the sight of him, she jumped down from the stool and passed through a curtain into the workshop behind, calling for her father.

William Thiene was there a minute later, a small man with wiry arms and toughened fingers, his leather apron on and his sleeves rolled up. There was a stoop to his back, so that he seemed to regard Campbell suspiciously from the start.

'What is your need, Sir? I have no clergyman's boots here. Williams on Sermon Lane is where you want to go for that.'

'I am not here for clergyman's boots,' said Campbell. 'I will be travelling soon, to the Caribbean, Barbados, and am in the market for supplies to sustain me there.'

The man wiped his hands on his apron, spoke carefully. 'The requirements of a clergyman are different in the Caribbean to what they are here in London, I am sure.'

'That's what I have been told,' replied Campbell. 'My glebe at home in Scotland was easily enough worked to supply my wife and me in our manse with our wants, but in Barbados I am to have a hundred acres, and sugar cane is a different crop from peas and kale.'

The shoemaker was still careful. 'No doubt you will have men to work your land for you, as all the gentlemen do.'

'Indeed,' said Campbell. 'That is my wish, but it is a question of where to find them, and for that I am presently at a loss.'

The shoemaker's daughter, who had been standing by the curtain all this time, said to her father, 'Should I tell mother to light the fire in the parlour?'

'Aye,' said her father, removing his apron and watching Campbell all the while. 'And you fetch two glasses and my Madeira wine. I am sure the gentleman would take a sip of my Madeira wine?'

Campbell nodded once and followed the shoemaker.

There were three apprentices busy in the workshop – one carefully cutting a length of leather with a small and lethal knife, a second bent over the last, and a third hammering a heel to a left boot. They had all looked up when their master entered the workshop, and all looked away as quickly when they saw his apron was off and that he had someone with him who was on other business than theirs.

Thiene led the way up a wooden staircase at the back of the workshop, and noticed Campbell glancing at a small, heavily bolted door set under it as he did so. 'Cellar. I'm careful of my goods, Mr . . .?'

'Morrison,' said the Scotsman, 'The Reverend Walter Morrison.'

The details were agreed quickly enough. Eight men and two women, all to be over fourteen years of age, the men below fifty, the women free of disease and below forty. It would be forty shillings apiece – Thiene had his overheads, and the risk was all his, after all. He would have to pay his Spirits fifteen shillings apiece at the very least, and then there would be the paperwork. The paperwork must be done right, the signatures or the marks secured. That was why they called him the office-keeper – everything would be right. There was hardly a living to be made in it nowadays, if he was being honest. 'Not like the old days, the war and all.'

'The war?' asked Campbell.

'Aye. A ready supply for the plantations was to be had then. You see, the Irish are all very well to be cleared out and shipped off, leave that country to proper Christian government. All fine and good for Ireland, but the gentlemen of the plantations have learned their measure and I'll tell you straight – they don't want 'em. Start a fight in an empty barrel, half of them, not to be trusted. And always mumbling in that heathen tongue. Idolaters, Sir. Your own countrymen were better, at least they were proper Christians, Sir. But that all stopped when the war stopped – no more prisoners being marched down from the North. Made a few fortunes, that did.'

'Oh?' said Campbell, surveying the miserable parlour with a degree of scepticism.

'Oh, not me, Sir,' laughed Thiene. 'Did all right, though; learned my trade then properly, the buying and selling, the merchants that would give the best prices, how to keep the costs down, keep the paperwork right. A middleman you might call me. You ask any of them, some of the most respectable gents in the town,' and he named some of the merchants for whom he acted after Dunbar and Worcester, 'and they'll tell you: you can trust William Thiene.' He leaned towards Campbell, grinning over his foul Madeira like a gargoyle with a goblet: 'Made them fortunes, I did. Fortunes.' As he reminisced on the ships he had filled, and for whom, and the ships he had filled again, to meet the relentless demands of the tobacco plant and the sugar cane, Campbell wished for his business to be swiftly concluded.

'Some of the merchants don't seem to understand, though, that it's a different game now,' went on Thiene.

'Government won't allow children from the streets and Bridewells any more – what else is to be done with them, I ask you? No easy supply of battle leftovers either, and the gents in Virginia aren't too keen in obliging us in the emptying of our gaols. They still want the labour though, and that's where Will Thiene has to take the risks.'

'How so?' asked Campbell, feigning an agreeable level of ignorance.

Thiene leaned closer, his sour breath mingling with the acrid smoke of the mediocre fire between them. 'The Spirits. Mine are the best in the business. Follow drunken men from taverns, or new-arrived strangers from the coffee houses. Befriend them, offer them a roof for the night, good employment. Women out on their own – well, they ask for it, don't they? And then they bring them here, this very room, and I get them to sign the papers. They'll be down that cellar before they know it, and shipped down to Wapping or St Katharine's at the bottom of a cart-load of hides the next day. They're in the hull of a ship before anyone notices they're missing, if they notice at all. Not legal, Sir – not strictly legal, and that's the risk. I might see myself in the magistrates' court, and risk a fine, but don't you worry, Sir, I'd never name my gentlemen.'

Later, at Kent's, Campbell warmed his hands around a piping dish of coffee. He paid little attention to the conversations going on around him, taken up instead with the thoughts racing around in his own mind. He must be careful, careful, plan everything exactly. And there was his sermon still to write too, well, he knew his text for that. The words whirled themselves together in his head, though, and the ideas came to him at such speed that he had scarcely the time to write them down on the paper he had demanded from the coffee house boy. He wrote until the last of the other drinkers rose to leave, and Samuel told him it was time that he, too, went to his lodgings. And yet, despite the hours he had spent there, while the brewing coffee had sent its charred and bitter scents out on to the streets, and pipe after pipe of best Virginia tobacco had been smoked so that one end of the coffee room was scarcely to be seen from the other, when he finally passed through the doorway and out into the night, Archibald Campbell still carried the smell of Smithfield about his person.

In the fine house on Cheapside, as Mirjam slept, George Tavener paced the floor, checking locks on doors and window shutters. He would not sleep tonight.

'For God's sake, Tavener,' Seeker had said when Tavener had told him of it that afternoon, 'why do you think your house is being watched? You are a rich man in a city where men watch their wives starve and see their children go with rags on their backs. Have you more than you need? Aye, that you have. Take order with yourself, put better locks on your doors, hire watchmen for the night. Have a pistol by your bed if you must, but I have greater concerns than protecting your gold.'

'As have I,' Tavener had insisted. 'It is my wife, not my gold that he watches.'

Seeker had been silent a moment, and the air, the bustle of the street around them outside Kent's, had seemed to still, until it was only those two in this whole city of half a million souls that breathed, that spoke. There had been something in Seeker's expression that Tavener had never seen there before. 'Then look to your wife,' the soldier had said at last, 'because if another man is watching her, and she takes a mind to watch him back, it may be the last you ever see of her.'

And so two men of the Watch were at the back door of his house, another two at the front. Another walked the lane behind their garden, for George Tavener had the money to pay for it all. But still he would not sleep. He would watch over Mirjam himself: no other could be trusted, and somewhere in his mind, George Tavener knew that he had brought this on her.

*

In Knight Ryder Street, the carpenter did not sleep either. His room was too quiet, too empty without the dog. But the beast was keeping watch over the girl in Dove Court, and would do so until told otherwise. Thoughts of other things came into his mind, and he knew he would not sleep until he had banished them. He took his knife, and a piece of wood from the basket in the corner, and began to carve.

EIGHTEEN

Dreamer of Dreams

8 November

In his chambers overlooking the Cockpit in Whitehall Palace, Damian Seeker was reading a sermon with Archibald Campbell's name at the top of it, the one he had seen Will Fiddler deliver to the printer on Ivy Lane just the previous day. It had been brought to him in the early morning – the printer was no fool, and had cleared his presses of all other work until the soldier's commission was completed.

Seeker turned the pages that had kept Clarkson and his pressmen up until the early hours, and he could feel his blood quickening. Something was not right. He pulled open the door to the ante-chamber where only one young officer was in attendance at this time. 'Bring me a bible,' he said. 'Now.'

As ever with the Presbyterians, the sermon was littered with biblical quotations, lengthily exposited upon, to vindicate the minister's own vision of man and God. But when Seeker looked at the texts accompanying the later quotations, he knew that they were wrong: in number and title they were wrong.

It was a King James Bible – Cromwell had not meddled with that, and it was clear from the early, correct quotations in the sermon that that was what Campbell had been using too.

Seeker took the sheets of the printed sermon and the bible, with its tiny type, over to a table beneath a window, where the low winter sun was casting some welcome light. From here he could see down on to the edges of the park and the beginnings of green, open spaces. He seldom allowed himself to gaze too long upon those spaces.

He took the sermon line by line, slowly at first, but then, as he grew certain, more quickly. From about a third of the way in, the references were all wrong, some out by a line, some out by three or more. What also became increasingly clear to Seeker, when he consulted the notes of the two soldiers he had sent to listen to Campbell that night, was that the references had not been wrong when Campbell had first penned his sermon. The misattributions were a cypher, added between the delivery of the sermon to the Scotsman's delightedly terrified congregation and the delivery of its text to the printer's workshop off Paternoster Row.

Seeker slowly put down his eyeglass. 'Will Fiddler.'

He was still seated in that attitude of contemplation by the window when Thurloe arrived three minutes later.

'Well?' said the Secretary.

Seeker passed him the sermon. 'It's a coded message. I

don't know the cypher yet, but it's contained in the biblical references. They are not accurate and don't correspond to the sermon as delivered by Archibald Campbell in his church.'

Thurloe didn't ask how Seeker could be so sure of this, Thurloe rarely wasted time asking Seeker to justify himself. 'And the use of the sermon?'

'Twenty copies ordered from Clarkson's off Paternoster Row, by Will Fiddler.'

Thurloe frowned. 'Twenty? Hardly worth the printer's while, surely.'

'He paid the price for a hundred, but only wanted twenty made up.'

'But the peddler? You are certain?'

Seeker worked his jaw. 'I am. He is to collect them from the printer this afternoon. I'll warrant they are for dissemination to selected parties.'

Thurloe was already turning towards the door. 'Have him brought to me when you bring him in.'

'I had not intended to bring him in,' said Seeker.

Thurloe stopped, turned back. 'Seeker, you cannot leave this man in play.'

'Another day yet. That's all I'll need.'

'They'll take longer than that in the Cypher Room.'

Seeker shook his head. 'Dr Wallis arrived in town from Oxford yesterday; he's at his house in Fenchurch Street. He'll have the thing broken by dinnertime. Fiddler won't tell us anything if we bring him in now. I'm for letting him pick up the sermons from the printer's, and watching who he gives them to, where they're delivered, then picking the whole crew up; we'll have twenty men instead of one, and of those twenty, I guarantee I'll break at least a dozen.'

A considered nod showed Thurloe could see the sense in the plan.

'In the meantime,' continued Seeker, 'Campbell is to give another sermon tonight. We'll see if Fiddler takes it to the printer's again and how he alters it. By that time we'll have the cypher, and learn a good deal more about whatever he and his co-conspirators intend to undertake. Then we'll have to take him in, any longer and their plot might begin to gather force.'

Thurloe was now convinced. 'You have all the men you need?'

'Another dozen.'

Thurloe nodded. A copy of the sermon was in his hand. 'I'll get this to Wallis now.'

Less than an hour later, Seeker was again at Clarkson's print shop, giving the printer his instructions. He was to pass the twenty copies of the sermon as ordered to Will Fiddler when the peddler came for them that afternoon. Should anyone else come to collect them, the printer's devil was to go immediately out into the street and tell Seeker's man, who would be opposite the end of the lane in the guise of a stockfishmonger, and point the fellow out to him when he emerged back out of the alley with the sermons. Not the slightest breath of this was to reach Will Fiddler, on the pain of both their lives. The penalties for abetting a traitor were, he reminded them, worthy of their grimmest woodcut.

More, when Fiddler came to them with a new sermon from the Scottish minister, they were to waste no time in handing it to Seeker's man, manuscript as it was, instantly. They were not to as much as begin preparing it for print. They were not even to read it.

By the time Seeker had finished issuing his instructions, utter silence had fallen in the print shop. Though they didn't understand what they'd become involved in, the gravity of it was all too clear to the master printer and his workmen. Most had faces white as parchment and not a word to say, but then, as Seeker was about to leave, the master braved a word.

'The Sparrow is out then, I see. Who have you got instead for John Winter?'

Seeker froze. 'What did you say?'

The man shrank back a step, evidently regretting having spoken. He held a shaking hand towards Seeker, in which was held a slight and badly printed pamphlet. 'This,' he said. 'Started appearing around St Paul's this morning. See' – he pointed to the bottom of the title page – 'it's marked "the Sparrow".'

The girl was almost of a mind to call in the dog.

'I bid you lower your voice. I would not have my neighbours know my every business.'

'Your business?' Seeker slammed the pamphlet down on

the table. 'They have but to stop the nearest street-hawker, step into the first coffee house they come to, to know your business. What were you thinking of?'

It had taken Seeker very little time indeed to track down the author of the latest pamphlet purported to have been written by the Sparrow. The printer on Sermon Lane whose mark had been on the back page hadn't even considered dissembling: Ellingworth's sister had brought it to him. When Seeker had arrived at Dove Court, Maria had boldly confirmed that she had penned the thing.

'I—'

But he was not ready for her to say anything more yet. 'Is this the first time you have done this? Or do you write all your brother's pamphlets? Have you any idea the danger you set yourself in? The threats the Protectorate faces? Your brother is held in the Tower over the murder of a senior army officer; a plot against the Protector, involving men your brother was known to have spoken with in Kent's, has just been uncovered in Oxford; another by another of his acquaintance from that coffee house found to be brewing, and you think this the time for the Sparrow's sister to set herself up as a critic of the state?'

Maria's interest was taken. 'Another plot? Who?'

Seeker had gone too far. 'Nothing. You must say nothing of it, but for God's sake woman, what do you mean by this?' He picked up the pamphlet he had thrown down, scanned it again, and read, 'Tyrant in a Prophet's clothing: Oliver Cromwell, Dreamer of Dreams.'

'It is a play upon the book of Deuteronomy, where it warns against the rise of a prophet, a dreamer of dreams.'

'I *know* what it is,' said Seeker.

'Well, you cannot deny that the Protector has set himself up as such, it is in every speech he makes.'

Seeker ignored this. 'Do you know how that passage progresses? Do you know what it advocates?'

She bridled a little. 'I know my Bible well enough, Mr Seeker.'

'I do not think so,' he said.

'How so?' she challenged him.

He laid the pamphlet aside again. 'The passage speaks of a false prophet, "and that prophet, that dreamer of dreams, shall be put to death". Is that what you seek, Maria, is that what you wish to stir up?'

She sat down in her chair, genuinely shocked. 'Surely you cannot believe that?'

He sighed heavily and sat down opposite her, the first time he had done so in that room. 'No, but that is how it will be read.'

'I only wanted to rouse people, to help Elias, to show how Cromwell's promises have come to nothing, when an innocent man finds himself in peril of execution . . .'

Seeker knew now that she had done nothing like this before, that there was a naïvety in her that, for all his revolutionary ardour, her brother lacked. He brought his voice very low, conscious, as she had said, that little could be kept private in these rabbit warrens of city houses, room piled upon room, floor upon floor, with little thought in their construction than should they fall down, they could be thrown up again, and filled up again as cheaply, lives and all. 'You cannot speak of rousing the people. It will be taken for sedition. The army – and I know whereof I speak – is at a state of tension and waiting to snap. The murder of John Winter has left all uneasy. Should anything befall Cromwell, your brother's throat will be the first cut. You must do nothing more to draw attention to yourself, do you understand me?'

She nodded, lost. 'I don't think there is anything else to be done for him.'

Seeker did not move to contradict her. Thurloe had made it plain that, proof or not, Ellingworth would be scapegoated sooner or later, and that Seeker's objections had had their time. The only thing now keeping Elias Ellingworth from a traitor's death – and Cromwell had promised that that was what it would be – was Winter's widow's insistence that her husband had died in her arms, before Ellingworth could ever have come upon him. But Anne Winter's stock in Whitehall, dependent entirely on her husband, had never been very high and was tumbling by the minute.

'What has she told you about that night?'

Maria Ellingworth came out of her reverie. 'Who?'

'Winter's wife.'

She looked puzzled. 'Nothing, we don't speak of it.'

'But you must be alone together often.'

'Yes,' she conceded, 'in the room with Grace, but we don't speak of her husband's death. We spoke briefly of Elias, but she does not like to do it in front of Grace because she fears it upsets her and I think she is right. Mind you, I don't think the medicine she brings her does much good either.'

Samuel had also spoken of medicine, but Seeker had paid it little attention at the time.

'I've come upon her once or twice in the act of dropping some liquid from a phial into Grace's mouth. She says it is simply a calming infusion of chamomile and cloves. Elias and I seldom have recourse to the apothecary, but I would not have thought such an infusion could have such a powerful effect.'

Seeker's mind went to what George Tavener had heard of the auction at Bleeding Heart Yard, of the apothecary with whom Anne Winter's addiction had entangled her, of the substances he sold. 'You think she's lying to you?'

Maria had clearly not considered this. 'I can smell the cloves, but as to the rest . . .'

It could be anything. Seeker remembered dried berries, powdered roots, herbs with a hundred different names. There'd been an old witch by Kielder Water who could procure any effect you might wish to pay for. She'd have been long burned by now, that woman. He thought about what Maria had said. 'And how does Grace Kent progress?' he asked at last.

Maria drew a deep breath. 'Very slowly. Her fever is gone, and she sleeps, but it is an agitated sleep.'

'And when she wakes, what does she say?'

Maria was thinking. Eventually, she looked at Seeker, puzzled, the realisation just come to her. 'I don't know. I haven't seen her awake since the day she had her fainting fit under your interrogation in the coffee house.'

Seeker pushed his chair back and began to pace the room in frustration. 'But she must wake. Good God, I mean it has been how many days? Five? How does she eat?' He was unwontedly awkward: 'Make water and all the rest? When is she washed?'

'Anne Winter,' Maria said slowly. 'The night nurse George Tavener got in says Grace never stirs from dusk till dawn, so it's Anne Winter that sees to it. The clockmaker's wife from across the lane helps her sometimes, but sometimes it's just Lady Anne. She comes at the same time every day, just as Grace is showing discomfort and stirring. She tells me to go and help Samuel in the coffee room, that it is no trouble to her to manage, with the old woman to help her. And I go.'

Seeker passed a hand over his brow in frustration: something was only now becoming clear to him that he should have realised a long while ago. 'I have not the time,' he muttered to himself. 'I have not the time.'

Maria got up, took a tentative pace towards him. 'What is it? What do you need me to do?'

Half an hour later, Maria Ellingworth took off her cape and hung it over the back of the chair in Grace Kent's chamber.

The clockmaker's wife had made to leave when she arrived, but Maria stopped her.

'I would talk with you a moment.'

'Talk away, my dear. Haddon doesn't expect me home another hour yet.'

'I want to know what happens when Grace wakes.'

The old woman pursed her lips then smiled. 'Well, my dear, we feed her and clean her and put her to the pot. Like a babe, she is, poor girl.'

'You and Lady Anne.'

'Yes,' the woman affirmed. 'Now, I didn't much take to her at first, I'll tell you, but she's very solicitous of Grace. Mourning takes us all different – I should know, I've buried two husbands before I ever knew my Haddon. It's my view she's pouring all the love for her dead husband into Grace. Caring for her because it's too late to care for him more. And so the world balances out, for your poor brother cannot care for the girl now.'

Maria bit her lip and remembered what Seeker had told her. She must not be drawn on Elias, by anyone, and she must concern herself only with the questions he sought answers to.

'What does Grace say when she wakes?'

'Say?' The old woman thought, and then gave a rueful smile. 'That I can't tell you, my dear. You know, I'm sure she says something, but my ears are an old woman's ears, and I cannot sort through the mumbles and moans for proper words. Besides – now I hope you'll not tell her I say so, for I mean no harm by it – Lady Anne is never done talking to her, like to a babe. Talking her through it all, "What we do now, what we are to do next, there, take your broth, there, sip this, there, sit now while we change your shift, there, all is well, do not trouble yourself, all is well." On and on she runs, soothing, and all I can make out of what poor Grace says is that she asks for Elias.'

The old woman shook her head sadly, and Maria let her go, promising she would wait with Grace until Anne Winter arrived.

NINETEEN

The Watchers and the Watched

On the barge carrying him downriver to Greenwich Seeker felt the breath of ice on the wind and wondered if the Thames would freeze this year. It would do nothing for the order of the city if it did, and make a causeway for all manner of miscreants and rebels. He ran his eye over the instructions from Thurloe. The celebration for the Lady Frances's birthday would take place in two days' time, having been moved from the Banqueting House at Whitehall to what was still called the Queen's House at Greenwich. Seeker was to liaise with the Captains of the Life and Foot Guards over the security of the Protectoral Family.

'Why the change of location so late in the day?' he had asked Thurloe.

'John Winter,' Thurloe had replied. 'If Anne Winter's telling the truth, and Ellingworth didn't kill him, then we have an assassin who already knows his way around Whitehall. We still don't know for certain that the Dutchman Hendricks has left England, and that's a concern. Cromwell's whole family is going to be at this performance, and they'll be exposed. The Committee decided it would be better to move the event away from Westminster, and further from the city, to somewhere more isolated, more easily controlled.'

'Hmmph.' Seeker had not been convinced. He'd studied the lists Thurloe had given him naming everyone who was to be at the Queen's House in two days' time, from the Protector himself down to the meanest scullery maid. Now on the barge on his way downriver, Seeker scrutinised the names again, making a new list of his own, noting the inconsistencies, the improbabilities, and the ill-advised. Oliver delighted in such gatherings, but the thing would be a purgatory for the Lady Protectress; he wondered that Oliver couldn't see it, but she would endure, as she always did.

All the Council of State and leading army officers presently in London would be there; a selection of parliamentarians with whom the generals had not yet quite lost patience; the Secretaries like Thurloe, Meadow, Milton, and more junior officers in their departments: Dorislaus, Marvell. Then there were the 'court' names, for Oliver did have a court. It was a weakness in him, Seeker thought. It was always a weakness, when a leader wished to be loved. Cromwell had won the government of England by conviction and the sword; he had not courted flattery, but now it courted him. A yeoman he had been, who found himself now on a footing with the aristocracy, those who had taken care not to tie themselves too firmly to Charles Stuart's foundering ship. There was Lady Ranelagh, and her brother, Boyle – Seeker knew him for one of the Oxford coffee house mob – his name went on to Seeker's own list of those suspect. And then there was the city: the great, the good, the powerful, the wealthy – all the same in the city. It was no great surprise to Seeker to see George Tavener's name amongst those invited. Besides, Seeker knew Cromwell enjoyed Tavener's company – 'an Englishman's Englishman,' he had told him once. Seeker did not much mind Tavener, but he was not disposed to trust people simply because Oliver liked them. He considered a while, but did not write Tavener's name on his own list.

One name he had had no hesitation about, though, was that of Lady Anne Winter. The invitations had gone out before Winter's death, and as his wife she had been included as a matter of course, for all that it was common knowledge at Whitehall that she was as much for Charles Stuart now as ever she had been. 'Aye, but she'll not come now that her husband is gone,' Thurloe had said. Nevertheless, Seeker had added her name to his list.

What unsettled Seeker most of all though about the gathering at Greenwich was the entertainment itself. A musical recital, an arrangement of songs by Henry Lawes, all under the direction of Sir William Davenant.

'Davenant is hardly five minutes out of the Tower,' Seeker had said.

'By pardon of his Highness,' Thurloe had replied. 'Bulstrode Whitlocke, Henry Lawes, even John Milton had all been petitioning on his behalf long enough. He's an old scoundrel, I'll grant you: dissolute and debauched, but of no more danger than your gloves there.' Thurloe had released a rare smile. 'Less, I should imagine.'

The joke had been lost on Seeker. 'He's a known Royalist, inveterate; Lieutenant-general of ordnance in Newcastle's army, emissary of Henrietta Maria, a smuggler, taken in outright piracy . . .'

'Those days are gone,' Thurloe had interrupted. 'The hospitality of the Tower has done much to improve his view on the world. The man is little more than a laughing stock, a syphilitic old poet who knows when the game's up. He's spent years trying to curry favour with Parliament and now the Protector himself. Oliver thinks this a good opportunity to display his leniency to those prepared to abandon their former allegiances. And besides, the promise of the music intrigues him. If Davenant wishes to find favour with Oliver, he has hit on exactly the way to do it.'

Seeker was still not convinced of the soundness of the plan, but he had other matters to pursue. 'And the players?'

'Dutch,' Thurloe had replied. 'From a performance at their church in Austin Friars. Thoroughly looked into, every one of them. You need not concern yourself with them, Seeker.'

After Thurloe had left, Seeker had thought a long time about their conversation. In particular, he'd thought about the Dutch players and singers who'd performed at the

Sweelinck recital at Austin Friars. He'd thought about those who'd attended, what he himself had seen. Perhaps half an hour after the end of his conversation with Thurloe, Seeker added Mirjam Tavener's name to his list.

And now, as the chill of the river nipped at his fingers, he went over the reports he'd requested on each of the names on that list. Nothing. Nothing he had not already known or that was of any help to him in the present circumstances. But in truth, it was another enquiry that was troubling him most at that moment, more than the biting cold or the sluggardly pace of the oarsmen in their desultory battle with the wind blowing up from the marshes. Before he had left Oxford, he had sent agents into the West Country to make enquiries about John Winter, or rather about John Winter's family. He had sent them to the village of Elstowe, the small settlement where Winter, according to his wife, had once told her he'd grown up. The agents' report had been at the bottom of a pile handed to him by his adjutant that morning, and he had only now been able to read it. No one in Elstowe, nor any other village for a radius of twenty miles, had ever heard of John Winter. And that might have been the end of it, had it not been for the comment of one elderly man in nearby Dunster, scribbled at the bottom of his report by the youngest agent as an afterthought. ' "There were a lad ten year ago or so, disappeared from that village one day, in the time when Goring was besieging Taunton. Some said he went to join Prince Rupert, others that he was for Parliament. No one ever heard more of him, but it was a time when people were happy enough to forget things. His name wasn't Winter though, it was Snow, Evan Snow." '

Seeker read again the name of the village, and sought it in his mind until he found the memory of where he had heard it before.

George Tavener's mind had not been properly on business since Seeker had told him of Hendricks' approach to Mirjam on the night of the Sweelinck recital; since Mirjam revealed a man had been watching her, he had hardly slept. He had repeated to himself over and over again her assertion that she hadn't recognised the man, but it was no good: fears, and suspicions even, had wormed their way into his mind and there begun to gnaw. He summoned the maid Esther to his counting room and dismissed his clerks.

He waited until the door to the counting room had been firmly closed before speaking.

'I want you to tell me about the man who was watching my wife.'

The girl opened her mouth to speak. A slight look of panic came over her face. 'I . . . I don't know who he was, Sir, I swear it.'

'Describe him to me.'

Her cheeks coloured, and, haltingly, she began to repeat once more the vague description of dark clothing, cloak, hood pulled low that he had already had from both her and Mirjam.

'What was his height?' he asked her. 'The quality of his

shoes? No hat but a hood – you are certain?' The girl closed her eyes, as if thinking harder might bring her better answers, but Tavener was not disposed to wait. 'When he was in the garden, you must have had a better view of him then. What of his hair – short or long? His colouring – pale or sallow?'

Tears were now dripping on to the girl's cheeks. She said something he could hardly make out.

'What?'

She tried again. 'It was not the same man.'

George Tavener spoke very slowly. 'What do you mean?' he said.

She looked to the floor as if to find her resolve there and said, 'The man the mistress saw in the garden; he was not the same one I had seen watching the house from across the street.'

Tavener leaned in towards her, terrifying. 'Are you certain?'

She nodded frantically, afraid to look at him.

'And why,' he asked, his voice dangerously low, 'do you tell me this only now?'

Her reply was so badly mumbled he could not make her out.

'Speak up, girl!' he roared.

Half out of her skin, she blurted, 'I didn't wish to contradict the Mistress, to frighten her further.'

'But she had already seen the watcher on the street, had she not?'

A nod.

'So why should she mistake him in the garden?'

The girl was sniffing now, but had raised her eyes from floor to waist level.

'I don't know, Sir. She—perhaps she hadn't such a good view as I, I saw him twice across the street, and she only the once, and then I had a better view of the man in the garden – I was on the second landing, looking out at the window as I was going up the stair with a bucket of coals for your bedchamber. I think the mistress's view must have been obscured by the mulberry bush, but I could see clear over the top of it.'

'And what did you see?' he asked slowly.

'I . . . I think – the way he was dressed – he might have been Dutch, and . . .'

'Out with it!'

She looked at him directly now, her courage taking her to where there was no going back from. 'I saw him watching her, call something. I saw her turn her head in his direction. He called again and she started to walk towards the apple tree, by which he stood. But then Jem came out at the back door and through the yard, and the Mistress seemed to take fright. She looked towards where the man was and . . .'

'And?'

'And she shook her head, Sir, and ran back towards the house.'

The exertion of saying what she had not wanted to say

had left the girl breathless and her face crimson, but the effect of her words on George Tavener was quite different: the colour drained from him and he became unnaturally still. Then his head dropped and his shoulders fell.

'Sir, shall I fetch you something? Mr Tavener, Sir? Some brandy, perhaps?'

But she got no answer. Tavener had forgotten she was there. All he could see was the image of his wife waiting for Jakob Hendricks in his own garden.

The maid set a footstool in front of the chair into which he had slumped, and went quietly from the room. An hour later, the watchmen George Tavener had hired to look to the security of his house had all been paid off and let go to their other business, and a note bearing the words, 'The matter I spoke to you of yesterday is finished now, and I will speak of it no more,' with Tavener's signature at the bottom, was on its way to the chambers of Damian Seeker in Whitehall Palace.

Seeker had arrived in Greenwich, and was making his tour of a house finer than almost any he had entered. He had never been inside the Queen's House before; he'd spent a little time in the garrison of the old royal lodge at Greenwich Castle, and watching Oliver exercise his favourite horses in the tilt yards, but never been inside the house. Oliver had wanted it for a residence, but Thurloe and others had objected: there was too much open parkland to the south, any foreigner of evil intent coming up the Thames would have found little to stop them before Greenwich: the place was not safe enough.

'Not safe enough then and not safe enough now,' murmured Seeker as he made his tour. And yet, for all that, it seemed to him that the Queen's House was like a jewel, a box for jewels, all for one woman, Charles Stuart's queen. Denuded of its painted and sculpted treasures, and of that one woman who now begged her bread from her nephew in Paris, Seeker thought the house must be all the better for it: simple, and clean and beautiful. People who thought they knew him believed he understood little of beauty, that nothing other than function and utility were of interest to him. They had no cause to know it, nor he the wish to tell them. The soldiers who watched him as he stood at the bottom of the magnificent spiral staircase that was girded with iron lilies did not consider for a moment that he did so for any reason other than to assess the difficulties that stairway might put in the way of his protection of Cromwell, the exits and entrances it might allow an assassin. Seeker knew this, and indeed, the security risks of the stairway would have to be assessed. Yet, as he first set eyes on it, he felt for the first time in nine years the sensation of wanting to share that sight, his wonder at it, with someone else. The feeling passed as quickly as it had come, and he continued on his reconnaissance of the place that, for one day and one night, he must render a fortress.

★

Samuel Kent, who had troubles enough, would have wished Archibald Campbell in any other establishment in the city but his. The minister's clothing was becoming grimier by the day, and Samuel could discern a wildness in the man that the drinking of his coffee only seemed to render worse. His discomfort was deepened when Campbell was joined by William Thiene. Samuel had encountered Thiene before, and there was something in the shoemaker from Smithfield that he truly did not like. He wondered what the two might have to do with one another. Thiene took no coffee but some bracket and a pipe. He eyed the coffee boy in such a way that Samuel remembered the rumours he had heard about how Thiene made his money.

'Gabriel,' he said to the boy after Thiene had demanded another pipe, 'do not you go near that end of the table again tonight, the minister and the shoemaker, you understand? And if ever you should see that shoemaker in the street, you run right home here and you don't look back.'

'Is it a wicked man, Samuel?'

'Aye, boy, as wicked as they come.'

The boy did as he was told, and Samuel hobbled to that end of the table to see to those two himself. It was a relief to him when Will Fiddler appeared in the coffee room, and by some contrivance managed to seat himself near to the minister and the shoemaker.

'You're a long way from Smithfield, William Thiene,' Samuel heard Fiddler say.

'And what's that to you?' replied Thiene. 'I may take my pipe where I please, may I not?'

'As long as that's all you take,' Fiddler answered him. 'There's many here would not like the fit of your shoes.'

Thiene would have responded, but Campbell stopped him. 'Ignore that man,' he said. 'I have not the time to waste on his trade of words.'

Fiddler inclined his head to the minister and turned his attention to the coffee-drinkers on the other side of him, who were swapping tales of the young Charles Stuart's debauches abroad. The packman was soon laughing along with the rest, ignoring whatever business the minister and shoemaker were so earnestly contracting.

And that they were engaged on business was evident to Samuel.

'The same amount,' said Campbell.

'For *one*?' said Thiene, somewhat disbelieving.

The minister leaned forward. 'But it must be the right one, the *right* one, or not a penny.'

Ten minutes later, Thiene was gone, leaving Campbell well-satisfied with the exchange.

After Kent's, Campbell returned to wait in his cold church, and watch as his congregation began to press in; he felt his lip curl in distaste at the careful minuet they performed with one another to gain precedence in the pews. There were more of them tonight, drawn no doubt by tales of his vehemence and zeal: that was a satisfaction to him, that more would hear him give his last sermon, his last oration in a house of God.

As the chanting of the first psalm built in power, Campbell took the opportunity to look into their faces. Perhaps there was one in there that God might have sent as an agent of His conciliation, His mercy? More apprentices tonight, huddled together, waiting, eager. But what could they know of conciliation, mercy, revenge?

And then, as the psalm fell silent, Archibald Campbell opened his bible and began to read to them from the book of Exodus, of the bondage of the children of Israel. The congregation listened, already pleased. They knew the story well, they had heard it often enough, in so many sermons on the freedom of the English people from the bonds of the Stuart kings. There was the question of course over who was their Moses, and the fear of false gods: no doubt their gifted new minister would resolve each to their satisfaction and comfort. But, an hour and a half later – sooner than they had expected, but they were glad of it – the congregation stumbled from the church, forgetful of their carefully established precedence, the words of the shrieking Scotsman still ringing in their ears.

It had begun unexpectedly. 'You! You are Egypt!' he informed them. 'You' – he singled out a prosperous-looking merchant, known to have made his fortune in Virginia – 'you are Egypt! "I have surely seen the affliction of my people which are in Egypt and have heard their cry by reason of their taskmasters."' He had lowered his hand and waited a moment, resting his eyes on his confused congregation and said, in a low and terrible voice, '"For I know their sorrows." ' Another merchant was then selected, one not long returned from seeing to his investments in Bermuda. ' "And you will grieve, for I will stretch out my hand and smite Egypt with all my wonders." ' And for the next hour and a half, Archibald Campbell had regaled his listeners, in shocking and astonishing detail, with promises of rivers turned to blood, plagues of frogs, lice and flies, diseases of beasts, pestilence, hail, locusts, darkness and the deaths of their firstborn.

Women fainted, outraged aldermen pulled their families from the pews, schoolboys gaped in awe. On the faces of one or two apprentices was a satisfaction, a delight, born of years of overwork and beatings, on others a blanched horror. The two young apprentices he had noticed there before were sitting together, close to the front and unknown, it appeared, to anyone else. They reminded Campbell of soldiers, and were the last to leave as the near-speechless members of the church council began finding ways to blame each other for this disaster. None dared approach their minister, who was left alone, declaiming to an empty church, the punishments of Leviticus, 'eye for eye'.

Seeker was weary after a long day discussing with the Captain of the Protector's Life Guard how they might render Greenwich a fortress. Satisfied that the Captain had the logistics of that, at least, in hand, Seeker refused the offer of a billet for the night, and took to the fog-bound river once more, pleading matters awaiting his attention in Westminster. And there were indeed matters awaiting his attention there, and food and a warm fire if he should want them.

The lights of Southwark glowed through the freezing fog to the left of him, to his right he fancied his eyes discerned the Tower. Cold stone, damp running down the walls, the unsettling fog snaking under doorways and through windows to bring all manner of insidious suggestions to the prisoner's ears. Was that what it was like tonight for Elias Ellingworth in Sale Tower? Was he at the point yet when the death Seeker was striving to spare him would seem instead like a deliverance? Was he screaming, or did he sit alone in silence?

For London was a place in thrall to silence tonight. The sound of the city bells was muffled by the fog, and the murmur that usually rose from the mass of huddled houses and lanes seemed to have been silenced under it. Seeker wondered about silence, about things unsaid. Kent's coffee house, where there was so much noise, human and mechanic, so much hubbub, was a place of silences. Anne Winter: he had seldom met a woman so capable of, so at ease with, sheer silence. And then there was Grace Kent, who tried to talk, but was not heard. And John Winter himself, who had left behind him what? Nothing. No mark. A silence where tales of childhood and of youth should be.

'Let me off by Fishmongers' Hall,' he said suddenly, 'I have business in the city.'

★

Samuel had been about to close up for the night when Seeker appeared at the door of the coffee house. The soldier accepted a hot liquor of betony.

'Will do good for your head, Captain. I see the way you pass your hand across your forehead. You're troubled.'

Seeker afforded Samuel a brief smile. 'We're all troubled, Samuel. There are too many knots, too many things to untangle in this business of John Winter. Tell me, you came from Exmoor too, did you not? You never heard of a man named Evan Snow?'

Samuel shook his head. 'Means nothing to me,' said Samuel. 'Mind you, I left the place myself before I were twenty. Land wouldn't support two families, and I had no interest in it anyway – left it to my brother, and good luck to him. I wanted to see the world, not spend my life looking at an ox's arse. Saw the world, too, or as much of it as I cared to. Soldiering – you can pick or choose, can't you, Captain? There's always someone'll take on a soldier. But Evan Snow? No, never heard that name before.' Samuel regarded the other man, and saw the soldier. 'You hungry, Captain?'

Seeker appeared to think about it a moment then shook his head. 'No. Thank you,' and Samuel left him to his drink.

As the boy went past with his broom, Seeker stopped him.

'How does Mistress Grace tonight?' he asked.

Gabriel shrugged. 'Same.'

'Is there someone with her now?'

'Just Maria, but she'll be going soon, to her own place.'

'Who sees her back there?'

'Maria? Won't let anyone. Samuel's afraid for her, afraid of the Spirits – Will Thiene was in tonight.'

'Will Thiene? What was he doing in here?'

'Talking to that Scottish minister. Will Fiddler would have joined in with them but they gave him the brush-off quick smart. Samuel says Will Thiene's a runner of Spirits, but even the Spirits wouldn't get past that dog of Maria's.'

'The great hound across the street?'

'Beast must be frozen, but he won't come in. Just lies there all day, watching everything, till she's ready for home.'

Samuel made no objection when Seeker said he wished to look in on Grace again. 'But knock first, Captain. I wouldn't have Maria frightened.'

The room was not as stiflingly hot as it had been on his previous visit, but it still smelled of greenery and fresh herbs.

'You are late about, Mr Seeker,' said Maria, only half glancing round as he stooped beneath the lintel of the door.

'I have been to Greenwich.'

'Not to the Tower then,' she said, looking determinedly at the book she was reading.

'Your brother's trial is set for four days from now. I will see him again tomorrow morning, and try him one more time at the truth. Have you any message for him?'

She thought carefully. 'To hold fast to what is right.'

'And if that message sends him to the gibbet on Tower Hill?'

'Then he will have died honest,' she said.

He made no response, but went to the other side of the bed to look more closely at Grace.

'Has she stirred while you've been here?'

'No,' said Maria, before telling him what she had learned from the clockmaker's wife.

'So Anne Winter will not allow her to be heard.' Seeker was silent a moment, watching the sleeping girl, wondering what dreams she dreamt. His voice was low. 'What is it she will not allow you to tell us, Grace?'

'You think it is that?' said Maria.

'I am certain of it. Anne Winter takes great care that none but herself should know what Grace Kent has to say when she wakes.' He looked at the side table and then the mantel-piece. 'Does she leave any of the medicine?'

'No, she always sees that Grace finishes it; one dose a day.' A sudden fear flitted across Maria's eyes. 'You don't think she's poisoning her?'

'I don't know,' said Seeker. 'I know little enough about poisons, but I cannot imagine there are many that would be this long in taking their effect. Does she ever leave the phial here?'

Maria shook her head.

'Then she must be prevented from administering any more of the compound until its nature is established.'

'How is that to be done?' asked Maria.

'I'll tell Samuel Kent to forbid her access to his niece

unless there is someone else there. You must stop her if he cannot. As for the medicine, I'll see to that.'

Matters of business arranged, the silence that now fell hung heavy between them.

'You read to her?' said Seeker at last, nodding towards the book.

'Sometimes,' she said. 'Although not this. I think she might find it a little disturbing.' She passed him the volume in her hands.

'Mmph. Carleton,' he said, leafing carelessly through it. 'Tales of conspiracies and plots to scare good Protestants to their beds.'

She raised an eyebrow, half mocking, half intrigued. 'And are you not a good Protestant then, Mr Seeker?'

'I am no Papist, if that's what you mean,' he replied, uncomfortable.

She regarded him a moment. 'They say you are from the North.'

'Aye,' he said, his chin up. 'What of it?'

'Many of the sects, in their wild days, before Cromwell put a stop to them with his blasphemy laws, came out of the North did they not?'

'Some.'

'Elias used to speak of it – the woodsmen, itinerant craftsmen and labourers, the dispossessed – they came from the North to the cities and brought with them their ideas, their theories of freedom in religion . . .'

'Those ideas and theories led to the Ranters,' he said, 'with their running around proclaiming themselves Christ, their debauchery, their denial of any way to perfection except through sin.'

'And was there not freedom in it?'

'What? Aye, freedom to drink until they were senseless, to lie with any woman they chose, to live off the work of others – not much freedom for the women they abused, the men they cuckolded, the children they fathered and abandoned to the care of others. You think the objects of their profanities felt themselves free?'

He could see from the astonished look on her face that his vehemence had surprised her.

'But the Ranters came in a time of madness,' she said, 'when the order of the world was turned on its head and the towns and cities filled with masterless men. Before them though, Elias told me, there were sects in the North that had survived centuries – Familists, Quietists, Anabaptists, Seekers—' She stopped. 'You,' she said, 'your name. You were a Seeker.'

He didn't reply.

'I am right though, am I not? You were of one of those sects in the North. You or your family?'

He started to walk towards the door, then stopped. 'The Seekers believe that Heaven and Hell are here amongst us, in this world. Hell, I have seen, but Heaven I have yet to encounter.' He reached for the latch on the door. Maria rose half out of her chair.

'But, I thought – you are taught to wait, are you not, for the suffering Christ to be resurrected within you, for the light? Did you never look for the light?'

'I looked,' he said.

'And?'

He was motionless, his back still to her. 'There was nothing there.'

Back downstairs, Seeker left Samuel more money than was needed for the drink he had had, and made for the door without further conversation, pausing only to put on his helmet before he went out again into the night. The dog gave a low, sustained growl as he passed, but he ignored it, as he did the watchmen and the few travellers abroad on Cornhill. Those who didn't have to be out weren't: the fog brought fear with it, cloaking the comfortable and familiar, leaving instead paths and passageways known only to rats and slithering things, and the malefactors of the night.

Seeker wanted to go home, to be home, to sleep, but the coffee boy's mention of William Thiene, of the Spirits, came back to him and so, at the end of a passageway along from the top of Birchin Lane, he waited and he watched; he watched the end of Birchin Lane and he watched the hound that guarded it. The bells of St Michael's struck a dull ten and soon afterwards the dog stood up, alert, trotting down the lane and emerging again at the heels of Maria Ellingworth. Seeker remained at his post until hound and girl were almost obscured by the fog, and then he began to follow. He could sense the beast listening for him. As the pair turned up Grocer's Hall Court some drunkard lurched out of a tavern and made a grab for Maria. The dog had the man on the ground in seconds, and stood over him, snarling, until the fellow was dragged away by his suddenly sobered companions. The episode was enough for Seeker, and he turned from his silent shadowing and back down to the main thoroughfare, weary for his bed.

It had been a long service at the Dutch church at Austin Friars, and Mirjam Tavener had had to use a great deal of guile, in which she was unpractised, to see off the solicitous attentions of her friends, who had brought her to the church and who would have her come home with them, or accept a ride in their carriage, rather than walk the streets of the city back down to her home on Cheapside. That was not to be thought of. Mirjam had countered one offer with the claim of another, until at last all her friends were gone, each believing her to be safely in the care of someone else.

And then, when she was sure that all who knew her were gone, she had begun to thread her way across the courtyard and through the old cloisters of the Austin Friars, until she found at last the little garden and the well of which the letter had spoken. She could hear creatures moving in the undergrowth and felt suddenly frightened, as she had done as a small child, when her nurse had blown out the candle by her bedside. She had not been frightened in the Weesehouse, for there she had never been alone. The fog had come down heavy even here, encircling the pillars of the cloisters and masking trees and bushes so she could almost believe the monks of centuries ago still walked their precincts. And then one of the figures that she had thought some immovable object did take a step towards her, and as he emerged from the swathes of mist surrounding him, Mirjam Tavener felt the intervening years drift away from her, and she was fifteen again.

TWENTY

Cyphers and Keys

9 November

As ever, a pile of documents – letters, reports, notes from Thurloe – awaited Seeker when he entered his chambers early next morning. He read through them quickly, adding a comment to each before passing it on to those who were to carry out his instructions.

A copy of the transcript of Campbell's sermon of the previous evening was also in front of him, its contents agreed and cross-checked by the two young soldiers he had sent in the guise of apprentices to Goldsmith's Court chapel the previous evening. Seeker raised an eyebrow at the tenor of the minister's lesson – as the soldiers had informed him, Campbell was clearly mad. He paid most careful attention to the biblical references alongside Campbell's graphic and increasingly demented exposition. They all made sense in terms of what Campbell elaborated upon in his text.

'When did he take it to the printer's?'

The man he had left watching over the alley to Clarkson's print shop was still in the guise of a stockfishmonger.

'First light,' said the man. 'Woke the printer with it.'

'And Clarkson has not read it, nor attempted to begin work on it?' asked Seeker.

The man shook his head emphatically. 'Handed it straight to me, Sir.'

Seeker glanced again down the list of references, only two of them scored out this time, and more hurriedly than before.

'Dr Wallis is at the Cypher Office?'

Another soldier by the door nodded.

'Take that to him,' said Seeker, handing the man the copy of the sermon, with the altered references starred. 'Tell him it is of the greatest urgency – the moment it is ready, a copy is to be made for Secretary Thurloe, and another brought to me at the Tower.' He barked at another adjutant: 'You, send to Secretary Thurloe's office – I want warrants out for the arrest of the peddler Will Fiddler.' As he was pulling his cloak from the door he shouted, 'And someone make ready my horse.'

Of all the impediments between Westminster and the Tower, it was the commotion on Cheapside that brought Seeker to a halt. Half the Watch of Cheap ward was congregated at George Tavener's front door, the rest, it soon became apparent, along with some of the city's most prominent aldermen, were inside. Seeker dismounted and handed his horse's reins to the trooper behind him, and the crowd quickly separated to allow him through.

'What's going on here?' he said to the constable who was trying but failing to guard the front door. Before the man could answer him, Seeker began to see for himself. Splintered wood, broken glass, a green Chinese vase smashed on to the black and white Dutch tiles of the entrance hall, and, splattered everywhere, blood.

'Where is George Tavener?' Seeker demanded.

The constable said nothing but directed Seeker with his eyes to the darkened interior of the house. Mirjam Tavener was sitting, like a small ghost, on the bottom step of the great stairway of the house, and she was terrified. In her hands she held the torn remnant of a bloodstained lace cuff. 'This is his. It was caught on the handle of the door.'

Seeker soon had those with no business to be there cleared from the house and from the street in front of it. He questioned the constable of the Watch and then let the fellow get on with his ineffectual work. He sent word that Tavener's clerks were to lock up the counting house and allow no one else in there until he could speak to them himself, then he had Mirjam Tavener's maid light a fire in the small parlour, where he would question her mistress.

'And bring her a posset of something,' he said. 'The woman looks frozen and half-starved.'

He turned then to Mirjam, but did not immediately ask about her husband. 'I think you have been ill, Mistress Tavener.'

'I . . . no, it is the shock . . .'

He stopped her. 'A shock of ten hours' standing does not cause the flesh to drop from a woman's bones and the sheen to go from her hair as yours has done this past week, Mistress. I think whatever has caused your illness is of longer duration than the night just passed.'

'This week? I—'

Again he forestalled her, uninterested in whatever half-prepared lies she might offer him. 'Since the night of the organ recital at your church in Austin Friars. The woman I saw arrive there on her husband's arm, like a bright and sparkling ornament, is not the woman I am looking at now.'

She looked at her feet. Had no answer for him.

'Where were you, Mistress Tavener? Where were you until ten last night, when you returned to this house to find all in uproar and your husband's blood washing the floor?'

'I . . .' Her voice was scarcely audible.

'Speak up.'

'I was at my church. There was a service.'

'Until ten o'clock at night?'

She moved her head slightly, her eyes, thinking. So many people he had seen like this, desperately searching for some plausible falsehood. 'I was caught up in talk with some friends; I did not realise the time.'

'On a night like last night? And those friends allowed you to walk back here alone? Do better, Mistress.'

She shook her head and began to weep. 'I cannot.'

'He is still here, is he not?'

She looked up, startled at the finality in his voice. 'Who?'

'Jakob Hendricks,' he said.

She crumpled completely. Seeker sighed impatiently and let go the back of the chair he had been leaning on, walked to the window, surveyed the street. Her discomposure irritated him more even than Anne Winter's coolness in the face of her husband's murder had done. He would take honest indifference over insincere grief.

'Compose yourself,' he said eventually, when his patience was at an end. 'I expect you to answer my questions clearly and with accuracy. Any further dissemblance will do nothing to assist Hendricks or your husband, if he is still alive, and may well condemn you yourself to the stake at Smithfield.'

'The stake?' Her voice was scarcely audible.

'The punishment for a woman found to have a hand in the murder of her husband is to be burned alive.'

'Murder George? How can you think it?'

'The ease with which I can think such things would surprise you, Mistress Tavener.' He turned briskly away from the street window. 'Now, to the matter in hand. It was Jakob Hendricks you were with last night, was it not?'

She nodded.

'Where is he now?'

'I don't know,' she said.

'Mistress, I have warned you . . .'

She leaned forward, beseeching him. 'But it is the truth.'

'Tell me the rest,' he said, 'from the beginning, and speedily.'

'I am thirty-two years old, Mr Seeker, my husband forty-nine. I was born of a wealthy merchant family in Amsterdam that lost everything and my parents left me orphaned at fifteen. It was my fortune to be taken into the Weesehouse in Amsterdam, given bed and board and taught skills that would prepare me to be a good wife. When I was seventeen, an English merchant in search of a wife came to the Weesehouse.'

'George Tavener?' said Seeker.

'Yes. And he chose me. He is a handsome man now, and he was even more so then. I went willingly, gladly, and have never one day regretted that I did so. He has been the best of husbands to me, and I have tried to be a good wife.'

'And Jakob Hendricks?'

'Jakob Hendricks was a boy who used to send me notes and flowers in those fairy-tale days when I had a family and was a child. I kept the notes and flowers but never answered them – it would have been shocking to do so, and my father would not have liked it. I kept them all through my time at the Weesehouse, and at first I used to think that he would come there and find me, but then I realised he would not.'

'Do you have them now?'

Her grief-ravaged face broke into an unexpected smile. 'No, it was a girl's foolishness, and I left that foolishness behind the day I walked from the Weesehouse at my husband's side.'

'And so?'

'Nothing. Nothing until one week ago, when I was leaving the Sweelinck recital and a man stepped from the shadows and tried to talk to me.'

'Hendricks?'

'Yes. I knew him at once, but my husband's servants would not let him come close, and I was too confused to acknowledge him.'

'When did you see him again?'

'Three days ago, in the garden of our house. He was waiting behind some fruit trees, but I could not speak to him because there were servants everywhere. I returned later and I found a note in a bird house hanging from the apple tree.' Again she smiled. 'It was his old method, when we were young, in Amsterdam. It said nothing more but a place – the well in the old herb garden of the Austin Friars, and the time – nine o'clock last night.'

'What did he want?'

She twisted her wedding ring and lifted her eyes to Seeker. 'Surely even you know what a man who has been in love with a woman for twenty years wants when he sees her again? He wanted us to be young again, me to be free and willing to go with him.'

'And yet you are here,' said Seeker.

'Where else would I be? I love my husband.'

'So why did you go to meet Jakob Hendricks?'

'It was for his sake, Hendricks'. For myself, it was to bid farewell to an old dream, from another life. But, for him, I was determined that he should understand, for once and all, that I have chosen this one.'

'Where is he now?'

She shook her head. 'I don't know, truly I do not. But George – you do not think Jakob – no.'

'No, I don't think that. But the fact remains that your husband was taken from this house while you were at your rendezvous with an enemy of the state, taken by the front door, from which he had removed the watchman earlier hired for your protection. If you are ever to see your husband again, do not even think of practising any further deceptions.'

He made for the door. 'The Lord Mayor has called up the trained bands to search for your husband. I have other business to attend to now, but I will return in a few hours. Have your husband's clerks make ready his books, and a list of all his debtors. And you think of anyone you know who for any reason might mean him harm.'

The contrast between Tavener's house on Cheapside and where Seeker later found himself could hardly have been greater, yet each was a receptacle of misery. It was cold in the Tower, and the damp that hung in the air had about it the odour of centuries. How many men had spent their last days, years, here? How many men had died here? How many had Seeker known die here?

The coughing rag in the corner of the cell on the uppermost floor of Sale Tower was Elias Ellingworth. He looked up as Seeker entered the cell, bringing the light from a candle with him. In the look Seeker saw the eyes of Maria Ellingworth, but haunted.

'Is it time?' asked Elias, his voice hoarse.

'Time for what?'

Elias began to laugh, a laugh that turned again to a cough. 'For my trial.'

'It is set for two days from now, at Westminster,' said Seeker. 'After that I can do nothing more for you.'

The lawyer summoned what strength he had to straighten himself, and also managed a smile. 'You will forgive me, Mr Seeker if I wonder what you have already done.'

Seeker did not tell him of the protection he had arranged for him, of the ease with which the guards might otherwise have turned a blind eye to other soldiers, set upon exacting vengeance for the killing of the beloved Winter. He did not tell him that had he not argued for a postponement of the trial, to allow further evidence to be taken, he, Elias Ellingworth, would have been dead already.

'You saw the killer of John Winter, didn't you?'

'No, Seeker, that I did not.'

'What do you know of Winter's wife?'

Ellingworth frowned. 'That she is a strange, strange woman, and I cannot fathom her, but there is goodness there, somewhere.'

'When she came to see you here in the Tower, did she mention to you a man named Evan Snow?'

Ellingworth shook his head. 'I have never heard of him.'

'And you persist in claiming to know nothing of Sir Gwyllm Crowther?'

Again the smile. 'Alas, my career being what it was, I did not move in those circles, if Crowther ever set foot in Kent's coffee house he never made himself known to me.' But then, even through his weakness, Ellingworth became animated. 'The plot – the painting – what happened?'

Seeker gave him the brief details of the foiling of the Oxford plot and of the fates of the conspirators. 'That you made your suspicions of the painting known may stand you in good stead.'

'I will not get a pardon.'

'No,' conceded Seeker, 'but perhaps an easier death.'

Then Seeker questioned Elias about the relationship between Will Fiddler and Archibald Campbell.

'There was none. In fact, I think they took an instant dislike to one another.'

'Would it surprise you to know, then, that Will Fiddler is using corrupted versions of Campbell's sermons to send coded messages to Royalist conspirators about the country?'

Ellingworth's eyes were wide. 'Surprise me? It would astonish me. Come, Seeker, you must know – you *do* know surely – that for years Will Fiddler has disseminated pamphlets such as my own about the country, arguing the claims of the people, the Republic. You think he has turned-coat now?'

'No, I don't know yet what is the nature of the game he plays,' said Seeker. 'Anyhow,' he recalled himself to the matter in hand, 'none of that is your concern, and I have no more time to waste upon you.'

'I am surprised,' said Ellingworth, 'that you wasted any at all. Why have you, Seeker?'

'Because I believe in truth, and justice, but I no longer believe you completely innocent. If you cannot be moved by justice, then consider your sister. She barely gets by in that hovel with your support. How do you think she will fare without it?'

'You have seen Maria?'

'Aye.'

'And how does she fare?'

Seeker paused in his passage to the cell door. 'She is determined, and proud, and, truth be told, not without the help of friends. But she suffers for you, and one such as your sister should not have to rely upon the charity of strangers.'

Ellingworth regarded him strangely for a moment. 'And has she any message for me?'

'Not one you should pay any heed to.'

'But you will tell me, I think, for her sake.'

'She urges you not to forsake what you believe to be right.'

'Whereas you would? I don't think so, Seeker.'

'The difference between your understanding of right and mine is where our problem lies, Ellingworth.'

And Seeker left, suspecting it was the last time he would see Elias Ellingworth alive.

★

By the time he got back to Whitehall, Thurloe was already waiting for him.

'Wallis has broken the cypher – it gave him no great difficulty, as it was a thing done in haste. Evidently the failure of the Oxford plot has forced them into more desperate, precipitate action.' He handed a sheet to Seeker.

Gather your troops and commence your ride upon Jerusalem. The chief matter will be accomplished by midnight on the night of the 10th of November. At that hour, the second sermon will be released. The gates of the city will be opened to you. All will be in disarray and you must seize the hour.

Seeker glanced up from the paper. 'Tomorrow night.'

Thurloe handed him the note of the second sermon. Seeker read it, three words:

Herod is dead.

'Cromwell,' he said.

'And London,' said Thurloe, indicating the first paper.

'Does Oliver know?'

Thurloe nodded.

'And?'

'I sometimes think he has too much faith in our ability to keep him alive.' Thurloe was not making a very good fist of masking his frustration.

'So the journey to Greenwich goes ahead?'

'He will not countenance a change in the arrangements

313

for his daughter's birthday. Several foreign ambassadors are to be in attendance. He will not have them report back to their sovereigns that Oliver Cromwell cowers in Charles Stuart's palace like a frightened mouse. The Protectorate family travels by barge to Greenwich on the morrow, and the performance is to take place as planned. He will have the Life Guard around him, of course. But from the moment he walks into that hall, I don't want you further than three feet from him. You understand?'

Seeker nodded. He understood. Any bullet, any blade, intended for Cromwell would have to pass through him before it ever came near the Protector. There was nothing more to say on that score.

'The peddlers are being followed?'

Thurloe nodded. 'Twenty of them. Hell's fire, Seeker! Twenty – how might that translate into horses and men should the pamphlets reach their destinations?'

'But they will not, surely?'

'No. The recipient of each sermon will be arrested the moment it is handed to him. And then we shall have them, and break them.'

'Where is Will Fiddler being held? The Tower?'

Thurloe turned away from Seeker. 'He is not held.'

'What?'

Thurloe spun on his heel, spoke quickly. 'There is more to be learned by watching him, who he talks to, where he goes, what he does when he collects the second sermon . . .'

Seeker wondered if the Secretary had gone insane. 'The second sermon? I gave clear instructions to the printer not to print it. If the cypher is known to any malcontents in the city – and Fiddler will have seen by now that it is – they would spread the word in the streets. If the people thought Oliver was dead, there would be uproar, panic. We could not contain it.'

'It will not come to that.'

'But we cannot leave Fiddler free to walk the streets any longer. He'll realise soon enough his plan is uncovered, and then he will make himself disappear. The man is the most dangerous, duplicitous—'

'You must not take this so to heart, Damian, we have all been fooled at some time.'

'Not for three years,' Seeker said. 'Three years he was my informant, I had him come to this very room and tell me what he knew, what he saw, heard. He took my coin and he played me for a fool.' He shut his eyes, rubbing his hand into his temple in a way very few people had been allowed to see him do. He thought back to the last time Fiddler had been in this room, making his report of the comings and goings at Kent's, unaware that Seeker had had his pack searched by one of his men in the ante-chamber. 'But he gave me things – he gave up Hendricks, Seaton.'

'He didn't give you Hendricks,' Thurloe reminded him. 'It was the painting in Kent's, with its pointers to Oxford, that made you seize on Hendricks as a suspect amongst all those named as having been in Kent's that day. And Seaton?

A happy diversion for him from the Dutchman and his mission. Fiddler was not to know the Scotsman would also go there. He gave up Zander Seaton to rid himself a while of you.'

Inside her bedchamber, Mirjam Tavener sat staring at the fire she had allowed her maid to light, and trying to think how she had brought this catastrophe upon herself and her husband. In the city, at the Exchange, on the wharves, in the coffee houses, all the talk was of George Tavener. He was at the bottom of the Thames, he was in the Tower, he was on one of his own ships, halfway to the Channel already, his coffers emptied. Rivals were already negotiating for his trade, debtors quietly congratulating themselves on their good fortune, creditors and investors converging on the door of the house on Cheapside, while inside concerned Dutch matrons fluttered, taking order of the house and kitchens, and sending up to her tea that would not be drunk.

Damian Seeker, who they said did not know the word love, was now her greatest hope. She considered what he had said – enemies? No more than any successful man, and the clerks were making up their lists. And then her eye was drawn to the door in the far corner of the room, the door that led to George's private study, and the beautiful, locked Italian chest.

She was still sitting there an hour later when Seeker at last returned. His mood was foul and somewhat distracted, but he listened to her carefully all the same.

'You have not looked in it?'

'I do not have the key.'

'Where is it?'

'Around my husband's neck,' she said.

Seeker took a small knife from his pocket, saw her flinch, put it back and cast around the room for something else. On Mirjam Tavener's French walnut dressing table were some silver clasps and hairpins. He picked them up and started to work them with his fingers, bending them back and then reshaping them until he was satisfied with them.

She followed him through to the study. To her surprise, he said, 'It's good workmanship,' before bending one knee to the floor and beginning the process of unlocking all the drawers and compartments of the cabinet. One by one he picked a lock, opened a door or a drawer, lifted the contents from it and held them up to her. Time and again, her only response was, 'I don't know.' A diamond, uncut, almost the size of his thumbnail; deeds to enough houses to fill a street – Kent's coffee house among them; a journal, records of his meetings at Whitehall and with whom – this Seeker flicked through and then set aside, for later perusal; titles to land in Virginia, Maryland; commissions to raise settlers for those lands; a forest in Ireland; an ingot of Spanish gold; letters, from correspondents in Amsterdam, Madrid, Venice, the Americas – again a swift read through, again Seeker set them aside. And then his search was complete.

He returned money and jewels to the cabinet, and made a note of the deeds pertaining to houses in the city before returning them too. The journal and letters he put in his bag. 'It seems your husband is the wealth of England embodied, Mistress. He has done very well from our nation's late troubles.'

'As have others,' she replied. 'Were it not for your nation's late troubles, as you call them, your mighty Cromwell would be nought but a fenland farmer, trailing the mud of his fields into the corridors of Westminster, to seek licence to drain his tenants' lands.'

Seeker ignored the remark. The light in the room had been fading with the day, and his attention was taken by a glint of gilt cast by a new-lit candle he had moved from the top of the chest to a table beside him. The gilt was around the heart of a black bee at the bottom of the cabinet, and at its centre, a hole. He brought down the candle and knelt again before the cabinet with his twisted pin. He slipped it into the heart of the black bee, turned it slightly, and then slid open a drawer that Mirjam Tavener had never noticed before. From the drawer he lifted a slim red ledger. Again Mirjam shook her head.

Seeker opened the ledger and began to read, and as he did so, the words of Archibald Campbell's sermon began to whisper, and then to thunder, in his ears.

TWENTY-ONE

The Quality of Mercy

There was a different feel to the air of the city today, a restlessness beyond that which was usual. Anne Winter had begun to feel it in herself within moments of walking through the Holbein Gate, eastwards, away from the Palace of Whitehall. The deer in the park felt it, she had seen it in them, the imminence of freedom. A few more days, and the last of her affairs would be arranged, a few more days, and her last, her only true promise to her dead husband would be fulfilled. That morning, she had looked into the glass in her bedchamber in the apartments that she would soon be leaving, and begun to recognise the woman looking back at her. In that moment, looking at the peddler on Cornhill, realising who he was, she had finally made up her mind about what she would do, who she would be.

The morning was crisp and the fog of the previous night had lifted, and it was a glory to her to walk, unfettered by attendants or the watchful eyes of guards and Palace spies. With a smile, she declined the proffered services of the hackney-drivers and the chairmen with their sedans. She didn't mind the increase in traffic at Charing Cross, the carriages coming from the Strand, bearing their cargo of the wealthy for their progress in the park, the carters from St Giles-in-the-Fields, and the countryside beyond Piccadilly bringing their wares into the city. The fine shops of the New Exchange had never held any great attraction for her, but today she caught herself glancing at the arcaded fronts as she passed by, beginning to consider how she might furnish her new home. Anne Winter felt the shackles dropping from her, and a new freedom in her step.

By the time she reached Whitefriars, her boots now somewhat dirty and the hem of her dress spattered a little by passing coach- and cartwheels, the sense of enervation in the air had become something else, a tension, simmering, threatening. It was as if the desperation housed within the Fleet Prison had found its way through the walls and laid hold of the very breath of those who passed nearby.

There was something different, too, in the sound in the streets, a different rhythm. The usual overwhelming clamour for business, for trade, for news, had become instead a rumour, growing in certainty, in definition as she passed. Eventually, she could hear it clear: 'George Tavener, George Tavener.' 'George Tavener has disappeared. George Tavener is murdered.' In her mind's eye, Anne Winter saw the merchant at his seat in Kent's coffee house, had a memory of him by dim candlelight, the slight rise of his hand in a basement auction in Bleeding Heart Yard, of his passing her on his way out of the Lord Protector's presence chamber only three days ago. The open, clear-blue sky that had greeted her as she'd walked from the Palace gates that morning was gone now, obscured by tall and teetering buildings that overhung the street below, cutting out what sky might have yet to be occluded by the reeking smoke of the living city. The morning freshness had turned to the chill damp of a gloomy noon. Anne Winter quickened her step; there was much for her still to do and time pressed.

Magpie Alley seemed dingier and more hopeless than ever to Anne Winter now, perhaps because she saw it for what it was. Another three days and she would never have to set foot in this vile place again.

Practised in their art, two soldiers, in apprentices' guise, lounged one at either end of the alleyway and waited for her to emerge from the apothecary's, which she did after a very little while, slipping some small item into the pocket that hung from her waist. As she hastily retraced her steps back out on to the lane, the apprentice apparently emerging from a nearby pastry booth made ready to follow her, while the other slipped quietly into the apothecary's shop and closed the door firmly behind him.

Anne Winter hurried along the lane and by the Fleet Conduit up Ludgate Hill. Even in the press of people around St Paul's, her shadow did not lose her; indeed, it became easier to follow her now, up close. It was evident that she was going where Seeker had said she would go: Kent's coffee house.

★

It had become Anne Winter's habit, on Samuel's request and Maria Ellingworth's forthright instruction, to enter and leave the coffee house by the back way, on St Michael's Alley, but she did not do so today. Today, as she had done on her first visits, she entered through the main street door. As was usual, her appearance caused a hush, a lull in the conversation. She ignored it and scanned the table for faces she knew: no one. The discomfiting Scottish minister was, thank God, not there; the Dutchman, Hendricks, gone; the Scotsman Seaton, she had heard, dead; the lawyer, Ellingworth, in the Tower; the peddler was nowhere to be seen. The boy, Gabriel, came hurrying towards her, to guide her swiftly through the room to the stairs, but she did not move. 'Is it true? Is George Tavener murdered?'

'Nobody knows, your Ladyship. They're saying all sorts of things, but there's been no sign of Will Fiddler today and Samuel says we don't know what to believe. Go up to Mistress Grace now, Lady Anne, please, but don't say anything of it in front of her, for pity's sake.'

Upstairs in the little bedchamber, removing her cloak, she made the usual enquiries of the clockmaker's wife.

'You are earlier today, your Ladyship.'

'I woke early. I don't like to be in the Palace and so came here.'

The old woman seemed puzzled by her. 'But surely there is somewhere else you can go. Do you not like to ride in the Park, or take the ferry over to the Spring Gardens, or call upon your friends?'

Anne Winter felt no need to hide her thoughts from the woman. 'Cromwell has closed the Spring Gardens, and besides, I have no friends in those places.'

'Oh.' The old woman seemed at a loss for a moment, then: 'Since you are early then, you will not mind if I go now. Maria won't be long in coming, I'm sure, and it's a while yet till she will wake.'

'Yes. Go. Thank you, I can manage well enough until Maria gets here.'

The clockmaker's wife put on her shawl and made to leave but paused to look at Grace. 'She's getting thinner, isn't she, poor girl?'

'Her heart is strong though.'

'No, your Ladyship. Her heart is broken. I doubt our vigil will go on much longer.'

Only when she heard the tread of the old woman's step on the bottom stair did Anne Winter move. She went quickly to the door and turned the key in the lock and then took the phial from her pocket. It was too soon, she knew, but the girl Ellingworth might arrive any minute and Anne Winter felt Maria's eyes on her more and more each time they were in this place together. With more difficulty than she had expected, she raised Grace's head and shoulders from her pillows and put a bolster behind them the better to support her. Some wisps of Grace's hair had fallen loose from her cap and Anne Winter brushed them carefully away. She lifted a beaker of cordial from the small cabinet by the bed and tried to make Grace drink. Very little of the liquid found her mouth, most rolling from her dry and cracked lips down her chin to dampen the neck cord of her night shift. Anne Winter tried to lift her further, but there was no hope of moving her from the bed by herself. She should have got the old woman to help her before she had let her go, but then she would surely have argued that it was too soon, that it wanted an hour or more for Grace's usual waking time. So be it.

She tried again with the cordial, but again more ran down the girl's chin and neck than entered her mouth. Eventually, Grace murmured, and Anne said, 'Ssh, now, ssh. It will not be much longer. But you must take your medicine. Open your mouth for me, Grace. That's right, that's good. Now swallow.'

Outside, on the streets, Seeker could feel it: the mood was changing again, restlessness had become anticipation, uncertainty purpose and a realisation that the action was now afoot. Troops of soldiers on foot and horseback had been dispatched to the liberties of London and the villages around it. Cornets bearing messages the length of the country had been sent in search of the peddler. And where Will Fiddler was England's business, George Tavener was London's. Seeker had sent word to the Lord Mayor and aldermen of where exactly their militia should look. Everywhere, on both sides of the Thames, the Spirits were being flushed out, houses being raided, arrests made, cellars forced open. A bookbinder's by St Paul's, a butcher's in St Giles, a pepper merchant's in Southwark, an inn on Holborn, a coal merchant at Dulwich, a brewer at Queen's Hythe – ostensibly respectable citizens and householders were being arrested and taken to their nearest gaol. An appearance before the magistrates, a fine, and then home again. For all but one of them. Damian Seeker had learned the worth of listening to what a coffee house boy might have to say, and so one Spirit in particular would deal first with Seeker before he ever set himself at a magistrate's mercy. And there would be no hope of a simple fine for him.

The stench of Smithfield disgusted Seeker. It brought to his mind images of human carnage, of Naseby, Dunbar, Worcester. The cries of the beasts were unnatural: his horse tensed beneath him. Up from the heart of the city, the rush of rumour and news came on Damian Seeker's heels and so had not quite reached the small lane on which the shoemaker plied his lawful trade, but by the time Seeker and his troop had pulled up outside the shoemaker's shop, there was a crowd of people behind them, anxious to see whatever entertainment the misfortune of another might have to offer.

He was hardly two paces through the door before the shoemaker's daughter had run through the curtain to the workshop to tell her father the news that some giant or devil, or Oliver Cromwell even, had just come in from the street. The laughter of his apprentices was quick in dying when they looked up to see who had followed her through the curtain.

Seeker glanced at the girl. 'Send her upstairs,' he said to Thiene.

'But—' the shoemaker began to protest.

Seeker gestured to the soldier behind him, who stepped forward, scooped up the child and carried her to an upper room, in which she was instructed in no uncertain terms to remain.

One of the apprentices attempted to make use of the distraction to make a bolt for the back door but Seeker floored him with one swing of the boot to the side of his leg. 'No one will leave this house without my permission.' He turned again to Thiene.

'Where is George Tavener?'

'George?' The man affected surprise in as far as his terror would allow him.

Seeker brought a fist down on the workbench with such force that a hammer resting near its edge fell to the floor. 'Do not waste my time. Where is he?'

The man started to babble, but his apprentices were not yet trained well enough, and Seeker saw one of them glance at the locked cellar door beneath the stairs.

'Keys!' he demanded.

Again Thiene began to babble. Seeker merely stooped to pick up the fallen hammer from the floor and swung it at the lock, which sheared off the door at the second contact. He then stood back while two of his men kicked the cellar doors in. He called for a light and began to descend the steps into the foul and filthy dungeon beneath William Thiene's house.

There were eight people in the place. In one corner, a huddle of street children, three boys and a girl, who might have been anything from ten to fifteen years of age. They had the dead eyes of those to whom the worst has already happened. Two well-dressed but bruised and dirty young men, taken no doubt on their way from a tavern or card game, stumbled forward, swearing in the sudden light. A woman, gaudily dressed but no longer brightly painted, with scabbed mouth and hands, regarded Seeker coolly, no surprise registering on her face, and in the corner farthest from the hatch, bleeding and his clothing torn, watched George Tavener.

'And so,' said Seeker, 'this is what your riches have bought you.'

Four men had been sent to the Black Swan on Fetter Lane before Seeker had even closed the ledger he had found in the drawer of George Tavener's cabinet. The innkeeper denied any knowledge of where the Scottish minister might be, and protested that he kept an honest house. He was still protesting it, to abuse and mockery from his own customers, as the soldiers marched down the lane towards Goldsmith's Court.

The courtyard was empty, save for an old woman and her grandchild, scraping carrots over a bucket at her back door.

'Oh, aye, what now?' she said.

'Nothing for you to trouble over, grandmother. Get the child inside a while though, and stay there yourself, too.'

'Well,' she said, easing herself up from the steps, 'if it's that mad preacher you're after, you won't find him in there, he's gone.'

'Gone? Where?'

'How should I know?' she said impatiently. 'Half an hour since, down towards the river. Not in his preacher clothes, mind. Dressed up in good Flemish cloth too big for him, and an old woollen blanket like an Irishman.' She spat. 'Making for Ireland, like as not.' She lifted the child and the pot of carrots and turned down the passageway of her dwelling.

'Did he say anything?' the soldier shouted after her.

'Muttering something about an eye for an eye. Frighten you out of your wits, he would.'

It was at the Custom House quay that they found him. He didn't see them at first, so keenly was he watching the loading of a ship bound that day for Barbados. It was the carts he was most interested in, and he enquired of each carter where he had come from until the shore men cursed him out of their way.

The soldiers positioned themselves in a square, cutting off every exit route and began to walk towards Campbell. They were within ten yards of him before he noticed. He clenched his fists and started to murmur something. His head, his whole body, was shaking and as they drew closer to him they heard what he was saying, time and again: 'I'm not going back on the ship,' he said. 'Do what you will, but I'm not going back on that ship.'

★

Seeker had ordered that when found, Archibald Campbell should not be taken to the nearest city gaol, but to his church, and kept there under guard until Seeker should arrive, and so it was done. It was a good long time before Seeker was free of his other business: the children from Thiene's cellar were sent to Bridewell along with the whore, for what care and correction they might merit; the names of the two young men of quality were taken and they were cautioned to refrain from such haunts and pastimes as had brought them here. Seeker would have let them go then, for want of the leisure to deal otherwise with them, but an ill-considered glance of assurance, of entitlement, exchanged between the two caught his notice, and they too were thrown in a cart for Newgate, to await their appearance before the magistrates. It was dusk before he walked into the plain little chapel in Goldsmith's Court, where his men had long since grown weary of the company of their prisoner. Cold though it was, they were glad when he gestured to them with a movement of his head that they should take up their posts outside, at the door to the chapel.

Campbell sat rocking himself on the bare flagstone floor, his back towards his pulpit. He held Seaton's blanket tightly round him, and was quoting to himself from the Scriptures. He gave no sign of having noticed Seeker's arrival, nor the departure of three of the four guards. It was only when Seeker drew up a wooden chair and positioned it opposite him that he seemed aware that there was anyone else in the place at all. He looked up briefly. 'There is nothing for you here, but you know that. I can see it in you. Go away and don't trouble yourself more.'

'I haven't come for guidance,' said Seeker.

'Oh?' said Campbell, looking at him again, his eyes red. 'Then what?'

'Tell me about George Tavener.'

'Tavener? He'll go to Hell – I have sent him there. If he's boarded. Is he boarded yet?'

'The ship is still in dock.'

Some of the anxiety passed from Campbell's face. 'There's time yet then.'

Seeker nodded. 'Tell me about Hell.'

'You have not been to Hell? Perhaps not. It's full of Christians. Master and servant, overseer and slave. Eighteen hours a day, labouring under the sun, labouring at the sugar cane.' He looked up sharply. 'Never take sugar in your drink, it's full of blood! Aye.' He nodded. 'No comfort, no comfort, only work and beatings and no release.' Suddenly, he threw off his blanket, began to wrestle with the too-big clothing of his former travelling companion. 'I will show you my back.'

As he struggled, Seeker said, 'I do not need to see your back.'

'Aye, but you will see it!'

Eventually, he had worked off jacket and waistcoat and shift and turned to Seeker a back scored with livid scars and sores that looked as if they had never properly healed.

Seeker said nothing for a moment, and then: 'George Tavener brought you to Barbados.'

Campbell nodded. '*The Eagle*. It was after Dunbar. You were at Dunbar?'

Seeker nodded.

'Your Cromwell – he knew the right Psalms! Ten thousand of us taken prisoner. Do you know what he did with us?'

Seeker knew. Half had been in too bad a case to be of any further danger, or value, and so set free. The rest, five thousand of them, had been marched to Durham. Only half of them ever reached it, over two thousand of their countrymen left dead from starvation, exhaustion and sickness on the way. And then, while they waited for their transports to servitude in Ireland and the New World, they had been herded like cattle into whatever prison could be found for them.

'I was in the cathedral,' said Campbell. 'A fine place to contemplate the works of God. And I saw them, there. For six weeks, to the glory of God and Oliver Cromwell, I watched men starve, freeze to death, fester in their noxious infections until even the flies would have none of them. We ripped out your pews, tore down your pulpits, anything that could be burned. But there was no warmth to be had. And so to deliverance, when the merchants came, who had bought us, to take us on their ships to England's paradise, and there sell us on again. I had thought Durham was Hell, but that was before I ever knew Barbados.'

'George Tavener bought you?'

'As I have lately discovered. The thought that I would find him out and render unto him what he had rendered unto me is all that kept me from madness these last four years.' And so he had found his way to Will Thiene in Smithfield and paid him to do to George Tavener what Tavener had done to him.

'You were freed then?'

Again Campbell shook his head. 'Escaped. My third attempt . . .' He turned his back slightly towards Seeker again. 'Only two sets of lashes, you see. A Scottish mer-chantman, Argyll-born, like myself, took me home. Six months ago. Home from Hell.' He smiled. 'Home from Hell,' and he began to rock himself as he had been doing when Seeker had first entered the chapel.

The one guard who had remained in the chapel finally spoke. 'But it's no crime, is it, Captain? George Tavener was in his rights, if he bought his licence. What else was to be done with them?'

'No,' said Seeker rising, and setting the blanket around Campbell's shoulders once more. He picked up the ledger dated December 1650, in which George Tavener had recorded Archibald Campbell's name amid the many other items of human cargo that had made his fortune. 'It's no crime.'

Back in his chambers in Whitehall, Seeker examined the small bottle that had been waiting for him on his return.

'He wouldn't tell you what is in it?'

'A tonic for the nerves, he said. Says Lady Anne comes by every day for her tonic.'

'Anne Winter? Nerves? The woman does not even feel. Arrest him, shut the place down.'

'And the tonic?'

Seeker fingered the bottle thoughtfully.

'Leave it with me,' he said.

An hour later, all business for the next day made ready, Seeker saw to the last of his tasks before giving himself over to the few hours' sleep he could spare in the night. It had been long dark by the time he came to the door of the Stone House on Knight Ryder Street. This first home of the College of Physicians, two rooms on the street frontage, had been given up by them forty years ago, but since then a succession of apothecaries, slighted by the physicians, had, generation by generation, plied their trade here. They were known to Seeker, and it was not the first time he had had to call upon the services of one in particular. A close oversight of John Drake's alchemical studies was maintained by the Committee of Safety but Seeker had never had cause to mistrust him.

Drake held and turned the bottle in his hand. Examined the colours of the liquid by the light, careful not to hold it too close to the heat of the burning flame. The room felt to Seeker more akin to a place of worship than had Campbell's bleak chapel. The air was heavy with scents that were not of natural provenance, and candlelight threw into relief vessels of pewter and burnished copper whose uses Seeker could only guess at, alembics and burners of varying dimensions which might have played a role in some ancient eastern devotion for all he knew. Attired as he habitually was in his black robe and cap, to mark him out for his trade, Drake, with his sallow skin, dark hooded eyes and cavernous cheeks, had the air of the high priest of some ancient mystery. There were those who said he was a papist, others a Greek. Seeker knew him for a Jew, clandestine in his religion and of no threat to the state.

'Where did it come from?' asked the apothecary after regarding the bottle a while.

Seeker told him.

'Magpie Alley? Then its purpose will be nothing good,' responded Drake. 'It will take me a few hours, but I should have it by first light. Shall I bring it to you then?'

Seeker shook his head. 'I will be gone long before. Send word to me at Greenwich, the Queen's House.'

'As you will.'

'I bid you good night then, Drake.'

The apothecary turned to his workbench, phial in one hand while the fingers of the other traced the contents list of an old and well-used book. By the time he came to himself enough to murmur 'Good night, Captain,' Seeker was already walking down the corridor towards the street.

TWENTY-TWO

Tempest

10 November

By first light, the waters of the Thames were almost still. Inside Whitehall Palace, as the Protector made his devotions, there was a fluttering of lace and silk, felt boots and satin slippers. Cloaks trimmed with mink and miniver were laid out; in the kitchens, the aroma of warm spices and mulled wine drifted upwards as heated possets were prepared. By the Privy Stairs, the barge was being made ready, garlands of ivy were being strung around the bows and a velvet canopy stretched over its frame. Baskets of nuts, fruits and sweet pastries were set beneath it, furs loaded.

Will Fiddler was abroad early, well-disguised and careful to keep to the hidden places. He had heard of the descent into madness of the Scottish minister, but that was of no concern to him now, for Archibald Campbell had already played his unwitting role in the great enterprise, and today would be the day for the sending out of the second sermon.

But when the boy Will had sent came back and told him what the printer Clarkson had said, that there was no sermon, would be no more sermons from that printing house, and if Will Fiddler looked for further explanation he should betake himself to Damian Seeker, the packman knew he had a choice: to sneak away, quietly and for ever, or to take the one last, desperate chance remaining to him.

In Birchin Lane, Gabriel was beginning to set the fire under the pan, Samuel just making his weary way to the store-room to select the day's beans for roasting. In the upper room of the coffee house, where Grace Kent slept on, Maria Ellingworth removed her cloak and began her vigil. However early Anne Winter might arrive today, Maria would be there, waiting, and she would see to it that Anne Winter would not be left alone with Grace a moment. The hours in the sickroom were long, and Maria could not keep her thoughts from dwelling on the sufferings of her brother, the thought of him in some desperate cell in the Tower. What had it come to in their lives, when their only hope was in Damian Seeker?

By first light, Seeker was already at Greenwich. Every inch of the Queen's House had been searched and searched again: there had been no intelligence of the planning or planting of explosives, but even Thurloe's intelligence was not fail-safe. The Protector, despite his objections, was safer on the water than on the roads; the Lady Protectress was to be thanked for having persuaded him. The Life Guard would escort them on the river, and from the landing to the court-yard of this house, and then all would be at Seeker's direction, all that might go wrong his responsibility.

The Hall, designed by Inigo Jones, who had been respon-sible for so many of the fantastical masques, with their moving scenery, descending clouds, explosions of light and sound, in which the Stuarts had so delighted to spend their time and the nation's wealth, was today almost a chaste, pure thing. Seeker could admire the sparse precision in the setting of the white Italian and black Flemish tiled floor, the geometry of it. Above him, the gilded wooden frame on the ceiling, mirroring the pattern of the floor below, enclosed empty white spaces where once mythical depic-tions of the Stuarts' rule had been. The paintings were long gone – reserved for the people, it was said, after the execu-tion of Charles Stuart, but Seeker thought the people would think themselves better served by the stark simplicity he was looking on now.

Already, in the galleries, the musicians he had seen in the Dutch Church were claiming their places, shifting their positions, tuning their instruments, all under the direc-tion of Henry Lawes. Seeker had no great dislike of the composer – he and his brother had earned their bread com-posing for the royal court, but now one was dead and the other lived quiet enough, careful that his songs and private musical evenings should give no offence, and willing to turn his talents to the use of the Protectorate when so required.

London was full of former Royalists hoping not to draw attention to themselves, to see out their days quietly as their former sins were gradually forgotten, and Oliver was content enough to let them do so.

The singers, though, were another matter, for they were being rehearsed by Sir William Davenant, and here, Seeker, thought, Oliver had allowed his love for music to push his leniency too far. It was Seeker's firm view, as stated the other day to Thurloe, that Davenant should have been dead long ago. His ravaged nose, the butt and cause of half the jokes in London for over twenty years, bore testimony both to the syphilitic adventures of his youth and the desperate mercury cure that had so disfigured and almost killed him. No idle Cavalier sloping off to some continental corner to debauch his life in peace, Davenant had stuck to the Stuart guns long after they'd stopped firing. An emissary of the Queen in exile to her now dead King, when their cause had been all but lost, he had turned his talents to outright piracy. He had been caught, eventually, and few men, it was said, merited the executioner's axe more than William Davenant. And yet, somehow, after four years of imprisonment, here he was, the showman, the irrepressible spirit, released only a few months ago, after a barefaced appeal to the Protector himself. Even now though, despite the powerful friends who had canvassed for him, Davenant still had something of the whiff of the Tower about him, and Seeker was certain he more than once saw the playwright's hand rub absently at some unseen irritation on his neck. At

Seeker's insistence, Thurloe had had Davenant's every move, every contact, every correspondence since the plot encoded in the sermons had come to light scrutinised, but nothing suggesting complicity of any sort on his part had been found. The singers he had hired were examined one by one, none found to be of any concern. Davenant had sworn on the peril of a swift return to the Tower that he knew nothing of a peddler called Will Fiddler. Nonetheless, Seeker had set two of his men at the Queen's House to watch the old playwright's every move.

Seeker left the hall and went to see that all was as it should be in the kitchens. They had made fun at first, the Londoners, of the Lady Protectress and her thrifty table: they would not make fun now. Images came unbidden to Seeker's mind of the steaming cook shops he had walked past so early that morning, beginning already to boil up their scraps of meat, their potages of grain and roots and whatever herbs might be found, of the street children emerging from their cellars and damp doorways, to start their day of begging for money, begging for food.

Seeker went next to the loggia on the first floor, looking out over the park. Already soldiers were stationed all around, their eyes alert for any unexpected movement in the green expanse before them. He descended again by Henrietta Maria's lily staircase to the Great Hall. And waited.

Upriver, in the city, Anne Winter, dressed in her simple widow's habit, her favoured outfit now for her ventures into the city, had ascended the rough-set stairway, little more than a slanted wooden ladder, to enter for the last time the tiny narrow bedchamber of Grace Kent, beneath the eaves of the coffee house on Birchin Lane. She had an hour, at most, before the coach would appear at the top of the lane, her maid inside with clothing more appropriate to the events that would follow later that day. It had all been arranged, timed, planned with care, but what Anne Winter had not accounted for was that Maria Ellingworth would already be at Grace Kent's bedside when she arrived. The young lawyer's sister seemed to have been expecting her.

'You are out and about before your time today, Lady Anne.'

She hesitated in the doorway, uncertain of how to proceed. 'I have business at Greenwich this afternoon. I wanted to visit Grace before I set out on my journey.'

Maria got up and threw another coal on the fire. With her back turned to Anne Winter she said, 'There is no need. Mistress Haddon will be here to assist me when Grace wakes today. She has been very restless in her sleep – I think she may waken sooner today, and for longer, God willing.'

Anne Winter made no response, and Maria turned to look at her.

'Do you not think it would be a good thing if she woke longer, Lady Anne?'

Anne Winter hesitated before replying. 'I think it is perhaps better for her that she doesn't know what passes in the world, what is to pass.'

Maria's face, so confident and challenging less than a minute before, lost something of its assurance. Her eyes fell away from Anne Winter. 'You mean Elias?'

'Your brother's trial is set for tomorrow, is it not?'

Maria nodded.

They both knew what would happen: Elias would be found guilty of the murder of John Winter. He would be sentenced to death – hanging, because he was not high enough born for the executioner's axe, and then he would be trundled through the streets of the city on a cart, from Westminster to Tower Hill, and hanged there before the curious mob, a traitor to the Protectorate. Anne Winter was right: it would do Grace little good to know that; better perhaps that she should wake instead to learn that there was truly no hope, that Elias was already dead.

'What will you do?' Anne Winter asked her. 'Have you any other family?'

Maria shook her head. 'No, but we do not want for friends. George Tavener's wife has pressed me to come and live with them, as a sister.' She looked up at Anne. 'Can you imagine it? Such kindness? And I know, for he has offered it often enough, that Samuel would have me be here and eke a living with him and Grace.'

'And yet I do not think you wish for either.'

Anne Winter had spoken to her as to an equal and she answered her as an equal. 'No. I would be warmer and better fed in either household, have more company than I have ever had at home, but what I wish for is my brother free and scribbling into the night in our garret, leaving his papers strewn over the table so I can hardly find space to set down a cup or dish. He cares not if his food is hot or cold, his shirt clean or dirty.' She lifted her head, anxious that the other woman should understand. 'I am *more free* than any woman I know. I would give all Samuel's kindness or George Tavener's wealth to listen again as Elias rages at one pamphlet, scoffs at another, to be able to stop him as he goes out the door to remind him that he has not tied up his boots properly, to be able to go through his writing as he sleeps and amend those parts that will surely see him hanged . . .'

And the word, with all its finality, was there between them.

Anne could not hold the desolate look in Maria's eyes. She took off her black woollen jacket and sat down across from her at Grace's bed. She took the sleeping girl's hand – it was warm and softened by its unaccustomed rest from work. She spoke soothing words a few minutes and then slipped her hand behind the pillow and began to lift the girl up. Maria went instinctively to help her, but then stopped.

'What are you doing?'

Anne Winter spoke hesitantly. 'As I must be away this afternoon, I thought to give her her medicine a little early.' She spoke as carelessly as she could. 'I will need your help to see that she swallows it.'

But Maria shook her head. 'No.'

'What?'

'No. You are to give her no more.'

'But why? Surely . . .'

'It is by order of Captain Seeker; you are to give her no more.'

Anne Winter was stunned. 'But what has Damian Seeker to do with this? What is he to you?'

Maria seemed confused, her answer hesitant. 'I . . . he has tried to help Elias, that is all, but he says I am to prevent you from giving Grace any more of your physic. Hand me the phial, Lady Anne.'

But Anne Winter was already on her feet, the phial unstoppered. She tried to force what she could of the liquid down Grace's throat.

An instant later Maria was using all her strength to push the other woman's hand away from Grace's mouth, calling for help. By the time that Gabriel came running up the stairs, the bedding below Grace Kent's chin was sodden, and the reddened imprints of Maria's gripping fingers rising on Anne Winter's arm. As the terrified boy looked from one woman to the other, Anne Winter took up her discarded jacket and hurried past him. She cast one last glance, something desperate in it, at Maria as she left the room, but could find nothing more to say to her.

At the bottom of the stairs, old Samuel was waiting anxiously.

'My Lady . . .'

She shook her head. 'It's no use Samuel, and I am truly sorry for it.'

★

Jakob Hendricks should have been long gone. It was as if there were something in the air of this city that made his judgement fail him. He should never have come back here after Oxford. What had he thought – that Mirjam Tavener would come away with him, to live a life of secrecy, duplicity, rootlessness? That would never happen and he would have been gone, without question, by now, had he not received intelligence from Sir Gwyllm Crowther that, one way or the other, all would be done with tonight. But if their plan should fail, which, though God forbid, it might well do, then new arrangements would have to be made, new structures put in place. Crowther had always known when to seize the moment, and on this, of all occasions, he had done his job well: the money was promised, the purchase in hand. The property on Crutched Friars had been well chosen, its location a good one, with easy access to the river and to the eastern exits of the city. He had taken some time exploring and mapping the house – each cupboard, each stairway, each corridor carefully sketched and noted. Wall cabinets, compartments, hatches, attics, cellars, all were recorded, twice. There would be nothing left wanting when the architects and engineers set to work on the place – it would become the setting for a living masque, played out under the very noses of the Protectorate. Here, those well-affected to the King would meet, have their orders, pass information one to another, change identity, slip secretly away if need be, all in the safety of the home of a quiet-living Royalist widow who had withdrawn from public life. His sketches and notes finished, Hendricks folded one set carefully and secreted it in the inner lining of his boot, the other he placed, as agreed, in the hollowed out space beneath a floorboard next to the hearth in the main upper room of the house. There was nothing more to do. He left the house by the basement kitchen door, taking care to lock it as he did so. He slipped quietly out of the backyard gate, the very image of an old gardener, which was his guise for today, and checked in his leather satchel for the hunk of bread. The key to the house was still in his hand, and he carefully reached it down into the satchel and pressed it into the hunk of bread. He was relieved to see that at the end of the lane, as arranged, a young urchin was begging. Hendricks passed the boy the hunk of bread from his bag, and leaned closer to whisper to him the coded name of the person to whom it was to be delivered. Then he hurried down to the river and the barque that was waiting to take him home, smiling and tipping his hat to any who caught his eye, a kindly old Dutch market gardener returning to Holland for more seeds and bulbs to trade.

As the barque set for Amsterdam passed Greenwich and the lovely house built for the exiled Queen he still served, Jakob Hendricks respectfully tipped his old gardener's hat one last time.

Almost all the guests invited there to celebrate the forthcoming birthday of a fenland farmer's daughter had arrived. As the members of each party made their entrance into the

Great Hall, they found themselves under the unflinching and unabashedly open scrutiny of Damian Seeker.

They were all there, almost all: members of the Council of State, generals not in far-flung postings, younger lieutenants with an eye to promotion, secretaries to the committees. There was Thurloe, who seemed, as ever, to be in all places and none. There was Milton, helped in, smiling at the prospect of the evening to come, laughing – Milton! – at some remark by Davenant, who felt his element grow around him. With a glance, Seeker reminded his men that they were to know where Davenant was and what he did at every moment. There was Dean Owen down from Oxford, seething with imminent disapproval and the grievances he had been brewing, having travelled from the University no doubt in the company of Warden Wilkins, whose cheerful disposition drew as many to him as Owen's withering scowl repulsed. The gentry and aristocracy who had had the sense to throw their lot in with Cromwell took their places with an air of entitlement that even the events of the last twelve years had not taught them to discard. Lady Ranelagh was there, being feted by the Protector: Seeker wondered if the depredations or sufferings of her fellow Irish were topics for her garden parties and salons. As he surveyed the gathered, chattering crowd, Seeker wondered how much it differed from those who might have thronged this room in days past, watching the ludicrous masques produced by Davenant, Jones, Johnson, for the flattery of a foolish king. He studied them again, thought about them. No: this gathering was different. For the most, they were here, like the Protector himself, on their merit and not on their birth.

There was Colonel John Hutchinson, sporting as fine a set of lovelocks as any Cavalier he might have brought down in the war, and his fiery wife, Lucy – a clever woman and one not known for holding her tongue. Keeping a close watch on the Protector all the while, Seeker moved a little closer to Lucy Hutchinson. She was one of the few people in the room that he knew he did not intimidate. She smiled as she saw him approach.

'Captain Seeker! I had not counted you a music lover. There are many layers to your mystery.'

Hutchinson glowered at her. 'You must not mind my wife, Seeker. She has not enough to do with her time and so resorts to mischief.'

Seeker's face betrayed not the faintest glimmer of humour as he said, 'Then surely, Colonel, you must buy the lady a new pen.'

He was rewarded with a deep curtsey from the woman regarded as one of the sharpest wits and most uncompromising writers in England.

'But tell me, Seeker,' she said, her face now serious, 'what is Davenant doing here? I hardly know what Cromwell is thinking of, to let him out of the Tower, never mind to allow him here.'

'Come, Lucy,' chided her husband, 'he knows his good fortune, and he is a fine poet, after all. And you know how Oliver loves a good song.'

'Nonetheless, the man is tainted, beyond redemption, and I am not talking about his fearsome visage.'

Hutchinson sighed, but his wife was not to be stopped. 'Masques, dancing, stage plays, drunkenness and bawds – all designed to keep men of wit or influence from knowing the poverty, the injustices at their very doors. And it is rumoured that he dreams of resurrecting his godfather's *Tempest*.'

Seeker never heard Hutchinson's response, for just at that moment the growing babble around the Great Hall was suddenly silenced by a communal intake of breath. Seeker turned his eyes in the direction that all others in the room were looking; just emerging from the foot of the wrought-iron lily staircase, unescorted, was Lady Anne Winter. She had been invited, of course, four weeks since when the invitations had first been sent out, for as John Winter's wife it could hardly be avoided, but John Winter was dead, so very recently dead, and no one, for a moment, had thought that his widow would still come.

But come she had, and not in widow's weeds either. The black wired lace cap with matching gown she had sullenly haunted the corridors of Whitehall in these last few days were gone, and she stood framed in the entrance to the Great Hall of the Queen's House a blaze of colour. Anne Winter had never mimicked the immodesty of the Stuart queens, and she made no display of female flesh here to outrage the Puritan sensibilities of Cromwell's court, but she came into the Great Hall of the Queen's House in Greenwich a sensation of luxury and light. Her gown was of deep red velvet, the sleeves and bodice embroidered with flowers of gold with tiny white seed pearls at their heart. Beneath her gown, a gold lace gauze covered skirts of the purest white satin that skimmed the red velvet satin slippers on her feet. Surveying the room a moment she made her curtsey to the dumbfounded Protectoral Family, before silently taking her seat.

The air was heavy with the desperation to say something, and it was clear from the wave of low muttering and the occasional louder, barbed remark that many gave in to it. But it was not the clothing worn by Anne Winter that took the attention of Damian Seeker – he had known from the start that her show of mourning for her husband was just that. What he was looking at, and what really should not have been there, was the ruby and pearl brooch at her breast.

It lasted for hours: Seeker had spent more contented evenings on watch in sodden ditches or blasted hilltops in the wars than he was doing tonight. The great majority of the faces around him were rapt in listening to the latest collaborations of Davenant and Lawes, and the fine voices of the singers. A glance at the clock in the upper gallery told Seeker it was almost eight o'clock, and the performance must soon draw to an end, at which point the assembled dignitaries would flock to their supper upstairs, in the gilded blue chamber that had been the Queen's withdrawing room. From his position behind an enraptured Oliver, he glanced at the programme in the wearying Lady Protectress's hand, and saw that there remained but one item left – a new arrangement by Davenant in honour of the Lady Frances.

Seeker's mind and attention were much taken up by Davenant, too much, perhaps, he thought later, for a little way into the song a discordant movement amongst the musicians in the upper gallery caught his eye. One of the recorder-players, a small, bearded fellow in a broad-brimmed Dutch hat, whom Seeker suddenly realised he had not seen amongst the players at the Sweelinck recital at Austin Friars, laid down his instrument, to the evident confusion of the conductor. It was the registering of the confusion in the conductor's body movements that alerted Seeker, and he found the recorder-player again in time to see him raise another long-barrelled instrument, which he pointed almost directly at Seeker.

There was no time to think, hardly time to move. With an almighty shove, Seeker overturned the gilt chair in which Oliver Cromwell, directly in front of him, was seated, and, pushing the Lady Protectress sideways at the same time, flung himself on top of the Protector's prone body. The sound of the musket fire and the bullet that whistled through the air was unmistakable through the screams and uproar that broke out in the Great Hall. For all his years out of the field, Cromwell still had the strength of a bullock, and it was with some difficulty that Seeker managed to hold him down. Only when he finally became conscious of the searing sharp pain of the bullet that had lodged itself just below his left shoulder did Seeker at last begin to relinquish his grip.

Up in the gallery, the final song of the programme had come to an inharmonious end in a cacophony of shock. The soldiers whom Seeker had posted at the end of every walkway had the recorder-player in their grasp. The man did not struggle, but as he was hauled towards the stairs gave Seeker a familiar, self-deprecating smile that made Seeker's stomach lurch in a sudden horror of realisation. The man who was being marched down Henrietta Maria's lily stairs, whose hat and false beard had been torn off by the soldiers in whose grasp he was, had been Damian Seeker's city informant for three years.

Seeker, now bleeding heavily, had managed to get to his feet, as had Cromwell, by the time the man was hauled before the Protector. Oliver, shaken, had only one word in response. 'Tower.'

The soldiers surrounding the failed assassin stamped their feet in assent, but somehow, in all the confusion of the last few moments, Anne Winter had managed to interpose herself between Seeker and the man who had so cleverly deceived him. Smiling, she dropped a deep curtsey, deeper than any she had ever deigned to make to Oliver or his wife, and said, 'My compliments, Sir Gwyllm, on a magnificent performance.'

Seeker watched as Will Fiddler returned her gesture with an attempt at a bow. 'My pleasure, your Ladyship. My only sorrow is that, in the end, I missed my note.'

Despite the searing pain radiating from his shoulder, Seeker felt suddenly frozen. The realisation of what had so nearly happened, and how close Anne Winter had come, in that first, opium-addled conversation after her husband's death, to giving him Fiddler's true identity almost took from him the ability to breathe. By the time he had mastered his breathing and regained some clarity of thought, not only was Gwyllm Crowther gone, on his way to the Tower, but Anne Winter, too, had disappeared, and in the shock and commotion of the last few minutes, no one Seeker asked had seen her leave.

TWENTY-THREE

Evan Snow

It was like no field hospital that Seeker had ever known. The hard board on which he lay was dry, and smelled of beeswax. The sounds of music and bullets were all in his memory, and low voices, some female, filled the room. There was a surgeon somewhere, Seeker could smell the heating knife, and steeled himself for the pain that would come, for this was not the first Royalist bullet that had been gouged from his flesh. A hand gripped his, a strong, firm, man's grip. Oliver.

'Hold fast, Seeker, 'tis but a splinter.'

There was kindness in the eyes, and concern too. Seeker's resolve strengthened, and he made no sound, did not move his jaw even, as Cromwell's finest surgeon expertly cut the bullet from its resting place.

His resolve held too, as more instruments were heated, to seal the skin, and ointments applied to the wound.

'And will he mend?' enquired the Protector of his surgeon.

'This time, at least, but I would prescribe no more musical entertainment for the Seeker.'

'Aye, it was a rough tune to hear on such a day. Poor Frances is distraught at your hurt, Seeker, and Lady Cromwell can scarce be kept from attending to you herself.'

'Her Highness has always treated me too kindly.'

'No, Damian, it is you have always used her as a lady, where others have not, and that is not a thing she forgets, nor I. Heal well, we have need of you.'

With some final remarks to the surgeon, Cromwell left, leaving instructions that the Seeker was to be attended to where he was, until such time as he was fit to be removed to his usual chambers in Whitehall.

As Cromwell's physician assisted the surgeon in dressing his wound, Seeker felt heat and chill begin to alternate in waves throughout his body. He looked upwards, expecting to see the beam and plaster ceiling of his own chamber and struggled to make sense of what he was seeing instead. Far, far above him, in reds, blues and golds, he saw the story of Daedalus and Icarus, and the terrible fate of one who had flown too close to the sun.

'Where am I?' he asked.

The physician frowned. 'Lie still. You are in the former Queen's bedchamber at her house in Greenwich.'

Yes. Where else could it have been, with this image of the Stuarts who thought themselves to be the centre of the Universe? Little wonder that Oliver had not wanted to spend time in this room. Seeker tried to get up again.

'Will you lie still, man?' said the physician. 'Another two

minutes and we will be finished, and then we'll give you physic to help with the pain.'

'Physic?' said Seeker. 'What physic?'

'A preparation of the Protector's own apothecary; it will numb the pain around the wound and help you sleep.'

Apothecary. Seeker impatiently waved the surgeon away and began to manoeuvre himself from the table. He called to one of his own soldiers who was standing by the door.

'Has any word come from Drake on Knight Ryder Street?'

The young man opened the door and called to another guarding the end of the corridor. Soon, Seeker was reading the message there had not earlier been the chance to give him.

'Ready my horse,' he shouted. 'And where is my shirt? In God's name, will someone bring me my shirt!'

All protestations of surgeon and physician, and indeed of the Lady Protectress herself, availed them nothing. Oliver was already long gone, being bundled back to Westminster with his Life Guard. Thurloe was on his way to the Tower, where along with Colonel Barkstead, Lieutenant of the Tower, he would soon be at work on Will Fiddler, or Sir Gwyllm Crowther, whichever he might be. But it was not the double-dealing of his informant that occupied Seeker as he stiffly took his horse's reins: his business was in the very heart of the city.

His men did not ask him where they were going, there was no time to do anything but follow, and tonight Seeker was riding as hard as they had ever seen him, as if more than one life depended on it.

By the time they reached Southwark, Seeker could already feel the blood of his wound seep through the surgeon's dressing. No matter, he had ridden harder, for longer, with worse. The Watch at one end of the Bridge held them up no longer than did that at the other when they saw who it was that demanded passage. Once on the north side of the river, the riding necessarily became slower amongst the narrower streets and their many crowding obstacles. Those who looked out from upper windows and doorways on Seeker and his helmeted riders, made ghostly in the glow of light from the street lamps, withdrew quickly and closed their casements.

In the coffee house, Samuel had not been sleeping: while upstairs the night nurse watched over Grace, below in the coffee room he was resolved to sit and watch through the night, with Maria, her brother's last night on this earth. Tomorrow they would see him tried, and soon after hanged. And it would be done quickly, for there was trouble and restlessness in the town, in Whitehall and Westminster, in the West Country and, who could tell, maybe even in the North?

Since the last pot had been scrubbed, and the door bolted behind the last customer, they had been sitting by the fire, talking of Elias. Samuel had watched over many comrades in their last hours, and in his mind's eye he saw the fiery lawyer, alone in his cold and barren cell in the Tower. Samuel was a simple man, and had heard more than he cared to of religion, but as he listened to Maria speak, about anything, everything, he willed God to send strength to the girl's brother.

It must have been nearing midnight when their peaceful vigil was broken by a desperate hammering at the door. The boy Gabriel leaped from his box bed, to which he had been sent, protesting, by Maria an hour before, and, taking hold of Samuel's stick, went ahead of her to ask who it might be that so disturbed them.

A moment later, the door opened and hastily re-bolted, Lady Anne Winter stood before them, half-frozen and her skirts and scarlet slippers spattered with mud.

Maria forgot herself. 'Good God, woman, are you finally gone mad? What brings you here at this hour?'

Anne Winter was shivering and breathless. 'I stole a horse.'

'A horse!'

'I have come to warn you. Damian Seeker will be on his way here. If he asks you anything about Will Fiddler, deny it all!'

'Will Fiddler? But how should we deny Will, that we have known since ever we set up here?'

She was regaining her composure. 'That is all you know of him?'

'What does anyone know of Will? He is a packman, that is all.'

'That is truly all you know?'

'Yes? What is this?'

But she wasn't listening. 'Thank God. But Grace – has she woken?'

'Only for a while,' said Maria slowly, 'and no sense to be had of her. Why?'

Anne Winter was shaking her head. 'When she truly wakes, you must not let the Seeker see her. Do you understand me? Whatever else you do, do not let Damian Seeker come anywhere near her.'

But it was too late: by the time the women had ascended the stairs and sent the night nurse back to her own home, Samuel and Gabriel could already hear the hooves approaching the top of the alley. Samuel made no attempt to have the boy keep them out, and soon the place was filled with soldiers.

Heavy footsteps took the stairs two at a time, and Maria knew it was Seeker. She knew no more than anyone else at Kent's what his arrival there at that hour meant, but on first sight of him as he entered Grace's room, it was something in the man himself, rather than the fact of his being there, that struck her. Even in his act of reaching up to remove his helmet, Maria could see that something was wrong. There was a stiffness, a hesitation, she had never before remarked in his movements and when she looked at his face she saw there was barely any colour in it. She opened her mouth to say something, but then closed it; the Damian Seeker she had

glimpsed in her sparse garret wasn't known to the other
people in the room, and it was with them that he evidently
had business.

A momentary look of confusion passed over his face to
see Anne Winter there, in all her muddied finery. Without
even glancing at Maria, he spoke directly to the woman in
the torn skirts and filthy scarlet slippers.

'How did you come here?'

'I stole a horse.'

He didn't look surprised. 'You should know there is a
warrant given out for your arrest. You are wanted for interrogation by the Committee of Examination on the matter
of the attempt on the Protector's life. Thurloe's men have
gone to your apartments in Whitehall.'

'I cannot think you are here to warn me,' she replied,
affecting an unconcern she could not truly feel.

'No. My men will escort you to Whitehall once we have
finished our business here.'

'And what is that business?' It was Maria who spoke.

It was only now that Seeker appeared to notice her.
Again, for a very fleeting moment, she glimpsed pain in his
eyes, a brief haggardness in his face, before he straightened
himself to reply. 'It is a matter concerning the Lady Anne,
and Grace.'

'Though not me?'

'No.' He dropped his voice, and she saw the man who
had sometimes stood in her garret. 'Will you leave us a
while, Maria?'

Finding herself completely trusting of him, she nodded, and quietly got up and left. As she was about to pass Seeker at the door, he put his hand on her wrist to stop her: not a grip, but a light touch. 'Has she given her anything?'

Maria shook her head slightly. 'Not since yesterday.'

'Good.' He left his fingers resting on her wrist a little longer than was needful, before she did as he bid her, closing the door behind her.

The door of Grace's chamber once closed, Damian Seeker was again a soldier.

'Just us now, then, Seeker. Have you come to tell me my doom?'

'Your doom is none of my concern, not tonight.' He nodded in the direction of the girl on the bed. 'Tell me why you have been drugging Grace Kent.'

'Drugging? I have not—'

'Do not waste my time, Lady Anne: a man's life is in the balance, and you know you are the one who can tip it, one way or the other. I thought at first you were poisoning her, for fear of something she knew.'

Anne Winter was shaking her head, but Seeker was not ready to let her speak.

'This paper, though, tells me otherwise.'

She glanced very briefly at the paper. 'What is it?'

'It is a note from John Drake in the old Physicians' Hall on Knight Ryder Street. It is his analysis of the compound you have been administering to Grace Kent since first she learned of Elias Ellingworth's arrest for your husband's murder.'

'How do you . . .?'

'How do I know what is in it? Lady Anne, I think you take me for a fool. Certainly, the mountebank from whom you bought your preparations knows otherwise. My men had no trouble in persuading him to hand over to them what he had been selling to you. I took the preparation to Drake and this is what he found: henbane.'

She shook her head but he was not to be interrupted. 'Not to poison her, but enough that would induce a deep sleep, and confuse her recent memories.' He looked fixedly at Anne Winter. 'Your every effort has been to keep Grace Kent from waking enough that others might hear what she said.'

Anne Winter made no reply and so he continued. 'I thought then that she must have seen something, heard something, here in the coffee house that would witness to your guilt in your husband's murder, and that you sought to silence her until such time as another hanged for it and the world moved on. And that is what you aim at, isn't it, Lady Anne, that Elias Ellingworth should hang for your husband's murder before Grace can wake and make anyone hear her long enough to know the truth?'

'I bear the lawyer no ill-will.'

'No,' said Seeker, 'but you would see him hang, to protect that girl there.'

Anne Winter stared at him; he could see the struggle in

her for some response, some denial, but none came. Her shoulders slumped and she looked away from him. Her voice was not much beyond a whisper. 'How did you know?'

'It was tonight, when you made your grand defiant entrance to the Great Hall in Greenwich. In your anxiety to mock the Protector's grief for your husband, you told me who his killer was.'

'But how?' and even as she said it, her hand went involuntarily to the ruby and pearl brooch at her breast.

He nodded slowly. 'Elias Ellingworth himself told me, when I first went to see him in the Tower the day after your husband's murder, although at the time neither he nor I knew the importance of what he said: he mentioned the brooch you are wearing tonight, and I think it is the proof that will free him. I should have realised it sooner, but I was taken up with some other information I would have him give me and paid the thing little heed.'

'I don't understand,' she said.

'The day you first came to the coffee house, you had that brooch with you, and you lost it, dropped it in the private booth of the room below us.'

'But . . .'

She was scrambling for the words, to understand herself. 'I—didn't know it. I didn't realise until . . .' Again her hand went towards her breast, lingered on the brooch. 'I had forgotten.'

'As, for too long, had I. But when Elias Ellingworth

crossed the floor of the coffee room below us to look upon the picture Samuel Kent had bought from a stranger only the day before, he saw Grace find that brooch amongst the cushions in the booth. It was but a matter of hours before your husband was murdered.'

Again Lady Anne was thinking, casting her eyes about the room for some way out. 'I—I found the brooch here, after I heard the girl had fallen ill, when I first came to attend to her.'

Seeker walked towards her and brought his face down closer to hers. 'With every lie you tell me, you harm yourself, and her, more.'

'I am not—'

He cut her off. 'Elias Ellingworth saw Grace Kent find that brooch here a few hours before your husband was murdered. I saw that very same brooch, lying on a cabinet in your chamber early the next morning, while your husband was scarcely cold and you still had his blood on your shift. It was returned to you sometime in the night, and do not try to tell me it was Ellingworth who brought it back to you, because I know he did not.'

She stared at the small room's fire, knowing that it was over. 'She brought it to me when she came here. She told the guards she was my maid, and showed them the brooch as proof.'

'Did she give it to you before or after?'

She looked at him, uncomprehending.

'Before or after she stabbed your husband,' he said.

'After,' she said, searching her memory, 'when I found her with him.'

'He was still alive?'

She nodded. 'She was still holding the knife, and his blood was on the neck and sleeves of the linen shift beneath her gown. I gave her one of mine, in case anyone saw her.'

'Do you know why Grace Kent murdered your husband, Lady Anne?'

She looked to the bed, where the girl was becoming more restless, starting to murmur something. 'I think she is waking.' She got up and walked towards the door. 'I have done what I can. She will tell you herself.'

Seeker ordered Anne Winter downstairs, with instructions to Gabriel to fetch her something warm to drink to keep off the cold and shock that was now finally taking hold. It was almost an hour later that Grace Kent was at last able to tell Damian Seeker what he already knew.

The room was over-warm for him, and he had taken off his cloak on first entering it, but now, with Maria gone, he felt able to remove his jerkin. The pain of the movement shot through him like a bolt and he winced, getting a sudden noxious whiff of his own blood. Taking care to keep as much out of the light as he could, he took up his place by Grace Kent's bed.

Supported by pillows, in a fresh nightgown and cap with her hair lank but brushed and tied with a white ribbon, she had been watching him in silence.

'You have come,' she said. Her voice was a little hoarse and cracked, and he saw she had some difficulty in speaking yet.

'Yes, I have come. I need you to tell me about Evan Snow.'

And, over the next hour, with many stops at his instruction to sip at the cordial or rest her voice, but with a clear mind and without rancour, she did.

Grace had grown up at a forge in the West Country. Her mother had died when Grace was still a young child, but she had been happy enough, and she and her father and brother cared for well enough by their grandmother at the forge. When the troubles between Parliament and King had broken out, the lord of their manor had declared for the Parliament, and joined Waller's army in the West, taking her father with him. Her father had been killed at Devizes. He'd never known that Samuel Kent had also been there, in a different regiment, and it was a thing that Samuel did not like to think of. Her grandmother was also dead by now, and she and her brother had sought shelter in a nearby village, and for a time things had gone well enough, until the Royalists took hold in the West Country, and Goring's men wreaked devastation everywhere they went. It was at this point in her tale that Grace's voice became bitter. 'For all they called themselves Cavalier, they were men without compassion, men without honour.' Men who wrote songs, poetry. Men who murdered in the night, who raped. Village by village they had gone to in the night, burning and destroying everything they found, if they could not be bought off. When it came the turn of her village, and they had known well enough that their turn was coming, there was nothing to buy them off with. No money, little food, no plate, furs, silks. And so the men in the village chose what they could give: her. Her brother swore the Cavaliers would come nowhere near his sister; the men in the village bound him in shackles he himself had made, gagged him, hid him in a cellar until the thing was done. And so the night-men had come and the village had given her to them. And in the morning, when she was bleeding and scarce able to walk, those same village men had not been able to look at her, but turned her out with the name of whore. She had been fifteen years old.

Seeker's mind went again to the tales he had heard in the Golden Cross inn in Oxford, when the older man at the table next to him had silenced an angry young ostler by reminding him of the depredations of the Royalists under Goring and Grenville in the West – of the pillage, and arbitrary hangings, and debauchery: murder and rape in the name of war.

'And Evan Snow was one of the Cavaliers?'

'No. He was my brother's best friend. I had known him all my life. He had argued against my brother's binding and gagging, but one slap from his father had silenced him.' Here she looked at Seeker, her eyes burning. 'One slap.'

'And then?'

'He stood by while I was given to the soldiers. He turned away when I went towards him the next morning, pleading for his help. He could not look at me.'

Seeker let her words rest in the room a while. The sound of the crackling logs in the fire seemed to comfort and fascinate her.

'And when did you next see Evan Snow?'

She gave him a rueful smile. 'Not for many years, until he walked into my uncle's coffee house, calling himself John Winter and asking for his wife.'

And so, after nine years, the sins of Evan Snow had found him out. There had been no atonement.

She seemed to gain strength from being able to tell her story at last. 'I spent so long, running from that village, scared ever to look back. Nine years, telling no one.' Then she corrected herself: 'Save Elias. I told Elias a little of it, but not all, and he has never pressed me. But then, Evan Snow walked through that door, and a few minutes later, I came on his wife's brooch among the cushions, and I decided to stop running and face him with it instead. I took the brooch to get me into Whitehall.'

'And you killed him to avenge yourself.'

'No,' she shook her head. 'I had taken the knife for my protection travelling through the city and across the liberties to Westminster. But then, when I saw him, I could think only of my brother. I killed John Winter to avenge my brother, Mr Seeker: he had heard my screams in the first hours of the night, and the next morning, after they released him, he walked out of the village and hanged himself.'

Back down in the coffee room, Seeker sat down across from Anne Winter in the booth.

'She has told you?'

'Yes. You knew what happened to her?'

'John told me one night, years ago, when I asked him why he had married me. He told me it was for love, and in hope of atonement for his sins. He told me what had happened in his village, what he had done, not done, the death of his friend, the shame he had lived with ever since. At Baxton Hall, when the parliamentary soldiers murdered my brother and sacked the house, they would have had me too, had John not intervened. He saved me from Grace Kent's fate. He never told me her name, until the night I came upon him lying outside the door of our apartments in Whitehall, Grace still with the knife in her hand. He looked at me and said, "It is her, Anne. See to it that she does not pay, for she has paid enough already." '

And now he saw for the first time that in spite of herself, Anne Winter had loved her dead husband. 'I did that last thing for him; I gave him my promise, and so he died in peace.'

'And Elias Ellingworth? How did he become involved?'

She lifted her hands. 'Providence? Once I had got Grace tidied a little, given her a clean shift, I showed her out by a different stairs, told her to tell the guards she was my maid setting out on an early errand. Elias must have come along the corridor looking for John only a few minutes later, and you found him there. He knew nothing of Grace's involvement until I visited him in the Tower and told him of it, and she none of his until you yourself told her of his arrest.'

The woman was exhausted, and there was nothing more she could tell him. Whether or not she had had foreknowledge of Gwyllm Crowther's plot would be for the Committee of Examinations to decide. He stood up and called over two of his guards.

'Take her back to Whitehall and keep her there, under guard, until she is sent for.'

As she passed out of the booth to go with her captors, Anne Winter looked over to where Samuel Kent and Maria Ellingworth were seated together by the fire, each looking at Seeker with a desperate kind of hope.

The last thing she said to him before the soldiers led her away was: 'And what will you do, Damian Seeker?'

TWENTY-FOUR

Trial

11 November

It must have been near three in the morning by the time he returned to his chamber. The fire was long, long cold in the grate, and there was nothing to eat. He was entirely alone. Two of his guards he had left at the coffee house, although he had told neither Samuel Kent nor Maria Ellingworth the truth as to why. Samuel had accepted that it was for Maria's safety, until the time of her brother's trial, and Maria had been too lost in defeat to care.

'So, it is over then,' she had said to him after Anne Winter had been led away. Seeker had told them that whatever else John Winter's wife might be guilty of, it was not his murder. 'There is nothing to be done for Elias now.'

'There may yet be something,' he said, pulling on his cloak once more. 'The night is not over.' The hound, still guarding the entrance to the coffee house, watched him as he passed.

'What will you do, Damian Seeker?' Anne Winter had asked him, challenged him. 'What will you do?'

Two weeks ago he would not have hesitated. Grace Kent had murdered John Winter, Grace Kent would hang for it. It was not for Elias Ellingworth, shackled in the Tower, to decide, for love, that her punishment would instead be his. 'What do you know of love?' Anne Winter had also asked him, some time ago now, as he had held out to her the divorce pamphlet some concerned acquaintance had pressed upon her husband. He knew what havoc love could wreak; he saw it at work in Samuel Kent, in Maria, in Elias, in Grace; even, though few might believe it, in Anne Winter. He had felt its work on himself, on his every understanding of the world: it had wrought its devastation on him and made him something else. Order, discipline, was all that had given his life meaning for years now. There was none of either in love.

As he paced his small, bare chamber, Anne Winter's voice sounded again and again in his ear. 'What will you do, Damian Seeker?' He pictured Samuel Kent, old parliamentary soldier, who asked little from the world but had given much. What would it add to the sum of good, to the stability of the state, if his niece should die on the gibbet, an entertainment for the crowd on Tyburn Hill? Her crime would not be undone, and according to the dying words of the man she had killed, she had already paid her price. But how then could he let an innocent man die in her place? Ellingworth would be no great loss to the Commonwealth – too radical, he would never be satisfied, and his words, his writings, could tend only to instability. He would be a loss to no one but Maria. And how would Maria Ellingworth fare, a woman alone with no means but her wits in the city of London? Maria should not be a consideration, though. Seeker resolved himself: she was not a consideration; it was enough that Elias Ellingworth was innocent of the death of John Winter and Seeker would not see him hang for it.

By a quarter past three in the morning, Seeker's chamber was empty again. Day by day, the weather had grown colder: autumn was gone. The ice was hard set on the streets, hanging from rafters, freezing over gutters and wells. Seeker liked the loneliness of the city at night, and not much more than half an hour would see him to the Tower.

The guards were accustomed to see arrivals at any hour, and tonight, they knew, after the attempt on Oliver, there might be many more. No one liked Tower duty; it was like no other prison, no other stronghold, in Europe. It nurtured within its stones the spirit of despair, an essence of hopelessness that might have been brought here, seeping, from the river, centuries ago, or that might have imbued the very earth on which the place was built.

Seeker's interview with Elias Ellingworth had not lasted long. As he had expected, the lawyer was not sleeping, but spending the last night before his trial and inevitable condemnation in writing by the meagre light of the one candle he had been permitted. Seeker had read of men who claimed their imprisonment had set their minds free, that the fact of their imprisonment gave them control over their keepers, and indeed Ellingworth exhibited no sense of any need for caution now, if ever he had done – perhaps it had always been Maria who had excised the most inflammatory of his thoughts from the written page. Seeker glanced at one or two of the pages already dried: polemics against property, the corruption of power, injustices in the law, a rage against Leviathan. Condemned men were permitted a last speech at the gallows; Ellingworth, it seemed, was determined that his voice should still be heard long after he had finished his final dance.

At first the lawyer had been reluctant even to put down his pen, to acknowledge Seeker in the room. Only when Seeker had finally said, 'Grace has woken,' did he at last pause in his scribbling.

'She has told me everything, and there is no point in your lying any more to protect her. I had it from her own lips and those of Anne Winter; I know why Grace did what she did, and I know why Anne Winter tried to conceal the fact, and I think I know why you are lying for her too.'

'I killed John Winter.'

'You did not, and to say so will not spare Grace the gallows. Nothing would be gained by it. You dying in her place would condemn her to a life of guilt and regret.'

'You know what was done to her? When she was fifteen years old?'

373

Seeker nodded.

'And so you will hang her anyway? What kind of a man are you, Damian Seeker?'

Seeker said nothing for a moment, was choosing his words carefully. 'If you are intent on protesting that you are the one who murdered John Winter there is nothing I can do for you, or her.'

The emphasis had been on the final two words. Ellingworth laid flat his quill pen and gave Seeker his full attention. 'What would you have me do, then?'

And so, keeping his voice low, so that the guards on the door might not hear, Damian Seeker told him.

The conversation with Ellingworth had not taken long, and yet it wanted little more than an hour till dawn when Damian Seeker finally left the Tower of London, having made one more visit, conducted one more interview, before stopping a short while to take a bowl of porridge and a cup of ale by the brazier in the guard room. Afterwards, he went by the river, commanding the bargemen to take him to Whitehall by all speed. It was a journey he had made many times before, on colder days than this, but now it seemed the frost in the early-morning air was investing the blood in his veins. He could not remember when he had last slept. He knew why Thurloe valued him above all his other operatives and agents: truth. Damian Seeker never lied. What men knew of his history, his life before he joined Fairfax's army in the North, they might write on a paper not half the size of their hands, and they had long given up asking him, but for his service to Thurloe, to the Commonwealth, the Protector, his word was never questioned.

At precisely ten o'clock that morning, as the bells of London announced the news to each other, Damian Seeker, mounted on Acheron, passed beneath the portcullis of Aldgate and into the city, ahead of the cart carrying Elias Ellingworth to Westminster and his trial for the murder of Lieutenant John Winter. Seeker knew that despite the events of the previous day, Oliver Cromwell himself would be waiting, to see justice done. Thurloe had told him; the Protector could feel his enemies closing around him: he had known, he had said it more than once, that the murder of John Winter had been but a prelude, an opening gambit, the latest in so many schemes, to an attempt on his own life. Seeker was determined that no fanatic looking to curry favour with Oliver should get to Ellingworth before he even reached Westminster.

'Oliver believes that the Lord's providence has been with us,' Thurloe had told him when he was admitted to the Secretary's chambers a little before dawn, 'but that we must not risk His wrath by slackening in our watchfulness. He urges that there should be no complacency.' Thurloe had sighed, and Seeker could see just how tired the man was.

'We have never been complacent,' Seeker reminded him.

'No. But things have been coming too close. The Oxford plotters came close to furthering their plan, and had you not been alert to the attempt on the Protector at Greenwich all would now be chaos. I fear the cloak of security we study to throw around Cromwell has too many threads hanging from it, when a lawyer we have had under our surveillance for years can plan and execute the assassination of a high army officer without us having the slightest intelligence of it in advance.'

'It wasn't Ellingworth.'

Thurloe had sighed with impatience. 'Still this, Seeker? I told you—'

Seeker had stopped him. 'I have the proof. Here in my hand.'

Fifteen minutes later, having read the document over three times, and questioned Seeker on it, Thurloe had sat back in his chair, rubbing his chin in thought. 'It is neater,' he'd said at last. 'It is certainly neater, and less like to set the city up in arms. The trial cannot be stopped – due process must have its day – but it will be a short one.'

The procession arrived at Westminster, the prisoner was taken from his cart, and all was ready for the trial. Ellingworth would be his own defence; Anne Winter his only witness. The courtroom was small – purposely so – it was better that the lawyer's audience was a small one. The attempt on Oliver the previous day gave what little excuse was needed to keep all not well-affected to the regime away from its hearing. There would be no shouts of scorn and abuse from the gallery to interrupt these proceedings. Bulstrode Whitelocke had agreed to preside – it looked better not to have an army man sit in judgement over the killer of an army man – the people had become sensitive to these things, and Whitelocke still carried about him a hint of Parliament. It should keep the people happy enough.

Seated on the far side of the courtroom from Thurloe and Seeker was Anne Winter, no scarlet robes and slippers for her today, no treacherous brooch, but a simple black woollen gown and cap. At her neck was a plain white linen collar.

'She might be a Quaker today,' observed Seeker.

'You think? To me she has the look of one ripe for the executioner's axe,' replied Thurloe, grimly.

Seeker turned to look at him. 'Has Will Fiddler given her up?'

Thurloe shook his head. 'No, and we have no evidence against her. She sticks to her story that her mind was addled with opium when first she saw him at Kent's, and that she did not recognise him as Crowther until he made his attempt on the Protector yesterday.'

Seeker remembered: Anne Winter's mind might well have been addled the first time she had mentioned Crowther – addled enough to almost let slip who he was – but once it had cleared, she had known exactly who the peddler at Kent's was, and had had the presence of mind from then on to deny any knowledge of her fellow Royalist.

'She made her feelings very clear all the same, though,' he said.

'Aye,' said Thurloe, 'but Oliver feels leniency, for the

moment, will do less harm than being seen to persecute her would. I have already had the story put out that she is sick in heart and mind with grief – the news-sheets will like that. She'll be turned out of Whitehall by the end of the week.'

'And then?'

Thurloe smiled. 'And then, my friend, we will watch her like a hawk.'

The court, army officers almost all, rose as Oliver made his entrance with Bulstrode Whitelocke. Seeker noticed that in a corner, from which he could observe everyone he considered of interest, was Marchamont Nedham, editor and chief writer of the government organ *Mercurius Politicus*, and as different a journalist to Elias Ellingworth as could be found in all of London. Nedham would write what he was told to write by whoever was in power and prepared to pay him. Whatever record he made of the proceedings of this court would be embellished with all the mockery, scorn and insinuation of danger required to keep the populace in an attitude of manufactured outrage, that they might not think to question their masters. Nedham was a poison, and Seeker did not like that the regime he served should have recourse to such a one. He watched Nedham, followed his eyes, and they took him to the corner of the upper gallery, nearest to the stair, where, unnoticed by him before, Maria Ellingworth sat with George Tavener by her side. Seeker hadn't seen Tavener since he'd freed him from William Thiene's basement in Smithfield, and had not expected to see the merchant here today. He felt a sort of grudging admiration for the man – battered, one black eye still half-closed, his story known to all of London by now, he had nonetheless come to show support for his friend: only one with such close connections as he could have got Elias Ellingworth's sister past the guards at his trial. An unpleasant smile spread across Nedham's already unpleasant face, and soon he was scribbling with inspired satisfaction. Seeker promised himself that this week's edition of the *Politicus* would get nowhere near the censors, never mind the presses, until he had first personally scrutinised every word of it.

Tavener was talking to Maria but she did not look as if she were listening. She was staring, unmoving, at a small door behind the judges' bench through which, very soon after the Protector's arrival, her brother was brought. Ellingworth, always gaunt, was gaunter still after his sojourn in the Tower. The habitual black circles beneath his eyes were deepened, his cheeks more sunken. His hands, so rarely at peace, were bound firmly behind his back. Nonetheless, as he surveyed the court, a look something akin to excitement came into his eyes, a glimmer of something: awe. Ellingworth's wonder was caught not by the nature of his surroundings – a medium-sized, wood-panelled assembly room in Westminster, no more imposing than any other – but by the presence of Oliver Cromwell. Seeker had seen it before, in other men, had known it in himself, the wonder of finding oneself in the presence of one singled out by God for greatness. For a moment, all polemic, all disappointment, all criticism of the regime went out of Elias

Ellingworth's head, and all he knew was that he was standing before the man for whom a few years earlier, in the time
of hope, he would have died. Seeker wondered if Cromwell
saw it too.

The preliminaries over, the court was brought to order
and Bulstrode Whitelocke read the charge: that in the early
hours of the morning of 3 November, Elias Ellingworth,
lawyer, of Cheap ward in the City of London, under a false
name and pretence of bringing intelligence of interest to
Lieutenant John Winter, did obtain entry to the Palace of
Whitehall, where he did seek out and most foully murder
the said lieutenant. How did he plead?

This was Elias's moment. He looked around the court,
looked up to the gallery, saw his sister. Maria, a guard next
to her, leaned forward and mouthed one word: Please. She
didn't need to say any more. Elias knew, Seeker knew,
everyone knew what she meant. Please plead, as, for eight
days, Elias had refused to plead at all. Unwilling though he
had been to take a chance of incriminating Grace by pleading 'not guilty', he had not himself been prepared to lie in
court. His respect for the law was too great to plead 'guilty'
when he was not, so he had, through all his days in the
Tower, other than in his last conversation with Seeker,
refused to plead at all. Maria knew, should he persist in this,
he would be taken to a dungeon in Newgate gaol, where he
would be crushed to a slow death between the two great
weights of the mechanical device kept there for the correction of those who would not answer to the majesty of the

law. 'Please,' she repeated, and this time, her brother did not fail her.

'Not guilty.'

There was outrage in court. The army had come for blood, they had been promised blood, promised retribution for their murdered colleague. Cromwell had come for reassurance that another enemy would be put beyond the capacity to harm his regime. A look of confusion passed over Anne Winter's face, and she cast a frozen look of condemnation at Damian Seeker. Bulstrode Whitelocke, in the President's chair, was a picture of consternation. Elias had been caught with the bloodied knife in his hand, over John Winter's still-warm body. For eight days in the Tower he had refused to assert his innocence. How could he now plead not guilty?

It was at this point that John Thurloe, Secretary to the Council of State, stepped forward.

'If I might beg the indulgence of the court, your Honour, I have new evidence that I would present.'

Bulstrode Whitelocke looked helplessly to Cromwell, who, with a face like thunder, could do little more than twitch his assent.

Thurloe went past Ellingworth and presented himself before the bench. 'I have in my possession a document which will assert the innocence of Elias Ellingworth and the guilt of another. It was obtained in the early hours of this morning by Captain Damian Seeker of the Guard of the Committee of Security, and only very lately put into my hands.'

As Thurloe passed the paper across the bench to Whitelocke, the look Seeker felt upon him from Anne Winter was
heavy with loathing. He could do nothing to avoid it, nor,
in so public a place, could he turn his eyes upwards to where,
anyone else might have seen, Maria Ellingworth was also
looking at him in unconcealed wonder.

Whitelocke opened the paper, his eyes widening, then
passed it to Cromwell. All precedent and procedure was
now forgotten as Cromwell looked beyond Thurloe to
Seeker.

'The signature is genuine?'

Seeker nodded. 'Yes, your Highness.'

'Then we have no further need for this court.' He stood
up and began to walk towards the door behind the judge's
makeshift bench, by which he had come in. Only as it was
opened in front of him did Cromwell think to turn to an
utterly bewildered Whitelocke, gesture towards Ellingworth in the dock, and say, 'Let him go.'

TWENTY-FIVE

On the Wings of Mercury

12 November

The coffee houses were agog. The presses had been at work all night, broadsheets and news-books flying around the town faster than the censors could reach out their hands to grasp them. *The Weekly Post*, *The Faithful Scout*, above all *Mercurius Politicus*, thundered in ever more lurid language of how close England's enemies had come to bringing the state to catastrophe: the notorious Welsh traitor Sir Gwyllm Crowther, in the guise of a city peddler, had brutally murdered Lieutenant John Winter and then made an attempt on the life of the Lord Protector himself.

In Kent's, the shock was greater than in any other coffee house in London. 'I cannot believe it,' said Samuel Kent, who had not had to wait to see a news-book to discover what had passed at Elias Ellingworth's trial. 'Nigh on four years, I knew him. Four years, served him coffee, filled his pipe. Heard his stories, told him mine. Four years, and yet I never knew him at all.'

'I too counted him a friend,' said George Tavener. 'Will Fiddler, who would have believed it? A Royalist spy.'

'Aye,' said Samuel bitterly, 'and a traitor to his friends.'

'How so?' asked a soap-merchant, not long sat down.

'How so?' asked Samuel in disbelief. 'Because he would have let Elias *hang* for the murder of John Winter. He came here, pretending friendship to us all, solicitous for Elias, for Maria, for Grace, my Grace. And all the while he *knew*.' He spat at the fire. 'Will Fiddler, Gwyllm Crowther, whoever he might be: never let me hear his name spoken in this house again.'

Crowther had been in a sorry state, in the early hours of the morning before Elias Ellingworth's trial, when Damian Seeker had finally been let in to see him in his prison in the Flint tower. He'd been shackled, arms and feet, to the wall and floor of the cell, his blood darkening the straw beneath him. Seeker had thought for a moment that he wasn't conscious, but when he'd lifted Crowther's chin he'd seen the insolent grin with which the packman, Will Fiddler, his informant of three years, had always greeted him.

'And so, Seeker,' he'd gurgled, 'you have come to hear the last of my secrets, but I don't think I will tell them to you. Even Colonel Barkstead has given up on me, for now.' He'd treated Seeker to a broken-toothed smile which had split a wound on his lip and set it to bleeding down his chin once more.

Seeker had let go of his chin and watched the man's head

flop down on to his chest. 'Thurloe will have your secrets from you. There are ways of keeping a man alive long enough. And you have given up others in the past.'

'For the greater good,' Crowther had slurred.

'Even those you gave to me?'

The Welshman had gurgled a bloody laugh. 'Sometimes, it was necessary, to divert you from other things. For the greater good.'

'Even Seaton? Hendricks? You gave me them both when I asked you who had been at Kent's that first day.'

Crowther had made to shake his head and then thought the better of it. 'I gave you Seaton,' he'd said. 'He was lost anyway, finished, looking to die in the cause. He was alone, part of no network, his capture or death would compromise no one. It was a gift to me when he walked into that coffee house that day and I knew I could hand him to you, as a distraction.'

'From Hendricks?'

Crowther had taken a moment to get his strength, grunted his assent. 'Yes, but I never gave you Hendricks – you worked that one out yourself, more's the pity.' He'd opened a bruised eye and regarded Seeker with a kind of amused esteem. 'How did you do that, by the way?'

'Elias Ellingworth. He saw the painting, that was why he went to Whitehall that night, to see John Winter: he wanted to tell him what he'd seen in the painting. I take it you had had it placed there for Hendricks?'

Crowther had nodded slightly, again made a sound that

might have been a laugh. 'Our new code was not quite as ingenious as we had thought, then.'

'What? A church called St Peter's? Oxen at a ford, the time on the clock, the appointed date and the names of the conspirators on the graves? This is how best you thought to inform Hendricks of the identities of his co-conspirators and where he should find them?' Seeker had been scornful. 'It was the work of amateurs. It was even badly painted.'

'Granted, it was not my finest work,' Crowther had replied, 'but the fellow who'd agreed to approach Samuel with it was getting cold feet, and anxious to be away from London, so the thing had to be rushed somewhat.'

'Who was it?'

'That placed it? A nobody. As Samuel said, a poor fellow without a shilling. There is no shortage of hungry men in this city, ready to take a risk and disappear.' Crowther had evidently taken some satisfaction from this. 'But tell me, Seeker, how did you come to know in the first place that the message was to be left in Kent's?'

This time it had been Seeker's turn to smile. 'You surely don't think Charles Stuart snores in his sleep in Cologne without it disturbs Thurloe in his bed in Whitehall?'

'You have spies in the King's court? Who?'

Now Seeker had actually laughed. 'You think I would tell you that before I was certain you had been dead at least three days?'

'May they burn in Hell,' Crowther had said.

Seeker had grunted. 'After a year or two in the company of Charles Stuart, they probably will.'

'Hmmph.' Crowther had then become serious, almost honest. 'We'll all burn, one way or the other, Seeker, you, and I, and Thurloe – maybe even the King himself. There are few innocents in this game of ours. But Elias . . . that I do not understand, that I would never have expected. Why did he kill him?'

'Kill who?'

'John Winter.'

Seeker had thought, irrationally, that somehow Crowther would know.

'He didn't. It was Grace Kent who murdered John Winter.'

It had only been later, as he was going over the conversation in his head, that Seeker had realised what had been strange in Crowther's reaction to this news: at no point had he expressed shock or disbelief that it should have been so. All he had said at the beginning was: 'Tell me,' and so, in straightforward manner, Seeker had.

After the tale had been told, Crowther had remained silent a few minutes. 'I should have realised. For the last few years, I travelled everywhere in the West Country, heard everything. I have heard the like in more than one place. I should have realised when I heard her name, knew where she came from.' He'd looked towards the meagre shaft of moonlight that came through the slit window into his cell. 'I think I didn't want to know.'

Seeker had waited. Anne Winter's challenge to him, 'What will you do, Damian Seeker?', hung in the balance, there, in that condemned man's cell.

'She has not gone to trial?' Crowther had asked suddenly.

'No. Ellingworth does, tomorrow. He will not give her up, nor will Anne Winter, who has known the truth all along.'

Crowther had smiled at this. 'That is a better woman than people know.'

Seeker had let the remark pass.

'Who else knows the truth?' Crowther had continued.

'Only we two in this room.'

'Then no one else ever will,' the Welshman had said.

Even afterwards, Damian Seeker would never have said that Sir Gwyllm Crowther, who had come so close to killing Cromwell, was a good man, or a man of honour, but as he'd walked from the traitor's cell half an hour later, carrying the fabricated confession to the murder of John Winter, drafted in his own hand and freely signed by Crowther in his, Seeker had found himself wishing, unlikely though it was, that his false informant's death might be a quick one.

In the chapel in Goldsmith's Court, off Fetter Lane, all was silent. Another preacher would be found, soon enough, God willing, to minister to the good Presbyterians of the city and preach to them the word of God. They would take more care, this time, to find one whose mind had not been loosed and frayed by the corruption of the wars. Some way away, out past Bishopsgate, behind the locked doors and high walls of Bethlehem hospital, Archibald Campbell would have given much to hear that silence, but there was no silence in Bedlam. He would have covered his ears with his hands, but his hands were bound so tight he could not move them. He would have scratched at these new manacles, if he could have reached them. Truly, in a place such as this, a man might go mad.

In his house on Cheapside, George Tavener wondered, for a while, if he had been mad, to think Mirjam could ever have betrayed him with another man. He wondered how he could have doubted what he had known the first time he had laid eyes upon her in the Weesehouse of Amsterdam: she would be a good wife; she was a good wife.

He had never told Mirjam all the details of his business, and she had never asked: she was, after all, herself a merchant's daughter. There had been no shame, though, in the trade of men: the wealth of the nation was coming more and more to depend on it – how else were the plantations to be worked? And there had been no crime, either, in law – Parliament had been glad to rid itself of rebels, Irish, Scots, street children, vagabonds, in any way it might: there had been no turning of a blind eye; it had, for a time, while the war raged, been acceptable to do it in plain sight. But then George Tavener had crossed a line – foolish, foolish – he had begun to buy his slaves from the Spirits, and never ask where they had got them from. He had had time, cold and damp and tormented by rats in William Thiene's cellar, to consider all of this, and the thought that he had done to other men what was now being done to him had sickened him. But he would do something. He would make amends. He took a sip of his claret and watched as Mirjam put her hand to her neck and felt the cold brass of the little key that hung there, the new key he had had made for the repaired locks of her Florentine cabinet.

Anne Winter, too, was holding a key in her hand. She stood before the street door and looked up at the three stories of the house on Crutched Friars, the one storey over-reaching the other. She smiled: she liked it very well. She would plant herbs in boxes in the upper windows, and put new pantiles on the roof. The door she would have painted green, and have a brass knocker put there, in the mould of her father's crest. The key turned with little difficulty, and telling the chairmen who had carried her here from White-hall to wait, she went in. She felt like a child on its birthday, but before she could properly explore the house, there was one thing she had to do. She went up to the second floor as instructed, and took the first door on her left into what would be her withdrawing room. She went to the further side of the hearth and bent down. The floorboard came up with only a little resistance under the pressure of her fin-gers, and there, as she had been told they would be, were the plans sketched out by Jakob Hendricks. In a few days, the letter would arrive from Cologne, with the architect who would ensure the improvements to the house would be made, to the exact specifications required.

It was difficult to believe it was only a few days since the peddler Will Fiddler had stopped her just after she'd left Kent's, and she had realised for certain this time that he was Sir Gwyllm Crowther, her dead brother's friend. She had also realised, there and then, that Crowther must in some way have been acting for the King, and had resolved, in that moment, that she too would play her part. Crowther would die, and there was nothing she could do about that, but he had found her this house, and now, in her hand, she had the plans that would turn it into a safe house for agents of the King, where they might meet, plan, hide, pass information, all under the guise of old friends or servants of the lieutenant's widow. Slipping the plans into the lining of her heavily padded bodice, Anne Winter left the room and continued the examination of her new home.

By the time he had reached Cologne, Jakob Hendricks had provided himself with a new suit, suitable to a courtier of the King, however shabby the court of Charles Stuart in exile might in truth be. Room after room he passed through, scullery, kitchen, boot-room, narrow corridors where dejected Royalists in worn and dated fashions huddled in small groups trying to remember they had once been wits. One or two eyebrows were raised in surprise as Hendricks passed.

'We had thought you dead,' one erstwhile Cavalier ventured.

'No doubt,' returned Hendricks, without taking the trouble to glance in the man's direction. Admitted, with a tired affectation of solemnity, to what passed for the King's presence chamber, he surveyed the faces of those laughing at Charles's jokes and jockeying for nearness to his person, and wondered which might be the one in Thurloe's pay, the one who had betrayed him.

EPILOGUE

Seeker's Morning

Dusk was falling over London and what little light was wont to find its way into the garret of Dove Court had abandoned its efforts for the day.

Maria was brisk. 'Samuel insisted upon it – Elias is to stay at Kent's until he is restored to full health. He would brook no argument. I heard him say something about the great debt they owe him, but there is none that I can think of – if anyone owed Elias a crooked penny, rather than it be the other way round, he would think himself a rich man.'

And so, Seeker realised, Grace must have told her uncle everything: what she had done, what Elias had been pre-pared to do to save her. It was as well, he thought, for if the two people she most loved knew the truth, then it was a burden she would no longer have to carry with her, and he would have wagered the last drop of blood in his veins that neither Samuel Kent nor Elias Ellingworth would ever tell another living soul what Grace Kent had done.

Maria was too busy struggling with the carcass of an unfortunate-looking chicken to notice his pensiveness.

'Samuel says a night in our cold garret here would be the end of him.'

Looking round at the sparse, damp room with its cheerless fire, Seeker could not think but the old soldier was right.

'And yet *you* are here,' he observed.

Maria gave up on whatever she was trying to do to the chicken and thrust it into a pot. 'They would have had me there too – he and Grace, for she improves by the hour, you know – but I have had over-much company of late, and wanted a little time to myself.'

'Oh, I see,' he said, picking up his helmet from the table on which he only now noticed she had set a small jug of winter green and berries in decoration. Two scrubbed wooden trenchers waited on the sideboard, and she had poured ale into a glazed earthenware jug. 'I will keep you no longer.'

She stopped in the process of dropping some soaked barley into the pot. 'You are not going to stay?'

He gestured awkwardly towards the table. 'I would not spoil your evening. I see that you are expecting company.'

'Aye, and that company is here, or so I thought,' she said, annoyed, 'unless you would have me feed this chicken to the dog?'

'No,' he stepped towards her, alarmed. 'The bones would choke him.'

'And you as well no doubt,' she said, in an unaccountable fury.

'I . . . but . . .'

She threw down the bunch of parsley in her hand. 'I

thought to thank you for what you did for Elias, persuading Will Fiddler to confess at last, but I see my efforts are not welcome to one used to dining with Cromwell.'

Astonished, he went a step closer and, unthinking, put a hand on her wrist. 'Do I look as if I am used to dining with the Lord Protector?'

She gazed at him, and he saw that she was just retreating from the brink of tears. 'No,' she said at last, 'you look half-starved.'

Relieved, he let his hand drop and took a pace backwards again. 'I can't remember when I last had a proper meal. Your chicken will be very nice.'

They watched each other, each completely at a loss for what seemed like a good few minutes, until Maria nodded. 'Well, you had better sit down then.'

And so he did, awkwardly, glad that she had not noticed him wince as he untied his jacket and put his helmet under his chair this time, for want of a better idea.

She worked in silence a while and he watched her, wondering how the bird would ever cook tonight over such a fire, and beginning to understand a little better why Elias Ellingworth might be so thin.

'A few days ago, at Kent's,' she said lightly, her back still to him, 'we spoke of you having been a Seeker.'

'It is nothing but a name to me now,' he answered evenly.

She put down her knife and turned to look at him. 'But it was once?'

He swallowed some of his ale. 'I was brought up in that

sect. My family had travelled the North for generations, finding work on farms and villages, shelter and sustenance in the woods. We troubled no one, and were let to live our own way, to worship our own way, without parish or priest. We were taught to look for the kingdom within ourselves, amongst ourselves, and understood Heaven and Hell as present here on this earth.'

'You were free,' she said.

He wasn't looking at her. 'We thought so. Perhaps we were, or simply deluding ourselves. But then other sects, lone preachers, started to spread over the country and come among us.'

'Ranters?'

'Aye, them and others. There was no sin, they said eventually. No rules to bind and govern us. All was permitted, nothing forbidden. Nothing made that could not be broken. Soon there was no order.'

'And so you left your home and family and joined with the New Model Army for order? Dear God, Seeker, can order matter so much?'

In his mind he travelled far to the North, and nine years back, to a meeting house, trim, clean, simple, at the edge of a wood. Before all the congregation, a woman stands up, a young woman, with flowing blonde hair and a three-year-old girl on her hip. She declares before the community gathered there that she will divorce her husband and take to her another. At first there is silence. She stands, defiant, then heads nod in acquiescence. Let it be so; this is their freedom, their right. Though some avoid his eye, most face him boldly. Only in the eyes of a very few does he glimpse compassion. The silence lies heavy on the meeting house until the man turns and walks to the door and opens it. He steps out and closes it again behind him. The moonlight is on the path and the carpenter begins to walk.

Seeker was still looking past Maria when he finally answered her. 'Without order, there is nothing at all.'

It was some time later, when they had decided that they might at least risk a little broth from the pot, and taken it with a hunk of the bread that was to have been Maria's breakfast, and Maria had fussed with herbs about the wound at his shoulder, that she suddenly noticed.

'The dog,' she said, looking at the large shaggy hound absorbing what little heat was to be had from the fire.

Seeker looked over at it. 'What of it?'

'Tonight, when you came up the stairs, he did not bark at you.'

'I know,' he said. 'He will only growl at me if I am wearing my helmet.'

'I don't understand,' she said, her face registering her incomprehension.

He smiled and reached his hand towards the beast, who came over to him and nuzzled against it. 'I trained him to behave so. It is my dog.'

And all about the market the next day, Kitty Jennet said she had seen Damian Seeker go in at Elias Ellingworth's house on Dove Court by moonlight, and not come out again till near dawn, and further, that she herself had seen Maria Ellingworth soon afterwards, in her nightshift, draw water at the pump in Dove Court, a strange smile upon her lips. But London was a town full of rumour in those days, and none paid any heed to Kitty Jennet.